Chris Ryan Extreme
Hard Target

25.6.24

Chris Ryan was born near Newcastle in 1961. He joined the SAS in 1984. During his ten years there he was involved in overt and covert operations and was also sniper team commander of the anti-terrorist team. During the Gulf War, Chris Ryan was the only member of an eight-man unit to escape from Iraq, where three colleagues were killed and four captured. It was the longest escape and evasion in the history of the SAS. For this he was awarded the Military Medal.

He wrote about his experiences in the bestseller *The One That Got Away*, which was adapted for screen and since then has written three other works of non-fiction, fifteen bestselling novels, a series of childrens' books and a number one bestselling series of ebooks. Chris Ryan's novel *Strike Back* has been adapted into the hit Sky series of the same name.

Chris Ryan Extreme: Hard Target

Chris Ryan

CORONET

First published in Great Britain in 2012 by Coronet
An imprint of Hodder & Stoughton
An Hachette UK company

First published in paperback in 2012

10

A CIP catalogue record for this title is available from the British Library

B Format ISBN 9 781 444 72946 7
A Format ISBN 9781444756401

Typeset in Plantin Light by Hewertext Uk Ltd, Edinburgh
Printed in Great Britain by Clays Ltd, St Ives plc

Hodder & Stoughton policy is to use papers that are natural, renewable
and recyclable products and made from wood grown in sustainable
forests. The logging and manufacturing processes are expected to
conform to the environmental regulations of the country of origin.

Hodder & Stoughton Ltd
338 Euston Road
London NW1 3BH

www.hodder.co.uk

acknowledgements

To my agent Barbara Levy, publisher Mark Booth, Charlotte Hardman, Eleni Lawrence and the rest of the team at Coronet.

one

Mardan, Pakistan. 03.00 hours.

The car was a Toyota Land Cruiser and the gun on Joe Gardner's lap was an AK-47. Outside, the full moon flashlit the street and surrounding desert the same shade of grey, like a pool of floating ashes. Forty-five kilometres due north of Peshawar, smack bang in Taliban country, and the four-man team in the Cruiser was about to get surgical.

Gardner killed the engine and unfolded himself from the driver's seat. He was the last operator to debus the Cruiser, his Gore-tex Timberlands softly crunching against the stone-baked ground. A wad of forty-eight-degree heat blistered his face and choked his lungs. Gardner tightened his fingers around the AK-47 grip. His left hand was stippled with mozzie bites and he had to suppress the urge to itch them.

The Cruiser was parked up at the side of a ragged road that cut through the south-west of the Pakistani city. The Khyber mountains dominated the western horizon, baring their jagged black teeth to an asphalt sky.

John Bald manoeuvred next to Gardner and said, 'Forty metres. Last house on the right.'

He was pointing south down the road. Gardner gazed beyond the bulky shoulder of his best mate and studied the building Bald was gesturing at. It was an unlit, two-storey structure flanked on its right by scrawny trees, drab grass and acacia shrubs. A row of electronic and mobile-phone shops stood to its left. The shops were closed but their displays dispensed a thin light over the street.

'You're sure this is it?' Dave Hands whispered hoarsely, nodding at the ECM tracking device Bald was holding.

'Hundred fucking per cent.'

The flashing red light on the tracker reflected on the hard ridges of Bald's face. He and Gardner had been mates ever since the day they had both passed Selection. At the end of the brutal simulated-torture exercise Gardner had been ushered into a room with the other candidates, and Bald had winked at him and said, 'Piece of piss, that.' The man had more Scots in him than a crate of Irn-Bru and a smile permanently poised somewhere between amused and crafty. Now Gardner looked intently at the tracking device in Bald's hand. It was the size and width of an iPhone but in his mucker's giant, calloused grip it looked as if it had shrunk in the wash.

Dave Hands screwed up his face at the building.

'Looks fucking empty to me.'

'Tariq Afridi's the leader of the Pakistani Taliban,' replied Bald, tucking the tracking device into the pocket of his salwar trousers. 'He's a big deal, Davey boy, and we know exactly where he is. Right inside there.'

All the Blades were dressed in local clothes. But hidden under his kameez coat each man had a Viper special forces assault vest with four pouches for spare ammo clips and three utility pouches loaded with survival gear: compass, map, lighter, gold coins, water-purification tablets, penknife, para cord.

They were now fifty metres away from the building on the other side of the road leading to Ragesh, a strip of rutted asphalt that was ninety per cent potholes and mud. Bald led the way, Hands second and Gardner third. The fourth man in the team was a Yank. Anthony Shaw was a Navy SEAL with a dead-eyed expression that made him look colder than an ice-cold beer and pencil-thin lips that only parted when he was quoting Corinthians. The Regiment lads weren't religious and had taken the piss out of Shaw the moment he started Bible-bashing. Preacher Man, they called him. To be fair, the Yank took it in good spirits. He'd been assigned to the team because the op was a joint US–UK effort, but Gardner and Bald had privately wondered if he might prove a liability to the mission. Rumours had been flying about that Shaw hadn't made the cut for the bin Laden gig because SEAL commanders considered the six-foot-six, 300lb African-American to be a hothead under fire, prone to rushes of blood to the head.

'Christ,' Bald had said to Gardner when the two of them were alone and preparing for the op. 'If the bloody Yanks think he's too gung-ho, imagine how trigger-happy the guy must be.'

They were moving fast, passing a field of ripe rapeseed that stretched towards the hilly north-eastern side of Mardan. Each man maintained an irregular distance from the man in front – a uniform distance between four moving objects would be instantly noticeable to the human eye.

Twenty metres to the building. The four-man team collected in the shadow of a clump of blue pine trees eighteen metres down from the building. The pine needles drooped in a breeze that offered little respite from the heat. They also provided the lads with valuable cover. From where they were positioned none of Afridi's goons in the building would be able to get a mark-one eyeball on them.

The lads were carrying variant AK-47s of the type used by the Albanian counterterrorist unit. The ASH-78 Tip-3 model had three firing modes: single-shot, three-round burst and fully automatic. Hands had a grenade launcher fitted to the underside of the barrel of his weapon. Gardner's weapon had a six-inch crack on the wooden buttstock and duct tape wrapped around the ammo clip to stop the rounds from spilling out.

Gardner gestured to Hands and Shaw.

'Flank around to the rear,' he said. 'The signal will be our attack from the front. Once you hear us hit them, get in through the back door and slot any fucker dumb enough to get in your way.'

'What if there isn't a back door?' Hands asked.

'Then choose a window, you bastard. John and I will clear the ground floor. You and Everton make your way up to the first floor.'

Gardner led the way out from behind the pines. The team went into silent-running mode. No one was to speak. They didn't want to disturb Afridi and his toughs. A voice in the back of Gardner's head warned, *Don't cock this up.* This was a high-stakes op. Because inside the building was Tariq Afridi, leader of the Tehrik-i-Taliban terrorist group.

The Pakistani Taliban was the evil twin brother of the Afghan franchise. It was responsible for directing a spate of cross-border attacks on coalition forces along the Durand Line. AfPak, the pen-pushers at the MoD called it: the blurred line between Afghanistan and Pakistan that had become a safe haven for the Taliban.

At that moment, Gardner knew, Afridi's personal security detail would be ushering a TV news crew into a sparsely decorated room with a dirt floor. After months of negotiating, Afridi had agreed to an interview with a local news station sympathetic to the Taliban cause.

What Afridi and his crew didn't realize, however, was that the cameraman was an MI6 plant. Secreted inside the shotgun mike of the Sony DSR-300 camcorder was an ECM transmitter. And at that very moment it was leading Gardner's team straight to the big prize.

Twelve metres between the Blades and their target. Gardner glanced over his shoulder at Hands and Shaw. He motioned for them to break right and manoeuvre down to the side of the building. Though they knew about the TV crew, the bottom line was the lads were going in half-cocked. They had no idea how many guards Afridi had on his security detail, so they had to adopt a cautious approach.

Hands and Shaw spun off and made their way past a shuttered tobacco shop. Meanwhile Gardner and Bald made a beeline for the door. Now Gardner increased his stride and surged on ahead past Bald. Twelve metres became ten.

Then they saw the front door swing open. Gardner flung himself out of sight, into the ornamental porch of the store next to the building, Bald doing the same a split second later. They hunkered down low in the criss-crossed shadows and observed a guard emerge from the building. He closed the door behind him.

Nine metres between him and Gardner. The guard was stumpy. Blobby features, no shoes. He slung his RPK assault rifle over his shoulder and cupped his hands to his face. The tip of his cigarette glowed like an ember. He was facing away from Gardner and Bald, oblivious to their presence.

Slowly, carefully, Gardner unsheathed the Fairbairn-Sykes combat knife from the utility belt hanging beneath his kameez. He could feel Bald's breath on his shoulder as it came in shallow, tepid waves. Knife in his right hand, he edged out from the porch and crept towards the guard.

Six metres. The guard scratched his elbow. Smoke wafted from his nostrils. Gardner was four metres from him ... Three ... Blood was rushing in his ears, his warm breath seeping out. Still the guard seemed unaware of Gardner. He flexed his gnarled toes.

Two metres ...

Gardner caught his breath in his throat. It formed an icy block.

One . . .

Silently straightening up from his crouching position until he was almost vertical, with his knees slightly bent and his back slightly arched, Gardner twisted his thumb and forefinger so that the tip of the smooth, slim blade was pointing away from him and at the target.

The moonlight reflected on the blade. The word 'ENGLAND' was stamped on the crosspiece.

Do it.

In one smooth motion Gardner plunged the knife up and hard into the base of the man's skull.

The incision was deadly. The tip of the blade pierced beneath the bottom of the skull and forced its way up into the cerebral cortex. Gardner could feel the tip strike something hardish yet pliable, like putty. He clasped his left hand over the guard's mouth. He flicked his wrist to give the knife a twist. The guard's body trembled. Blood oozed out of his head wound like crude oil. Gardner eased the body to the ground, rolled him over on to his chest, then wrenched the knife from his skull. Bits of brain matter clung to the blade. Gardner wiped it on the topsoil but blood still smeared the grooves.

Bald was with Gardner now, taking up a position to the right of the door. Gardner re-sheathed his knife and slid to the opposite side of the door. He caught his breath in his mouth. The door was wooden with a beam slanted across the divide. To Gardner it looked flimsy. Bald nodded at him, thinking the same. Gardner flashed three fingers at him.

Three seconds . . .

Bald adjusted his legs, spreading them out to a little beyond shoulder width to give himself a solid, sturdy firing stance. Then Gardner stepped out into the open and faced the door head-on, shifting his weight on to his left foot. He hoisted his right leg up and back and flicked it at the door at chest height.

The rubber sole of his Timberland was an inch from the door when the explosion rocked his world.

two

The door shot off its hinges and slammed into Gardner like a two-ton truck. Flying backwards, he landed on his back four metres from the entrance. Splinters from the door needled his hands and face. A red-hot wind blitzed him. His ears were ringing like a tuning fork.

Booby trap, he thought as he lay there. But then he scraped himself off the ground and peered into the fog. Bald was already charging through the door. Gardner staggered through a second later. The *ca-rack* of single-round gunshots riddled the hot air. Someone inside was shouting.

Gardner manoeuvred through the heavy smoke, his eyes watering. But he could see rugs on the walls, a stockpile of ammo belts and RPGs in one corner and a simple tandoor oven in the other.

Blood streaks on the dirt floor, mixing in with shrapnel.

The smoke thinned a little. Gardner spied a hand on the floor. The smoke thinned a little more. The hand was attached to the arm of an Arabic-looking man lying face down in the dirt. Gardner grabbed a clump of the man's black hair, lifting up the head. He found himself face to face with the MI6 guy. Except now the guy had no face. There was a glistening black hole where his eyes should have been, as if someone had scooped them out. Somehow he was still alive, his chest inflating and collapsing spasmodically, his spittle-flecked mouth snatching for air. He was trying to say something. Gardner kneeled beside him and detected a soft flopping sound in his chest.

'Who did this?' Gardner said.

'Afridi,' the guy throated. 'He killed . . . every . . .' He didn't finish the sentence. Choking, he hocked up thick black goo. Gardner left him to gargle his way to the dark side. He caught more gunshots – a single shot followed by an urgent three-round burst.

'Fuck!'

The voice belonged to Hands. Gardner pushed on towards an arched entrance that led out from the back of the room, and entered a dark corridor so narrow his shoulders were scraping against the walls. At the end was a plain wooden staircase. He hurried down the corridor, two more *ca-racks* sounding in the air. These gunshots were getting louder. Upstairs, Gardner figured. He raced towards the staircase. But then, to his left, he noticed a low opening – more like an alcove than a room. Sparkling, snowflake-sized dots studded the floor. Diamonds. And Bald. His mucker was on one knee beside the diamonds, raking them in with his free hand. Bald had his back turned to Gardner.

'What the fuck, John?'

Bald froze. Gathering himself, he shot to his feet.

'I was just—'

'For God's sake,' Gardner snapped, cutting him off. 'Where are our mates?'

'You should see the stash Afridi's got here,' said Bald, kicking dirt over the diamonds and pretending not to hear Gardner's question. 'It's like fucking De Beers.'

'Forget it. We're taking the stairs.'

Gardner led the way, clearing the steps two at a time. He reached the landing in six long strides, Bald a couple of metres behind him. Sweat formed at the nape of Gardner's neck and waterfalled down his back.

'Hands? Shaw?' he called. Nothing but silence – along with the sulphurous smell of a discharged weapon that thriller writers always mistook for cordite. It tasted like burnt chlorine on his tongue.

Gardner swept right, his index finger applying slight pressure to the trigger mechanism, primed to slot any fucker in his sights.

The landing was room-sized. Against the far wall was a cache of AK-47s, RPGs and a stack of grenades. A door to his left. Corpse in the mouth of the door. Hole in the back of his head, big and deep and round. The kind of hole you could nestle an orange in. A second body lay slumped by the weapons. His brown kameez was punctured with bullet holes, the wall peppered with half a dozen more, spent brass littering the floor by his naked feet.

Dave Hands was to the right of the X-rays slapping a fresh thirty-round clip into his assault rifle. Shaw stood next to him, his mountainous frame dominating the window that looked out on to the Ragesh road.

'No sign of Afridi?'

'Not a bloody peep.' Hands shook his head ruefully.

Bald clicked his tongue. 'He knew we were coming.'

Gardner said nothing.

Shaw turned away from the window to face Gardner. 'We've got company.'

three

'How many X-rays?' said Gardner.

'Twelve,' Shaw replied.

Gardner blinked gritty sweat out of his eyes and checked out the situation on the street for himself. The X-rays had dispersed as quickly as Shaw had identified them. Gardner could just make out three silhouettes flitting between the shadows of the buildings and a row of Daihatsus and Nissans parked sixty metres to the east down the street. The silhouettes were using the vehicles for cover. They were hunched behind the vehicles' wheels, which told Gardner they weren't amateurs. Only experienced fighters with proper training would have known that the front and rear tyres were impervious to bullet penetration. Anywhere else on the chassis and the target risked having a round pass straight through the car and rupturing his flesh.

'What do you see?' Bald asked.

Gardner watched one of the silhouettes peel away from the vehicles and sprint down the street on a parallel course from the building. He was gunning for a side street thirty metres east of the building. Because he had studied satellite images and Google Earth blow-ups of Mardan before insertion, Gardner knew that that little street gave access to the rear of the building they were in. And if the Taliban managed to hit the rear, the Blades would be fighting on two fronts. They'd be fucked.

'They're going to mount a flanking attack,' said Gardner.

He took a deep breath, closed his eyes for a second and worked out their options. The metallic grip of the AK-47 felt hot and sticky in his hand. Twelve X-rays. Maybe more in reserve. Versus four Regiment operators.

They had four clips of ammo each, which amounted to 120 rounds total per man, and their only getaway was the Land Cruiser. If they'd been in the Afghan Gardner would squash this attack in a finger-click. He'd get on the comms and put a request to the head shed for fast air, then wait for the F16s to flatten the place back to the Stone Age. But this was Pakistan. This was a deniable op. He couldn't request fast air because, as far as the pen-pushers at Whitehall were concerned, Gardner and his mates weren't even in Pakistan.

So what's the plan, Joe? he wondered.

He turned to Bald. The Scot's eyes were trained on the approaching Taliban forces.

'Put suppressive fire down on the bastards. Keep them rooted to the spot. Can't let them flank us.'

Shaw immediately discharged a torrent of three-burst rounds at the targets. The sound was hypnotic, deafening. Shaw had it covered. On the third burst Gardner turned and made for the stairs, Bald and Hands at his back.

Back to the front room. The air was thick with the putrid smell of burnt flesh and hot brass. The doorway was charred black. Debris littered the dirt floor, clumps of mortar and stray cartridges. The MI6 guy's face was locked in the weird look of the newly dead – not scared or distressed, but mildly surprised, like a man standing outside his house who suddenly realizes he's lost his door key. Gardner sidestepped the trashed camcorder and took up a position at the front-facing window, dropping to one knee to give himself a stable firing position with the window at chest height. They had a clean line of sight down the Ragesh road. At their ten o'clock stood the vehicles the Taliban were using as cover.

Bald drew up alongside Hands at the side of the doorway, thumbing the fire selector on his AK-47 to semi-automatic. Hands gripped the GP-25 underslung grenade launcher. The UGL was a Russian variant addition fitted on a rail system beneath the barrel. They were carrying Russian firearms for the same reason they were decked out in local clobber – because it was a false-flag op. The war needed to be won, and the bad guys were the wrong side of the Khyber Pass.

Of course, the Regiment had to defer to Whitehall and cover its tracks in case the shit hit the fan. So they carried nothing to identify them as SAS operators. They didn't use Regiment equipment, guns or gear.

The GP-25 had a grooved surface with a trigger mechanism at the rear of the unit and a quadrant sight fixed to the left side of the mount. Reaching into a Russian military-issue pouch secured around his waist, Hands pulled out a VOG-25 caseless grenade and shoved it into the launcher. The mount made a clicking sound as it locked the round into place. The VOG-25 had an effective range of 150 metres and upon impact created a lethal kill zone of five metres. Hands was packing the 'P' version of the grenades. These were loaded with a special charge in the nose so that they bounced up from the ground and exploded at the target's mid-section, slicing and dicing their guts like a supercharged cat o' nine tails.

Figures were now scuttling down the road towards the side street. The road was unlit at that point and Gardner counted six blurred, indistinct shadows. Their only identifying features were the barrels of their AK-47s. The nearest X-ray, he saw, was shouldering an RPG.

Gardner peered down the iron sights of the AK-47 and tucked the buttstock tight into his shoulder. The grip felt good. The guy with the RPG was running towards the side street. He was fifteen metres from reaching cover and disappearing. His mates weren't far behind.

Gardner depressed the trigger.

The gun jolted in his grip, lighting up the fetid darkness and issuing an ear-splitting *ca-rack*. The round thunderbolted through the air and smacked into the X-ray's neck. He jerked, flinched, stumbled. Momentum propelled him a few metres further. Blood sprayed out of his neck. The 7.62×44mm bullet had severed his jugular vein. Then the guy dropped.

His mate to the left was throwing a grenade. Bald promptly discharged three rounds into his torso. The grenade rolled out of his hand.

'Get down!' Gardner shouted.

The grenade kicked off with a crump. Scorched earth and stones came flying through the windows and doorway. A second later Gardner popped his head above the wall and looked out of the window. Another X-ray was standing upright a metre to the right of the detonated grenade. The explosion had lacerated his torso. His bowels were hanging out like the inner tube of a sliced car tyre. The X-ray dumbly tried shoving his innards back into the gaping wound. Gardner watched out of the corner of his eye as Bald issued a single round. The throat of his AK-47 barked and the round punched a bolt-hole through the X-ray's forehead.

Three more fighters dashing down the Ragesh road. Hands unleashed the UGL at them. The VP-205 round made a satisfying *whump* as it landed at the feet of the middle X-ray. He watched the grenade bounce up into the air. It seemed to be suspended for a long time, hovering in front of the X-ray's chest. Then it erupted. All three Taliban disappeared behind a ball of smoke. When the smoke had cleared, Gardner found himself looking at a bunch of limbs and blood and fabric. The X-ray on the right was doused in his mates' blood and guts and howling at his severed torso. His legs were beside him, feet level with his shoulders. His entrails uncoiled on the ground.

'That's six down,' Bald said, his voice interrupted by the

relentless noise of Shaw putting down suppressive fire on the half-dozen Taliban fighters who remained hunkered behind the vehicles. Their zapped mates had made them wary about charging out of cover. But Gardner knew it would only take one or two to make it to the back of the building for the Blades to be in the soup big time.

Distracted by movement to his right, he shot a look over his shoulder at Bald. He could barely believe what he was seeing. Bald had turned around and was patting down the pockets of Afridi's personal security guard.

A pair of hands shoved Bald back so he lost his balance and hit the floor. Shaw was staring daggers at Bald. The vein on his shaven head was pumped and prominent, like he had a length of garden hose beneath the skin. He said, 'What the hell do you think you're doing?'

'Get your hands off me,' yelled Bald, kicking away the reams of spent brass and empty clips. 'I could ask you the same question. You're supposed to be upstairs.'

Shaw shot Bald an arctic stare. The Scot returned the look – with interest.

'Stealing is a sin,' Shaw said. 'Exodus 20:15.'

'Mind your fucking business.'

Shaw glared at Bald for a moment longer. Then he angled his head at Gardner and said, 'I'm out of ammo.'

'Here,' Gardner replied, chucking him one of his two spare clips. 'Take mine. Better make those rounds count, mate.'

Shaw rushed back up the stairs.

'Pious prick,' Bald said, wiping blood from his mouth after the Yank was out of sight.

'What now?' Hands shouted to Gardner from his position at the front window. 'We've still got six of those fuckers left to deal with, and I reckon they'll have sounded the alarm to their Taliban buddies. We're not gonna be able to hold them off for much longer, Joe.'

Gardner saw Bald stash something into his pocket and then return to his position at the window. Something was going on with him, but now wasn't the time to worry about it.

'Hold position here,' Gardner told Hands. 'When I give the word, we're bugging out. John, come with me.'

He shuttled down the corridor and up the stairs. Bald paced alongside him. They hit the landing. Shaw had stationed himself back at the window. He didn't turn to acknowledge either man. Instead he was staring down the sights of his AK-47. He was completely absorbed in the business of acquiring targets. Gardner and Bald joined him at the window. Shaw's line of sight overlooked the street below and the six remaining Taliban fighters, conscious of his firing position, had squatted down behind the vehicles so as not to present him with an easy shot. Gardner could make out a foot trailing out from behind a wheel. Another fighter's head was visible behind the windscreen of a battered old Corsa. Shaw was training the sights on the second figure's skull.

Good luck hitting that fucker, Gardner thought. The AK-47 was said to have an effective range of 300 metres in semi-automatic mode but he'd always reckoned that was too generous. The AK-47 wasn't famed for its accuracy. It had been designed with an emphasis on rapid fire and close-range kill potential. It wasn't the kind of firearm used by snipers. He doubted Shaw could register a hit on a difficult target fifty-plus metres away in poor visibility.

Then Shaw discharged a single shot – the figure's head burst like a pumpkin – and Gardner was forced to reconsider. He swapped a look of admiration with Bald.

'You're kidding me,' he said to Shaw.

'Finished first in my class at sniper school,' Shaw replied. 'Should have been me putting one through Osama's head.'

Gardner watched the other five Taliban fighters crawl deeper behind the vehicles.

Shaw switched to his next target. A Taliban fighter had sprung out from the vehicles and was sprinting towards the side street in a zigzag fashion, head low and moving fast. Shaw struck the guy in the neck at the first time of asking. Blood spurted from his throat. Bald looked at Gardner. The crafty smile that Gardner knew so well.

This guy can shoot, Gardner thought. 'Still four targets left,' he said. 'We've got to abort the mission, and get out of here. There's no way we're finding Afridi now.'

Then Gardner saw Bald staring into the doorway. Gardner followed his gaze. There was a window at the back of the room overlooking the streets behind them. Breeze-block buildings with corrugated-iron roofs, courtyards with dogs and goats tethered to wooden poles. Tangles of electricity cables and phone lines sagging from poles more slanted than the tower of Pisa. And, on the nearest rooftop, a figure scrambling into the distance.

Bald got the word out before Gardner could open his mouth. 'Afridi.'

four

'Displace out the back door,' Gardner told Shaw as Bald shot out of the window. 'Relay that to Hands. RV point is the mosque south-west of our location. Now fucking go!'

Gardner followed Bald through the window. It yawned out into a cracked-tiled balcony suspended nine metres above a litter-strewn backyard. Bald was in front of him and poised on the balcony ledge. Afridi was fully twenty metres beyond Bald, brandishing an AK-47 and clambering across a wide, low roof cluttered with half a dozen satellite dishes. He didn't pause to look back at his pursuers. Gardner thought he saw a diamond drop from his pocket. Then something glimmered on the roof like a fallen star.

Bald started to hoist himself up on to the roof of the adjoining house, directly opposite the balcony. The edge was two metres above his head, yet somehow he made it look easy. His forearms were tense and sinewy like a pair of coiled steel cables. His thickset fingers clamped themselves around the edge of the corrugated iron and his lats and shoulder muscles did the heavy lifting. The roof he was hauling himself up on to formed part of a grid of tin and tile roofs that covered the city.

Bald was nearly there. Then he suddenly lost his grip. His right hand slipped, his legs dangled like slack rope. He summoned all his strength to thrust his right hand back up to the edge of the roof. But it fell agonizingly short. He tried again. This time his fingertips reached it and grasped it. He grunted as he pushed his body up. Once he had slid his Timberlands over the edge of the roof, he rolled on to his front and offered Gardner a gimme.

Gardner went to clasp his left hand around Bald's, then remembered how much it was stinging from the mozzie bites. He thrust his right up at Bald instead, resting the balls of his toes on the balcony's edge, pushing himself up first with his calves and then with his lats. Blood pumped into his dorsal muscles, swelling them. It felt like each muscle was being shredded with the tension.

At last he was up. Bald spun around and raced across the rooftop, then Gardner picked up the chase. Their boots clanked against the corrugated iron. Afridi was already two rooftops down the line, at least twenty-five metres away, his silhouette framed on top of a ramshackle structure, all exposed breeze-blocks and glassless windows. Bald slowed to a quick walk and tucked the AK-47 stock tight against his shoulder.

He took aim at Afridi.

Slot him now, Gardner thought, and it was mission accomplished.

The barrel of Bald's rifle kicked up as he discharged a single round. Sparks flicked up on the roof. He'd missed. The Taliban leader stopped in his tracks and stared back at Bald. Then he lifted his AK-47 and sprayed a wild volley of rounds at both men. The muzzle flash briefly illumed his face. His skin was stretched and wrinkled like tanned leather.

Bald and Gardner picked themselves off the ground in time to see Afridi leaping off the roof. Disappeared from view.

'Fucker's dropped down,' Bald said. 'Someone forgot to tell him that we always win, Joe.'

With that Bald ran to the edge of the roof and without seeming to look, jumped down to the ground below. Gardner peered over the brink. No sign of Afridi. The drop was deeper than he'd anticipated. Had to be twelve metres, he figured. Bald was scraping himself off the ground. Gardner clamped his eyes shut and lowered himself from the rooftop. He landed with a bump, collapsing on his hands and feet, then rolling over on to his side. A plume of dust belched up from the ground and into his eyes.

'Quickly.' Bald gestured to a sequence of fresh footprints stamped into the dirt. They were in a backstreet that snaked between a dozen courtyards. The ground was bare except for patches of dry grass, the occasional puddle and tin bottle tops. The footprints tapered off to the south, leading out of the backstreet and into a warren of alleyways.

Gardner was running on Bald's shoulder, passing scabbed walls and gutters overflowing with raw sewage. They soon reached the end of the street.

'I see him,' said Bald, his voice impatient, hard as frozen gravel.

Afridi was slipping into the shadows down the alley at their three o'clock. He had a long stride on him and instead of slowing down he seemed to be sprinting further ahead. More like forty metres now between Afridi and them.

'One thing the Talibs are good at,' grinned Bald. 'Running like hell.'

They chased as Afridi sped down the alley. Thirty-six hours in-country, no sleep and hard tabbing and Gardner's eyelids were heavy as hockey pucks. A vicious stitch speared his right side and crawled up to his armpit. He was sure Bald was flagging too, even if he wasn't showing it. He knew they had to push themselves all the way on this mission if they wanted to slot Afridi and decapitate the Tehrik-i-Taliban.

Exposed rubbish festered in the streets, and Gardner fought his gag reflex. Afridi was already at the next alley turn, twenty-five metres away. He threaded his way along the rubble-strewn passage. But soon that rubble was blocking his path, forcing him to slow down and pick his way around it. They were gaining on him at last.

Moonlight flooded the alleyway, turning the ground into a purple ribbon. Gardner paused to peer down the sights of his AK-47 and train the cross hairs on Afridi's temple. One headshot to strike a fatal blow to the Pakistani Taliban.

He breathed out.

Pulled the trigger.

A round slapped into the wall behind Afridi.

Missed.

Forget it, Gardner told himself. It was a one-in-a-hundred shot. Keep going. Don't stop now. He was sucking in deep breaths and trying hard not to focus on the countless pains queuing up at his pain receptors, demanding to get their tickets punched every last fucking one of them.

Now they were into a square and twenty-five metres away, on the other side of it, was the mosque, its minaret picked out against the sky, the moon suspended above it, bathing the building in white light.

But Afridi was nowhere to be seen.

'Where the fuck is he?' growled Bald, slowing his stride.

Shadows wormed out of the mosque's courtyard. They drew closer and closer until Gardner could make out the features of Dave Hands. That broken nose, the ears that looked like a dog had chewed on them, the blemished skin: an unmistakable package. Shaw was next to him, sweat teeming down his enormous figure. Shoulder to shoulder, the two men looked like the opposite ends of a set of Russian dolls.

'Afridi?'

Hands jerked his shoulders. 'Thought you boys were taking care of him.'

Distant catcalls of gunfire interrupted them.

'Fucking great,' said Bald, pricking his ears. 'More Talibs on the way by the sounds of it.' He nodded at Gardner.

'We don't have much time. Joe, you and Dave go get the Cruiser.'

Gardner nodded his agreement. Bald's plan made sense. They had to nail Afridi, but they also needed to plan how they'd bug out from Mardan before the next wave of Taliban arrived.

'Preacher Man, you and me are going Talib hunting,' said Bald, resting a hand on Shaw's shoulder. 'Joe, our RV will be the Maktoub road. We'll see you there once we've given Afridi the good news.'

Bald and Shaw paired off, tracing a route down the alley leading away from the mosque. Gardner and Hands began marching in the opposite direction. The mosque faced the Maktoub road, which ran north-west of the Ragesh road they had originally travelled along in the Land Cruiser. They navigated to the left of the mosque, skating around its courtyard.

Then they took a left, past a procession of low, flat houses, the road as dry as the bed of a drained river. The heat was oppressive, smothering their faces like hot towels.

'Maybe the cameraman couldn't keep his gob shut?'

The air, already thick, filled with the stench of incinerated human flesh.

'He worked for MI6,' Gardner said, 'and those guys are heavily vetted. And anyway Afridi zapped him too.'

At the Maktoub–Ragesh intersection, Gardner hung another left. Forty metres up the street stood the building or what was left of it. The immediate area was carpet-bombed with twelve Taliban corpses. They were sprawled unnaturally, mottled arms and legs twisted at unusual angles. The soil was coated a darker shade of brown. Gardner scanned the street, looking for any signs of live X-rays. He couldn't see any movement.

As he headed straight for the Land Cruiser, he spotted an X-ray dragging himself towards the roadside. Black, bubbly flesh covered his face. His skin looked like the lungs of a sixty-a-day smoker. He was nine-tenths dead and from the look of things the other tenth wasn't far off. Gardner turned away and picked up his stride.

They neared the Land Cruiser. Gardner prised open the driver's door and dumped his AK-47 on the dashboard. Hands threw himself on to the rear passenger seat. There was the satisfying thump of car doors being slammed.

Then Gardner heard a metallic clatter. He looked down at his feet. His last spare clip had somehow slipped out of his tactical vest pouch. He bent down to pick it up, planting his left hand on the driver's seat to support him. He straightened up and put the clip back in his pouch, making sure the button was properly fastened this time.

But then there was another noise. Something was hissing.

A pain flared up in Gardner's left hand, sudden and excruciating. Gardner's eyes flicked down and settled on a snake uncoiled on the front passenger seat. The fucker was sinking its teeth into the back of his hand. The slitted eyes and sharp fangs marked it out as a pit viper.

Gardner went rigid with terror. Then Hands spotted the snake too. He leaned forward and hit it sharply with the stock of his AK-47. The half-metre-long viper whipped its tail, loosening its jaw from Gardner's hand and directing its rage on to Hands, who responded by jabbing his stock at it repeatedly. As the snake slid towards the driver's door, Gardner sprung open the latch. The viper hissed again as it slithered out of the Cruiser and into the darkness.

Gardner breathed out. A pair of bite marks had sprouted on his hand. They were red and sore, like needle pricks. A tingling sensation worked its way from his pinkie to his thumb. Gardner shook it off, twisted the key in the ignition and shunted the Cruiser into Drive.

'You see them diamonds inside?' Hands said above the engine's growl.

'The ones Bald had his mitts on?' Gardner said. 'Yeah, I saw them all right.'

'Must be worth a lot of money.'

'So?'

'Just saying.'

Gardner kept his foot to the floor as they neared the turn-off leading to the mosque. Hands was in his ear again, saying that the house where they'd seen Bald scraping up the diamonds was two minutes' drive away. But Gardner was distracted by an object winking in the rear-view mirror. It was coming from the far end of the road. The lighting was poor but Gardner could make out the outline of a Toyota Hilux pickup truck 140 metres back. It wasn't catching up with them, despite the fact that Gardner had the Cruiser doing eighty kilometres per hour.

Three guys were clinging on to the rigging on the cargo bed. Something was resting there between the guys. It was metallic and shaped like an aircraft turbine. In the darkness Gardner couldn't quite identify it.

'Taliban reinforcements,' he said. One of the figures on the cargo bed was firing an assault rifle into the sky.

'Hope you're a better driver than my ex-wife,' Hands said.

'This is before or after she tried to run you over?' Gardner said as he headed on to the Maktoub road, wrestling the wheel all the way to the right. The cab swerved around the bend. The tyres squealed like dying rabbits. For a second Gardner thought they would smash into a convenience store. But in the next instant they were straightening out, and the tyres stopped screaming and the cab stopped shaking.

'I see John,' Hands said.

Gardner saw him too. He was twenty metres ahead.

'Where's Shaw?'

Bald was racing out from the mosque courtyard on roughly the same course that Gardner and Hands had just taken. He froze in the middle of the road and waved his hands at the Land Cruiser. Bald didn't appear to have seen the Hilux to the rear of it.

Gardner had to slow down on the approach to Bald, and the sudden drop in the Cruiser's speed allowed the Hilux to get to within eighty metres of it. Now Gardner and Hands could see more clearly the metallic, engine-shaped object mounted on the rear cargo bed.

'Fuck me, it's a Minigun,' said Hands.

The GAU-17/A Minigun was mounted on a specialized gun pod. The guy who'd been firing his assault rifle into the sky had ditched his weapon and was seizing the handles at the rear of the barrel. Gardner's bowels did a somersault as the barrel began to rotate and whine, warming up to deliver its 3000 rounds per minute of hot 7.62-51mm-calibre devastation.

Stay way ahead of the Hilux, Gardner thought. Allow the Minigun to train its sights on you and you'll be punched with more holes than a box of Krispy Kremes.

Looking ahead, Gardner saw that Bald had only just clocked the Hilux. The Cruiser headlights jumped and glided around him.

Ten metres became seven. Gardner reached across and flung open the front passenger door. Bald was lacquered in blood. His face, his arms, his neck. Slick and wet and varnished, from a distance it almost appeared like war paint, except Gardner had seen too many pints of the red stuff to mistake it for anything else.

Gardner slowed down to thirty-five. Bald sprinted the last few metres to the front passenger door and grabbed hold of the door frame. Gripping the underside of the roof, he eased his left foot on to the seat. Then his right. The Cruiser lurched over a pothole and shuddered, causing the door to thump shut and flinging Bald fully into the Cruiser.

'Fucking drive!' he roared.

'Where's Shaw?'

'No time, Joe.'

'Where's your weapon?'

'Just get us out of here!'

Gardner gunned the engine. The Cruiser growled. They started chewing up road. The speedometer clawed its way past the fifty mark. But the Hilux was still on their backs and any second now, Gardner knew, that Minigun would erupt.

'Fucking hell,' Gardner muttered.

With Gardner at the wheel and Bald bloodied and battered, Dave Hands took control of the situation. He rolled down his passenger window and rotated himself so his back was pushed against the front seat and his feet planted against the rear seat. Then he leaned his profile out of the open window and levelled his AK-47 at the Hilux. He rattled off a three-round burst. The rounds hit the dirt around the Hilux. The Cruiser was jerking and shuddering. Hands was struggling to get a stable shot off.

'Hurry the fuck up!' Gardner shouted.

Hands let off another three rounds. The first shot was wide, but the second and third struck the front-left tyre and the rubber came off like the peel off an orange. The Hilux buckled and screeched. Gripping the wheel, the driver looked like he was wrestling with the hind legs of a dog. Too fucking late, thought Gardner as he glanced in the mirror. The Hilux veered off the road and crashed head-on into the wall of the mobile-phone shop. Impacting the building at 110 kilometres per hour, the front end of the Hilux was crushed like a Coke can. Two figures were flung through the windscreen and slapped into the wall. Noxious smoke billowed out of the bonnet as the engine sputtered and died.

'Still got it,' said Hands, easing back into the rear seat and kissing the stock of his assault rifle.

The Blades left the Hilux for dead on the horizon, the

pickup truck melting into the blackness and followed fast by the buildings and scar-tissue roads of Mardan. Six minutes later they reached the cold silence of open country. No one said anything for the longest time.

Finally Gardner said, 'What happened to Shaw?'

'Dead,' Bald monotoned, his face blank, unreadable. 'Afridi got him. There was nothing I could do.'

Gardner hit the brakes. The Cruiser lurched, shuddered, stopped.

'What the fuck are you doing?' Bald eyeballed Gardner as he shunted the Cruiser into reverse.

'We have to go back for him,' said Gardner.

'With half the Taliban on our case? Fuck that.'

'John's right,' Hands put in, pulling himself upright.

The Cruiser sat on the road for a long second while Gardner weighed up what to do. On the one hand, the Regiment never left its own behind – that was the code. But the lizard part of his brain told him Bald and Hands had a valid point. It would be a virtual suicide mission to head back into Mardan. The place would be crawling with Taliban reinforcements. Reluctantly Gardner put the Cruiser into drive and hit the accelerator. He slammed the palms of his hands against the steering wheel in frustration.

Bald screwed his eyes shut. They sped west towards the final RV point, a field on the outskirts of a tiny village called Aparzi, forty-three kilometres due west of their current location. Forty-three kilometres to freedom. In two hours and eight minutes' time, at precisely 06.00 hours, a Chinook would arrive at the RV and evacuate the lads back to Camp Bastion, the British military base deep inside Helmand Province.

As he ratcheted the Cruiser up to 130 kilometres per hour, Gardner allowed himself the small satisfaction of thinking that the extraction was about the only part of the plan that hadn't turned to a complete clusterfuck.

five

Gardner had his foot pressed all the way down. The speedo was twitching at the 140 mark. Mardan had been replaced with a barren landscape populated by a few threadbare shanty homes and interspersed with the occasional bland mosque.

No one said a word.

Hands worked the radio transmitter. The unit's comms gear consisted of a secure radio, Iridium 9555 satellite phone with an internally stowed antenna, and the GPS unit that allowed the command centre to track their every move.

The secure radio ran on an Ultra-High Frequency (UHF) encrypted line and was designed for Low Probability Intercept and Recognition (LPIR), using a burst transmission capability. This allowed messages to be compressed into short transmissions and made them harder to detect by enemy SIGINT. The signal provided an encrypted line back to the command and communications centre for special operations based at Bastion.

The blood on Bald's face had dried into thin smears, as if someone had used his face as a thumbprint.

'I'm sorry, Joe.'

Gardner said nothing.

'Afridi jumped out of nowhere. He came at me. Knocked my AK clean out of my hands. Then he went for Shaw. Had this big fucking knife – speared his heart.'

Gardner gripped the steering wheel so hard he thought it might snap in his hands.

'I went for Afridi but it was already too late for the Yank. I killed Afridi with my bare hands. You should've seen the look on his face, Joe.' He cleared his throat. 'We took him down. That's what we came to do, and we bloody well did it.'

Gardner still said nothing.

But he was thinking: all my years in the Regiment, every shithole part of the world I've fought in, every operation I've taken part in, I've never once lost a man.

Until now.

'Tell you what,' Bald said. 'At least we won't have to put up with Shaw quoting fucking Bible passages any more.' He smiled weakly. First at Gardner, then at Hands. Neither man returned the smile. The atmosphere was too grim even for Hands. Bald dropped the smile and stared at Gardner's left hand.

'What happened to you, Joe?'

Gardner bit his tongue. He couldn't focus. A pressure was building in his skull, pain humming inside his temples.

'Looks like a snake bite,' Bald added.

The pressure swelled behind Gardner's eyes.

'Pit viper bit him,' said Hands.

'I'll be fine,' Gardner snapped.

But in truth he was feeling far from fine. His lips were numb, he was freezing cold despite the slow-cooked dawn heat, and he had a headache that felt like he had a colony of ants burrowing into his skull. Christ no, he didn't feel fine at all, and he was sure as fuck he didn't look it either.

'Let me take a look at it, Joe.' As the designated first-aid specialist on the mission, Bald was responsible for treating any trauma wounds or infections.

'I said I'm fine.'

Bald shrugged and settled for staring out of the window at the ticker-tape landscape. He closed his eyes again.

'Fuck!' Hands broke the silence and switched off the radio unit. He had a disgusted look on his face, like he'd been sucking on a bag of dicks.

'What is it?'

'Well, the good news is that the Chinook's on its way.'

'And the bad?'

'Head shed says Camp Bastion is coming under heavy attack from the Talibs. Sounds like we're to help repel the fuckers. It ain't gonna be an easy ride home.'

'And I was really looking forward to that fucking pint,' said Bald.

Gardner tensed his forearms. A road sign announced that Aparzi was still twenty-four kilometres away. He chose not to share his dark thoughts with his muckers.

six

Dawn was breaking over a parched lunar landscape. Gardner brought the Land Cruiser to an abrupt halt 300 metres below the RV point. The RV itself was a raised, platform-like square of land located a hundred metres above the desert floor, on the sloping edge of a mountain shaped like a torn knuckle. At forty by forty metres it was big enough for a Chinook, but high and inaccessible enough to deter any curious passers-by.

'This is as far as we can go,' Gardner said above the metallic tap-tap of the cooling engine. 'Rest of the way we're on foot.'

'How long?' Bald asked.

Gardner checked his NATO-approved MX10 Nite watch. Hands and Bald were wearing the same model. They'd all synched their timepieces at the beginning of the mission. The PVD-coated stainless-steel case of Gardner's watch was flecked with grains of sand.

'Nine minutes to the chopper ETA.'

Hands, fiddling with the sat phone, said, 'I hope they ain't fucking late because the head shed's saying we've got about fifty Taliban on our case.'

Gardner scratched his sore hand.

'Where? I don't see anyone.'

'Other side of the mountains. Coming straight for us.'

Gardner frowned at the mountain range.

'How long till they get here?'

'Head shed reckons ten minutes.'

Bald tugged the latch of the passenger door. 'We'd better get a fucking move on, then.'

The men debussed. Hands stashed the comms gear in a backpack and hoisted it over his back. Checking that they had left nothing behind, Gardner paced around to the boot and clicked it open. Inside was a go-bag containing four glow-stick markers and a flare gun for launching a distress signal.

'Shit,' muttered Bald, drawing up to the boot and reaching for an object wrapped in newspaper beside the go-bag. 'Almost forgot this bad boy.'

Gardner shook his head as his mate unwrapped the object. It was an Excalibur Exocet 200 hunting crossbow. The resin mould was painted in desert camo colours and was capable of firing its 20-inch bolts at a range of over fifty metres. Ever since he'd become a paid-in-full Blade, Bald had insisted on taking the crossbow with him on ops. It was like his lucky charm. He had modded the Excalibur to fire bolts whose tips were loaded with the primary explosive acetone peroxide, or TATP, operating on a two-second delayed reaction.

Bald grabbed the case of explosive bolts and tapped the crossbow.

'I might not have a rifle,' he said. 'But this will do the job nicely.'

Gardner saw Bald eyeballing the car lights in the distance as they closed in. He was gripping the medieval-style cross-bow in his right hand. Something about his face unsettled Gardner. There were streaks of blood at the corners of his lips, like a badly drawn clown's smile. He faced Gardner and said, 'Remember Selection?'

Gardner nodded at the memory.

Phase One of Selection took place in the rugged Brecon Beacons in South Wales. The hardest tab of their lives was up the unforgiving Pen-y-Fan mountain, rain lashing down on the cold and hungry candidates as they strove to reach the next RV. Gardner had pushed hard all the way to the summit. When he finally made it, his lungs had turned to sandpaper and his quad muscles were mush. He beat Bald on that first phase. Beat him by a whole eight minutes.

'Piece of piss,' Bald had said at the end of Selection.

Now Gardner broke into a run. He began scaling the mountain. The going was tough. The soil was loose and he found it difficult to secure a foothold. It was like running up a salt deposit. Matchsticks lit his calves; he figured the incline had to be at least fifteen per cent. He leaned forward, groping around for rocks to grip on to. But the rocks were loose and crumbling like wet chalk, and visibility was poor in the grainy dawn. Bald was ahead of him, forty metres further up the side of the mountain.

Gardner picked up the pace. He was exhausted and wondered how Bald was doing.

And then he recalled the rumours that had done the rounds back home. Rumours that said no man could have waltzed through Selection like Bald did. That he must have cut corners along the way. One failed candidate swore he'd seen Bald taking blatant short cuts on the Brecon Beacons course. The head shed dismissed the candidate's accusations out of hand. Bad blood from someone who wasn't good enough to make the grade, they said.

Gardner had just closed the gap between himself and Bald to twenty metres when a dull *phtt* ripped through the air. A faint star sparked on the upper edge of the mountain high above the RV. Dirt kicked up in front of Gardner.

Sniper.

'Get the fuck down!' Bald shouted. The three operators instinctively hit the ground at the same time. Gardner was lying prone on his chest. He propped the AK-47 up in front of him.

Gardner scrambled towards a clump of rocks at his ten o'clock. Bald was making his way to the same cover. Hands was at Gardner's three, hidden in a low scrape.

A second *phtt*. This shot zipped past Gardner. Close enough that he could feel the carriage of heat coming off the bullet. Soil erupted a few metres behind him. The sniper was adjusting his range.

Getting closer.

Gardner crawled as fast as he could towards the rocks. The sniper had been getting his range with the first two shots. The third, Gardner knew, would be on the money. He was seven metres from the rocks. Sweat percolated down his back, hot and sticky.

The third shot came just as Gardner reached cover. The round smacked into the spot he'd occupied half a second earlier.

'Just in time,' Bald grinned.

The fourth shot came three seconds later. It thumped against the rocks, showering Gardner and Bald with granite shards. But they didn't panic; they planned. Gardner pricked his ears and absorbed the sound of the shot. The *phtt* told him that the sniper had a suppressor fitted to the barrel of his sniper rifle. That also explained the lack of visible muzzle flash.

'I put him at our one o'clock,' he told Bald.

'Do you hear how clear the shot is? Fucker can't be more than 200 metres away.'

'Maybe one-fifty?'

'Yeah, maybe.'

Scanning the mountains, Gardner imagined where he would set up shop if he wanted to slot a bunch of X-rays.

'There,' he said, keeping his voice low. 'That smooth ledge with the large boulder.'

'I see it,' Bald replied, then spat on the ground. His phlegm was quickly absorbed into the scalding desert floor. 'Good angle. Excellent cover.'

'Perfect firing position.'

They stared at the spot and waited.

Then they saw him. A coal-black silhouette moving out from the boulder and bounding towards another boulder to the west that offered a clear line of sight over the rocks behind which Gardner and Bald were hidden.

'We've got to take him down now,' Gardner said. 'Before the fuckers across the mountain get here. I don't know about you, but I don't fancy my chances against fifty of the pricks with a single clip.'

'Save your ammo,' said Bald. 'I'll handle the sniper.'

'With that piece of shit?' Gardner pulled a face at the crossbow.

'Watch and learn, Joe. Watch and fucking learn.'

Bald had consistently proved himself to be the top marksman in the Regiment. The standard range for a crossbow bolt was between forty and fifty metres, with the bolt travelling at some 300 feet per second. An expert operator, using the crossbow in perfect conditions, can hit a target at a hundred metres. Bald was aiming at a moving target in low visibility at a distance of 150 metres.

Sinking to a prone firing position, Bald edged towards the rocks. His breath stilled. There was a long pause of silence as he tracked the sniper. The silhouette was almost at the next boulder.

Then Gardner heard a light *pop* as the crossbow fired its explosive arrow bolt. He traced the trajectory of the arrow. It rose high in the air, its tail fins spinning. Then it dipped sharply.

The arrow's tip pierced the shooter's right leg. He gave a yelp and stooped low, pawing at the wound. He was trying to pull the bolt out when the TATP detonated. The sniper was swamped by smoke.

Then his body imploded.

Flaps of skin, bits of bone and gristle and burnt fabric were blown across the rock face towards Gardner and Bald. Even in the half-light they could see that there was nothing left of the shooter except the stub of his left leg and a bag of bones.

Bald sprang to his feet.

'Always wanted to do that.'

Hands was approaching them, sat down, phone pressed tight to his ear.

'ETA in thirty seconds.'

'How far away are the X-rays?'

Hands consulted the head shed on the phone once more.

'They're closing in fast,' he reported back to Gardner. 'In fact we'll get a mark-one visual on them any second.'

The three of them doubled their pace, scaling the mountain until they were nearly on top of the RV. The rising sun coloured the platform with purples and reds. Gardner had never seen such a stunning patch of land.

The Chinook announced itself with a faint *whump-whump* that grew ever louder. Gardner cracked open the glow sticks and handed one to Bald and another to Hands. They arranged them in a W shape to signal to the chopper's pilot that they were ready for extraction. The *whump-whump* grew so loud Gardner could feel his eardrums bleeding. He arched his neck up and saw the Chinook breaking through the slate-grey clouds grouped in batches on the horizon.

Gardner spied movement midway up the eastern side of the mountain, at their three o'clock. Ten silhouettes were framed against the sky. They were negotiating a rugged path on the mountain, climbing around the rocks and hollering at Gardner. He put them at 300 metres away. Two of the X-rays paused and unleashed sporadic bursts of semi-automatic fire at the Chinook. At a range of 300 metres they had more chance of winning the lottery twice in a row than downing the chopper.

The Chinook circled impassively over the RV. Then it

hovered directly above the SAS men, its blades blowing dirt and rocks into a giant whirlwind below.

Gardner discharged six quick rounds on the silhouettes. On the sixth he winced and dropped the AK-47. His left hand was burning up. Then he scooped up the assault rifle in his right hand and inspected his left. He was no medical expert, but he understood that he was in serious fucking trouble. His hand was distended and purple. The two bite marks had turned black, like fish eyes. He could no longer feel his fingertips. His lips were numb and when he closed his eyes weird coloured spots danced in front of his eyelids.

The viper's venom was working its way through his bloodstream.

The Chinook lowered its Marlow rope. They were bugging out using the new RPX system. Rapid Personnel eXtraction relied on a super lightweight rope with an ascender attached to one end and used a two-loop integrated safety system. The rope was deployed from the Chinook, then hauled the operators up in a sort of reverse rappelling action. Gardner let Hands latch himself on to the rope first and indicated to the crew to begin winching him up.

The X-rays were too late. They discharged a few futile, wayward bursts at the Chinook. But the Blades were getting out of Dodge and there was fuck-all the Taliban could do about it. It was game over.

Gardner just hoped to God that there was an antidote at Camp Bastion.

seven

As they landed on the outskirts of the base, the rear-loading cargo ramp on the Chinook opened up like a whale's mouth.

Gardner stood at the edge of the lowered ramp and surveyed the surrounding area. The Chinook had descended a hundred metres west of Camp Bastion, as close as it dared to get to the firefight kicking off at the base. Gunfire cracked and popped above the incessant drone of the Chinook engines. Frag smoke formed a kind of clinging, dirty fog above the camp. Home to more than 10,000 squaddies, Bastion was a hunched enclave of field tents, shipping containers and prefab military barracks hemmed in on all sides by HESCO blocks. Separate from these was the field hospital. The camp's airfield consisted of a row of aircraft hangars and a 2350-metre-long concrete runway scorched in places from perpetual mortar attacks. Gardner remembered reading somewhere that Bastion airfield was the fifth-busiest UK-operated airport in the world. But landing at the runway was impossible now: Taliban forces had breached the runway's perimeter and were taking potshots at the coalition soldiers entrenched in the shadow of the hangars.

'This is as close as I can get her,' the pilot said over the intercom. As if to emphasize the message, an RPG detonated in the air directly above them and shock waves from the blast shook the Chinook.

'Jesus Christ, it's hot,' the pilot added.

'Just the way we like it, mate,' Bald shouted back.

Gardner was first down the ramp. His Timberlands crunched hot dust. The chopper's blades kicked dust up into the air, reducing his visibility. Bald and Hands quickly shadowed him off the ramp. The Chinook didn't waste any time fucking about. It was thundering towards the horizon faster than a Blade could work up a hot brew.

The dust frothed and evaporated. Gardner established his bearings. He could make out the jagged line of HESCO blocks at his three o'clock, backgrounded by gnarled mountains. The clatter of AK-47 gunfire was spliced with louder single-shot *ca-racks* which he suspected were the squaddies inside Bastion putting down rounds. The land separating them from the base was littered with the carcasses of burnt-out jeeps and chunks of shrapnel shaped like shark teeth.

Gardner saw a figure rushing towards him. He was decked out in the squaddie get-up of digicam in desert colours, the sleeves rolled up to his biceps. He moved clumsily, weighed down by his Modular Tactical Vest and his lightweight helmet. Gardner reckoned the kid was all of nineteen.

'Private First-Class Danny Grant, 1st Battalion, Royal Anglian Regiment,' said the squaddie, gripping Gardner's hand in awe. 'You're the SAS guys, right?'

'Tell me what the hell is going on,' Gardner said, shaking the kid out of his stupor.

The squaddie looked surprised. Then he turned serious. 'The Talibs have been bombing us since 03.00 hours. Had us properly under the cosh. We're used to the mortars, but they've been coming at us on the ground now too.' He shook his head. 'It's a bloody mess.'

'Who's in charge on the ground? We need to talk to them.'

'Colonel Turrell,' the kid said, eyes flicking from Gardner to Bald and back again. 'We'll have to take a short cut around the airfield. The Talibs are bombing the crap out of the front gates. Hope that's OK.'

'Fine, take us there.'

They paced east, parallel to the airfield, Gardner maintaining a four-metre distance to the rear of Grant, Bald and Hands. It was more of a habit than anything else – just wider than the kill zone of a landmine or IED.

'You know, I was thinking of trying Selection myself,' said Grant.

'Just concentrate on getting us to Turrell.'

'Yeah, all right. But maybe after you could give me some tips about passing through?'

Gardner sighed inwardly. If he'd had a quid for every squaddie who thought himself worthy of wearing the famous dagger crest, he'd be living in a gold-painted mansion and wiping his arse with Egyptian silk. He felt sorry for Grant. The kid was bright-eyed and green. Probably been in-theatre for a few weeks at most, he thought.

But Gardner had bigger worries on his mind than the wet-behind-the-ears private. He was beginning to doubt whether he was in a fit condition to fight. He was feeling feverish and lame. The discoloration on his hand had spread up his forearm all the way to his elbow. His pulse seemed weak and irregular. Merely keeping pace with Grant left him feeling dizzy and exhausted.

Rounds whistled past his face. The Taliban assaulting the airfield had obviously spotted them. Gardner hit the deck. He clocked Grant standing upright and blinking at the volley of bullets raining down on them. The confused look on his face told Gardner that the private hadn't grasped they were coming under heavy fire.

Gardner launched himself at Grant, about to shout at him to get the fuck down.

He got no further than 'Get—'

They were being hit by a tidal wave. A throat-burning,

ear-lancing tidal wave. The world turned ten shades darker than midnight.

Gardner was knocked for six. He saw Grant being tossed through the air like a rag doll. Then Gardner was lifted off his feet too. The landscape unravelled in an ochre blur. He didn't know which way was up, which way was down. He felt something punch him in his left hand. A dozen blows pounded on the small of his back. A wave of pain exploded down his spine.

The world silenced and stilled.

Gardner opened his eyes. He was lying flat on his back. The silence faded. It was replaced by a cry, guttural but human, high-pitched but glottal. Who was screaming like that? Someone's injured, he thought. His leader's instincts kicked in. He glanced over his shoulder in an effort to see who'd been wounded.

Then Gardner realized the screams were coming from his own mouth.

The pain in his left hand had gone. He blinked grains of soil out of his eyes. Looked at his hand. He had no hand to speak of. His arm ended at the wrist. It didn't even look like a wrist any more. Just a tangle of serrated flesh. Bones, muscle and sinew were jutting out of the hole. Like he'd shoved his hand into a meat grinder.

Another scream. This one came from his right. Gardner looked across and saw Grant lying a few metres away. The kid had taken the brunt of the blast. His skin was punctured in a thousand places by ball bearings, his belly stitched by the same. His legs and groin had been blown away. All that was left was a pair of shattered femurs and a dark patch where his bollocks used to be.

The Taliban carried on putting rounds down on the operators. Bullets hopped and skipped around Gardner. One thwacked into Grant's belly. Blood sluiced out of the neat ten-pence-sized hole.

'Joe! Fucking hell!'

The voice sounded far off. Distorted. As if the speaker was underwater.

'Joe! Joe!'

The voice grew more distinct with every hoarse repeating of his name. Finally he understood that it belonged to Bald. He hacked up blood and sand. Dear God, he'd never been so thirsty in his whole life. Spittle gathered at the corners of his cracked lips. He managed to roll on to his right side, his left arm flopping around uselessly. Then he looked at the scrubby area directly behind him. Five seconds ago he'd been hurrying across it with a fresh-faced squaddie. Now that same squaddie was ripped in half not four metres away. The soil was a concertina of shrapnel scars, bitter smoke and streaky blood.

Amid the carnage, Gardner spotted his detached thumb and forefinger.

Bald materialized through the smoke.

'What are you doing? John? Fucking get back!' Hands screamed from behind the smoke curtain. And a voice sounded in Gardner's skull, saying, 'Hands is right.' Standard operating procedure was to wait for the clearance team to arrive when an operator was maimed in a landmine or IED attack. Trying to rescue Gardner now would only expose Bald to enemy fire. Bald wasn't just acting recklessly, he was being suicidal.

'John!' Hands roared again.

To no avail. Bald bounded along the desert floor. Enemy guns rattled furiously as they zeroed in on him. Round after round smacked into the ground in his wake, like a sequence of firecrackers kicking off in his footprints. He was gunning straight for Gardner. To his right, Grant was faintly bleating.

Bald reached Gardner, casting a six-foot-three shadow over him.

'Don't worry, mate,' Bald said, kneeling down beside his mate. 'I'm getting you out of here.'

Gardner tried to form a word, but it died in his throat.

'Save your energy, Joe. You're gonna be OK.'

While Hands put down suppressive fire on the Taliban at the airfield, Bald set to work on Gardner's trauma wound. He ripped a sleeve off his kameez coat and wrapped the material tight around the elbow, plugging the blood flowing from the wound. Gardner felt a dull, aching pain drill its way down his forearm. Bald applied a gauze dressing to the nub to keep it free of infection. Leave the wound exposed and the risk of septicaemia would increase rapidly. He manoeuvred Gardner on to his back, unscrewed his water canteen and tipped precious fluid into Gardner's mouth. It tasted better than the best beer in the world.

'Hold on, Joe. Just one minute, OK?'

Gardner barely nodded.

Bald shuffled over to Grant. The squaddie was in terrible pain, groaning like a stray dog hit by a car. Bald shushed him.

'My teeth . . .' the kid said. 'So cold . . .'

'Easy, lad.'

'So cold . . .'

The kid was delirious. His eyes were dancing in their sockets. His breathing was erratic. Gardner looked on as Bald removed a set of morphine injections from his tactical vest, tore open the packets and plunged them one by one into the kid's flaccid, pallid arm. The kid didn't protest. He knew he was fucked. No legs, no dick, a monstrous gash where his torso ended – he'd bleed out before medevac could be sorted. Bald closed the kid's eyes and watched the life drain out of him like water out of a sink.

Bald scrabbled back to Gardner and slipped an arm around his back and helped him to his feet. Gardner was desperate to express his thanks, but still the words wouldn't come.

Bald said, 'You're gonna be fine, mate.'

Then he said something else and laughed, but Gardner couldn't hear him speak. Someone had put the world on mute.

He was falling in and out of consciousness. Red and yellow spots speckled his vision. The two men were going through the curtain of smoke. Passing through to the other side. Away from the incessant gunfire. Then it began expanding out like a giant puddle. He wondered if his eyes were playing tricks on him.

Eventually the world was reduced to a pinhole surrounded by darkness.

Then nothing at all.

eight

Hereford, UK. Three weeks later.

The Green Dragon in Hereford was famous for two things: reasonably priced London Pride, and Regiment groupies. It was hidden down a small street away from the town centre, and the lads had spent many an hour by the bar, knocking back pints of Pride and Greene King IPA courtesy of Stacey, the heavily mascaraed barmaid who was six months pregnant. With no idea who the father was, the lads had come up with a uniquely Regiment solution to the problem of fatherhood: they had a whip-round. Stacey now had a grand in cash for the kid, and every operator could breathe a sigh of relief at not having to shack up with the chavviest woman outside of Essex.

Gardner ordered a pint. He'd had to wait a good five minutes to be served by Stacey. Because tonight the Dragon was heaving with operators.

'Three quid, love,' Stacey said.

Gardner fished out some pocket shrapnel. A month ago such a simple action wouldn't have caused him any problems. But now he had a prosthetic limb where his left hand used to be. He had to rest the pint on the bar counter, then root around in his jeans pocket with his right. Finding three coins, he pressed them into Stacey's tattooed palm.

He did a one-eighty and saw Dave Hands standing right in front of him.

'Haven't seen you around in a while,' Hands said. 'What's up?'

'They call it "recuperation". Or decompression. Take your pick.' Gardner shrugged. 'It's all the fucking same thing.'

Hands nodded at the prosthetic limb. 'I heard that snake bite nearly finished you off.'

Gardner said nothing. Losing his left hand to the IED had only been the start of his problems. Medics on the Chinook stabilized his wound before sending him back to Selly Oak Hospital in Birmingham. Blood tests revealed a lethal dose of pit-viper venom in his system. He was given an intravenous antidote made from horse serum, which in turn caused serum sickness and knocked him out flat for a fortnight. Gardner was back on his feet again now, but struggling with the hand, the fact that he was on the Regiment scrap heap – and his mates' endless jokes about horse sperm. They'd got it into their heads that serum and sperm were the same thing.

'Well,' said Hands, filling the awkward silence, 'at least they didn't get your wanking paddle.'

Gardner sipped his beer. The pub was heaving with Blades both former and current, gathered to raise a glass to John Bald. Gardner spotted the man himself at the other end of the bar, beneath the TV showing the Sky News bulletin. The headline was something about the NHS. Bald was hanging with Major Pete Maston and a bunch of other head sheds that Gardner didn't recognize. Someone old and important-looking slapped Bald on the back. A young guy in a suit pointed to him and made the universal sign for another round, wrapping his hand around an invisible glass and arcing it to his mouth.

But Joe thought Bald looked uncomfortable. His smile looked more like a grimace and he was drinking unusually slowly while everyone else quickly got down to the important business of getting wrecked. Occasionally he would glance at Gardner for a brief moment before looking away.

'Reckon he'll be up for a medal or two,' said Hands, necking his Fosters, then pushing out an amber-nectar belch. 'No doubt he'll walk into some cosy security gig. Guarding Saudi princesses in Harrods for ten grand a week. Lucky bastard.'

Maston clinked a fork against his empty pint glass. The chatter subsided. Stacey lowered the volume on the TV. Everyone turned towards Bald. The Scot was still staring at the floor.

'I hate speeches almost as much as you lot,' Maston said. 'So I'll keep it short. John Bald is what this Regiment is all about. We train you all to be the best of the best. To never back down, to never give up. Thanks to John's extraordinary courage and sacrifice, the Tehrik-i-Taliban has been decapitated. In the struggle for a peaceful and bright future for the Afghan people, this is a decisive moment.'

Bald rubbed the back of his neck. Gardner thought he now looked pained rather than just uncomfortable in the spotlight. Maston cleared his throat and continued.

'But that's not all. As some of you may know, John also risked life and limb to save the life of his fellow soldier. Without his extraordinary courage, Warrant Officer Joe Gardner wouldn't be with us today. Medals will follow for Sergeant John Bald. But tonight is all about the honour that matters the most: the appreciation and respect of his fellow warriors.'

Maston raised his glass to a chorus of 'Hear, hear.'

Then Hands nudged Gardner and said, 'Look!'

Gardner stared up at the TV, along with everyone else in the pub. In response to shouted requests from across the room, Stacey cranked up the volume to full blast. The news report was of an exclusive live interview with the leader of the Pakistani Taliban.

'Afridi's been replaced?' Hands asked. 'Already?'

Gardner watched as the camera switched from the studio to the news report. The footage was low-res and grainy. The cameraman appeared to be ushered into a cave by a masked figure. Someone was waiting in the mouth of the cave. Torchlight flickered on the face of the new leader.

A pause of silence spread through the pub. Hands was the first to speak.

'I don't fucking believe it,' he said.

They were looking at Tariq Afridi.

He was alive and well.

Mutterings around the room. Maston's face turned shades of red. Gardner scanned the pub, trying to pick out Bald. Several other faces were doing the same.

What really happened back there in Mardan? Gardner asked himself. He remembered the diamonds scattered on the floor. He remembered the evil look Bald had shot Shaw when the Bible-bashing SEAL had confronted him. And the bad feeling he'd had.

Gardner and the rest of the crowd realized something at the same time.

Bald was nowhere to be seen.

nine

His phone rang.

Joe Gardner's phone never rang. When you lived off the grid, people soon forgot you even existed.

Not many people knew Gardner's name any more. Few enough that he was curious to know who was reaching out to him. He looked at the screen.

+00551171674519.

It was a number he didn't recognize.

And a voice he did.

'Mate, you've gotta help me,' someone shouted above a clatter of gunfire. The signal was weak. 'They're on my fucking case. Came out of nowhere. Millions of the fuckers. It's like vintage Baghdad.'

'John? Is that you, mate? You're breaking up.'

'We've called for backup but no one's arrived yet. Thumbs up bloody arses. You remember the Afghan, don't you? Now I'm in deep shit, Joe. You've gotta help me out.'

Gardner reached for his fake left hand with his good right. *Afghanistan.* The IED blowing up in his face. Smoke melting away, an exposed nub where his left hand was supposed to be, blood pumping out like oil from a burst pipe. John Bald it was who'd radioed in for a medevac under enemy fire. Saved Gardner's life. He owed Bald. Big time.

'Where the fuck are you?'

A pause for breath.

'John?'

He remembered the kid next to him. Twenty-one years old, his legs ripped off at the thigh, femur bones jutting out like a couple of split baseball bats. And the pints of blood – as if he'd been washing in a forty-gallon drum topped up with the stuff.

'Barbosa favela. Middle of fucking Rio de Janeiro. My location is my Troop times forty north, your Troop times twenty west from the Christ statue. Get here as soon as you can, Joe.'

'Mate, what's going—?'

The line died.

ten

The Cobra Hilton Plaza Hotel stood tall over the rotten favelas. The room was located on the twelfth floor and looked out to the south, away from the beaches and towards a metropolis of filth and human shit laid bare.

'I'm telling you, I don't know shit,' the guy chained to the radiator, Paulinho Nava, said.

'As you already explained, my friend.'

'Then why the fuck are you doing this?'

'You're beginning to piss me off.'

'You're fucking crazy,' Nava snorted.

Nestor Weiss pulled back the plunger, allowing the last liquid in the vial to fill into the syringe. Removing the syringe, he expelled any trapped air and gave the needle a tap.

'What's that?'

Weiss did not reply.

'When the other guys hear what you've done, you'll pay in blood. Anyone who harms a BOPE officer, they're marked for death, do you hear? *Marked.*' Nava's face was puffed up. He looked like he was suffering from a million bee stings.

Weiss was pleased with his earlier handiwork. He didn't throw many punches these days, but when he did, he could still beat a man real bad.

He held out the 12.7mm hypodermic needle.

'You're looking at 100ccs of sulphuric acid. Sure you want to piss me off?'

'Blind me then, you bastard.'

'Oh, but this isn't going in your eyes.'

The bravado was gone. Nava's veins rippled on his neck like tense rope as he tried to inch further and further away from Weiss, pressing himself up against the wall. He kicked out as Weiss came a little nearer.

'Stay away from me!'

'Did they teach you how to survive this in training school, my friend?'

Nava spat on to the textured silk carpet.

'Did they?'

Shifting to the left to sidestep Nava's flailing legs, Weiss knelt down beside him. The man's head was slumped forward. It was all he could do to fix his eyes on the needle.

'No, I didn't think so,' Weiss continued. 'When it comes to death, everyone's a first-timer.'

'If this is about money, I have . . . I can pay you—'

'You know it's not.'

'Women, then. Or boys. Fucking whatever. Shit, just name it and I'll get it for you, I swear.'

'None of these things interest me, my friend. The only thing that could keep you alive, you say you do not have.'

Nava's face dismantled. He would've cried, Weiss thought, if the BOPE commander hadn't already wrung every tear from his body. Pleading for his miserable life. 'I told you once – shit, a hundred times – I don't know where he is.'

'Then there's nothing else to talk about.'

'No, no. Please no.'

Weiss tested the syringe, squeezing a drop of acid on to the carpet. It made a sizzling noise on contact and burned its way through the fabric, all the way down to the floorboard.

Paulinho Nava, Lieutenant Colonel of the Special Operations Police Battalion, hero of the Siege of Reis favela, thrashed about wildly as he tried to yank the radiator off with his handcuffed arms.

All told, Weiss had killed more than six hundred men, women and children. Normally the victims seemed to accept death in their last moments, as if they were paralyzed, and Weiss was all-powerful, like a god. He got high off that feeling.

There's no such thing as a guy who loves killing, but then there's no such thing as a smoker who doesn't want to give up. Weiss still experienced guilt after each kill, still carried in his pocket a five-inch carving of the Basilica of Our Lady of Guadalupe which he rubbed for forgiveness. But killing, he thought, is also more addictive than heroin. Many hitmen, himself included, became aggravated if they did not kill for a while.

He shanked the needle into Nava's chest.

Depressing the plunger, Weiss flooded the heart muscle with corrosive acid. Nava's head shook violently from side to side. His bronze skin glowed ruby red. He foamed at the mouth. Boiling blood oozed out of every orifice. His nose, eyes, mouth and ears. Nava clenched his jaw and grunted.

He did what everyone did before they died, and shat his pants.

Nava stilled. A stream of blood trickled down his ear and on to a heavily tattooed right arm. Grim Reaper on the bicep, Frank Sinatra at the elbow, a 1930s playgirl on the forearm. He seemed to laugh, did the Reaper, as the images coloured red.

Satisfied this was dead meat, Weiss extracted the syringe, placed the cap on the needle and tucked it into his jacket pocket.

The first time he'd employed this particular method, Weiss had been curious as to the extent of the damage caused. So he bribed a coroner to prise open the ribcage and reveal the insides. He discovered that there was nothing left. Heart, lungs, kidneys, pectoral muscles, collarbone. As if someone had thrown a hand grenade inside the chest cavity.

Weiss glanced at his shitty digital watch, and remembered it didn't work. The clock on the wall, however, told him it was eight on a clear-eyed morning. Normally he worked as a contractor, no questions asked, doing business with the Juárez and Los Zetas cartels. They paid well. But today he was on the trail of thirty million dollars. The kind of money that could allow him to retire to the Cocos Islands, off Costa Rica. Drinking tequila on Chatham Beach. Wearing a more expensive watch, perhaps a Cartier, and having the finest pussy in all of Latin America. Weiss was tired of killing.

You've a chase on your hands now, he thought, as he tore off the hygienic gloves and tucked them in the pockets of his single-breasted, mid-calf-length duster coat, black denim. Nodded at Nava's corpse. Locked the room door and slipped the sign over the door knob. *Por favor não incomodar.* Do not disturb. Left the hotel and climbed into his rented BMW E90 sedan.

Have to find him today, Gardner figured. Otherwise it's too late.

Well. Time to pay a visit to a man who can help.

eleven

The Little Bird's rotary blades cut up the sky. Sunrise kicking in over Rio and Joe Gardner's hangover was along for the ride.

He had a beard that could strike a wet match and a nose that had more breaks in it than an American football game. Tied to a lanyard with his feet resting on the rail, he looked out at the favela two hundred metres below. Thousands of sprawling shanty huts built on top of each other, the huts fixed precariously on a rifle-green hillside, spitting distance from the financial district and high-rise apartments. To the west he could see the statue of Christ the Redeemer. Jesus didn't seem to give a fuck about the slum next door.

'Barbosa favela,' said Leon, sitting next to him.

Sounds like a Brazilian footballer, thought Gardner.

'Not much to look at, I know.'

'I grew up in Moss Side, mate. I've seen worse.'

'You think it looks bad from up here, wait till you hit the ground.'

The Little Bird began its rapid descent, diving sharply into the favela and ducking this way and that, turning on a sixpence. Gardner had ridden in Lynxes and Chinooks and Merlins, but the Navy crabs had no chopper as nippy as this. Now they were a hundred metres off the ground. Gardner clocked a gang of kids racing through the streets below. They were packing AK-47s and firing on an older group who fled east. BOPE had withdrawn from the favela, leaving the warring gangs to slog it out among themselves. Third World kids were getting ready for the Third World War.

Gardner, on the other hand, was going in half-cocked. Just him and a couple of scarred knuckles for company. His first task on landing at Galeão-Antônio Carlos Jobim International Airport had been to head away from the tourist hubs of the Leblon and Ipanema. Other people ventured south. Gardner had made his way west, to the poverty-ravaged district of Santa Cruz. A thirteen-year-old boy, a street hustler in a Brazil shirt with 'Robinho' on the back, said he could get anything for Gardner. For two hundred reals, he agreed to supply him with a black-market Sig Sauer P226. But the café the boy told Gardner to meet at was crawling with mean-looking cops, and anyway the kid never showed.

Inserting into a hostile environment without a gun, Gardner felt uneasy.

'It's all kicking off down there,' he said. 'Is this the best LZ you could find?'

'You'd better believe it. The gangs are shooting at anyone who moves. There's rumours that a couple of BOPE officers are cut off from the rest of their unit, and the kids smell blood. The surrounding streets are just too dangerous, amigo.'

'Dangerous for who? You and Mr Pilot here?'

Leon didn't answer. Fair play. The Bird was a favour from a mate of a mate, arranged at the last moment. Twenty-four hours earlier Gardner had been sleeping in a Hertfordshire bush. Since leaving 22 SAS he'd lived off the radar, as anonymous as a man could be in a Britain up to its eyeballs in CCTV. As a consequence, he allowed himself only two connections to the outside world, a Barclays cashcard and a mobile phone. The phone was to keep in touch with old Blades. Gardner wasn't the kind of guy who rang up and talked about his feelings or how his day had been. That wasn't his style. And so the phone never rang.

Until yesterday, when Bald had called him out of the blue.

He saved your life. The frayed nerve endings in his left hand reminded Gardner of the sacrifice Bald had made. So he had emptied his current account. Used the little bread he had to book a one-way ticket to Carnival City. Figured, if nothing else the weather had to be better than Stevenage.

He checked his mobile. Two messages. One from his operator, welcoming him to their local network partners. The second from the Brazilian partners themselves. Some waffle in Portuguese. More messages in one day than he'd received in a year.

'This Mr Bald, is he a friend of yours?' Leon asked.

'Why do you care?'

'You know, those BOPE guys are fearless. They don't give a shit. But if they get trapped by the gangs, it's game over. The gangs skin them alive, amigo.'

Gardner said nothing, because nothing needed saying.

The Little Bird hovered fifty metres above the ground. The chopper had more moves than a Soho prossy, but the cramped nature of the favela made venturing any lower too risky. Before boarding his flight Gardner had visited an internet café and studied the Barbosa favela and the surrounding area on Google Earth so he wouldn't be totally blind on the ground. But it was hard to absorb all the details, as the streets twisted and turned like a bowl of spaghetti. Barbosa favela crammed a quarter of a million people at the bottom of the food chain into an enclave the size of half a dozen Wembley Stadiums. Having boned up on his history, Gardner knew that the chaotic assembly had been created when veteran soldiers from the war of independence rocked up in Rio but, instead of being treated like heroes, were banished to the slums.

Know the feeling, Gardner thought.

The area immediately below them was obscured by a blanket of arsenic-grey smoke. Gardner could see less than nothing, but he could guess that whatever lurked beneath, it wasn't a fucking tea party. His heart hammered against his breastbone.

Sweat treacled from Gardner's brow on to his lips. He tasted salt, and last night's booze from the hotel bar, where he had hooked up with his number-one drinking buddy: drink. Gardner wiped his face with the sleeve of his T-shirt.

Leon smiled. 'Those caipirinhas taste nice, don't they?'

'Deadly.'

Gardner rested his feet on the side rail. He tossed a length of a coiled-up 44mm synthetic wire over the side. Then on to his right hand he slipped on a full-fingered abrasion-resistant abseiling glove. It took three attempts before he was able to do the same for his left. Mostly because the skin-tone carbon-fibre fingers didn't want to flex.

'Can you feel anything in that?' Leon asked.

'Nothing below the elbow, mate.'

'That's some real space-age shit.'

'A century ago they used to give blokes like me a hook on a stick. Now I can pick up grapes with this thing.'

With his palms facing inwards, Gardner locked his elbows and began sliding down over the side of the chopper and directly into the smoke.

It was like plunging into a big fuck-off barbecue. Fumes flooded his lungs and nostrils. He smelled cordite and burned flesh, and tasted hot metal on his tongue. It was a million degrees in the middle.

Fuck it, keep roping down, he told himself.

The drop was just forty-four metres to the ground according to the Little Bird's on-board altimeter. He wanted to scale down as quickly as possible – being suspended on the rope would leave you exposed to sniper attacks – but he had to use the friction on his gloves to control his descent. Fall too quick and you're liable to break a leg on impact. He didn't wrap his feet around the rope, because the leather on his Gore-Tex boots made the rope slippery.

Ten more metres and Gardner was clear of the smoke. Blinking tears and boozy sweat out of his eyes, he saw that the smoke was coming from a rooftop several metres to his right. Flames licked at a column of worn rubber tyres, toxic fumes disgorged into the air like from an old industrial chimney. Gardner looked at his feet.

Almost there. Just another couple of metres.

His feet hit the ground, but he couldn't get a firm grip. His boots scraped against something slick, and when he shuffled his feet he slipped backwards, banging the back of his head against the concrete, and, fuck, it hurt.

Ignore the pain. Don't give in to it, he told himself. Get up!

He released the rope and watched it withdraw through the smoke like a lightning bolt in reverse. The Little Bird was a noisy fucker for such a small chopper. As the bird pissed off, the *whock-whock* faded and the noise sank big time. Gardner scoped the LZ, glancing over his shoulders. He had landed in an L-shaped street at the base of the favela, two hundred metres from the Tutoia motorway. Might as well have been on the other side of the fucking world.

As he'd calculated, the gangs had swarmed on ahead and out of sight. Now the street was shabby and desolate. Two- and three-storey shanty huts and botched brick buildings lined the street. A lot of the homes seemed to get away with plastic or cardboard rigged up as roofs. Guess it rains less here than in Manchester, Gardner figured.

The sharp crack of rifle shots sounded off to the east. The direction the gang kids had scattered. The volley was furious, then silent.

As he picked himself up he noticed some kind of gunk beneath him, a big puddle, dark red, consistency of melted rubber. A single Timberland footprint marked the spot where Gardner had crashed. Right where his head had kissed concrete lay a pair of intestines, the large one brown and snake-like, the smaller one reddish and flattened by Gardner's bonce. He couldn't see a body. Whoever was stuck like a pig had fucked off to go and die in some alleyway.

First things first, he thought, rubbing his sticky hands down the sides of his sandstone combats. Bug out away from the rifle reports. Don't want your trip to Barbosa to be your last. He took off west, in the opposite direction to the gunfire.

twelve

It took Weiss an hour to worm his way through the traffic. He drove north, past the Maracana football stadium and, at the old Imperial Palace on Quinta da Boa Vista, he took a right, hit Avenue Osvaldo Aranha and edged along the gridlocked road for five kilometres. God himself could not make Brazilians hurry. Weiss thought some more about his next move.

All the way to Tardelli district.

Once off Aranha the traffic lightened. Weiss turned into Rua Pedro Cabral and followed it for two hundred metres until he reached the affluent Rua Buenos Aires. A row of houses reserved for rich people presented itself, each one opulent, whitewashed, gated. He made a beeline for the luxury villa at the end of the road, the biggest and grandest of the pile. The entry gate was painted gold and had a miniature video screen fixed above the comms panel. Someone had left it ajar. A gift.

Weiss parked out front and strode across the grounds, past a water feature big enough for a grand hotel and a column of palm trees green as the Amazon. Two men stood guard on the front steps. Armed with Uzi 9mm sub-machine-guns, weapon of choice for gangsters who watched too many Hollywood action movies, they were sharing a joint. Weiss walked unnoticed until he was thirty metres from them. He was a big guy, but light on his toes. One of the guys looked up, eyeballed Weiss and tossed the joint to the ground.

'Holy shit! Motherfucking Weiss!'

He couldn't run inside fast enough.

The second guy stuck to the spot, as if he had roots for feet.

'I need to speak to Big Teeth.'

'He's inside.'

Weiss yanked open the heavy teak door and let himself in.

The villa was lavish. It also stank of piss. A Rottweiler licked at a ring of its own faeces. On the walls, between antique mirrors, there were posters of *Scarface* and *The Godfather*, and bullet holes pocked the high ceiling. He had to watch his step to avoid the used condoms and crack pipes littering the marble-tiled floor. It was true what they said. No matter which way you dressed it up, or how rich it got, shit was always shit.

Weiss entered the lounge. It was like walking into a shadow. He squinted, saw a girl of sixteen or seventeen, spread-eagled on a red leather sofa. She could have been asleep, but her wide-open eyes had rolled back into her head. *Call of Duty: Modern Warfare 2* played on a widescreen TV. The air was redolent with the smell of marijuana and fear. Weiss counted twelve goons in total around the dark room, and he didn't need to look twice to realize that every one of them was busting a tool.

He relaxed. No goon dared point their weapon at him. Not unless they had a death wish.

Luis 'Big Teeth' Oliveira was sitting at a sofa in front of the TV. There was a coffee table in front of him with half of Colombia cut up on it, but it wasn't the coke making him jumpy. It was Weiss. Big Teeth furiously chained on a cigarette.

'Nestor,' he said, opening his arms, like he was preparing to hug a bear. 'What brings you down to Rio? Can't get enough of *Carioca* pussy, eh? You know what they say – once a man's tasted wine, he can't go back to water.'

'Your jokes bore me almost as much as your country,' replied Weiss, running a hand along the mantelpiece above a baroque fireplace. Dust coated his fingers.

Big Teeth shifted in his seat. 'Then . . . you're here because of the Carlitos thing?' His voice accelerated. 'I promise, we didn't have shit, not a shit, to do with Gonzales ripping him off. That boy is mad, amigo.'

'Calm down,' Weiss said, smiling, enjoying Big Teeth's fear. 'I'm not going to kill you. And this isn't about Gonzales.'

Big Teeth laughed nervously. His goofy, golden front teeth jutted out, like some kind of grotesque bunny. All that money, Weiss wondered, so why didn't the guy get his teeth fixed?

'I'm looking for someone.'

'We're all looking for someone special, eh?'

'*Enough* of your jokes, Luis.' Big Teeth looked at his feet, the TV, the comatose girl. Anywhere but Weiss. 'This man – he's a foreigner working with BOPE. A unit you keep a close eye on, I'm sure.'

'Forget it,' Big Teeth said, stubbing out his cigarette in a Jesus ashtray. 'We don't live in Barbosa no more, as you can see. Nowadays we're out of the drugs game. We're trying to go legit, man. Recording rap music and shit.' He blew out a last gust of smoke. 'I can't help you.'

Weiss angled his head, trying to lock his eyes on Big Teeth's.

'Luis, my friend, what's the problem? You seem very nervous. Is it me?'

Big Teeth held in his breath.

'Or maybe something else has you concerned.' Weiss looked at the coffee table, lacerated with knife marks. 'Is your gang in trouble, my friend?'

Big Teeth couldn't take it any more. He stood up and shouted at Weiss. 'What the fuck does this look like to you, man? We're just local players. Local, brother. And now you come here asking me about some out-of-town guy? Shit, I don't even have no fucking passport.'

Weiss sat on the edge of the opposite sofa, the one with the bitch. She didn't flinch. Not even the twitch of an eyelid. He stroked her hair.

'Luis. I know this man is with BOPE. There's only four hundred men in the unit, and I'll bet you know the names and addresses of each of them off by heart. And I *know* you're aware of him. You might think you're Mr Big Shot these days, with your swimming pool and nice car, but at heart you're still a *favelano*. You keep your ear close to the ground. So don't fuck me about.'

'Nestor, I swear—'

'We can do this the easy way or the hard way. I gave you my word I would not kill you today. And I will not. But tomorrow is a new day. Maybe I'll come again . . .' The threat lingered in the air.

Big Teeth watched out of the corner of his eyes as Weiss ran a hand down the girl's cheek. He seemed to be weighing something up in his head. 'OK, OK,' he said, stubbing out his Marlboro. 'What's his name?'

'John Bald. He's Scottish.'

'Shit. Fuck.' Big Teeth took a scrap of paper and a ballpen and scribbled something. A barrel-chested goon pressed it into Weiss's palm. He read a name and address, scrawled in appalling handwriting. Weiss was amazed Big Teeth could even write. He looked him square in his mismatched eyes, one brown, one green.

'This is where I can find him?'

Big Teeth shook his head. 'This is someone who might know where your guy is. I can't guarantee shit, though. You know how it plays in the favelas, all kinds of fucked-up stuff happening all the time.'

'I'll check it out. Pray this does not rebound on you, my friend.'

'It won't,' Big Teeth replied, finally going eye to eye with Weiss. 'But you need to worry about watching your fucking back in Barbosa. Those kids don't know you like we do. Shit's all different there.'

thirteen

His leg muscles throbbed from the intense vibration of the Little Bird. His olive-green T-shirt, drenched with sweat, clung to his back. Thirty minutes since his insertion into the favela, Gardner was breathing out of his arsehole.

He'd exited the LZ via a maze of walkways so narrow he couldn't even stretch his arms. A wrong turn almost saw him slip into a crater in the road filled with excrement. Unguarded rectangular holes, the best part of a metre wide and half a metre high, were fixed to the sides of each home and along public walls. From the foul smell wafting out of them, he figured they led directly into the local sewage system.

Gardner tabbed at a fast pace. He was conscious of the fact that the sooner he got to Bald, the better the chance he had of finding his old mucker in one piece. Five-eight, angular and bony, Bald was tough as old leather and built from the same granite as the houses in his native Aberdeen. With his face locked in a permanent frown, Bald looked stern and cold. Get a few jars of McEwan's down his neck, though, and he'd soon be scrapping civvies with the best of them. But in a place like Barbosa, Bald would need all of his evasion skills to survive, because he'd stand out like a fake tit.

Same for you too, mate, Gardner realized.

He emerged into a market square. Or what once counted as a market round these parts. It wasn't exactly fucking Lakeside.

Sunlight razed an area fifty metres deep and thirty wide. In the middle of the street was an abandoned police car, next to a fountain with a stream of clothes floating in it. Flames hissed from the roof of the police car. Gardner counted three bodies on the ground. Two weren't moving, their legs and arms contorted, red patches the size of coffee mugs on their chests. They were wearing the beige slacks of the state police. The third man coughed, shook his head and, spotting Gardner, began crawling towards him, digging his nails into the pock-marked concrete and dragging his rag-order legs behind him.

Gardner heard voices. Shouting. Single-burst shots.

Crack! Crack! Crack!

His instinct was to help the cop. But he was unarmed and knew he wouldn't be able to get to him in time. The shots were close, and all Gardner would achieve by rushing to the guy's aid would be to fuck both of them.

There were so many exits out from the street Gardner needed to take five just to get his bearings straight. Fucking hell, he thought, navigating here is tougher than the jungle.

Four exits from the market square. One to his six o'clock, the one he'd emerged from. Two open stairways to his left, twenty metres away. The fourth escape route was an alleyway opposite, partially obscured behind the torched car, where the tin-roofed buildings were so tightly bunched a man on a bike would have a hard time squeezing through. All he could make out was an endless warren of stairways, pavements and dirt tracks.

He looked for a reference point. The Jesus statue poked out above the shanty huts on the horizon, atop the Corcovado mountain to the north-east.

'My Troop times forty north. Your Troop times twenty west,' he remembered.

Gardner headed for a north-leading alleyway. He paused a few metres into the alley mouth, edged up to a grey wall with a half-washed portrait of Pablo Escobar along its length, hunkered down by the corner and peered back down the street. Though hidden, he was north-east from the van and saw a gang of six kids, none of them looking old enough to be on the Special Brew, springing out from the far alleyway. Red scarves covered the lower halves of their faces and they brandished their squaddie-proof AK-47s like they were water pistols, pointing them at each other when they spoke and waving them in the air. Careful to stay behind cover, Gardner looked on, wishing he had a juicy .50-cal heavy machine-gun to wallop these fuckers.

One of the kids shouted excitedly in Portuguese, pointing to the wounded cop. The brats laughed as they closed in on the poor sod. He moved on his hands and knees towards the car.

The tallest kid took out a fourteen-inch machete and slashed the guy's back with it twice, crossways, in an 'X'.

The cop screamed and reached down to his hip for a holstered pistol. Bad move. Two of the other kids pounced on him and pinned his arm down. The tall kid went to work. Using the rusted machete he began sawing through the wrist. Gardner shuddered as he heard the blade grind against bone. Blood spewed.

With a high-pitched scream the guy begged him to stop. He cursed. He cried.

But the kid kept on hacking away.

Halfway through, the guy gave up his squealing. When the kid was done playing surgeon for the day, he taunted the man by slapping his face with his own severed wank paddle. Another kid produced an old-school sawn-off and shot up the cop's arms and legs. Each time a subsonic *boom* accompanied the blast and the body spasmed, as though 10,000 volts were surging through him. The kids cheered. Then one urinated on him.

The tallest kid put the cop out of his misery. Holding a sledgehammer, he instructed the others to turn the man over so he was lying on his back. The guy tried to protest. But the kid wasn't interested. He raised the hammer with both hands.

And swung the black metal head down.

Gardner heard the shattering of the cranium from behind the steps, thirty metres away.

Staying behind the wall, he waited. The posse marched east, playing football with the dead cop's hand.

Keep heading north.

Get to Bald's location – before the kids do.

He U-turned. Went to climb the steps.

Found himself face to face with the business end of an assault rifle.

fourteen

The rifle was a Colt Commando. It was in crap nick, the paint-work chipped and brown masking tape wrapped around the mag to stop it from falling apart. The user wore a one-piece flame-retardant Nomex 3 assault suit, of the type used by the Regiment in Close-Quarter Battle ops.

He shouted something in Portuguese. Sounded more like a Brazilian football commentator.

'Easy, mate.' Gardner raised his hands. Fuck knows what the bloke is banging on about, he thought. But his face summed it up: trembling lips, knife-slit eyes darting left and right, the Colt Commando shaking in his hands. An edgy man with a gun more often than not led to an AD – accidental discharge.

'I'm not looking for any trouble,' said Gardner.

Someone else had already given this guy plenty of the stuff, by the looks of it. His face was mashed up, as if some-one had discharged a shotgun beneath his chin. A deep cut was drawn above his right eye, and when he spoke rivu-lets of blood trickled between his teeth. His skin was white. Though he'd been in Rio for less than six hours, Gardner just assumed everyone was more tanned than his pasty English arse. Not this guy.

'You're English?' the police officer asked in a perfect English accent that put Gardner's Manc to shame.

He nodded.

'Go back to the beaches. This isn't a tourist area,' the guy snapped.

'Says who?'

'BOPE,' he said, shifting his weight from one foot to the other. 'Captain Rafael Falcon, Second Squad. What's your name?'

Gardner lowered his hands to his sides, eyes on the BOPE captain. First impressions, he didn't rate the guy. He looked tense, jaws locked, like he was pushing out a massive fucking turd. Ruperts lacked the nerves of steel they demanded from their men.

'Heard you boys got caught in a shitstorm yesterday?' Gardner smiled.

Falcon's face hardened like concrete. 'You still didn't answer my question.'

'Say again, mate?'

'I asked you what your name was.'

'Joe Gardner.'

Falcon tilted his head back, revealing a thin neck smothered in blood. 'Gardner? That name sounds familiar.'

'I'm a mate of John Bald's.'

Falcon's facial muscles relaxed into a relieved smile, the kind a man paints when he sees a friendly face in a rotten place. He lowered the Colt Commando. Gardner was tempted to rush him and box the crap out of him, but decided against it.

'John mentioned you,' Falcon said. 'You were in the SAS too, yes?'

Gardner gave it the air-force shrug. 'He's an old friend.'

'He said you were a good warrior. One of the best.'

On a rooftop eighty metres to the north, two kids stacked worn car tyres one on top of the other. One of them produced a jerry can and started dousing the tyres in petrol.

'I got a call from John yesterday. He said he was in trouble. That all sorts of shit was going down, and he was stuck in this favela.'

'What time did he call?'

'Around five o'clock my time, so that's – what? – one o'clock local.'

Falcon chewed on it. 'That sounds about right. John was helping us train in explosive entry techniques up in Florida. He was out on patrol with us yesterday to put our training into action. John wasn't afraid to get his hands dirty, you know. He went out on missions to the favela whenever possible.'

'What the hell happened?'

'I'll explain later,' Falcon said dismissively. 'We have to get out of here first. The local gangs are going crazy. My unit retreated to wait for reinforcements.' He laughed out of the corner of his mouth, shaking his head. 'Can you believe, we have forty-nine *caveirãos* – Big Skulls – and we've only got twelve in working order. I swear, if we lose the drugs war, it's because we didn't have enough crank shafts and gearboxes.'

Flames gushed from the rooftop tyres. Pitch-black, toxic smoke belched into the sky. Gardner smelled burning rubber in the air. Heat shimmered across the horizon in waves.

'I don't give a fuck about your war,' Gardner said. 'I just want to find my mate.'

'All of the officers from yesterday are missing. Nine men, including our commander, Paulinho Nava. I hate to say it, but they're probably all dead, and that includes John.'

'Someone else told me that. All the same, I'd like to go and check for myself. He's an old mucker of mine, you see, and I owe him big time from back in the day. So how about you put your fucking piece down and let me go about my business.'

Falcon pointed the Colt Commando at the ground, and the knots in Gardner's stomach began to unwind. 'I've been separated from my unit,' said the BOPE captain. 'And John was part of my team.' He tapped Gardner on the shoulder. 'I'll help you find your friend. We can stick together. That way, we have a better chance against the gangs.'

'Ain't happening,' Gardner said. 'I'm a solo operator, mate.'

Squinting, Falcon said, 'You sound like you know where you're going.'

'I got a hunch,' replied Gardner.

Falcon screwed up his swollen lips. 'OK, and let's assume your . . . hunch is correct. Just where exactly are you headed?'

'North,' Gardner said. He nodded vaguely in the direction of the peak of the favela, several hundred metres distant and high. He didn't want to give too much away to some bloke he'd met only a few minutes ago.

'OK. So let's say you're heading north. How do you think you'll get there?'

Well, fuck. Falcon was right. Between Gardner and the statue stood a maze of alleys and criss-crossing roads, stairwells that seemed to lead nowhere, homes stacked on top of each other. Figuring out a route was impossible. He pictured himself bounding north, winding through the maze and losing his bearings.

'I know this favela better than I know my wife,' Falcon said. 'She'll tell you this herself, over pork and beans and a cold beer, after we escape from here.'

He removed his black assault vest and unzipped the top half of his assault suit. He was sweating like an Arab at customs. Underneath he wore a black T-shirt with 'I Belong to Jesus' on the front in big white letters. He tied the suit sleeves around his waist, then slipped the assault vest on top of his T-shirt.

'What happened to your hand?'

'Lawnmower accident,' Gardner replied.

'Huh.' Falcon gave a slight, sceptical nod. 'Come,' he said. 'I'll show you the quickest way.'

He led Gardner north, in the opposite direction from the corpses, yomping up a steep row of steps. The going was hard, each step caked in mud, the legacy of repeated mudslides. The passageways were claustrophobic, no more than a metre wide in places. Gardner saw a couple of dead civvies face down on the concrete, neat bullet holes in their backs. Running for cover, he thought.

Nothing in the favela was uniform. Metal walkways spliced the roofs. Washing lines obstructed every possible line of vision. Gardner had operated in Belfast, Baghdad and Kabul, but he had never seen anything like this.

Falcon glided up the steps. Clearly he'd had a bit of match practice. But Gardner matched him stride for stride. Unlike some ex-Blades, he kept himself in top shape. Being a drifter of no fixed abode meant that the everyday world was his gym. Daily runs, long walks, using park benches for push-ups and swing frames for wide-grip pull-ups. Gardner reckoned he was in better condition than some of the lads on active service. 'Like a condom stuffed with walnuts,' his last flame had described him.

He had Afghanistan on the mind again. At 0937 hours he'd been shooting the shit with the guy next to him, a cocky lad called Grant who wanted to win the war against the Taliban single-handed.

At 0938 hours Grant had femur bones instead of legs, his dick had been incinerated, his shredded ball-sack flapping in the hot wind. Shrapnel stitched across his belly and neck. Gardner was dazed by the explosion, to the point he looked at his own severed hand and felt no pain, and wondered only how long it'd take before he'd die of his wounds.

Normal protocol was to wait for a sweeping team and dogs to come in. The Talibs were cunning fuckers; they often planted secondary devices around the primary IED, nailing anyone who came to help. A sweep took time, something that neither man had. Bald raced across exposed ground to the crippled WMIK vehicle, flung open the door and dragged Grant across to safety, Gardner leaning against his shoulder. Stringy, purplish bowels gushed out of Grant as Bald tried to plug the gaping hole in his groin.

Gardner looked on as the lads grouped around Grant, the kid screaming for his mum, his fucking mum. As they shot him up with a morphine overdose, Gardner felt the blood loss from his hand. Blue and yellow blotches danced across his vision. A voice, Bald's, said, 'Don't worry, mate. Medevac's on the way.'

Falcon halted at the top of the steps, breaking Gardner out of his daydream.

'Stop,' he said. 'I see something.'

'What is it?' Gardner barely whispered.

No answer.

'Rafa?'

Gardner moved down on to his belly and slid alongside Falcon. Up ahead the alley widened out into a rubble-strewn yard, the extra space created by a ream of collapsed buildings. The area was vacant, probably because the locals were expecting it all to turn into a bag of bollocks any minute. Gardner scanned the rooftops and windows. No movement, but he couldn't help notice the bullet holes sprayed across the sides of most of the homes.

A bulky, black-painted van was parked thirty metres away, to their seven o'clock, on the lip of a winding road that zig-zagged west from the edge of the favela. The thing barely qualified as a road, more of a slick of caked mud, jutting rocks and knee-deep puddles.

'A *caveirão*,' Falcon said. 'From my unit.'

A foot-high slab of cement, with lengths of lead pipe jutting out, blockaded the Big Skull's path. Atop the vehicle, a warped turret revealed the evidence of a grenade lobbed inside. Two bodies lay next to the vehicle and from the way they were positioned, lying on their stomachs with their hands tied behind their backs, Gardner figured they were executed with a bullet through the head.

Gardner walked towards the bodies for a closer look. The stench was powerful. Like a spit-roasted pig smeared in shit. He checked the name tags. 'SGT. EDILSON.' 'SGT. CAMPOS.' Eight metres from the corpses, Gardner noticed something was missing.

Their heads.

He saw a pair of rugby-ball shaped objects speared to metal posts. If one of those heads is John's, he thought, I'll never forgive myself.

Gardner stopped in front of the severed heads. The eyeballs had been gouged out, the noses, ears and lips crudely sliced off. Their mouths had been forced wide open, and inside each one was a sawn-off cock and bollocks. The balls were greenish-brown and covered in glistening red crap. Flies buzzed. Maggots wriggled.

Returning his attention to the decapitated bodies, he spotted a pistol holder on one of them. Sinking to one knee, he hurriedly unhooked the strap. Browning Hi-Power. Fucking yes. He badly needed a tool and this was his chance to snare one.

The Browning Hi-Power was the classic semi-auto handgun. He pushed the release and ejected the clip to inspect the ammo. The Browning was loaded with 9mm rounds, less penetrative than the larger 7.64x21mm or .40 S&W brass the Hi-Power also took. Gardner didn't rate 9mm, reckoned that he pissed harder than nine-mils discharged.

He slapped the clip back in, stood up and tucked the Browning into the waistband of his combats just as Falcon swallowed his fear and approached the bodies.

A wooden placard was propped up by the posts.

'*Falta de Deus*,' Falcon read.

'I'm guessing that's not Portuguese for "Have a Nice Day",' Gardner said quietly.

'It means, "Lack of God". They are saying they are all against God.'

'Who's they?'

'One of the gangs.'

Falcon bowed his head and made the sign of the cross.

Even the Taliban weren't this evil, Gardner thought.

'Your friend—' the BOPE man began.

Gardner frowned. 'They might have taken him hostage. For ransom. The done thing round these parts, right?'

'Yes,' Falcon said vacantly.

'Focus, Rafa. This gang – they might have captured John?'

'If they have Bald, he's probably dead. And if they find us, they'll kill us too.'

'No they won't, mate. Not on my fucking watch.'

'You don't understand who we're dealing with. This is not an ordinary gang.'

Gardner wondered what constituted a normal outfit round these parts. Probably the little wankers who chopped up the officer.

'Tell me more about this gang,' he said.

'This was the work of Big Teeth's boys.'

'Who the fuck is that?'

'Luis Oliveira. People call him "Big Teeth". He doesn't operate in the favela personally, but he's the head of the largest gang in Barbosa, the Messengers of God. They control most of the drugs and weapons coming in and out of the favela. His number two is a guy called Roulette, and I'd bet my house on this being the work of Roulette's special murder crew.'

Gardner scanned north. Seems calm enough, he told himself. Still, he didn't want to take any chances. 'We should bug out, Rafa. Before we bump into them and they turn us into soup of the day.'

He tugged at Falcon. The BOPE rupert's eyes were fixed on a spot past his shoulder.

'We're too late,' he said. 'They've already found us.'

fifteen

Weiss breezed past the police. Four saloon cars were massed at the side of the road, a dozen pot-bellied cops scratching their stubble and kicking gravel, afraid to enter the favela without BOPE. They busied themselves with questioning people entering and leaving Barbosa, mostly white, middle-class kids looking to score weed. Weiss, on the other hand, went unnoticed. With his tattered Arizona Cardinals baseball cap and a Barcelona football shirt underneath the duster coat, the UNICEF logo smeared with old blood, he looked like the kind of guy who'd spent all his life in Barbosa.

The favelas were like prisons. They didn't care so much about who went in as who tried to break out.

Weiss had ventured only a hundred metres into the favela but he felt like he'd pitched up in another world.

Cracked old pipes poked out of each house, pumping shit into large puddles in the streets. Plastic bags and Coke bottles tumbleweeded across the road. Twenty-five metres further on a rickety man foraged through a heap of garbage, picking out wrinkled sheets of metal and dumping them in a shopping trolley. Motors stripped of their parts lined the street; telephone and electricity lines straddled its width like Chinese lanterns.

A hundred metres ahead, Weiss could see three teenagers sitting on upturned banana crates. Two of them appeared twelve or thirteen years old, skeletal frames, one in a loose-fitting Lakers basketball top and the other with his hair made up in cornrows, stabbing the crate with a blade.

The leader, Weiss figured, was the older boy. He looked about eighteen and sported spotless black-and-white Converses, with a golden crucifix dangling from his neck, a diamond-studded Jesus on the end. He sucked on a joint. At ten metres, Weiss smelled the pungent aroma, and felt three pairs of eyes burn holes through him.

'Stop right there,' the leader said.

Weiss kept on walking.

'Motherfucker, I said stop.'

The young guy took a final pull on the joint, jumped off his banana crate and stepped over to Weiss. He exhaled, blowing greenish-smoke into his face, eyefucking him.

'When I talk, you listen, bitch,' he growled, prodding a finger into Weiss's duster. 'You're in Batista's territory now. What I say, you do.'

Weiss slow-burned. He had places to be, people to grease, money to make. He didn't view the kid opposite him as a threat. More like a rat nibbling at his toes.

'Step aside, my friend, and I'll spare you.'

Batista grinned and lifted up his Chicago Bulls basketball jersey to reveal a pistol grip sticking out of the waistband of his jeans.

'Empty your pockets,' he said.

'You want it,' Weiss raising his hands, 'why don't you come and get it?'

He stuffed his hand into his right pocket and pulled out a whole lot of nothing except the bloodied surgical gloves. He did the same on the left and gave his evil eye to the Basilica statue. Batista blazed up like a flame to petrol.

'Some kind of a joke?'

'I'm not laughing,' Weiss replied. 'Are you?'

'Man, screw this goat-fucker. Gotta be a wallet somewhere.'

Weiss slowly peeled back his duster. Something held Batista's attention. Behind him, the two other kids leaned in for a closer look. Sewn into the inside fold of the coat were fourteen holstered syringes.

'*Puta que pariu.* This guy's a doctor or—'

Weiss snatched a needle with his left hand and in an instant plunged it into the side of Batista's neck.

White-eyed, wobbling on his feet, Batista stumbled backwards. He dropped like a pigeon in mid-flight, while the other kids looking on, bug-eyed.

The syringe was filled with a concentration of hydrocyanic acid. Weiss had a range of such syringes, the concentration of each one varied, depending on whether he wished the mark to suffer for ten minutes or sixty seconds. This Batista was an arrogant cunt, and in a perfect world he'd have stabbed him with the ten-minute needle. But Weiss was up against the clock, so he'd selected the one-minute syringe.

That was his idea of sympathy.

Batista jerked on the ground. His muscles flinched. He grimaced as they locked up, as if his body was shrinking in on itself, squeezing his guts. He drooled, his eyes were runny. After twenty seconds he voided his bowels. Thirty seconds and his breathing became short, raspy, rapid. Like a forty-a-day guy climbing a set of stairs. Cherry-red blood slid out of his eyes and ears. Funny how cyanide changed a man's blood colour, Weiss noted, as he watched the other two kids. They looked on, horrified but curious, like they'd discovered their parents fucking.

As Batista gargled and shat his way to death, Weiss pulled out a second syringe and lurched forward, grabbing the boy with the cornrows in a headlock, the needle point tickling his neck.

'This one carries infected blood,' he told Cornrow Kid. 'The homosexual disease. I push a little harder, and you will take many years to die. It will not be quick like your leader.'

The kid didn't answer. There was a piss patch the size of Africa on his jeans.

'I need to speak to the man called Xavier.'

Still nothing from the kid.

'Tell the man, Shorty,' Lakers Boy said.

'You're going to take me there, aren't you?'

'He'll do it,' Lakers Boy answered for him.

'Good. Because if he doesn't, I won't just kill you, but your families too.'

Shorty knew all the shortcuts. Many favela kids earned a few reals escorting French tourists around the favelas, unaware that their cash was going straight into the gangs' coffers.

They wove through the streets for twenty minutes until they were in the belly of the favela, where the police feared to tread. It was darker in these streets, the shacks ordered in a zigzag style, like going through sheet-metal trenches. He saw no one on the streets except gangsters decked out in shades and Mac-10s, and the occasional crack addict shuffling along.

'This is the place,' Shorty said. They were in front of a slum dwelling that looked smaller than a wardrobe in the Hilton. More like a lean-to with a brick front. The kid rapped his knuckles loudly on the door twice and shouted something.

Before Weiss could stop him, the kid was sprinting off.

No answer, so Weiss stepped inside.

He found himself in a square room. Thick dust blanketed the floor, and he seemed to crush a cockroach with every step he took. No windows and no furniture, just a wooden table at one end. Dead spiders hung from old cobwebs. Nobody had been living here for longer than a little while.

Weiss stopped.

About-turned.

Three figures blocked the doorway.

His eyes darted from one figure to the next. The man on the left was armed with a pair of brass knuckles. The second tapped a tyre iron against his leg. The guy on the right held a duo knife, both sides of the serrated blade extended.

·'I'm here for Xavier.'

'He's not home,' said the guy with the brass.

They closed in on him.

Weiss met duo-knife guy's eyes. 'Xavier's not really a person, is he?'

'Good fucking guess.'

sixteen

They ran as fast as their legs could carry them.

Sun in their faces and a dozen Messenger gang members a hundred and fifty metres to their rear, a ragtag army in Real Madrid shirts and Ray-Bans.

Looking for trouble.

Twenty minutes of scurrying through corkscrew alleys and rutted streets, and Gardner was so thirsty he could drink rat piss. Not a drop to drink since last night's booze, his stomach cramped, stitch piercing his abs like a screwdriver. Shut out the pain.

He glanced over his shoulder. The Messengers were no longer in sight, but their hooting and hollering carried over the rooftops.

Falcon was fucking knackered. He'd sprinted out in front of Gardner when the gangsters started slugging rounds off at them, but the vertical streets and right-angle turns had taken the wind out of his sails. Now he was three or four metres behind him.

'Which way takes us north?' Gardner asked Falcon.

'Keep going this way ... the alley ... it twists around,' Falcon panted. His already slack pace was slowing Gardner down, and cutting the distance to the Messengers. Go on like this much further, Gardner told himself, and the gang will be on your arse.

Best give them something to think about, he decided.

As they reached the end of alley number five million, Gardner swung to the right. He leaned up against the corner and nabbed Falcon as he jogged past, pushing him behind cover.

'Mate, soon as I start firing, get the fuck over the other side.'

Falcon didn't reply.

'You OK, Rafa?'

'Sure,' he said. 'Just it's—' His voice trailed like dust. 'Let's do it.'

'One—' Gardner said.

Gardner eased out from the corner, gripping the Browning in a double-handed stance, his right hand on the trigger, the prosthetic providing balance. His legs were shoulder-width apart to provide a stable firing platform. A Hi-Power box-mag, Gardner knew, held just thirteen rounds. The headless corpse hadn't been carrying any spare.

Thirteen precious rounds. Make every bullet count.

The alley was two metres wide and ran in a direct line for seventy. Gardner saw three Messengers rush into view, the advance party. They were kitted out with AK-47s. Seventy metres, but the Browning's maximum effective range was more like fifty.

'Two—'

The Messengers ran on. One of them unloaded a random two-round burst from the AK. He didn't see where the shots impacted; all Gardner gave a solid shit about was that they missed. These twats were in pray-and-spray mode, not taking the time to properly adjust their aim. And that was fine by him.

Sixty metres now.

Just a little closer, and I'll tell them what time of day it is.

Fifty-five.

With the 9mm rounds lacking the stopping power of a higher grade, full-metal-jacketed cartridge, Gardner would be relying on his shooting capabilities. Strike the guy in the right place, in the central region where his vital organs were contained, and he'd have a decent chance of dropping the fucker.

Get it wrong and they'd be close enough to spray 7.62mm madness in his face. At fifty metres or less, even a four-year-old could maim Gardner.

'Three! Fucking move!'

His Browning was the standard cop-issue SFS (Safe-Fast-Shooting) model designed specifically for police forces who had about as much weapons training as a chef in the Senior Service. Gardner took aim at the nearest fucker. The guy was running like Usain Bolt on speed, and was now forty-five metres away from his position. Gardner pressed the safety down with his thumb, the hammer sprang back into the single-action position, and he discharged three rounds from the Browning.

Tap-tap-tap.

The motion was fluid and the bullets surgical.

The first struck the kid in his left knee. Gardner had been aiming for the chest, but a knee shot was a good score. The round smashed the guy's cruciate ligaments to shit, opening up a hole that could house a plum. Singed muscle splattered his ankle and sparkling white trainers. If he'd dreamed of being the next Ronaldinho, he was fucked now. His leg folded.

The second shot embedded itself in his right shoulder. Impacted on the joint, his shoulder snapped loose, like a baguette broken in half. His arm bucked backwards with the force of the hit. Count the frazzled nerves and the chewed-up muscle ripped to shreds by the trajectory of the round, and he could forget about a career as Brazilian shot-put champion too.

Watching the kid stumble, Gardner figured he must be high on crack and impervious to the trauma of his bullet wounds.

He discharged round number three into his midriff. A puff of red and he finally collapsed, twelve metres from their position, AK-47 rattling against the concrete. His two mates, twenty metres behind, let off a volley of gunfire before darting into a home. Somewhere inside a woman screamed.

Meanwhile Falcon had transitioned to the left corner of the alley and started putting down rounds with the Colt Commando. He fired in three-round bursts. The second bunch of Messengers tried to advance, saw their dead mate and changed their minds.

Gardner kept his Browning trained on the dropped gangster. He risked a sprint forward, snatched the AK-47, the guy's right leg twitching, and retreated to cover.

'Right, we've bought ourselves some time,' Gardner said. 'Let's fucking leg it while we've got the opportunity to lose them.'

Falcon nodded vacantly.

'Rafa, mate. Fucking *now*.'

The rupert pointed to five brightly coloured kites soaring above the cardboard and tin roofs.

'Early-warning system,' Falcon said. 'The outer cordon of the gang is sending a message to the leaders that BOPE's on its way.' He turned to Gardner. 'The unit's coming back.'

He should be over the moon that his muckers are about to rock up, Gardner thought. So why the hell does he sound about as excited as a bloke being dragged along to Ikea on a Saturday afternoon?

'You want to head south and RV with your mates, go for it,' Gardner said.

'No, no,' said Falcon, gazing north. 'I'll come with you. If John's out there, I will help you find him.'

He couldn't quite place why, but that line didn't sit right with Gardner.

There was no time to argue. Three more figures appeared down the alley and Gardner and Falcon let them have it, two bursts sending the bastards scampering for cover.

They bugged out.

Gardner let Falcon lead the way. They skated down a couple of tight alleyways, keeping their eyes firmly locked on the ground. The concrete was studded with potholes the size of hubcaps, and plastic water pipes that snaked along the ground, leading up to blue storage units on the top of each housing block. It would be all too easy to fall and bust an ankle.

They climbed five flights of uneven stairs with a sheer drop all the way to the bottom of the favela on one side. It was a hard slog. The old muscle memory was kicking in now, reminding him of the endurance levels he'd built up during his years in the Regiment.

'Tell me,' Gardner said, 'what happened to Bald?'

Falcon stopped midway up the stairs to catch his breath. 'It's always the same when we enter the favelas. An outer cordon of gang members set off fireworks and fly kites. That's the signal for the inner cordon of snipers to take up positions, while a third team hides their drug stashes and money trains, unplugs any illegal satellite feeds, and so on. We roll into the favela in the *caveirãos*. Like the one you saw earlier.'

They came past a road with piles of bricks stacked up outside each house. Spent cartridges around the brickwork told Gardner these were defensive positions. Whether for civilians or gang members, he wasn't sure.

'This time we made our approach and – no kites. No fireworks. This is strange, yes?'

'Making you think you've caught them off guard,' Gardner said. 'Oldest trick in the book.'

'Our mission was to snatch Roulette,' Falcon continued, like he hadn't heard Gardner. 'The second-in-command of the Messengers of God. You know, the favela gangs, they kill people daily. OK, it's part of life here. But Roulette, he was one sick fuck. The guy had his own little hit squad. They'd kill people, cut off their heads and sew a pig's head to their neck. Or cut off their arms and legs, excavate the stomach and stick the limbs in there like a flower arrangement. I've seen stuff in my time, but these guys—'

His words trailed like surf.

'The streets were empty. We went deeper and deeper into the belly of Barbosa.'

He snatched at his breath, then went on, 'We arrived in the centre, and that's when our trouble began. RPGs. Sniper fire. Nine- and ten-year-old boys and girls throwing Molotov cocktails at the Skulls. They're big, you know, but you try being inside one when that happens. We went to fall back to safe ground, but they'd put up roadblocks everywhere.'

Gardner recalled the cement posts, the old cars.

'They were expecting trouble this time,' he said.

'What do you mean?'

'You said it yourself. The attack wasn't the standard shit. Someone had told the Messengers they were on the way, ahead of their kite system, so they decided to change their tactics. It was an ambush, Rafa. That kind of thing takes time and planning. You can't do it on the hoof.'

Falcon was quiet for several seconds. 'This is a war zone,' he said. 'The favelas are not slums. They are battlegrounds. A disaster such as this, it was bound to happen one day. All I care about is that two of my men are dead and the rest are missing. I just want to find whoever did this. And make them pay.'

The stairwell coughed them up at the back of a series of homes with a spectrum of gang tags sprayed over the walls. Falcon manoeuvred down a short alley and rested at the lip, hands on his thighs. A rectangular street lay ahead, flanked by grey-brick homes stacked like Lego pieces one on top of the other.

Gardner led the way across the street. He noticed a cream-coloured structure two hundred metres to the north, not far from the peak of the favela. Big caroba trees and khaki bushes shadowed the two-storey breeze-block building, which had whitewashed casement windows and a clay-tiled roof. Painted gates and a two-feet-tall metal fence bordered it.

'The school,' Falcon said, noticing where Gardner was looking.

'No shit, there's a school in the favela?'

Sticking out his bottom lip, Falcon replied, 'Government tries to integrate with the rest of the city. Schools, hospital, gyms. Even McDonald's.'

The building was pissing distance from the jungle.

To Gardner's south, Christ the Redeemer spread his soap-stone arms and faced east across the Atlantic seaboard. Falcon sucked in greedy breaths beside him.

'I think . . . we outran them,' he said.

Gardner didn't reply. He was focusing on the distances. A hilly expanse of land half a mile long and a mile wide divided the favela summit from the statue.

'My Troop times forty north.' John was in 14 Troop, the Mobility unit of D Squadron, 22 SAS. So, 560 metres north of Christ. 'Your Troop times twenty west.' Gardner had been in 11 Troop, D Squadron's four-man boat team. Although they were in different troops, D Squadron had deployed to Iraq, Afghanistan and, in 2002, Sri Lanka, where they trained up the country's elite security forces combating the Tamil Tigers.

His Troop by twenty – that put Bald at 220 metres west. The spot where the two measurements collided was a rough sequence of ridges canopied under secondary jungle.

'This is as far north as the favela goes,' Falcon said. 'There's nowhere else to go.'

'That's where you're wrong, mate.'

'What? I don't—'

A *clack-clack* of gunfire erupted at their six.

'The Messengers.'

'How they fuck did they gain on us so quick?' said Gardner.

'Shortcuts. There's dozens of ways to get around the favela. On the rooftops, under the ground—' Falcon paused, trying to control his tremulous voice. 'They're going to be here very soon. There's hundreds of kids in the gang. If they find me, they'll skin me alive, they'll—'

'Yeah, yeah, I get it. They don't like visitors.' Gardner flashed a devilish grin. 'Come on, we've still got the run on them.'

'But where to?'

'The jungle.'

They dashed across the street. Corrugated-iron sheets, a metre wide, ran diagonally along the square, connecting stacks of second- and third-storey buildings. An Isuzu pickup lay rusting thirty metres from the school gates.

Halfway down the street, Gardner heard a *crack*, split down the middle with a dull *thump*.

The inner cordon.

Sniper.

seventeen

Gardner took immediate action, diving behind the pickup for cover. He'd removed himself and Falcon from the line of fire, but now they were pinned down and fucking bollocks on toast. The Isuzu took a volley of 7.62mm abuse from the sniper to the east. This was different, a well-organized attack.

His ears were shredded by the sound of metal tearing through metal. The sniper was shooting up the Isuzu in the hope that a stray bullet would ricochet off the chassis and strike one of them. There wasn't much chance of that, but just to be sure Gardner pulled Falcon behind the rear wheel section and set himself against the front tyre. The front and back wheels on any vehicle were the best cover, as the engine parts provided a thick bulkhead.

'What now?' asked Falcon.

'Your BOPE mates – where the hell are they?'

Falcon got on his handheld radio. 'Twenty minutes.'

'Shit.'

'Too long to hold off the Messengers,' said Falcon, sounding panicky.

'Have a little faith, Rafa.'

The sniper had to be within three hundred metres because the *crack* and the *thump* were on top of each other, like they shared the same fucking bed. From the angle of entry of the bullets pebbledashing the Isuzu, Gardner knew the sniper had to be east. And he knew he had to take control of the situation. They had two or three minutes, max, till the sniper's Messenger mates rocked up to the party.

'Keep your eyes trained on the alley,' he instructed Falcon, grabbing the Colt Commando by the flat-top receiver and handing over the Bulgarian knock-off AK-47 in return. At medium range the AK was about as accurate as an Internet dating profile. The Colt, on the other hand, could clip the Queen's nose on a ten-pence piece from three hundred metres.

'Any Messenger tries it on, you give them the good news.'

'No, no, no.' Falcon shook his head. 'You don't understand. Roulette can call on hundreds of gangsters. I can't stop them.'

'How long now before your pals come to the rescue?'

'Till BOPE arrives?' Falcon checked his watch. 'Fifteen minutes. We can't hold out for that long.'

Again Gardner sensed that Falcon was in two minds about actually wanting to meet his BOPE mates. The urgency of the situation meant he had to park the thought.

'Did John never tell you what they taught us in the Regiment?'

Falcon blinked his ignorance.

'No such thing as can't, mate. We don't do failure. Now look sharp.'

A single shot crashed through the rear tyre. Air hissed out of the wheel.

One minute. Two more and you'll be overrun.

Gardner checked his new toy. Metallic stock, MIL-STD 1913 Picatinny rail with a mounted 4x day optical scope on top. He switched the Commando to semi-automatic on the fire-control notch, clicked open the door on the Isuzu passenger side and crawled into the pickup.

The seats had been ripped out, along with the steering wheel, gearbox and any other removable shit. He slid up to the driver-side door, facing east across the street, keeping his profile low beneath the bodywork. Gardner poked the barrel two inches out the driver's window, his prosthetic hand locked around the barrel and the stock tucked hard into his right shoulder.

In Baghdad, nailing snipers had been difficult. The wankers putting rounds down were armed irregulars with experience in the Republican Guard and the Iran–Iraq War, and had basic training: displacing after each shot, never using the same location twice. Guys like Juba the sniper, who claimed over a hundred American kills, proved elusive. You needed expert counter-sniper warfare to take them down.

Or if you were a Yank, you just lobbed about four tons of high explosive into the vicinity and let the grandma and kiddies fucking have it too.

Another report. No muzzle flash. He was using a suppressor, Gardner realized. Maybe the sniper wasn't as dumb as he'd hoped. Probably he had experience of slotting BOPE officers and knew exactly what to do: no need to worry about getting a direct hit on him or Falcon – just isolate them until the Messengers arrived to take care of business.

Two minutes. Almost out of time.

The concrete sparked as a bullet struck the ground in front of the pickup. The shooter was getting dangerously close. He was wise to the fact that Gardner was trying to isolate him.

I see something, Gardner thought. At my three o'clock.

An object glinted on the rooftop of a building. The glimmer came from deep within a mesh of satellite dishes and wires.

Years of being targeted by rooftop shooters meant Gardner was able to recognize the flash instantly, the metal barrel of a long-range rifle. It broke rule number one they taught in sniper school: paint your bloody gun, so it ain't reflecting the sun.

Gardner exhaled, relaxing his muscles, and gazed down the telescopic sights on the Commando. The magnified image of a gangster's head. Shaven-headed guy, skin the colour of ground coffee, lying on his stomach, dressed in jeans and a white vest. Gardner could even make out gold rings on his fingers.

Messengers clamoured in his right ear.

'They're coming,' Falcon said, urgent and trembling.

Gardner shut everything out. The gaggle of voices, the rupert's bitching, the blanketing heat and the sweat drenching his balls. He focused, then unloaded a single round.

The sniper's head exploded like a pumpkin, blood and chunks of skull and tissue splashing on to the rooftop. His body rolled onto its side, the exposed lower jaw facing the sky. The sniper's gnashers were lacquered in blood. The sun drenched the rooftop, making the blood sparkle.

Fucking take it, Gardner thought, debussing from the Isuzu. His feet had barely touched the ground when, through his peripheral vision, he glimpsed five figures at the mouth of the street, a hundred metres away.

Four of them, he was certain, were Messengers, because they wielded guns: state-of-the-art PP-2000 sub-machine-guns. Where the hell did they acquire those weapons? he briefly wondered. The thought was cut in half by Falcon discharging a three-round burst from the AK-47. Two rounds smacked into a Messenger. His grey tracksuit bottoms reddened and his mates retreated, leaving him to try and plug the hole in his mangled cock.

The third struck a man several metres to the right of the Messenger. He was middle-aged and sported a tuft of hair white as the linen shirt he wore. The bullet entered the small of his back, and the guy flopped on to his belly, spilling the contents of a plastic bag he was carrying: pack of cigarettes, loaf of bread, lemons and parsley.

'Holy shit, Rafa. You fucking whacked a civvie.'

'Shit,' Falcon said, the AK-47 limp in his hand. 'I thought he was – it looked like he had a gun. I just thought—' His voice suddenly hardened. 'Fuck this cunt. It's his stupid fault. What the fuck is he doing out in the street anyway? Doesn't he know there's a war on? Fuck him.'

Bottle rockets screeched overhead.

'Fireworks. My unit's nearly here.'

'How long?'

'Five minutes.'

Gardner made a beeline for the school, Falcon tailing. Shake this wave of Messengers, he told himself, and you'll be free to reach Bald. He was more certain than ever that John had been able to escape the gang, and the last thing he wanted to do was lead a horde of the fuckers to his location. Once BOPE showed, he'd peel away and continue his mission.

A bullet struck to his left, and a voice squealed.

Falcon.

There was shit all over the concrete. His left ankle was doused in blood. The Messengers were trying their luck, braving the street. Gardner turned around, gave them four rounds from the Colt and, throwing an arm around Falcon's shoulder, helped him to hop on his good foot the final fifty metres to the school. Gardner was running on fumes, drawing on every grain of energy.

They were upon the school. The building cast a soot-coloured shadow over them. The temperature sagged from flame-grilled to plain hot. Gardner butted the padlock with the Colt stock. The lock was crude and the chain came apart with one clean blow. They went on through, Falcon yelping with every step.

'Hang on a little longer.'

Gardner gave a boot to the middle section of the door. An internal locking mechanism held the door in place, but the frame shuddered.

'Hurry, Jesus,' Falcon moaned.

A second kick. This time the door swung open. Gardner withdrew his support arm from Falcon, the BOPE rupert flaking out two metres inside the school on the lino floor. Spinning around to put a final burst down on the Messengers, Gardner counted ten kids, five of them armed with PP-2000s, the others with older pistols and revolvers.

He flicked the selector anti-clockwise to fully automatic, arcing the Colt horizontally across the thin line of Messengers. Bullets grazed walls, shredded a band of telephone wires. The gangsters ducked behind metre-high piles of bricks at the edges of the street. Gardner discharged eleven rounds, and got a hollow *click-click*. Shit. Out of ammo. He slammed the door shut, just as the Messengers returned fire.

'Elevate your leg,' he told Falcon, 'it'll stem some of the blood loss.'

Bullets bored into the door. Gardner fished two spare Colt mags from Falcon's utility belt, slapped one into the mag feed and stuffed the second in the leg pouch on his combats.

Forty rounds of ammo. Gardner shattered a window pane to the right of the door, raking the glass out with the Colt's barrel and unleashing a burst into the street. Shielded by the bricks, the Messengers were popping off rounds without aiming.

'Five minutes is up, Rafa. Where the fuck's BOPE?'

'Perhaps the smoke and the gunfire are too much.'

'Sod it. We've got to hope they're on their way.'

But all that stood between the two of them and getting walloped were thirty-six bullets.

eighteen

Weiss guessed they'd go easy on him at first and he was right. The guy with the knuckledusters fucked him up a bit with a right uppercut that sent him flying. Cold steel cracked his jawbone so bad it felt like someone had sewn razor blades into his face. Then it was the turn of the tyre-iron guy, who served up a whupping on both his legs, turning them red raw and swollen. All things considered, not so bad. He'd suffered worse. The big pain was saved for later. He expected nothing less.

They slipped a hessian sack over his head and tore the duster off his back. Then they escorted him through a weave of streets. The sack was dense and Weiss couldn't see where he was going. They carted him into another house and up a creaking flight of stairs. He listened out for noises, anything that placed him somewhere specific. A TV in the background played the theme tune to *24*. He thought he heard boys shouting.

They dumped him on a chair and bound his hands behind his back with plastic cord. Someone lifted the sack off. It took a moment for his eyes to adjust to the light, like opening his eyes underwater in a murky swamp. He found himself looking at a broad-shouldered, shredded figure sitting opposite in big round shades, Incredible Hulk T-shirt and sandals. He was sitting backwards on a metal chair and examining one of the syringes from Weiss's coat.

'So, you are the one they call the Needle Man.'

'And since there's no Xavier,' Weiss said, 'that makes you, let me see . . . Roulette. But fuck it. The name doesn't matter. You're still a dead man.'

Roulette laughed in his chest. 'That's fucking funny. You know, your name makes a lot of tough guys shit themselves. Me, I don't give a fuck. When Luis said you were coming here, I could hardly believe my good fortune. Tell me, what's in this one?'

Weiss screwed up his eyes.

'Thallium.'

'And what the fuck is that?'

'A poison.'

Roulette held out the syringe in his palm. Then Weiss realized they were not alone in the room. He could see two other men, dull-eyed, lean as poles at a strip club and dressed in slack jeans and T-shirts that reached their knees. They were like twins, except one wore a fake gold Rolex and the other had a Los Angeles Lakers basketball shirt. Rolex grabbed the syringe and tossed it to the ground. He crushed it underfoot.

'Tell me, is it true? What's it up to now, six hundred victims?'

'That depends,' Weiss replied.

'On what?'

'Whether you're counting yourself and your two fucking friends.'

Roulette shot to his feet.

'*Vai toma no cu!*' he barked, grabbing his crotch. 'There's only one more death the Needle Man takes part in – and that's his own.'

'You're making a big mistake, my friend. I'm worth more alive than dead.'

Roulette stepped to Weiss, so close he could see the pockmarks on the gangster's skin.

'You're wrong,' Roulette whispered. 'See, our leader, Luis, he's been in touch with some people who would love to see you dead. The Sinaola and Los Negros cartels in Mexico are especially keen to have your head on a plate. They've already made a, how do you say, down payment to Luis. It's over, big guy.'

Lakers removed Weiss's shoes. He fetched something from a shelf: a cordless orange power drill with a 10mm tungsten bit in the chuck. Weiss gritted his teeth and tried to concentrate on his breathing pattern. It was the only way he was going to get through this. If he passed out from the pain, he might never wake up again. But he couldn't take his eyes off the drill.

'If you do this,' Weiss told Lakers, 'I'll find you and kill you and your whole family.'

A snakish smile broke out all over his face as he revved up the drill. As it whirred into life it reminded Weiss of trips to the dentist as a child.

'You won't get the chance –,' Roulette backing off, '– *my friend.*'

With Rolex pressing down on Weiss's foot, the third goon lowered the drill until the tungsten bit was touching the tip of his big toenail.

'Wait,' Roulette said. He dug out a clam-style mobile from his jeans pocket. Flicking it open, he pointed its camera directly at Weiss's toe. 'Big Teeth said he wants to see this.'

Lakers pressed the trigger. The chuck, rotating at 1100 rpm, began to pierce Weiss's toe.

The pain was excruciating, like someone ripping off his toenail a million times over. He did everything to shake his foot free, but the other guy was holding it firmly in place and he couldn't force any leeway. The toenail cracked down the middle as the drill pushed down into his flesh. His foot was covered in nail dust.

As the bit ate into his big toe, Weiss couldn't fight it any more.

They kept on drilling.

The drill shuddered as it tunnelled into his flexor bone. Lakers revved again and forced the bit deeper into his toe. Weiss fought hard to ride the pain, absorbing each wave of nausea and taking big gulps of air. It was crucial not to vomit.

He felt as if an invisible hand was choking him to death. That he might pass out at any given moment. And he knew that if he fainted he wouldn't escape with his life.

Dizziness overwhelmed him, like he was drowning in a bathtub. This is it, he thought, the moment of no return, and then a shrill, grinding sound stung his ears.

The bit had struck concrete.

He opened his eyes and peered down at the floor. Where his big toe once was lay a splatter of blood and curls of torn flesh. Dirty-white bone fragments covered in gristle, everything hanging together by a few limp muscle strings. He tried twitching it, but nothing happened. Bile burned his throat.

'Let's give him a rest,' Roulette said, flipping the mobile shut. 'We don't want him to miss the best part of the show.'

'Yeah, fucking see you in a while, man,' Rolex said. 'We're working on your teeth next.' He made a pliers-wrenching motion.

The three men left, locking the door behind them. Weiss heard the stairs squeal like dying rabbits as they trampled down them, and a woman shouting, Roulette calling her a fucking ass-licker and a whore with a pussy the size of Argentina. Another door slammed, this one further away. The front one, he guessed.

Weiss spat on the ground. His mucous membranes were bright red. Somehow the pain and anger failed to register inside him. Ever since he was a child he had lacked basic empathy. A shrink would probably link it to his abusive upbringing, to the times he witnessed his alcoholic father rape his mum, or the day *Padre* swung his fists at his little sister, Maria, until she died of a brain haemorrhage. But the whys didn't interest Weiss. He only knew that he felt no emotion towards anyone else – but, most of all, himself.

So it was that Weiss didn't pity his situation, or rue his bad luck.

Instead, he focused on escaping.

nineteen

Gardner had slotted five Messengers but they'd kept on coming
and their number had swelled to twenty. Each one decked out
in the gang's unofficial uniform of Ray-Bans, football shirts
and PP-2000s. To conserve ammo, Gardner restricted himself
to single shots whenever a Messenger slid his head above one
of the four brick parapets strewn about the street.

Two guys, a few years older than the rest, yelled at each
other. They suddenly leapt out from behind separate spots of
cover. Mounted red-dot sights lasered the window. Gardner
crouched, just as they pulled the triggers in tandem. Cooked
air stroked the back of his head as the Luger rounds pelted
the frame, slapping into a metre-high china statue of the
Virgin Mary. Five seconds of fury, then Gardner detected a
lull. Must be reloading, he thought, as the statue disintegrated
into a dust cloud.

The lull was only two seconds, but that was all he needed.
He shot to his feet and saw the two guys feeding fresh clips
into the housing receivers. One of them was a fraction ahead
of his mate, tugging the bolt lever into the closed position at
the rear of the barrel. Poised to let Gardner have it. Gardner
peered down the Colt's iron sights and gave the bastard a .223
black eye.

The bullet entered the Messenger's right socket, flinging brain matter and skull out the back of his head in a

frenzied spurt, like uncorked champagne. His mate ditched his PP-2000 and scarpered.

With the other Messengers content to put down rounds from their concealed positions, Gardner pulled back from the window and tended to Falcon.

'Wal-ah,' Falcon said. Gardner could see his lips were dry as bread crust. He retrieved Falcon's canteen and tipped a precious few drops into his open mouth. Falcon swallowed greedily. Gardner had a sip himself. Wished it contained something a little stronger.

Falcon was slipping in and out of consciousness now, his eyes glazed over. Gardner gave him a hard slap on both chops.

'Wakey, wakey. We need to get arses into gear.'

'Where am I?'

'In Rio, mate.'

'I'm dying.'

'Bollocks. You'll be fine.'

Falcon mumbled something that sounded like a prayer.

'Do yourself a favour and look at the ceiling,' Gardner said, as isolated bullets pinged against the front of the school. He rolled up Falcon's left trouser leg, unlacing the combat boot to get a close-up view of the trauma wound.

'How is it . . . bad?'

Gardner didn't reply.

The lower portion of Falcon's leg was totally fucked.

Beneath his knee the skin was singed and covered in burn marks, like his leg had been used as an ashtray. The bullet wound was a smooth, inch-wide circle bang in the centre of his shin, blowing out the bone and everything else with it – muscle, skin, a piece of his trousers. The lower half of his leg flopped like a rag doll.

'Want the good news first, or the bad?'

'I'll take the good.'

'It could have been worse,' Gardner said. 'You've been shot in a part of your body that's mostly bone. If the fucker caught you higher up the leg, at the knee or thigh, they'd have burst your popliteal or femoral artery and caused you to bleed out.'

'So I'm not going to—?' asked Falcon, risking a sideways glance at his leg.

'No, mate. You'll live.' Gardner smiled. 'The bad news is, until we get you to a doctor, it's gonna feel like you got an arrow stuck through your ankle, and there's no morphine to numb the pain.'

The rate of gunfire suddenly increased. Dozens of bullets struck the door, like a hundred sets of hands rapping against the woodwork. Rounds whizzed through the exposed window. The noise lacerated Gardner's ears.

I need a distraction, he thought. Something to give us a chance to bug out. He rummaged through the pouches on Falcon's assault vest and located an M67 frag grenade. A little buzz of excitement rose inside him. Trailing back to the window, he tore the safety pin from the clip, maintaining a firm grasp on the spoon to stop the grenade igniting. He released the spoon, waited two seconds for the cook-off, and then raced past the window, lobbing the grenade thirty metres into the street. The M67 rolled.

Four metres short of a Messenger's foot, it came to rest.

Gardner stepped away from the window as the Messenger moved to pick up the grenade. He was going to chuck it back to its sender, like they did in the movies. But the grenade had less than a second to detonate, and as he disappeared from view Gardner heard a powerful *whump*, accompanied by the sound of hot steel splintering flesh and concrete, like a million stones spilling. Someone screamed at the top of his voice and suddenly Gardner was back in Sangin, listening to the life bleed out of the delirious kid to his right.

'What about a tourniquet?' Falcon asked.

'On that? Fat chance, mate. Cutting off the blood supply will do more harm than good. Leave it exposed for now, until we can get it properly seen to.'

'Shit, my lungs. I – I can't breathe.' Falcon looked at Gardner's outstretched hand, seized it. 'Fuck. Those bastards keep coming. They won't stop, not until we're both hanging by our legs.'

'We'll pull back to the rear. The school's not far from the jungle, right?'

'A hundred metres, maybe less. Why?'

'That's where John Bald is.'

Gardner shouldered Falcon and led the way down the cool main corridor, joining the entrance to the rear of the building sixty metres away. Three classrooms flanked either side of the corridor, with lino floors, chicken wire over the classroom windows. The strong smell of disinfectant stung his nostrils.

They were thirty metres from the rear exit.

Twenty.

'Shit! I forgot my rifle,' Falcon shouted above the racket.

'Can't go back now, mate. You got a secondary?'

'A what?'

'A backup weapon – handgun, anything like that?'

Falcon nodded, opening his leg holster and removing a stainless-steel Taurus PT92 semi-automatic. Not bad for a secondary, Gardner reckoned.

A loud bang to his rear. He glanced over his shoulder. The front doors swung open. Gardner clocked the Isuzu in the street. And a guy's torso, the body charred black as burned toast. He recognized the footwear on a pair of legs to the right. Same fucker who'd reached for the M67.

Three shadows sprinted into the corridor.

Ten metres from the rear exit and in the cool of the corridor, Gardner's mag was empty. Hurrying, he ejected the mag and manually pulled the bolt lever, loading the final clip of Remington brass into the receiver. Twenty rounds – all you've fucking got, he thought. He tugged the bolt a second time, chambering the first .223 round.

He focused on the nearest target. Forty metres distant. Broad and with a distinctive Mohican. Gardner adjusted his aim, dead centre on the target's chest area.

Crack!

Smoke fluted out of the Colt's barrel. It was as if the target had swallowed a packet of C4. His chest cavity ruptured, a hole the size of an apple punched in his breastbone. Grey and black shit slopped out, like an uncoiling snake. The guy flopped forward. Blood spewed on to the lino floor.

'What have you got?' Falcon shouted, discharging his Taurus at the middle target. 'Show me what you fucking got!'

His aim was wild, the rounds sparking off the brick walls, like a dozen firecrackers going off. Glass on the classroom windows cascaded. The air thickened with mortar dust.

The target was twenty metres away, fifteen now, and Gardner fought to maintain his composure. Some guys went batshit in the middle of a firefight. Others, like him, seemed to reach a new plane of calm.

Deep intake of breath, exhale, loosen your shoulder, he told himself.

The target's face disappeared behind a carmine mist as the bullet erased his eyes, nose and mouth.

Falcon pumped four rounds in quick succession at the third target. The 9x19mm Parabellum chopped the guy in half, unzipping his guts. He stopped, dropped his PP-2000 and dumbly tried to shove his intestines back inside his stomach. Too late: Falcon dropped him with a neck shot, blood spraying across the kids' drawings adorning the walls.

'That's what happens, bitches. That's what fucking happens!'

'Cool it, Rafa. Two more at the twelve.'

Gardner felt a pain sear the point between his neck and jaw. He raised a hand to the wound. Blood seeped from his ear; a bullet had grazed him, slicing off the lower tip of his ear, and dear God, it fucking stung.

In a frenzy now, Falcon pummelled bullets at the two Messengers. Five shots in each. He shot the second guy long after he'd dropped, rounds shredding his arms and legs, swearing at him in Portuguese.

'Through the exit,' Gardner shouted. 'While we've got the chance.'

'You see that asshole die?' Falcon asked as they ventured out the back, into a playground of bleached grass, swings and roundabouts. 'He took it real good, you know?'

'Button it. I'm not interested. Just tell me the quickest way to the jungle.'

Falcon nodded left, like he was in a silent movie. To a small row of shacks to the left and up from the school. A low cattle fence separated the shacks from the flourishing undergrowth.

Almost there, Gardner thought.

Voices. Danger close. He peered around the corner. Four Messengers, forty metres away. Led by a guy with pecs the size of boxing gloves and biceps that looked as if he'd plugged his veins with cannonballs.

The sky bellowed a faint *whup-whup*.

'What is it?' Falcon said, seeing Gardner back-pedalling.

'They're outflanking us, mate. Head in the other direction.'

Gardner rushed to the opposite corner. Three Messengers appeared from that direction.

'Pincer,' he said, kneeling to unload a burst against the three targets. 'Fuckers are coming at us around the sides. Rafa, take the left.'

The *whup-whup* grew louder. Incessant.

Gardner chopped down two of the Messengers, but the third had lined up his PP-2000. No time left to put down another burst. The guy released the catch.

Thwack!

Blood arced out of the Messenger's chest, spraying Gardner in the face. Warm, salty fluid splattered his lips. His vision was dotted red. The Messenger sank to his knees, pawing at his throat. Gardner saw a Bell Ranger 206 helicopter, thirty metres off the ground, and a sniper tied to a lanyard, buzzing like an F1 car around a racetrack.

BOPE had arrived.

Gunshots to his six. He spun around. The Bell Ranger was chewing up the four Messengers attacking from the other flank. They fell like fucking skittles.

Gardner hauled Falcon to his feet.

'Looks like your mates arrived in the nick of time. Let's go and find a medic, get you patched up.'

'I'll be OK.'

'Cheer up. They came back for you. Another few minutes and you – fuck it, we – would've been royally fucked. We owe them all a pint. Besides' – he gestured to the ankle – 'if you don't tend to that, it'll turn septic. Then you'll be in a world of shit.'

Gardner scooped up his Colt Commando and escorted Falcon around the side of the building, the weapon aimed ahead in case any Messengers were desperate to get some.

The Bell Ranger circled the school building, sniper walloping Messengers in the back as they ran for cover. Three Big Skulls roared into the street, disgorging a dozen BOPE operators. They wasted no time putting rounds down, kicking in the doors of nearby houses. From inside each one Gardner heard the shriek of women and the crackle of gunshots. Across the street, two kids, thirteen or fourteen, unarmed, attempted to run into an alleyway. A BOPE operator unloaded his Heckler & Koch G3 sub-machine-gun, taking chunks out of the kids' heads. When he approached them he kicked their bodies.

The Messengers moved back a hundred metres. A few stragglers sought cover behind bollards and on the rooftops.

Then Gardner looked on as a neat line of schoolchildren, dressed in pristine white shirts, pressed navy-blue shorts and polished shoes, brown satchels draped over their shoulders, walked through the street from sixty metres away.

'Sponsored schoolchildren,' Falcon said. 'Their parents work as nannies or housekeepers for the rich people in Rio. Schooling is divided by address of residence, you see.' He winced, trying to relieve pressure on his ankle. 'These children are sponsored to go to school outside the favela.'

An eerie silence followed. Gardner realized that BOPE and the Messengers were participating in some sort of unspoken ceasefire. No one dared engage while the kids walked past, oblivious to the bloodshed and the Bell Ranger and the spent cartridges.

'I need to sit down,' Falcon said. He hobbled over to rest by the roadside. Gardner watched the surreal progress of schoolchildren along the street until it curved to the left ninety metres up, and they disappeared.

Once the kids had departed, the gunfire resumed.

Gardner spotted an ambulance bringing up the rear of the BOPE train. He turned to his left – and stopped in his tracks.

Falcon was gone.

twenty

The pain was not so bad, Weiss thought. He had read somewhere that a man's pain threshold was greater than a woman's, despite the fact women had to experience childbirth. His ability to endure, he believed, was greater than most. As they pulled out his toenails one by one, he thought about how good it would feel to kill them.

He examined the tips of his nine surviving toes. Curly, hairlike matrixes remained, looking like the roots of upturned plants. They had rinsed him thoroughly: his toenails, the sliced left ear where his outer lobe had been sawn off, and the soft, moist ruptures in his mouth, which, an hour ago, housed four sets of perfectly good molars.

'Not so tough now, huh, Mr Needle Man?'

Roulette sat on the metal chair, cupping a Swisher Sweet cigarillo between his hands. A spicy aroma wafted through the stale air.

'Would you care for one?'

'I don't smoke,' Weiss replied.

Roulette turned to the two goons. Lakers clutched a box cutter, Rolex a pair of tempered steel snips. Weiss wondered which one was next, as Roulette's phone sparked up. He read the message, grinned and nodded to Rolex.

'I've got some business to take care of,' Roulette said. 'Go with the snips first. Big Teeth says use it on his testicles.' He nodded to Lakers. 'While I'm busy you can go fetch the saw. Big Teeth wants his head by sundown.'

He blew smoke out his nostrils, then stood up.

'Enjoy it, Needle Man,' he said, and left, Lakers in tow.

'Just you and me,' Rolex said. He practised with the snips. 'I'll give you a choice. Fingers or toes?'

'Let me think about it,' Weiss replied.

Twenty years ago, when he was a fresh-faced contract killer, Weiss had made an almost fatal error. A mark he was trailing hired a bunch of thugs to pounce on him, and he had found himself bound up in a basement. Only a friend's quick thinking saved him that day. Ever since, Weiss had taken precautions against being captured. He carried a four-inch blade tucked into the buckle on his belt.

But it was out of reach.

'So, what's it gonna be?'

'Your friend did my toe already,' Weiss said. 'How about a finger to match.'

Rolex did a head-shake smile. 'You're one crazy motherfucker.'

Weiss had no other get-out clause, no alternative exit plan. He wished he was in a James Bond movie, then he'd have some ridiculous gadget secreted on his body somewhere; maybe a poisonous spray screwed inside his watch.

But he had nothing. Just his statue of Our Lady of Guadalupe. She'd delivered him safely through six hundred murders. Weiss had evaded hundreds of cops, other contract killers, violent gangs and vengeful relatives. Now he'd got caught again. Perhaps he was getting too old for this line of work. Just as well that this was his last mission. He consoled himself with the thought that the pain was bad, but the reward – all thirty million of it – would more than make up for it.

Rolex stepped towards Weiss. 'Shit, amigo. Looks like you puked up real bad. You've ruined your shirt.' Acidic yellow and brown chunks were sprayed down Weiss's shirt front. Rolex paraded around to the back of him and stopped. The plastic cord was fastened so tight around Weiss's hands that the blood supply was constricted and his fingers were bloated.

'Jeez, these fucking fingers . . . We tied you up *tight*,' said Rolex. 'Might take a couple of tries before I cut one off.'

'This is your last chance,' Weiss told him, trying to sound confident, in control of the situation. 'If you let me go now, I'll spare your family. I can't promise your life, but your brothers and sisters and parents, they don't have to suffer.'

Rolex laughed as he examined Weiss's fingers.

'I don't got no family, man. How about this one?' He isolated Weiss's right index digit. 'The trigger finger, amigo. Or in your case, needle.'

The touch of Rolex's hand was replaced by something cold and metallic.

Weiss caught the sound of feet on the treads. The goons returning. He'd counted the stairs when they first dragged him up. There were twelve steps, he knew. They'd already cleared six.

'Just a minute,' Rolex shouted to the door, snips clamped loosely around Weiss's finger.

'I'm about to make a deal happen,' Weiss said. 'Thirty million. Work with me on it. Fifty-fifty split. Fifteen million dollars apiece.' Pride prevented him from begging – he was always disgusted by those victims who broke down into a whimpering mess. But he thought that a gang kid low down the food chain, as Rolex undoubtedly was, might bite at such a big offer.

Rolex clicked his tongue. 'Bullshit.'

'It's true, I swear. Why the fuck else would I be here?'

He paused.

The footsteps stopped.

'Eighty-twenty, my favour.'

The door opened.

'Fifty-fifty or nothing—'

Gun reports blasted Weiss's ears. The snips fell away from his finger and he felt something warm and moist splash up against the nape of his neck, then trickle down his back. A distant clatter of gunfire, at the bottom of the stairs. Women, men, their voices cut short by the staccato bursts from automatic rifles.

BOPE operators flooded the room. Weiss counted four of them. Finding no one else inside the building, they turned to leave. Weiss's hands suddenly sprang free and he let them flop by his sides. His arms were numb below the elbow. He felt the blood rushing through constricted veins, like a tunnel flooding. The operator who'd freed him knelt down beside him. He was wearing a handkerchief to disguise his identity; some BOPE operators, Weiss knew, also lived in the favelas.

'Are you OK?' The eyes were green, the forehead copper.

'Yes, yes,' Weiss replied in perfect Portuguese. He didn't want to sound foreign, because an out-of-towner wandering around the favela would make the operator suspicious. Gang torture, though – that was common enough.

'He's dead, now. The others too.'

'So . . . I'm free to go?'

'Who are you?'

'I fix cars, that's all.'

'Then I suggest you leave. You want my advice, stay clear of the school area. There's a bunch of Messengers up there, and they're not giving up without a fight.'

Weiss stood up. He was unsteady. He turned around to see Rolex holding his hands to his face. Melted eyeball seeped between his fingers, like fried egg white. Warm blood spewed out of a fist-sized puncture in his neck. The bullet had sliced the jugular vein. He was still alive, sucking in tiny breaths of air that flowed back out of the exposed wound.

'Goodbye, my friend.'

Weiss picked up his coat and slipped on his boots. The right quickly became squidgy inside, as his big toe oozed blood.

He made for the stairs.

The living room had been turned into a shooting gallery. Two obese women lay slumped on the armchair next to the TV. Both equally shot to shit. Weiss had to watch his step on the stairs, where Lakers sprawled face down. The BOPE operators seemed to ignore Weiss. And why wouldn't they? As far as they were concerned, the Messengers were the only targets in town.

Weiss seized up as he made for the front door, raised a hand to his temple. An enormous pressure throbbed between his ears, as if a family of spiders was scuttling around his skull. He closed his eyes for a second and the spell seemed to clear.

His mind on the $30 million bounty, he said a prayer of thanks to the Virgin Mary. Once again, she'd come good for him. And he afforded himself a little smile, thinking how BOPE hadn't just let a contract killer slip through their midst, but had actually helped him with his mission.

He followed the path to the school.

twenty-one

Gardner cleared the low fence bordering the shacks, using its wooden posts as a lever to swing his body clear of the barbed wire. A smell of manure and ginger gagged him, watering his eyes.

The fence gave way to a thin line of caroba trees, piassava palms and khaki bushes. Gardner steered between their lone, prickly branches and pushed into the thicker vegetation. The buzzing of the Bell Ranger hushed, replaced by the squawks of macaws and parakeets. He felt the air swell with oxygen, prising open his lungs. Vine thickets shut out the light. His palms sweated, he could feel fear rising in him. The fear of a tight, dark space.

At last he emerged into a dome of secondary jungle. He wiped grime away from his eyes and, taking a look over his left shoulder, got his bearings. He'd entered the jungle at the north-west tip of Barbosa favela. When he'd inserted into the slum, he recalled, the jungle tapered north-west up a steep mountain to a summit several hundred metres above sea level. Six hundred metres to the south lay Corcovado mountain, its hunchback shape jutting against the skyline. If he adjusted his route westward and carried on for a couple of hundred metres, he'd be in line with the coded coordinates Bald had given him.

Fuck, Gardner thought. That phone call seemed like a year ago.

His stomach echoed like a cave. He hadn't touched a morsel of grub since the previous night, but, juiced up with the knowledge he was nearly upon Bald, he got a second wind. He turned down the volume on the hunger, forgot about the aches and pains in his calves, and pounded on through the understory of the jungle.

He didn't make as much progress as he would have liked, his pace hindered by the fact that the jungle floor was a dense mess of overgrown weeds, thorns, ferns, canes and shrubs. In primary jungle and deciduous forest, where tall canopies cut out much of the sunlight, the undergrowth is limited. But in this secondary jungle, where the canopies had been chopped down, sunlight had a clear run to the ground, and the vegetation flourished into a greasy tangle, as if the plants were knotted at the roots, forcing Gardner to concentrate on his every step. He wished he had a knife to hack through the overhanging vines and thickets. He just had to use the stock of his Colt to push aside spiky bushes.

In a way, Falcon had done Gardner a favour with his disappearing act. He'd served his purpose in leading him to the edge of the jungle. Still, something ate at him. Why the hell was Falcon so desperate to avoid his BOPE muckers?

Another thought scratched at the base of his skull: who had kitted out the Messengers with hi-tech PP-2000s? The Russian-manufactured sub-machine-gun was the darling of elite forces and special police units, not the kind of firearm that was easy to buy on the black market – and he doubted they came cheap whatever the source.

Gardner stopped. He'd managed to get himself hooked up on the edges of a rattan bush, known in the Regiment as the 'wait-a-while' bush, on account of how long it took to free yourself from one. All I fucking need, he thought, as he began to work the needles loose from his clothing. Millions of the fuckers, it seemed.

No sooner had he untangled himself than his ears pricked. He paused.

A campfire crackled. Thirty metres ahead, the thick vegetation retreated, giving way to a small clearing. A sweet smell greeted him, fruity and toasted. He instantly recognized that smell as belonging to the Cohiba cigars Bald was so fond of smoking.

I've found him!

Gardner stared ahead at the camp, and saw that, although he'd come out to Rio to help the mucker who'd once saved his life, this had also been a personal mission. About proving a point to the pen-pushers in Whitehall: that he still had the skills and the balls to be a Blade. They'd given him the boot because of his injuries. Flying here, negotiating the favela, rescuing his mate: he could still cut it.

His bowels roiled. He approached the clearing, listening and looking out for any signs of human habitation. John might be there, he reasoned, but a Messenger might have trailed him and could be lying in wait.

Ten metres from the clearing, he planted a boot in front of him and felt something squelch underneath and hiss like a deflating car tyre. His eyes shot down – and he jumped back. Boa constrictor. The snake's head shot forward, mouth wide open, teeth snapping at his ankle. Darting to the left to avoid its bite, he paced around the side of the vicious fucker, all seven feet of it. It hissed at him again, its blue tongue tasting the air, and slithered on.

Heart pounding, flies swarming around his face, Gardner entered the clearing.

The camp was empty. Signs left around the camp told him that whoever had been here had recently bugged out. Damp smoke drifted off a doused fire. A makeshift A-frame, set up at the northern end of the clearing with split atap vines thickly layered across the roof, was also empty. A latrine had been dug up twenty metres to the east of the A-frame. It was brimming with shit and piss that flies feasted on. Gardner spotted a half-full bottle of water hanging from a tree by a rope, and, next to the fire, the stub of a Cohiba cigar. He kneeled and picked it up. The leaves were wet at the mouth end.

The cigar, the fresh shit, the water. John must've bugged out less than an hour ago. An uneasy feeling clawed at his guts. The camp didn't feel right. Bald had the reputation of a vigilant Blade, the kind of bloke who was expert at covering his tracks, right down to bagging every last drop of piss. But the guy who'd lived here was lazy and hadn't made any effort to cover up his tracks.

Gunfire shattered his thoughts.

To your six o'clock, he figured.

He turned. Silhouettes. Ten of them, forty metres away. They sliced through the rattan bushes with machetes, chopping vines and shouting. He saw a figure point a shotgun at the understorey.

Boom!

Birds fluttered. The tail end of a boa constrictor was tossed into the air.

Messengers.

Gardner went into contact mode. He fell back to a caroba tree and knelt down behind the trunk, giving himself a clear line of sight, above the undergrowth, to the targets. Thirty metres to the Messengers. They were heading straight for the clearing. Bugging out was a non-starter; in this terrain he couldn't pick up speed, and they'd soon be on his case. So, time to give them the good news.

Fifteen rounds left in the Colt. He waited until the first target was ten metres from the edge of the clearing, and opened fire, single-shot. The target dropped, and his mates went batshit, spraying rounds in every direction. Gardner was partially concealed between the A-frame and the caroba tree, but he knew it was only a matter of time before they spotted him. He unleashed four rounds, two into the torso of a tall, gangly target, the others for his friend beside him, his body jerking like some weird street dance.

He was winning the fight. The Messengers couldn't get a fix on him. They were shitting themselves. Any minute now they'll fucking do one, he thought.

Splinters showered his face, throwing him on to his back.

He looked at the shredded caroba trunk. The shots hadn't come from the group to the east. Then another two rounds splashed into the soil around him, and Gardner was displacing to a shallow scrape behind the shit pit, cursing his bad luck.

A hundred metres north-east the jungle crested up into a ridgeline, where the undergrowth was stripped away, as if someone had given the ground a Brazilian. Rocky soil jutted out like a series of knuckle joints. And, exposed on the ridge, stood seven Messengers, taking potshots at Gardner.

Bullets flung maggot-riddled shit into the air. Gardner kept his head down, desperately thinking of a plan B. The Messengers to the east burst into the clearing, twenty metres distant. He chopped the first two down with his Colt, ducking to avoid the gunfire from the guys on the ridge.

You're pinned down and on your last eight rounds, he was thinking. Any second now you'll be overrun.

Three more gangsters raced into the clearing, thirty metres ahead.

The light, rapid crack of a Colt Commando silenced their shouts.

'Come to daddy,' a voice called out. 'You know you fucking want it.'

It was full-on cockney. Not Scottish, not John. Dry and hoarse, as if he'd necked a pint of sand. But unmistakable all the same.

Gardner peered out from the scrape. A rangy guy in a loose black T-shirt and grey combats, Bergen strapped to his back, raked gunfire down at the Messengers in the clearing. Their bodies formed a pile at the clearing mouth. He sliced up the final guy and slid over to Gardner's position.

'Well, say something, you silly cunt.'

Topped by Brylcreemed hair, the face had pockmarked cheeks and the rough horseshoe that was always the front-runner for the annual Credenhill shit tache competition.

'Dave?'

'Don't act so surprised, lad. It's me, not fucking Bono.'

'But what the—?'

'I'll explain it all, mate, soon as we've sent these wankers over to the dark side.'

Dave Hands was right. No time for questions. Hands vittled a few rounds over the top of the scrape, at a couple of injured Messengers trying to take cover.

'Reckon we need to pepper-pot back to a baseline.'

'All well and good, mate, but I'm down to my last few rounds.'

Hands nodded, fishing out a fresh clip from his utility belt. 'Don't ask, don't get. How many on the ridgeline?'

'Seven, total.' Gardner peered over the top, sighted a Messenger cross-graining the ridge on a downward slope towards the camp. Two taps on the trigger: slotted. 'Six. See that ditch just short of the ridge? Make that the baseline.'

'Bit of the old fire-and-move, yeah? Read my mind better than my ex-fucking-wife.' Hands checked his Commando. 'Right then. Thumbs out bloody arses.'

'Covering fire!'

Hands displaced from the scrape while Gardner concentrated the last six rounds of the clip on the Messengers on the ridge. The distraction worked. The Messengers returned fire on Gardner, ignoring Hands as he railed the western edge of the clearing, lying up at the ditch twenty metres ahead of Gardner. Now he went into contact mode, and Gardner sprang out from the shit-splayed scrape, racing diagonally across the clearing as fast as his tired leg muscles could carry him. Rounds smacked into the soil around him, flinging dirt into the air like geysers. Gardner hit the ditch.

As soon as he reached the baseline he saw Hands, down on his knees, spraying the Messengers. Gardner slapped in a new clip. The Messengers sought cover, but there was none. They must have realized the mistake of attacking from the ridgeline too late, as Hands sprayed arcs of lead mayhem along their position. Gardner fixed his eyes on Hands. The moment he eased his trigger finger, indicating he needed to reload, Gardner stood up and picked off Messengers with his remaining rounds. One, two, three: they dropped like Lehman Brothers' shares. Two final targets legged it.

'Fucking showed them the time of day,' said Hands, spitting.

'Let's break out of here before their mates get the scent. Millions of those bastards in the favela.'

But Hands didn't move. He stood up, propped his rifle against a tree trunk and fetched a pouch of Cutter's Choice baccy from his pocket. 'Relax, Joe. They ain't coming back. You know what they're like?' He lit the end of his Rizla paper. 'Catholics practising safe sex. First sign of trouble, they pull out.'

Gardner surveyed the carnage. Smoke mist clung to their legs. The air tasted of hot metal, cordite so thick he could chew on it, like gum. I wouldn't be so sure, he thought.

'What the fuck are you doing here anyway?' he said.

'Nice to see you too, mate.' Hands caned on his cigarette. 'I could ask you the same question. Suppose the two of us could waffle on for fucking ages, but you know what? Be easier if you hear everything from the man himself.'

'You mean—?'

'John's up the hill. He sent me to get you.'

twenty-two

1512 hours.

Weiss traipsed up the street. Towards the sound of gunfire. In the favela, if you wanted to find out the truth you followed the bullets.

But the cramps in his stomach and the convulsions in his legs had reduced his pace to a shuffle. He inched forward with one hand pressed against the bullet-flecked walls of the surrounding homes. It had taken forever to make his way from the torture house.

A hundred and fifty metres from the firefight now. Smoke clogged the air. The soft pulse of a helicopter. Hot ash parched his throat.

Son of Mary and Joseph, for a sip of water.

He stooped, and vomited. The fourth time in the past hour and his guts had no chunks left to hock up, just bitter yellowish liquid. He looked down. He'd puked on a chicken pen. The rainbow-coloured birds cawed their disgust.

As he drew near to the top of the favela the street inclined sharply. He wasn't sure if his legs could carry him much further. He stopped to catch his breath. His temperature had rocketed. The corners of his lips had cracked open, like paper cuts. Something is badly wrong, he thought. Maybe I've contracted a fever.

His mind cleared for a second. Fifty metres away, a blurred face came into focus, and he realized he'd hit the jackpot.

Roulette faced west, giving his back to Weiss. He'd not yet seen the Mexican. Roulette was barking orders at three goons. His voice was rasping, frantic. Weiss hushed his rapid breathing and hunched up against the wall.

'How many left?' Roulette asked.

'Alive, boss, or just the ones who can fight?'

'If they're alive, they'd better fight, or I'll fucking kill them myself.'

The goon hesitated. 'Twenty. They had the helicopter, we had nowhere to hide—'

'Son of a bitch,' Roulette cut in. 'And BOPE got the Russian guns from the bodies too. Which means that we're fucked, because they're going to understand where we got them from. Forget it. We can kill two birds with one stone. The guy who sold us the guns, he's the one who was going to rob us. We find him, it's done.'

'But, boss, the chopper—'

'The chopper can suck my dick. There's an RPG stash on the other side of the favela, in the safe house next to the hospital. The boys can take them. We'll shoot that fucking thing down. And Carlos –' Roulette clamped his fingers around the goon's neck '– make it quick. I don't want this bitch to escape.'

'Sure, whatever. What about you, boss?' asked the other goon.

'I'm going to finish off that *Mexicano* cunt.' He glanced at his watch. 'By now Alberto should have finished on his hands and dick. See you in an hour.'

The goons departed.

From his position behind the wall, Weiss spied Roulette pounding the street. Heading in his direction. Weiss reached into his duster. His left hand was shaking. He gripped the wrist with his right hand to control it, and produced a syringe. A thought picked at his frontal lobe, vanished before he could seize it.

Roulette was twenty-five metres off. With his left hand uncontrollable, Weiss chomped the syringe between his teeth and ripped off the cap. His guts made a squelching noise, as if his stomach was seeping acid into his bowels.

Ten metres.

Weiss steeled his hand. The needle glinted.

Five metres.

Roulette's shadow skated past.

Now.

Weiss swung around the corner and found Roulette almost on top of him. The Messenger leader collided with Weiss, who had to fight hard to stop himself toppling backwards. Roulette's eyes, a couple of black poker chips, blinked their surprise at him, then lowered and inspected the needle as it punched his stomach.

Roulette took two steps back and tugged the syringe out. Foaming at the mouth and swaying on his feet, he seized up.

'How does it feel?' Weiss asked, as Big Teeth's number two struggled for breath. 'Really, I'm curious. Do you know what's in your bloodstream?'

Roulette's eyes ballooned. He sweated feverishly, making a supreme effort to shake his head.

'I've injected you with Batrachotoxin. The name means nothing to you, naturally.' Roulette grunted his agreement. 'But perhaps you are familiar with the poison dart frog. The poison is the most deadly toxin known to man. It will attack your central nervous system first, paralysing your muscles one by one. You'll be in a state of helplessness as you lose control of your body. Your chest will feel like . . . like it's crushed underneath a cattle stampede. Breathing will become impossible. And you've shit yourself, I see. This . . . this is what you get for trying to *fuck* with—'

Weiss spewed blood, spraying Roulette's neck and shirt. He rested a hand on Roulette's shoulder to stop himself from falling over and dear God, his kidney was on fire.

He looked at Roulette and forgot about his pain. The Messenger's skin shifted pale blue. Many people panicked or cried in their last moments of life, and some even accepted death without complaint. But Roulette laughed. Weiss wasn't sure why. His eyes narrowed to dead matchsticks, his face screwing up in amusement.

It was the laugh of a man who intended his to be the last.

Weiss left Roulette on his knees, floundering in a pool of his own shit, and dragged himself up the street. The street peaked. He saw the bodies first, spread-eagled and deformed. Messy deaths, the kind Weiss disapproved of. It seemed strange when he considered it, but Weiss hated the sight of blood. That's why he used syringes.

The school. Nobody about. Decorated with bullet holes and cartridges, as if God had placed a storm cloud over Barbosa favela and made it hail brass.

He saw a Messenger fleeing from the north, running so fast his feet seemed not to touch the ground, and he knew instantly his destination.

The jungle.

That's where he'd hit pay dirt.

twenty-three

1600 hours.

Gardner and Hands moved low amid the undergrowth. They stuck to the most impenetrable route through the jungle – Gardner's idea, in case the Messengers picked up the chase again.

'This is pointless,' Hands moaned. 'I'm telling you, we're safe as bloody houses. You remember the crap insurgents in Basra? Shooting from the hip like they think they're in fucking Hollywood. These guys are ten times worse, mate.'

'I remember,' Gardner said, 'more than a hundred good soldiers died in Basra.'

'Yeah, but you always get one or two.'

Gardner took no notice of Hands and his spiel. He had spent fifteen years of his life hyper-alert and sticking to the cardinal rule – never underestimate your enemy – and he wasn't about to give up now. The jungle air was damp and moist, his clothes drenched, sticky. A trickling noise reached his ears, like coins jangling in his pocket. It came from the north-west. Energy coursed through him. He could hear the blood rushing through his head.

All the while he was keeping one eye on Hands. The man wasn't moving with care, snagging his Bergen against branches, trampling on tall grass and generally leaving the kind of sign that would make David Stirling roll in his grave.

'Been what, four, five years?' said Gardner.

'Five years, eight months and twelve days. Not that I'm counting.'

'So what's the buzz?'

Hands was quiet for a beat.

'Down here helping John. What's it fucking look like?'

Gardner raised an eyebrow. 'With BOPE?'

'Yeah, yeah.'

'I didn't know you and John kept in touch.'

Hands was silent again, as if they were talking over a bad phone line. 'Well, you know, we didn't for a while. He was doing this, I was tied up in a bit of that . . . You want the truth, Joe? No one fucking talked to me after, after – it. Not one fucking Blade. Not Pitman, not Grant, not even fucking *you*.'

He had turned on Gardner like a Rottweiler, eyeballing him ferociously. Gardner returned the compliment. Backing down wasn't in his DNA.

'Spare me the self-pity act, Dave. You fucked up the moment you tried to sell the drugs. Ten thousand ecstasy tablets, for fuck's sake. Once you made that choice, you deserved everything that came your way. And here's another thing. I don't give two shits whether you think it was me or any of the other lads who set you up with that undercover copper. Because, you know what? You made your bed. You fucking lie in it. There's no one to blame for what happened but yourself.'

'You can be a real dick sometimes, Joe,' said Hands, stepping into Gardner's face. 'Just because not everyone goes around licking Regiment arse, you think you got a right to fucking judge me.'

Gardner was suddenly conscious of the Colt by Hands' side. His finger paused on the trigger.

All alone, middle of nowhere, it would be so easy . . .

'And yeah, I got caught.' Hands' voice was becoming scratchy. 'No argument there. But I paid a heavy fucking price. Years after that, I couldn't get work wiping the shit off someone's arse. You don't know what I went through. No fucking idea. We all make mistakes, mate, but some of us take a harder fall. Know what I mean?'

Hands lifted his finger off the trigger. Then he smiled and extended his left hand. 'But I always say, past is past. I ain't got no grievance with you no more.'

Gardner shook hands with his prosthetic.

'Fuck it,' he said. 'Everyone deserves a second chance. If John's willing to trust you, that's good enough for me.'

He said it to put Hands at ease, not because he truly meant it. Hands, he knew, was prone to losing his cool. He'd once stuck his gun in the face of a guy who tried to overtake him on the A3. Threatened to shoot the driver and his bird on the spot. The CO of D Squadron, 22 SAS, Major Neil Buckie, severely reprimanded him, but Hands didn't shape up.

Then the drugs bust left Buckie with no choice but to give him the boot. And, in the years since, Regiment gossip had reached Gardner's ears of the dodgy dealings Hands was involved in. Pornography distribution, including kiddie porn and bestiality; counterfeit passports and credit card scams; drug dealing.

So why's John working with him? Gardner wondered, but he backburned the question.

They burrowed on through the jungle, Gardner's arms and legs in pain, his body cannibalizing its muscle for energy. Adrenalin supercharged his veins.

Two hundred metres further on, Gardner realized the origin of the jangling sound: up ahead, a fast-flowing creek running downhill along the basin of a pocked ridge.

'Home sweet home,' Hands said.

Everything clicked. The tracks at the camp. The fire. It wasn't laziness. 'The campsite,' Gardner said. 'No self-respecting Blade would leave such a mess. It was deliberate, wasn't it?'

Hands nodded. 'A decoy. John's idea. Put any nosy fuckers off the scent, know what I mean? He reckoned you'd figure it out for yourself.'

Thirty metres from the edge of the creek, which was tucked in behind a thick web of vines and ferns, Hands stopped. Gardner spotted a figure. The man was shaded by a nearby kopak tree that towered over the land, fifty metres high and half a metre thick. The trunk was crowded with buttresses.

Gardner paced ahead of Hands. The guy was sitting on a toppled tree trunk. He had a Fairbairn-Sykes fighting knife in one hand, slicing the double-edged blade along a length of bark in his other hand, tucking the dry shavings into a small pouch on his lap. Four Bergens were propped up against the trunk, coloured in digital camouflage.

The man's hands were black as soot, covered in welts and bruises. He was barefoot. A pair of brown socks hung from a long branch nearby. Gardner noticed that his right foot was swollen and purple, probably from where he'd been bitten by a spider or snake.

Gardner knew who he was, even before he stepped closer to him, when the jungle gloom eased and the face took on definition. His pale skin was masked by camo paint, eyes beaming like spotlights. He was bulkier than Gardner recalled, but still had the frown grooved into his forehead.

John Bald.

twenty-four

1633 hours.

He was close.

Weiss stumbled across the clearing and licked the air. It tasted zingy and heavy with topsoil. Like a bomb had gone off in his mouth. The battle that had raged in the clearing had occurred very recently, he figured. Smoke clung to his ankles, and the wounded had not yet died.

Make that 'one of the wounded', he thought as he approached the last survivor. The kid was not long for this earth. He was early twenties, a golden dollar-sign chain hanging from his neck, and a hole in his chest large enough to sink an orange.

Weiss squatted down beside him.

'If you want, I can make it quick,' he said, reaching a hand into his duster. 'Tell me which way he went.'

The kid shuddered. It was a bitch of a choice for any human being to make: die now, or live longer and suffer. The kid chose death. He pointed a finger west.

'Was he alone?' asked Weiss, now feeling for the syringe.

The kid curled his thumb and index finger into a ball, leaving two fingers in the air. So, the target had company. He had all the information he needed. Time to honour his end of the bargain.

Weiss frowned. He couldn't find what he was looking for. Pulling his coat wide open, he ran his peepers down the row of needles. He was missing a syringe, one loaded with a toxic alkaloid called aconitine. That's too bad, he said to himself. You probably dropped it when you escaped from Rolex and Lakers. Aconitine was one of his favourite compounds, and he made a mental note to touch base with his chemist on his return to Ciudad Juárez.

The kid wanted a quick death, and Weiss obliged. He administered a high dosage of succinylcholine to the neck. Within seconds the kid's muscles shrivelled up and he couldn't breathe. Something flopped in his chest. He went over to the dark side.

Weiss moved on. He got about halfway across the clearing before he doubled over in agony and his guts contracted, as if someone was yanking at him with a bungee cord. He coughed up black goo; shivered in spite of the jungle heat. The tips of his toes were numb, his fingers likewise.

You've got a fever, he reasoned. After what Roulette and his goons did to you earlier, are you surprised? But don't let it stop you. I won't, but Christ, it hurts. He steadied himself, fearing he'd faint.

One glance west and he was on his feet.

He noticed the snapped branches and the crushed twigs. The footprints and the damaged undergrowth. Someone had beaten a path through the foliage and left evidence of his route. It was God's will, he was sure of it. Thirty million dollars. So close now, he could almost smell the greenbacks.

Weiss ignored the fever and pushed on.

twenty-five

1701 hours.

John Bald looked at Gardner briefly, then went back to carving firewood from the wet bark. Crunching twigs sounded to his six o'clock. Hands drew near to him, and Bald put the bark to one side, knife dangling between his legs.

'Took your time, man,' Bald said.

Thinking the question was directed at him, Gardner made to answer. But Hands replied, 'We got held up. Messengers had a little welcome party for us, yeah? Nothing to get your knickers in a twist about. Me and Jason Statham here gave them what for.'

Bald ran his tongue around his mouth. 'Sure no one followed you?'

'Gimme a break,' Hands replied. 'Those gang pricks couldn't follow their own fucking shadows.'

Bald gave no indication of whether he agreed with Hands. Holding it up to the light, he examined the Fairbairn-Sykes. 'Well, you got here just in time. I think our mutual friend is about to pass out from the pain. I need you to clean his wound and get some fresh dressing on it. And a shot of morphine too, keep him quiet.'

Hands strode past Gardner to a figure at his peripheral vision. He noticed the foot first. The boot had been cut off, a grey blanket tied around it and a long forked branch that stretched from his armpit to below his foot, tied with vines around the ankle.

The foot belonged to Falcon.

Gardner did a double-take. Couldn't believe what he was seeing. He looked back towards Bald, who made no effort to explain anything to him, much less make eye contact. He seemed obsessed by the fighting knife.

'What, what's going—?'

'You must be exhausted, man. Here,' Bald said, tossing a canteen towards Gardner. 'It's from the stream. It's got a wee kick to it from the purification tablets.'

This isn't the John I know, Gardner thought. Bald never used two words when one would do the trick. But he was also warm and loyal. Now it seemed he was treating Gardner like a stranger. No 'thank you' for travelling halfway around the world.

Gardner unscrewed the cap on the canteen. Dark, filmy water sloshed about inside. He didn't raise it to his lips. Instead, he looked at the stuffed Bergens beside Bald – calm, relaxed Bald – and wondered.

He laughed.

'Something funny, Joe?'

'You tell me,' Gardner replied. 'The tablets, the fake camp, the Bergens. You don't mean to tell me you had all this kit with you for a patrol with BOPE? This took planning. Preparation. When you got jumped, all this shit was already in place.'

'Aye, man. You've a fair point,' Bald answered, his bottom lip weighing it up. 'The truth of the matter is, we had to take some precautions.'

'Who the fuck's "we"?'

Bald extended an arm towards Hands and Falcon. Hands rinsed out Falcon's wound with water, wiping it down with a gauze swab and wrapping a roll of sterile dressing around the open wound. The BOPE captain was feverish, fucking out of it like a pillhead in a rave club.

'Why, my business partners, of course.'

Gardner lit up like an oil field. He felt duped, had the urge to punch someone in revenge, but he wasn't sure who deserved a socking the most: Bald for his cry of help, Falcon for keeping shtum about his link to John, or Hands just for being, well, fucking Dave Hands.

'You reached out to me,' he said, pointing to Bald. 'You said you were in the shit, John. Knee-deep in the stuff. That's why I rushed out here at a fucking moment's notice. Because you were in trouble.'

Bald slipped on his dried socks and boots.

'But I am, Joe. I am. That's why I asked you here. Listen, I'll answer all your questions in a minute. First, I've got a question for *you*.'

He stabbed the Fairbairn-Sykes into the felled tree.

'Can you still drive a boat?'

twenty-six

Gardner didn't reply. He noticed Hands and Falcon edging towards Bald, hanging at his four o'clock. His brain tried to make sense of everything. The connection with dodgy Dave Hands. The need for a boat. The fake camp. Falcon's unease about his BOPE comrades. Each question only led to more questions.

'This is important,' Bald continued. 'Life or death. I need to know if you can help me.'

'Help with what?'

'Getting out, man. The airport's a no-go, there's checkpoints at the state borders, and it's a long haul to Santos by road anyway. Boat's the only option we have.'

'You're gonna have to be straight with me here, John. Either you've lost your passport, or there's something a lot darker that you're not telling me. I've come a long way – too far to be fucked about. So how about you cut to the chase?'

Bald chuckled and wagged a finger at Gardner. 'That's what I always liked about you, Joe. You call a spade a spade.'

He nodded to Hands. The skinny ex-Blade paced towards the Bergens and fiddled with the straps on the leftmost one, while Bald took from his pocket a tennis-ball-sized fruit, reddish and leathery, sliced it down the centre with his knife and popped one half into his mouth.

Then Hands tipped out the contents of the Bergen.

'This,' Bald said, 'is your spade.'

A stack of five packages spilled on to the floor, each the size of a paperback book, wrapped in white paper, with the image of a scorpion stamped on the top of the package. Gardner had conducted anti-drug-smuggling operations in Colombia and could identify a brick blindfolded. Each brick, he knew, was a solid kilo of pure cocaine.

Silence between the four men. Hands tucked the Bolivian marching powder back into the Bergen, and a single thought lodged at the front of Gardner's brain. What the fuck?

'The world is about opportunity,' Bald said, Gardner not even meeting his eyes. 'The winners seize it. The losers let it pass them by. You remember how it was in the Regiment, don't you, Joe? Strike when you have the chance.'

Gardner's eyes flitted between Bald and Hands. He didn't like the fact Hands was clutching his Colt Commando at waist height, barrel pointed at the ground. A quick swing of the carbine and he'd be aiming directly at Gardner's head. His own carbine dangled by his side, out of ammo and fucking useless.

'This here,' Bald said, waving his hand at the Bergens, 'this is what opportunity looks like.'

'You stole it from the Messengers of God.'

'Well, I prefer "liberated". Spoils of war and all that. It was actually Captain Falcon's idea.'

Gardner thought back to his first encounter with Falcon. 'The explosive entry course.'

'All I can say is, Florida's a good place to do business. There's fifty keys of cocaine in total, with a street value of thirty million dollars, American. We brought young David on board because of his contacts. He knows people who are desperate for premium-grade snow in Europe. Care for some?'

Bald held out the other half of the fruit. Gardner shook his head.

'Please yourself. The plan's worked out well so far. Rafael arranged to meet with some of the Messengers and make a weapons swap. A common enough exchange with BOPE and some of the army units. Corruption here, you see, it's part and parcel of daily life.'

'Some of the gang had PP-2000s,' said Gardner. 'Top-end firearms. You sold them to the Messengers.'

'The weapons exchange was just a front. After the deal went down we took the Messengers hostage and tortured them until they gave up the drug stash. They did – and quickly, too. Threaten to kill a man, he won't say a word. Shove a broom handle up his arsehole, you can't keep him quiet. But bugging out of the favela has proved more difficult.' Bald gestured at Gardner with the knife tip. 'Which is where you come in.'

Hands helped Falcon to his feet. The rupert tottered on his makeshift crutch to the side of Gardner, until he was at the fringes of his line of sight. Hands, Falcon and Bald were now spread out in a semicircle in front of him, the Scot playing it cool as Gardner slowly backed up on his heels.

'To return to my problem. I didn't sell you a bum steer, Joe. I really am in trouble. The Messengers know for sure we ripped them off, and Captain Falcon thinks his BOPE friends have their suspicions. Somehow we need to get this shipment down to the port of Santos, where David's contact will rendezvous with us. The only way we'll get there without being arrested is by boat. Rafael's got a contact who can rig us a Hacker-Craft at the port, topped up with diesel and ready to roll.'

Gardner met Bald's eyes. They were wide and shiny, like a man who'd just landed a prize catch.

'So, the question is: are you with us?'

Gardner felt three sets of eyes burning holes in him.

'Why the fuck would I want in?'

'I'm offering you a share of the profits,' Bald said, raising his palms. 'A three-way split becomes four. Just think. Seven and a half million big ones. It's yours. All you've got to do is pilot a boat two hundred and fifty kilometres down the coastline.' He paused, trying to gauge Gardner's reaction. 'And this is only the start of business together. Rafa here says there are literally hundreds of drug trains coming out of the favelas. We can clean up, Joe. You and me.'

'I don't know—'

'Life's not easy for an old Blade,' Bald cut in. He shook his head sadly. 'In the Roman Empire, soldiers were like gods. Today we're the shit on the heel of someone's boot. Look at the way the head shed treated you, fobbing you off with a pension that barely stretches to a chip buttie and a tin of beans. You, me – we deserve better.'

'I don't know,' Gardner said, 'who you are any more.'

Bald shifted on his feet.

'We used to see drug smugglers as the scum of the earth.'

'The world's changed,' Bald replied.

'No. Just you,' said Gardner, clocking Hands' face as it morphed from grin to scowl.

'Don't get all moral on me. This is snow, for fuck's sake. No one dies. If we didn't have it, the Messengers would sell it on themselves. What's the big deal?'

'Coke here, heroin in the Afghan. Drugs helped kill some of our mates. If the Taliban didn't get their profits from the poppies, maybe they'd never have had the resources to plant all those IEDs. Maybe good lads – guys we fought alongside – would still be alive. Sorry, John. I'm not perfect, but I'm better than a lowlife like Hands. I'm not getting my hands dirty.'

Bald crimsoned. Spit gathered at the corners of his mouth.

'You bloody well owe me. I risked my life to save you in the Afghan.'

'Yeah, I remember all right. But the Afghan was then; this is now. And my answer's still no.'

'Fuck you, then.'

The voice cut like a spear across Bald's shoulder. Hands had his Colt Commando raised level with Gardner's head. Falcon's right hand rested on his holstered Taurus, his other on the crutch.

'I told you bringing this cunt into the fold was a bad move.'

'Drop it, David,' Bald said.

'Nah, screw that shit. I don't know why you were so desperate to have him on the team in the first place. He's straighter than a fucking go-faster stripe, and he's supposed to get an equal share when we've done all the legwork?'

'We need him if we're to reach Santos.'

'I'll fucking walk it there myself. Better than letting this prick in on the action.'

'Another one of your bright ideas, Dave? Maybe you should offload a brick to a copper,' Gardner said. Wish I had a round in my rifle, he was thinking. Just a single bullet would do the trick. Put one right between Dave's eyes.

'Think you're funny, mate? You won't be laughing in a minute. And know what? Killing you will be the best decision I ever make.'

Hands peered down the sights of the Colt.

'Put the gun down,' Bald urged.

'Enjoy the ride, mate.'

Hands depressed the trigger.

His finger pulled halfway before it happened. Before Bald thrust at him. Before Bald, stocky with legs like tree trunks, but fleet of foot and agile, leapt the three metres to Hands, socked him on the jaw and knocked him backwards, the chambered round in the Colt kicking up into the sky, panicking a flock of macaws.

Falcon clumsily pulled out his Taurus. Gardner broke right, trying to put some ground between himself and Falcon's line of fire. A double *crack* split the air as he moved behind the kopak tree. He peered back towards the camp. Falcon's corpse on the floor, Bald shadowing him, cursing under his breath. Hands unconscious by his side. Bald turned to the tree. To Gardner.

'I make that twice, Joe. Christ, if I save your bacon again someone's gonna have to keep score. Tell you what, pilot the boat and we'll call it even-stevens. The good news is, I can offer you a three-way split, now that Rafael's . . . indisposed. And who knows, David might have to accept a pay cut. More for me and you.'

Gardner crouched behind the trunk. Unarmed. How the fuck do you get out of this one?

The answer came in the form of a gunshot. Bald unloading a round at the tree. Bark sprayed Gardner's face. Splinters nicked his hands.

'Sometimes I think about how different things would've been, you know? If we'd waited for the sweeping team to come in and scan the area. I mean, those sand monkeys had worked out the tolerance of landmine detectors and there could easily have been another device waiting to kick off in my face. But if I followed protocol, you'd have bled out.'

Gardner couldn't stand and fight. Not without a gun. He scanned the jungle.

'Remember the kid, Joe?'

'Connors. Pretty Boy Connors.'

Gardner kept him talking. Buying himself time. He looked towards the far side of the creek, where the land dropped off. Impossible to see how deep, or where it led to, but if he managed to get across there . . .

'Reckoned he had a Page Three stunner for a bird. Speak to him for more than a minute, out came the wallet and the picture of his missus. Then we found out she was actually from Page Three. Kid had just cut her picture out of the paper and scanned it into a photograph. Bloody joker.'

Bald's voice grew closer. Ten, maybe twelve metres away.

'Hard to watch a kid like that die. And it could so easily have been you, Joe. Do me a favour and—*What the fuck?*'

The clatter of a gunshot. Gardner heard Bald grunt, a separate set of footsteps rustling the dry leaves and a voice cussing in Portuguese. He ducked away from the kopak tree and saw a burly guy in a black duster coat, using his weight to pin Bald to the ground. Bald kicked and flailed at him, but the guy was immovable as a rock. His face was pale as the coke packets and his shaking hand held a needle ten inches from Bald's face.

'Son of a fucking bitch. Help me, Joe!'

For a split second Gardner's Regiment instincts kicked in, and he made towards Bald, fists clenched, ready to kick seven shades of shit out of the attacker. John's lied to me, he told himself. But he's still an ex-Blade, and I can't stand back and let him die.

A rush of air above. Whirl of blades, whip of an engine. Gardner arched his head up and saw the Bell Ranger overhead. Low, seventy feet, rails almost touching the canopy below. So low he could see the pilot's face, and the pattern on the sniper's sneakers.

The sniper was aiming directly at him.

He broke left just as the sniper pulled the trigger. The bullet thwacked into the butt of a tree. Then the chopper lifted and circled around the creek, the sniper indicating to his pilot that he needed a clearer shot.

Gardner's eyes followed it as it hovered to the east. Below, shadows moved along the ridgeline. They shouted and pointed towards Gardner. Bald still struggled with the guy in the duster. The shadows stopped seventy metres away. Two of them kneeled and aimed their weapons at Gardner.

Shit! Fucking surrounded.

He shot a final glance back towards Bald.

A needle suspended above his eyes.

'Joe, I'm fucked! Help!'

I can't, mate, Gardner thought as a crackle of gunfire erupted to his right. He ducked behind the eastern side of the kopak tree. He heard the furious splitting of bark as rounds smacked into the trunk.

Get out of here. You can't save Bald, but you can still save yourself.

His survival instincts kicked in. He darted towards the creek. Once there he stared at the drop. The decline was practically vertical, all the way down into another area of the Barbosa favela. He had a widescreen view of Rio, from the clutter of rooftops and electricity cables to the Hilton, to Copacabana beach.

He cross-grained diagonally along the drop. Ten metres down, he caught a scream at his rear, like someone strangling a dog. Bald. He pictured the needle plunging through John's eye socket, piercing his lizard brain. He didn't know who the attacker was, didn't give a crap.

Shake hands with the devil, expect him to stab you in the back.

The creek flowed directly past the favela, where it grew into impassable jungle. Half a dozen women were washing their clothes in the water. They stopped and stared at Gardner as he ran parallel to the creek. Twenty metres on, past a dead goat, he found a small fence, bounded over it and crossed the street. The Bell Ranger circled the air above. A Big Skull accelerated past, almost running over his foot. Slammed on the brakes. The passenger door swung open. An officer shouted at him.

You need to bug out, and quick, Gardner decided. The last thing he wanted was to be detained by BOPE. From what Bald said, Falcon wasn't the only corrupt guy in the unit, and the other dodgy officers wouldn't hesitate to execute a foreigner who knew too much.

Then he smelled shit and clocked a sewage hole on the side of an adjacent home. He had his escape plan.

twenty-seven

1811 hours.

Gardner crawled into a tunnel tight as a coffin.

His body slithered into hot, foul waste the consistency of mud. The shit-and-piss brew touched his chin, and he clamped his mouth tightly shut, fighting his gag reflex. The space was so narrow he had to tuck in his elbows; they scraped along the walls of the tunnel, scouring the skin.

He rowed with his arms, his fists acting as flat blades that pushed beneath the surface and splashed sewage against his face. He was forced to breathe in through his nose, and the smell was wet and vicious, like burned skunk. Shards of light from the sewage holes lighted up the crap he ploughed through. He saw used condoms, bloodied tampons, nappies, tissues and even a foetus. But most of all, he saw shit: a mass of brown, as if he was squirming behind a donkey with a bad case of Montezuma's revenge.

God, how long will it take to wade through this shit? Keep going until you're out of the favela, he told himself. But the favela's a mile long. A whole fucking mile. It's two miles to the beach. You have to get out of the area. It's not safe. Not with BOPE on your case. Fuck it, then.

He struggled on. The sewer flowed downward at an angle from the creek – three hundred metres above sea level – towards the beach. Occasionally a powerful surge of excrement rushed past him, pushing his head fully under the surface. Globs of shit filled his ears, his nostrils, prised at his clamped lips.

The holes in the street finished abruptly.

When the dark arrived, the fear rode its back.

And suddenly Gardner was back in the torpedo tubes during waterborne insertions training in Boat Troop. He watched the hatch batten shut, the darkness so complete he couldn't see his hands. The tube flooding with water, and the agonizing wait for the chamber to open, releasing him into the sea.

The fear burrowed into his spine, paralysing him. With every passing second it required greater effort to move forward. Every muscle in his body seemed to resist. The irrational part of his mind urged him to crawl backwards and exit the nearest street hole, but he fought hard against it. No, you have to push on. Like exploring caves, the darker and deeper you foraged into a mountain's guts, the closer you came to the other side.

He lost count of time. There was no way of judging how far he had slithered or how much further he had to go. It felt as if he was sinking into a bottomless pit. The sewage level rose, reaching his bottom lip. He thought he might choke and drown.

Squeaks pierced his ears. He saw a light, white and irresistible, like an onrushing train. The exit. The light energized him. He picked up the pace. Then the squeaks grew louder, and he spotted a pack of rats at the exit hole, swarms of the fuckers picking at the build-up of sewage. He came close to the exit. The rats were excited. They scuttled around the hole, jumping on to his hands. One landed on his head, and he shook wildly from side to side, screaming, the rat in his hair clawing at his scalp, but all he wanted was to escape the tunnel, to breathe fresh air, and he climbed through the hole and blinked in the sunlight.

He was out.

The rats scattered like pool balls at a break, and Gardner checked his surroundings.

He'd been coughed up in a backstreet of a residential neighbourhood. Split bin bags in a rubbish dump had attracted the rats. He followed the street to a main road. Pleasant whitewashed villas, tan apartment buildings and colonial architecture. In the background he made out Corcovado mountain. You've crawled through more than a mile of shit, he thought.

A street sign told Gardner he was on Rua Alfredo Chaves. From his memorized Google map of Rio, that placed him in Humaitá district, east of the statue and outside the cluster of favelas to the north: Barbosa, Santiago and the rest. A clock outside a shop told him it was seven-thirteen in the evening. The work crowd had retired for the night. There weren't many people about.

Not many, but a few. Across the street a fair-skinned girl in her twenties shot him a disgusted look and quickly moved on. Gardner glanced down at himself, and understood why. He was caked in shit from his toes to his neck. Some of the sewage was beginning to harden and fester in the heat.

Time for a wash, he told himself. He crossed Rua Humaitá, headed down a maze of tight roads and blue- and green-doored bungalows, drawing stares from the locals, and hit Rua Real Grandeza. Passing the São João Batista cemetery, its winged angel looking over the graves, he continued south for several hundred metres until he finally reached Avenida Atlantica and Copacabana beach.

He staggered across baking sand the colour of flax seeds. The beach wasn't so busy at this time of day; the tourists were wining and dining and heading out to town. Topless girls covered up their breasts and blokes in brightly coloured beach shorts stopped playing football, and stared. A group of teenagers shared a joint and pointed at him. Gardner didn't care. He looked ahead to the water, turquoise and foamy like cappuccino froth. The tide licked his feet. He shuffled into the Atlantic Ocean and swam out a hundred metres to a spot where no one could bother him. He let the cool water clean his body.

When he was done washing, he collapsed midway up the beach and let the fading sun dry his soaked, dirty clothes. Fuck me, he thought. Shaves don't come any closer. He'd come to Rio to rescue his mate and found himself tricked and ambushed by a man he'd once been proud to call his best friend. And he'd escaped. Now he was lying on a paradise beach surrounded by topless women with arses that would make a grown man cry. One girl, dark-haired and topaz-eyed and wearing just a black thong, grabbed his attention. That size, her tits have got to be fake, he reckoned. Either way, he admired the view.

Gardner laughed. Then closed his eyes. Sand grains blew across his face, clinging to his eyebrows and nose. For the longest time, his world was dark.

Then he felt the sun cool. He opened his eyes and saw a shadow standing over him.

twenty-eight

The shadow wore a suit, and the suit had a name.

'Leo Land,' the shadow said in an accent so posh it deserved a night at the opera. 'And you must be Joe Gardner. Don't forget my name, there's a good chap. I might be the last friend you ever have.'

Gardner squinted, shaken that the guy in the all-white linen suit knew his name. Land offered his hand. He looked younger than his accent. Land was classical posh: blond hair pushed back in a wave, right-angled jaw. He had a way about him, as if he owned the world and everyone in it, and his face stared out at Gardner from a thousand colonial photos.

Land helped Gardner to his feet and evidently caught a whiff of eau de sewer.

'I've told you my name,' he said. 'But perhaps you can guess my paymasters.'

'Foreign Office?'

'Not quite,' Land replied, shaking his head.

'You're definitely government.'

'Secret Intelligence Service. MI6 to the layman. Counter-Proliferation Section . . . Good God, that smell *is* rather strong.'

'Took the scenic route.'

'Well, it's been quite a day for you, hasn't it? Walk with me.'

'Buy a fucking dog.'

Land's face tightened. 'You're in hot water, Mr Gardner, and I'm the only person who can help you. So why don't you park that great big chip of yours by the door and come with me.' He smiled at Gardner. 'I hear the promenade's very pleasant at dusk.'

'Do I have a choice?'

'Of course,' Land said. But Gardner knew that if he blanked Land now, they'd find another way of cornering him. That was the Firm's style. Pretend to give you a choice, when you didn't really have any fucking choice at all.

They strolled up to the promenade. Wave patterns were carved into the black-and-white limestone. A dozen girls breezed past, scent of factor fifty and sex in their wake. Lamps lit up the Atlantic Ocean like a floodlit football pitch.

'Do you believe in second chances, Mr Gardner?'

'I believe in first chances. After that, it's in the lap of the gods.'

'Interesting . . . Personally, I think we all deserve a second bite at the cherry. But I'm getting ahead of myself.'

Land plucked a cigarette from a pack of red Pall Malls. Gardner clocked the Cartier watch on his wrist. The Firm must've given their boys a pay rise, he thought.

'Your little adventure in the favela is all over the news. Twenty-six killed, a further forty wounded. Bloodiest day in recent history, they're saying. No thanks to you.'

'In my defence, the other guys started it.'

'We need to talk in private,' Land said. He sucked greedily on his tab and the fumes wafted across Gardner's face.

'I'd love to, mate, but I got a plane to catch.'

Gardner paced away from the promenade.

'I'm afraid you won't get very far,' Land called after him. 'Dead men aren't usually allowed on planes.'

Gardner froze. His eyes rested on the bustling pavement in front of him. Cars drew tracer rounds in the gloom. People went about their evenings, giggling and holding hands while he reeked of seawater and shit, and an MI6 agent played mind games.

'You'll be curious to know,' Land went on, 'that one of the bodies BOPE recovered from Barbosa matches the photo on your passport. According to the paperwork, his name is Joe Gardner. In fact a surgeon is operating on the body even as we speak. He's attaching a prosthetic hand to the corpse, identical to the one you have.'

Land crushed the Pall Mall stub under his suede Oxford.

'You're officially dead.'

Gardner flipped like a burger. Felt a rush of steam in his veins. Suddenly he was in Land's face, so close he could taste the nicotine on his skin. Land tilted his head back.

'If you weren't in the Firm,' Gardner said, 'I wouldn't be the only dead guy on this promenade.'

'I'm staying at the Marriott. Come and have a drink and we'll talk some more.'

'Why the fuck should I trust you?'

'Because if you don't, my dear man, you won't make it to the end of the street.'

Gardner scanned the hotels and inns lined up along the Avenida Atlántica. The yellows, pinks and whites were bathed in a platinum glow from the streetlights and the traffic. The Marriott towered above the other buildings in a fuck-you gesture. Somewhere further down the road, Land's friends were waiting to kick Gardner's arse.

'Here,' said Land, tossing him a key card. 'Room 307. There's a fresh shirt and pair of jeans in the wardrobe. And for God's sake have a shower while you're at it. See you in the bar in twenty minutes.'

He showered and changed. Gardner swapped his Timberlands for black leather slip-ons and nabbed a pair of Ralph Lauren shades. He checked himself in the mirror. Looked as if he belonged in a reality show searching for his dream home.

The Terráneo lounge bar filled up with the pre-dinner crowd. Everyone was moneyed up. It didn't take Gardner long to find Land. The Firm's man in Brazil occupied a window table, admiring the view while swirling a glass of red in his hand. His jacket was draped tastefully over the back of the chair. The sleeves on his creased white shirt were rolled up to the elbow.

'Caipirinha?' Land asked as a waiter loitered.

'I'll take a beer,' Gardner said.

'Now that you've rejoined civilization,' said the MI6 man, 'I'm guessing you have lots of questions. Please, permit me to shed some light.' The waiter returned with a bottle of something called Antarctica.

Land folded his hands in his lap. 'It's very simple. From the moment you landed in Rio, the Firm has been watching you closely.'

Gardner gave his screw-face. Took a hit of Antarctica. The beer juiced his bloodstream.

'We intercepted Bald's phone call to you. No doubt he realized that BOPE monitor all calls and chatter coming in and out of the favela, which is why he spoke in code. But he neglected to consider who might be listening in at the other end of the line. It wasn't a very hard code for us to crack, of course, and we were delighted he reached out to you. John's been very quiet of late, you see.'

A smell of lemon and chilli greeted Gardner as a second waiter rocked up and carefully arranged plates of boiled mandioc, potato fritters, sautéed chicken livers and smoked red sausages seasoned with mixed herbs.

'I do hope you're hungry. Everything's delicious, but I strongly recommend the stewed cow's tongue.'

'Lost my appetite,' Gardner said, pushing the plates to one side. 'You knew about John from the start?'

'Yes, yes,' said Land, popping a fried cod ball into his mouth. 'His cocaine plot's been on the Firm's watchlist for the past six months, give or take. Seriously, you've no idea how much hassle you spared us by agreeing to help your friend.'

'Not any more he ain't. To me he's a stranger. *Was*,' said Gardner, correcting himself.

'That's where you're wrong, old chap. The fact is, Bald escaped from that hellish favela and is currently winging his way down the Atlantic on a rented Hacker-Craft piloted by an undercover agent. If we had a pair of binoculars we might even spot him passing by.'

Gardner steamed, as if he'd swallowed hot coals. 'John's alive, and you just let him waltz right out of there?'

'We had to. If we're to penetrate his drug-trafficking ring.'

He took another swig of beer. Three gulps and the bottle was half empty.

'John told me the plan was to transport the bricks to Santos by boat, and then a friend of Dave Hands was going to rendezvous with them and move it on. That's the ring you're talking about?'

Land nodded quickly. 'They're employing a rather unusual shipment route. The cocaine is due to be smuggled out on a Royal Navy frigate. The HMS *Lizard*. Our sources indicate that Bald has befriended a Wren by the name of Petty Officer Stephanie Wright. We suspect Hands may have acted as the go-between. The *Lizard*'s next port of call is Gibraltar, from where Bald will unload the cocaine and, presumably, sell it on—'

'To the next link in the chain.'

'Exactly. You see, Mr Gardner, why we don't want to pull the plug on Bald's grand plan just yet?'

Gardner stared out of the window. The bar's speakers gurgled Latin jazz. Hundreds of other voices in the background seemed to rise in volume, until they swelled inside his ear, as if he was standing next to a turbine engine.

'Where do I come into all of this?'

'Now we're getting to the nitty-gritty.' Land licked his fingers. 'We want you to follow Bald to Gibraltar. Once the exchange has been made with Wright, your orders are to take Bald by force. We need him alive. He knows the various links in the chain, and we'll have to break him to stand any chance of destroying the ring.'

Gardner thought about what Land said.

'You faked my death because otherwise John would think his deal had been compromised?'

'Just so. As for his accomplices, the BOPE captain is dead and Mr Hands is currently lying in a coma at the Copa d'Or hospital around the corner. At taxpayers' expense. I'm led to believe he has a nice view of the sea – if he ever wakes up.'

The waiter reappeared and cleared away the plates of half-eaten tapas. He gestured to the drained bottle of Antarctica. *Another?* Gardner shook his head and asked for a glass of water.

'I understand what you get out of busting the ring, but what's in it for me?'

Land wiped his lips with his napkin, and Gardner could have sworn he was hiding a smile beneath it. 'Spoken like a true opportunist. God, we train you chaps well, don't we? Name your price, Mr Gardner. I have mine, you no doubt have yours, and I'm sure we can meet somewhere in the middle.'

'I'm not interested in money.'

Land frowned. 'What, then?'

'I want a way back in.'

'To the Regiment?'

Gardner nodded.

'I'm afraid that's quite impossible. We carry a lot of clout around Whitehall, as you know, but breaking the rules on entry to the world's most elite unit is not in our gift. Perhaps

it wouldn't be such a problem, but that hand of yours, well—'
He shrugged the rest of the excuse.

'Sorry, mate. It's the Regiment or nothing.'

Land was quiet for a moment, eyes drifting over his wine glass.

'Possibly we could arrange something else. Not on the frontline. I mean as a grey man. Working in the shadows. Eliminating national security threats in countries under the radar. Strictly deniable, of course. You'd officially be in Regiment colours and rank, but answerable to the Firm. If I could wangle that, do we have a deal?'

A year on the sidelines had hardened Gardner, made him more cynical about the world and its workings. But fuck, the offer was tempting. A voice scratching at the base of his skull told him that he'd trusted the Firm before – and had got his fingers burned. Land's proposal sounded too good to be true.

'I've skimmed your file,' Land went on. 'Being a Blade, it's all you've ever known. I'm offering you a way back into the magic circle.'

'And if I say no?'

'Then you'll leave me with no option but to green-light your immediate termination. I speak of no idle threat. At this very moment dozens of agents are in Rio. Indeed, eight of them are based in this very hotel. As I said to you before, Bald cannot afford to think his plan has been put in jeopardy. Letting you walk away scot-free is not an option.'

Gardner hated to admit it, but Land had him by the bollocks. Even if he did evade the Firm in Rio, where would he go? They'd put the squeeze on him. With their vast resources and without a passport or access to funds, they'd slot him sooner or later.

Besides, he missed life in the Regiment. The camaraderie and sense of purpose. Adjusting to the outside world had proved difficult, which is why he'd become a drifter. Look what's on the table, he told himself. A once-in-a-lifetime opportunity to go back to doing what you do best.

'Fuck it,' he said. 'I'm in.'

'A wise choice. Welcome aboard.'

Land gestured over Gardner's shoulder for the bill.

'Now, I cannot overstate how crucial it is that Bald is captured alive – and after he's exchanged the cocaine. Nab him too early and we run the risk of granting him wriggle room in a court of law. He has to be caught red-handed.'

'No problem,' Gardner said. 'Just tell me where and when.'

'Go down to the Copinha bar on Rua Bolívar. Ask the owner for a lady called Carlotta. She'll be expecting you. Carlotta will hand you a package. New passport, sterling to exchange at the bureau and the keys to a hotel room on the Rock. There's also a mobile phone, secure line. You know the drill: don't call me, I'll call you. Understood? Good.'

Land stood up and casually dropped a black Amex card on the table.

'Life is all about second chances, Mr Gardner,' he said, pulling on his jacket. 'And you've just got yours.'

twenty-nine

Winston Churchill Avenue was closed for business. Traffic on the road connecting Gibraltar to the Spanish mainland honked its horns as red-and-white barricades lowered, cutting off the intersection between both ends of the road and the airport. A British Airways plane touched down and taxied along the runway, wingtips several metres from the lines of impatient cars. The plane's tail dipped behind a line of low buildings. The barricades lifted, the lights blazed green.

Shai Golan cruised on a bus to La Linea de la Concepción and walked the final kilometre or so to the border. He flashed his passport to the border guard, announcing himself as Alain Robbe. The guard nodded, took a quick peek inside his Nike gym bag and waved him through.

Had the guard stopped to quiz him, Golan was prepared. He looked the part; spoke it too. He was fluent in French, in addition to English, Mandarin, Russian and his native Hebrew. Golan was six foot five tall. His face was ninety per cent hair and his eyes black as pitted olives, as if they were permanently dilated. He could carry off the look of a dozen Mediterranean countries.

A policeman with a starch-white face monitored the expats and locals flooding in from La Concepción. Golan was glad he'd entered on foot rather than by car: the traffic was grid-locked, caused by a runway shorter than a Jap's dick. Each time a plane landed or took off, the road was shut off in both directions.

He trekked south along Winston Churchill Avenue, past the Victoria Stadium. After four hundred metres he reached the central roundabout and paced down Smith Dorrien Avenue for ten minutes, then took the first left, to join Main Street.

Golan considered himself a man of taste and culture. He appreciated the bustling, chaotic architecture lining Gibraltar's main arterial road. Moorish horseshoe arches sprouted over a sprinkling of shopfronts; other stores had painted shutters over the upper windows. In between stood white-stucco façades airlifted from Kensington. The effect was somewhat ruined by the shops themselves, a succession of branded fashion outlets and chain restaurants that left Golan feeling cold.

A taxi rank presented itself halfway down the granite-sett road. Golan hailed a cab and chucked his gym bag on to the back seat. He sat alongside it, resting a hand on the zip.

'Where to, mate?' the driver asked. He had olive skin and curly black hair, but his accent made him sound like a character in a British soap.

'The Botanic Gardens,' Golan said.

'Come for the wildlife, have you? Just be careful with the monkeys. They look harmless enough but they're vicious little bastards. I've seen one of them rip a young girl's hair out.'

Golan nodded.

'Name's José,' the driver continued. 'Lived here on and off for twenty-five years. Where did you say you were from?'

'I didn't,' said Golan, before adding, 'France. Paris.'

'Paris, eh?' The cabbie shot him a glance. 'Never been there personally. This is the place for me.'

He drummed his hands on the steering wheel, then pointed out of the passenger window to the west down King Street, beyond Linewall Road and Queensway, directing Golan's gaze towards the old fortifications lining the banks of the Strait of Gibraltar. Relics of the Great Siege.

'The thing about us, mate, is that we've got long memories. We remember the days of Franco and the terror. The closing of the border, yeah? We're only a small island but we're also the closest point between Europe and Africa. This place is special.' He glanced at Golan in the rear-view mirror. 'Do you see what I mean?'

Golan didn't, but he smiled his agreement.

The cabbie dropped him at the Alameda Botanical Gardens on Europa Road. Golan paid the fare and slung the gym bag over his shoulder. Once the taxi was out of sight, he trudged north-east up the steep Green Lane, past the O'Callaghan Hotel.

Age and experience had calmed Golan. His mentor, Zohar, took him aside one day and told him that either he exercised self-discipline or his contract would be torn up. But there were days when the old impulses stirred inside Golan and he hungered to be twenty again, wandering the Gaza Strip. The small scar on his neck, like an upside-down Nike swoosh, served as a daily reminder of – what? Why, the importance of being vigilant.

Green Lane arched north and then doubled back on Old Queen's Road. Golan made his way up a secluded trail lined with nettle and eucalyptus trees. Midway up the trail he detoured into the woodland until he hit a spot a little way down from an old artillery placement. Here the trees were dense enough for his needs, and he hunkered down beside the base of a ruptured trunk.

From the gym bag Golan removed a thermal-imaging camera equipped with a GPS unit, magnetic compass and laser rangefinder, capable of picking up and tracking human targets up to twenty kilometres away. The camera was also designed to survive extreme temperatures. He mounted the camera on the tree trunk and fixed a remote-controlled pan-and-tilt system to the set-up.

Golan aimed the camera towards the naval dockyard, next to the industrial park on the western edge of the peninsula. He spotted a Type-23 frigate, the HMS *Westminster*, sailing out through the breakwaters. Docked at the harbour was the HMS *Lizard*.

He paced north for thirty seconds and established a second camera site. No need to link the cameras with a cable of some kind; everything was connected wirelessly over a secure TCP/IP network. Golan slotted a remote network card into the back of both cameras. Then he fished a Dell laptop out of his bag and booted up to check the link had been established. Accessing the remote network prompted him to enter a password. He typed it in. The computer found both devices and opened up a pair of windows. Golan was treated to glowing thermal images of the *Lizard*. He pressed a key and the image on the left camera switched to a night-vision green. Another key caused the camera to zoom in. He dragged a finger over the mouse pad and the camera pitched on its mount.

Golan had killed his first man at the age of ten. Not a man, but a boy. A friend of his at the elite Château de Rosey boarding school in Rolle, Switzerland. Golan had no reason to murder Wei Chang, but he did it anyway, smashing his face in with a claw hammer behind the tennis courts. Killing Chang made Golan feel important in a way he'd never experienced. He had been a bad student, despite the hundreds of thousands of dollars his father, one of Israel's richest men, had lavished on the best schools and tutoring. Murder was different. He was good at it. Better than good. Exceptional.

Leaves crunched at his back. Golan spun around, fists clenched. Technically, he was unarmed. That's if you didn't count his body as a lethal weapon. There were many who did, and quite a few of them were dead.

He expected to see a police officer or perhaps a nosy tourist.

A Barbary macaque squatted a couple of metres away, hind legs tucked in as it chewed on a slice of apple. The apple seemed to be the monkey's whole world. The thing didn't so much as glance at Golan.

Sliding forward, Golan palm-struck the macaque in the face, the palm of his hand colliding with its flat nose. The monkey wobbled on its hind legs, swiping at his hand. Golan swiftly followed up with furious kicks to the belly. Sensing it was being overpowered, the macaque opted for flight over fight. Golan seized its trailing leg and smacked its skull against an olive tree, the monkey squawking, blood spattering up and down the bark, until it was silent, limp.

He retraced his route down the Rock and strolled a kilometre north back towards the town centre. On Cathedral Square, just one road from the clamour of Main Street, Golan checked into the Bristol Hotel as 'A. Robbe', paying in advance with cash. The chubby girl behind reception gave him the keys to a single room. Inside, he locked the door and pulled out a BlackBerry Storm from his gym bag, as well as a silver cigarette case filled with pin chips. Inserting one into the phone, he dialled the number from memory.

A man answered after the first ring.

'I'm in,' Golan said in Hebrew. The British government, he knew, used Gibraltar as a SIGINT listening post for communications from North Africa and the Middle East. Be careful, they'd told him. Keep things as brief as possible.

'You're late,' the other man said.

'I was held up. But everything's ready.'

Silence.

Golan was insulted. 'Have I ever let you down before?'

The reply was a dial tone. Fuck them, he thought, fishing the pin from the BlackBerry and flushing it down the toilet. They could tell him where to go, who to target, but they had no right to tell him how to do his job. He fired up the laptop. Accessed the imaging cameras fixed to the Upper Rock. And waited.

thirty

1400 hours.

Gardner kept the engine ticking over as he sat in the Grand Cherokee parked on Cumberland Road, up the street from the police club. A sleepy post-lunch hour on the Rock, and the Jeep's air con was working overtime.

He had an unrestricted view north-west across the harbour. Fifteen hundred metres distant and parallel to the airport runway stood the northern harbour, where cruise ships and ocean liners disgorged tourists. At the midway point was the private marina, where the locals stowed their quarter-of-a-mil yachts and speedboats. To his rear a Second World War artillery placement taunted the Spanish coastline at Algeciras.

The industrial dock was similar to those at Plymouth and Portsmouth and set two hundred metres away. HMS *Lizard* rested in the dock.

Peering through his Nikon Sporter EX 10x50 binoculars, Gardner watched the crew descending the walkway, mates in relaxed Dartmouth rig of polo shirt and chukka boots, psyched up for the run ashore.

He glanced at the passport-sized photo of Petty Office Stephanie Wright clipped to the front of a personnel folder. Nothing in her file indicated that the daughter of a Scottish carpenter and English teaching assistant was likely to be involved in drug smuggling. Good attendance at school, unblemished record in the Andrew since she passed out three years ago. But he kept coming back to her eyes. They were glassy and faded like denim. Impenetrable. Wright was hiding something.

Any minute now, she'd show up for her meeting with Bald.

The name tasted like hot tar on his tongue. Help me, Joe, Bald had said in the jungle. He'd help him all right. Help make that lying bastard pay.

Three days in Gibraltar, and Gardner was fighting an inner battle with himself. Part of him desperately wanted to exact revenge on Bald. And yet a ball of self-doubt lodged in his throat. John's not like Dave Hands, a voice said. He wasn't born dodgy. He must be caught up in something. And shit, maybe he does need your help.

Three days.

Gardner had touched down on the Rock in the dead of night, catching a redeye from Rio to Charles de Gaulle airport in Paris, where he had boarded a connecting flight to Heathrow and spent three hours nursing cups of tepid coffee and digesting the newspapers. The coffee barely dented his jet lag and the news was so depressing it made him want to eat his own face. Finally the last call came for BA490 direct to Gibraltar.

He had travelled with no luggage, but Land's parting instructions had been clear. Proceed to the carousel. Once the last remaining traveller has disappeared, a man will approach you. Do exactly as he says.

'We have no idea how wide or deep the network goes,' Land had said. 'It's not unreasonable to think they have eyes and ears all over the Rock. Assume you're being watched at all times, wherever you are.'

'Who knows about the mission?' Gardner had asked.

'No one's been informed about your presence on the island except myself, a field agent and my bosses. If you screw up, I'm afraid you're on your own.'

'Music to my ears. Where are you going to be in all this?'

'Not putting my feet up at Babylon-on-Thames, if that's what you're suggesting. The Firm is keen for this to be executed without any hitches. Since Mr Bald isn't familiar with me, it's considered both safe and, shall we say, agreeable that I stay on in Gibraltar in a supervisory capacity.'

Twenty minutes at the luggage carousel and Gardner had found himself alone with a guy in a flannel suit who looked a couple of quarter-pounders short of a heart attack. He was reading a paperback. A cartoonish action figure stood beneath a macho title. Only half the author's name was visible. Andy somebody. The guy's hand covered the rest.

'Come with me,' a voice had said to his back.

Gardner turned and saw a guy in a buttoned-up suit and shades. In forty-degree heat. He followed him across the polished marble floor to the terminal exit. A Grand Cherokee Jeep with fifty-per cent tinted windows sat in the parking lot.

'This is your motor,' the guy had told him. 'And this is your place.' He handed him an envelope along with the Jeep fob. Inside was a hotel key.

'Land said John's here already.'

'Flew in directly. Staying at the King's Hotel,' the guy said.

That had been three days ago. Now he refocused as a steady procession of boisterous matelots fucked off out of the dockyard and headed straight for the pubs in Casemates Square.

But no one matched the description of Stephanie Wright.

The last of the parties filed out of the frigate. Gardner swigged from a bottle of mineral water and watched a macaque scratch his balls beneath a palm tree's starburst shade.

At four-fifteen Wright finally appeared.

She came off the boat alone and decked out in a pressed white blouse with side lapels. Her top button was undone. She carried a laptop case.

A quick glance down the street, then Wright left the dock-yard and hailed a taxi.

Gardner dumped the binos. He urged the Jeep forward, racing down Rosia Road. When he was eight car lengths from the taxi, he eased off the accelerator. The cabbie was taking a seemingly random route around the Rock: a right on to Boyd Street, a quick left on to the narrow, winding Prince Edward's Road, left at the Castle Road intersection. A third left on Fraser's Ramp heading into Range Town, so that the taxi had, in short order, doubled back on itself.

Gibraltar's changed a lot, Gardner thought. On his first visit, as a wet-behind-the-ears Para, before he'd tried his hand at Selection, the place had been a chaotic mix of swarthy faces and red buses, olive sunshine and messy drinking establishments buried down sidestreets: the Hole in the Wall, the Angry Friar . . . Everything felt corporate now.

The taxi bypassed St Andrew's Church and continued down Prince Edward's Road, leading into Europa Road. Its rear brake lights blazed opposite the Alameda Botanic Gardens. Now Wright jumped out of the taxi and walked on towards the King's Hotel. Gardner pulled smartly into the side of the road.

Wright glanced furtively up and down the street. She climbed a set of steps flanked by bright green and pink flowers and disappeared inside the hotel, leaving Gardner staring at its art deco exterior. He knew from Land that Bald was staying in room 39.

Twenty minutes later Wright emerged and took a cab towards town.

Gardner followed her just for the hell of it, although he already knew the score. He'd been watching her for the past two days, and the routine was always the same, with a few minor differences. A ride around town, to throw anyone on her tail. Quick visit to the King's Hotel, then an hour or two wandering the main streets and sipping coffee, before a return to the frigate. On each occasion she lugged the laptop case.

He figured Wright was unloading small packages of the coke, secreted inside the carry case. Rather than risk one big shipment, she was taking the safer option and drip-feeding the snow to Bald.

She debussed at Convent Place, where the road collided with Main Street, bordered at the end by the Governor's residence. Bunting in pastel colours swayed in the sea breeze. He had to admit, she was pretty hot. Brunette hair, pin-straight with a kink at the ends. The way she walked, swinging her hips like she'd sprung from a jeans ad.

Gardner's secure iPhone sparked into life, shocking him out of his daydream. He answered, eyes trained on Wright as she window-shopped and lit a cigarette.

'Still tracking the Wren, are we?' Land's voice carried down the line like a door opening on to a blizzard.

'Another exchange just went down. Same place. I make that twelve in total.'

'She's certainly taking her time,' Land said. 'Listen up. The situation on the ground has changed dramatically. It appears that Bald is in serious trouble.'

Gardner looked at his watch. Five o'clock. Wright left a couple of hours between trips to Bald's hotel, so he doubted he'd see her again until seven or eight.

'I said, Bald's in—'

'Heard you the first time. But I've been back and forth from his hotel for the past forty-eight hours, and in all that time he hasn't shown his face once. The only thing he's in danger of is racking up a massive bill on the bar tab.'

'I'm afraid you're wrong on that score. Our intelligence friends received an anonymous tip-off. Three men arrived on the Rock this morning. They're planning to rob our friend of his product before he gets a chance to sell it on. If that happens, our hopes of uncovering the full smuggling ring are dead in the water.' Land coughed. 'How many more trips does our Wren have to make?'

'One or two max,' Gardner said. He guessed the laptop bag could hold a maximum of four kilos of Colombian snow, divided up into 500-gram tubes.

'Sounds about right,' Land replied. 'The *Lizard* is refuelled and due to set sail again tomorrow, so Wright's time is almost up. The word we have is that these men plan to attack Bald this evening.'

'Just after she's made her final trip.'

'We can't let them wreck the plan.'

Wright disappeared down a sidestreet. Gardner felt a bead of sweat slither all the way down his back to his arse. Something doesn't add up, he thought.

'Joe?'

Shit. He knew what was coming next.

'I need you to kill them.'

thirty-one

The Newman's Pub on Casemates Square was, according to a tourist pamphlet, an old favourite of the British Armed Forces personnel. Today it was brimming with married couples and screeching hen parties. Golan wasn't thrilled to be there. Given the choice, he'd rather be in an old-fashioned bar with some Thelonious Monk playing and a glass of Château Rollan in his hand.

He found her easily enough. The Rock-side cameras had filmed her disembarking and wandering towards town, and for him it was simply a case of scouting the bars around Main Street and Casemates. She brooded at a corner table, soaked in boozy shadows, nursing a glass of rosé. The moment was right. He moved in.

'Quite a party outside,' he said, stopping by her table.

'If you say so.' She necked the rest of her rosé, motioned to the bartender.

'Something the matter?' His voice was a masterclass in control. Soothing, concerned.

'No. Why would it be? I'm fine—' She shook her head. Angled it. 'Don't I recognize you from somewhere?'

'No.'

She laughed. '*No*?'

'No. You don't.'

The waiter brought over the bottle. 'But how can you be

so sure?' she said. 'Maybe I *did* see you somewhere, but you happened to be looking the other way. People are always spotting me out and about and telling me later.' She kept her eyes on him as she sipped from the fresh glass.

'What you say is impossible. I've only been in town a few hours.'

'So where were you before that?'

'France.'

'Your whole *life*?'

'If a man has to make a city his prison, Paris is as good as any.'

'And what did you say your name was?'

'I didn't.'

'There's that sure voice again. Never wrong, are you? Well, I'm Steph.'

'Alain.'

Golan had some more small talk lined up, when the doors swung open to his six and a gang of beefy women yelled at the waiter for more Jägerbombs. He frowned at them, pretending to ignore her reaching for the laptop case braced between her legs.

'We don't get women like that in Paris,' he said. Then he edged his hand closer to hers and smiled his best smile, the one where his chin, cheeks, lips melted into one another like beeswax. 'But I'm sure they have their own charm.'

'Not bloody likely. I have to share living quarters with about twenty of them.'

'You're Royal Navy?'

'Royal bitches, more likely.' She attacked her rosé. 'The other Wrens are at each other's throats night and flipping day. Who can drink the most. Who can lick a matelot in a fair scrap. I thought the boys were bad, but they've got nothing on the Wrens.'

'You sound like you want to leave?'

'And I will, soon enough,' she said. Her eyes slid from the

wine glass to a spot between her legs. 'Just a few little things to take care of first.'

His hand almost touched her trembling fingers. Suddenly he flinched, spilling the glass of rosé over her top.

'I'm so sorry,' he said.

'It's fine,' she replied, standing up and brushing her shirt. A waitress rushed over and wiped down the table. 'Shit. I need to wash it off.' Nodding at the case, she added, 'Do you mind watching this for me?'

'No problem. And again, my apologies.'

Two minutes later she returned, the rosé stain now a fleshy pink. She straightened her top and smiled awkwardly at Golan.

'I have to leave,' he said. 'Good luck with whatever you have to do.'

That smile lingered on her face. A tinge of regret maybe?

No matter. He'd got what he came for.

thirty-two

'The villa's on Sir Herbert Road,' Land had said. 'Other side of the Rock.'

'Who are they?'

'Cowboys. Mercenaries with time on their hands and no work. A growing problem for us.'

'American?'

'These particular cowboys are British.'

'I'm going to need a weapon.'

'I understand.'

'Because I'm guessing the targets are armed—'

'We think so.'

'—and they know how to use a gun.'

Rule number one in any contact situation, Gardner reflected: Never underestimate your enemy.

'Go to your apartment. Our field agent's left a little present for you,' Land told him.

At the Charlatan Hotel, a two-star joint off Main Street, the room smelled as if a dog had died and nobody bothered to clean up after. He'd slept in ditches more comfortable than the single bed, and the shower veered between cold and freezing. Meanwhile Bald was living the high life at the King's. Another reminder of MoD cutbacks perhaps. On the plus side they'd supplied him with fresh pairs of combat trousers and a few polo shirts.

Fuck it. He wasn't here for the sightseeing.

He found the present under his pillow, and it was little. A double-action Sig Sauer P228, mag already loaded, with three spare clips of 9x19 mm Luger to keep him in business. He pressed the mag-release button, pulled the slide back and gazed down the chamber. Empty. Clean. He slapped the clip back into the feed, chambered a round and tucked the pistol into the band of his jeans. Unlike its more bulky cousin the P226, this model was easy to conceal.

Gardner trekked on foot to the eastern side of the Rock to Sir Herbert Road, and the villa where the cowboys were holed up. He didn't want to run the risk of a taxi or bus driver remembering his face. Land had spelled it out loud and clear that the Firm wouldn't help him out if he was caught knee-deep in dead people.

Devil's Tower Road eased into Catalan Bay Road and, after two miles, Sir Herbert Road. The east of the island was a parade of idyllic beach and rows of modern duplexes with balconies surveying the Mediterranean. A nice retirement spot.

The villa stood by itself, towards the southern end of Sir Herbert Road. As he passed a four-storey apartment complex, his senses heightened. He noted that most of the lights were off, holidaymakers enjoying a night out in town. A cruise ship glowed on the horizon. The beach was unlit, the road empty.

No one around to clock your face, he reassured himself.

Wet sand squelched underfoot as he neared the villa. Thirty metres. He spotted a grey BMW 3 Series parked on a gravel track out front. He raked his eyes across the porch. Lights went off in the reception.

They have to be out back.

Gardner found the perimeter wall, a four-foot-high block of whitewashed brickwork. He placed his weapon on the top of the wall and used both hands to lift himself up and over. At the rear of the villa, waves lapped against a deck fronting the beach. He stopped to recce the deck. Light poured out from a sliding door, colouring the ink-blot landscape. Chairs stood around a metal table littered with three plates of mauled chicken wings and opened Coke cans. To his right a glass sliding door, presently closed, linked the villa and the deck. Satisfied the deck was empty, he crept up to the side of the door.

Peering through the glass, he counted two targets in what seemed to be a master bedroom. Big guys, backs to him, hulking shadows. A black bag on the bed. Shapes that looked like handguns and a long, snake-like object he figured was a Benelli shotgun.

He removed the Sig Sauer from his jeans. He had plenty of experience using the P228, a Regiment favourite. He settled on a plan. Keep it stupid-simple: hit them hard and hit them fast.

The pistol had no safety lever. Gardner manually cocked the hammer to switch from double-action mode on the opening shot to single-fire. Firing the P228 was a joy: the first pressure on the trigger was ten pounds, and each subsequent pressure around half that. Once you got into the flow of discharging rounds, it felt as natural as breathing.

Gardner picked up a pebble and lobbed it at the table. The Coke cans rattled.

The muffled voices inside ceased. He had their attention.

A click as the latch on the sliding door unlocked.

Gardner balanced on the balls of his feet.

The door began to slide back. Sounds sharpened.

'Probably those fucking kids again,' a voice scratched.

The guy the voice belonged to emerged on to the deck. First he was a boot, Gore-Tex Caterpillar, all black, followed by a stocky leg. Then came the torso, chest like a forty-gallon drum and pecs fixed like spotlights on top.

Now.

Gardner lunged at his upper body, bending his left arm at the elbow, his fist tucked close to his chest, so the 'V' of his elbow pointed directly at the guy's neck. He shifted a step sideways and aimed his elbow at the nape. Now he swept his left foot along the ground in front of him, tripping the guy up. He reeled, losing his balance. At the same time Gardner straightened his left arm. His forearm smashed into the guy's neck, adding downward force and momentum to his fall. He heard the *thud* of skull meeting hardwood. As the guy hit the floor, Gardner pulled his left leg back, up, then down, like a hydraulic press, on to the groove of his spine. The guy grunted. He didn't know what the fuck had hit him.

Gardner turned his attention to the master bedroom. He raised the Sig Sauer level with his shoulder. Shit, where's the other guy? An arched entrance led to another room. Too dark to see much inside. A white door to the right. En-suite bathroom, he figured.

'*Fucking come out!*'

Nothing.

He aimed at the wall beside the door and fired. The shot punched a hole big enough to sink a fist into.

'*Last chance!*'

The door opened. A man stepped out of the bathroom, hands raised in the air. The big guy, writhing on the ground, made a play for Gardner's leg. He was built like a tighthead prop, and about as slow. Gardner swung his left foot into his balls, crushing them like a pair of ripe plums. The guy screamed like a baby.

Gardner kept his eyes on the other one. I recognize him, he thought.

Fuck, you'd clock that face anywhere. The grin that ate shit for breakfast, the crew-cut hair and peck-holes that passed themselves off as eyes.

'Joe? That you, mate?' said the man, lowering his hands.

'John Killen,' Gardner replied, not lowering his gun.

'Fuck me, what are you doing here?'

'I could ask you the same question.'

'We're on holiday, mate,' the guy replied in oozy Scouse. 'Come here for the fishing, like.' Seeing Gardner frown, he pointed to the bed. What Gardner had taken for firearms were a distance reel and a bite alarm, and a gym bag stuffed with a bait box. The shotgun was a hefty sea rod. 'Real good fishing here: bass, conger eel, mackerel . . . Do you mind not depriving Eddie of his manhood?'

Gardner glanced down at the guy with the squashed bollocks. He had a shaven head with a bulging vein running like a pipeline down his temple. His eyes were so close they almost met at the bridge of his nose.

'You remember Eddie Stone, Joe.' It was a statement of fact rather than a question. Sounded about right. No one was quite like Stone.

'How could I forget?' Gardner replied.

'Bastard,' Stone gasped as Gardner released his foot, his voice like trapped air gushing out of a puncture. 'I'll tear you a new arsehole!' he growled.

'Calm down, you big poof,' said Killen. 'Joe could've slotted you by now if he'd wanted to. Isn't that right, Joe? But exactly what *are* you playing at? Six months since we last shared a beer, and now you pop round here with a bit more than a friendly hello.' Killen was nodding at the Sig Sauer.

Killen. Stone. Once of the Maroon Machine, 3rd Battalion. They had worked alongside Gardner during his brief stint on the Circuit. A life of bounced cheques, shady contracts and broken promises. A life he'd been only too glad to leave behind.

'Someone told me you weren't just here to catch fish.' He kept it vague, not wanting to give away Land's name, or Bald's.

'Is that so?'

'Someone told me you came here to kill a man.'

Killen gave it the eyebrows.

'Seriously, mate? We're ex-Paras on our hols, not on some bloody top-secret Operation Flavius. Or perhaps we're going to go to the petrol station and slot a couple of Irish?'

'I don't know who to believe any more.'

'Put the gun down, mate. Whatever you've been told, it's not true. Look around the villa if you want. We've got nothing to hide.'

The certainty drained from Gardner's complexion. The gun wavered in his hand.

'All right, lad,' said Killen, helping Stone to his feet. The big guy with the small brain eyefucked Gardner. 'Easy now. Joe got his wires all crossed, is all. Isn't that right, mate?'

'Seems so,' Gardner replied. He scanned the master bedroom. Everything tied in with Killen's story. Fishing gear. Couple of bottles of Wells Bombardier bitter on the table next to a map of Gibraltar, a couple of red areas circled around the Strait. Sky News played on a TV. The news item featured a press conference held by the Iranian president, Fereydoon Karimi: 'We will not resist, we will not move, not one tiny step, on our sovereign right to nuclear technology . . .'

Gardner looked beyond the TV. Killen dusted plaster off his shoulders. Stone slumped in an armchair, rubbing his sore testicles. The scene picked at Gardner like a scab. He glanced over his shoulder at the deck. At the table. The Coke cans and the plates.

'. . . peace is important to us. Injustice is our enemy. And I want to assure the world, even on this momentous day in our nation's rich history, when we joined the ranks of nuclear powers: we do not seek to build a bomb.'

'Where's the other lad?'

Killen blinked.

'Who?'

Three Coke cans on the table. Three plates.

Three men arrived on the Rock this morning, Land had said.

'Don't mess me about, Johnny. Wherever you go, Eddie Stone goes. And wherever Fuck Face is, there's Terry Gill.'

'Terry's not here,' Stone said.

'Eddie's right. It's just the two of us. Now stop being a fucking tool and put the gun down.' Killen's Scouse sharpened. 'You're a mate, Joe, but you're beginning to piss me off.'

He's lying, Gardner decided. Both of them had become tetchy the moment he mentioned Terry Gill's name. Why would they lie about Terry's presence if they had nothing to hide?

'No,' Gardner said. 'You're playing me. Terry's here.'

Stone snorted and edged towards Gardner like a boulder.

'And what makes you think that?'

'Because that mug of yours is looking even uglier than normal.'

Stone lost it. He'd never really had it, but now he lost it big time. Stampeded at Gardner, head low, big hands reaching out to grab him. Brave tactics. Brave but stupid. Gardner slugged the barrel of the Sig against Stone's skull. Felt as if he was pistol-whipping solid lead. His wrist shuddered. Stone dropped on the spot, a divot next to his bulging vein.

'One chance,' Gardner said to Killen. 'That's all you've got. I suggest you come clean, unless you'd rather be six feet under.'

'Eat a dick, I don't know—'

Forcing Killen to his knees, Gardner placed the pistol alongside his ear and squeezed the trigger. Killen closed his eyes and clamped a hand to his ear.

'Fuck you, you cunt.'

'One more try,' Gardner said. 'Open wide.'

He shoved the Sig into Killen's mouth. Made him suck on it. The barrel was coated in stringy gunk fresh from Stone's head.

'This is it. I hear any more shit out of your piehole and you get to meet Ken Bigley.'

Killen was silent. Gardner cocked the hammer with his right thumb. Killen's eyes bulged out of their sockets, round and white as golf balls. His face was red. He mumbled something through the gun-gag.

Gardner pulled out the barrel, saliva clinging to it. Killen leaned forward and coughed.

'Jesus Christ, OK. Shit,' he spat. 'Terry's here. It was his idea anyway. He knows Dave Hands, worked with him on a blood-diamond gig in Sierra Leone.'

'Hands told Terry about the coke?'

'That prick has the loosest gob in England. Buy Hands a couple of pints and he'll tell you his fucking dick size.'

'Would have done,' Gardner corrected. 'Hands is dead.'

'Good fucking riddance. Terry's the one who planned to rob Bald. We were just tagging along as support, I swear to fuck. The plan was, he'd call us soon as he'd lifted the product.'

'Where is he now?'

Killen shot Gardner a defiant look.

'The King's Hotel. Where the fuck do you think?'

Gill was already on his way. No time to lose.

'Cunt,' Killen muttered under his breath.

'Say what, mate?'

'Do me a favour and get a new fucking hand, Joe.'

Gardner lamped him round the face with the Sig. Two solid thwacks and he was conked. He yanked a length of fancy rope from the curtains and bound up Killen and Stone. Then he locked the sliding doors, chucked the key into the sea and ran as fast as his legs could propel him. Kill them, Land had said. But they weren't a threat any more, and Gardner wasn't hot on slaying his own kind. They could stew here awhile until he figured out what to do with them. Who knows? he thought. They might even come in useful.

He rushed to the King's Hotel, praying he wasn't too late.

thirty-three

Petty Officer Stephanie Wright stood in front of the door to room 39 and steeled herself. Four large glasses of Zinfandel rosé sloshed around her head like a rough sea, and she found it difficult to focus. Wow, she thought, suppressing a hiccup. Gibraltar's bartenders didn't mess about with the measurements.

She went to knock. Hesitated. Her knuckles cast a ridged shadow over the spyhole.

At first the offer had seemed so simple. Take a package onboard the frigate, stash it in her locker – not that easy, considering how stingy the Senior Service was when it came to locker space and the endless dress codes required of the average Wren – unload the package the other side and collect payment.

There's always an *at first*, she told herself. *At first* it was a good idea to marry Danny, the guy she'd met two weeks before her sixteenth birthday. Danny, the boy in a man's skin who did lines of coke on their wedding night, and flirted with the hotel staff on their honeymoon in Corfu.

At first it seemed like a smart call to join the Navy.

Well. No more regrets. She'd already made up her mind that she wouldn't go back to Danny. And as for paying off his twenty-grand debt with the money from this job, forget it. No, this was her life now and no one else's.

She knocked on the door four times. Paused. Knocked twice again.

The stress of each trip back aboard the *Lizard* left her exhausted. Having to return to her locker, waiting for the coast to clear.

The crevice of light between the door and the carpet blackened.

He's standing the other side, she said to herself, taking a deep breath. John Bald scared her. Which was weird, when she thought about it. John was calm, softly spoken. Perhaps he reminded her of her father, the gentlest man in the world one minute and boxing her mother about the head the next.

The door opened and she stood there.

'Aren't you coming in?'

John was munching on a red apple, his frame filling the doorway.

Wright froze, glancing up and down the corridor. Vacant.

'This is the last package.'

'Tell the whole world, why don't you?'

Her eyes fell on the carpet.

'I'm joking, lass. You're just in time. I ordered room service for two.' He popped the core into his mouth, pips, stem and all. 'Hope you like fish, but I figured you spend most of your life on a boat.'

She smelled onion and tuna. Her tummy growled. God, I'm hungry, she realized. What with the hurry to unload the cocaine, she hadn't touched a morsel of food in the past twenty-four hours.

The room had a Twenties-style wooden desk and chair, a salmon-coloured carpet and an oriental ceiling fan that threw out waves of cool air. She propped herself on the edge of the bed and picked at food on a tray: white onion risotto, roasted sea scallops, seared bluefin tuna, all of it smelling delicious. John slid the laptop out of the case and laid it on the desk.

He fetched a screwdriver from the drawer and removed the screws at the base of the unit. Off came the cover. Inside, where a tangle of cables and circuit boards ought to have been, was a neat row of white tubes.

'That's everything?'

'Uh, let me see. No, I decided to keep some so I could go into dealing.' Wright rolled her eyes, picked at a scallop. 'Of course it's the lot. Unless you want to count and weigh 'em.'

'No, I believe you. Honestly, you did good.'

The voice was accompanied by a hand sliding across the middle of her back. She flinched a little. Flinched because his hands were colder than those of any man she'd known. A little, because she knew that resisting John was a bad idea. This wasn't part of the original deal, but the first night they rendezvoused in Rio, she'd been drunk and off guard and curious about the imposing Scotsman with the dark past and the darker features. She knew better now. But now was too late.

He let her unbutton her shirt and take off her shoes. A small mercy. She spent a couple of minutes undressing down to her panties and bra. It took far longer than she'd otherwise have done.

'When you get into something,' her mother had once told her, her face all puffed up, 'it's hard to pull yourself out of it.'

There were men who liked it rough, and there was John. He ripped off her bra at the seams. He was playful *at first*, because that's how he liked to start things. Then he slapped her. Then he smacked her. When they were both fully naked, he pushed close to her and gripped her neck with a gnarled hand. As she struggled to breathe he whispered in her ear the unspeakable things he'd do to her if she ever dared betray him.

She could hardly breathe as John fucked her. But she knew if she resisted, he'd only tighten his grip. She let him do his worst. He fucked her hard and his grip only loosened when he finally came inside her. Three minutes that felt more like thirty. She got through it by picturing herself disappearing out that hotel door and into the night, fifty grand in her back pocket. A new life.

The bed sighed as he rolled off her. Then she heard the jangle of his belt buckle as he slipped on his jeans.

'I need to go,' she said, her voice cracking like thin ice. 'We're off again tomorrow morning and all hands have to be on board by 0300.'

No response.

'You've got my money, right?'

'Right here,' John said, patting a travel bag resting on the armchair. He smiled at her. 'Relax. No one's suspected you of anything, have they?'

'I don't think so.'

'No, they haven't. Or else you'd have been detained by the police. Look at it this way: you're about to be £50,000 richer than you were this morning. All in all, that's not a bad deal.'

'I guess.'

'The Navy plays such an important role in the war on drugs. Ironic when you think about it.'

'Yeah,' she said distantly.

'All the time the *Lizard*'s seizing shipments, they've got the jackpot right on board.'

She stood up. The white bedsheet stroked her figure.

'Where do you think you're going?'

'Shower,' she said.

Hot water stabbed her skin. She blinked soapy water out of her eyes and saw a shape through the frosted-glass frame, half pink and half blue. John. What the *fuck* did that arsehole want now? Wright tugged on the cubicle slider. The glass revealed John grinning at her. Yes, *grinning*. Like she was the butt of some terrible joke.

'What is it?'

'Nothing,' he said.

The first punch knocked her backwards, water cascading on top of her. She tried to get up, but another fist to the face flattened her. Teeth loosened. Blood swam across her line of sight. Each blow vibrated around her skull. He punched and punched. Her world darkened to a bloody twilight.

She blacked out.

Woke up with no sense of time, or place. But she remembered John's face. He planned to kill her. Too badly injured to move, she moaned as John drew a razor blade across one of her wrists, then the other.

That man will be the death of me, her mother had said of her father.

The following week she died in a car crash.

That man will—

thirty-four

At its most south-easterly point Sir Herbert Road abruptly ended and the Rock became a sheer cliff, offering no passage along the south coast. Gardner knew he had no choice but to loop back north along the Devil's Tower Road. With Terry Gill already en route to the King's Hotel, Gardner needed to be there fucking yesterday. On foot wouldn't cut it.

A Ford Focus drifted towards him. The only car in sight. He hid the Sig behind his back and ambled into the middle of the road. The Focus came to a halt eight metres from Gardner, the headlights blinding him. Shielding his eyes with his left hand, he scoped the driver. Male, balding, forties. Beer gut threatening to burst out of his buttoned-up Hawaiian shirt. No threat.

'Help you?' the guy said as he stepped on to the road and approached Gardner.

'Give me your car.'

'Oh shit.'

The man was determined to leg it. By the time he'd returned to the car and flung open the door, Gardner had whipped out the Sig. The gun snatched the guy's attention. He paused, one foot inside the car, his body shivering with fear.

'Don't . . . don't kill me. I have a wife and two daughters.'

'Make yourself scarce then.'

The man ran towards the beach faster than his fat body had ever run. Gardner hopped into the car and raced back up

Devil's Tower Road and down Winston Churchill Avenue. He dumped the wheels outside the King's Hotel and scrambled up the steps.

The automatic doors couldn't open quickly enough. A woman at reception asked if she could help him.

'Maintenance,' he shouted back to her as he broke through the emergency doors to the right of reception, then bolted up the stairs. Screw this one up and you can wave goodbye to a future in the Regiment, he told himself.

I won't.

Three flights up. His calves and quads had healed since the gruelling slog through the favela, muscle fibres enlarging as they repaired themselves. He scaled the treads effortlessly. His palms depressed the crash bar. The door obliged.

He faced a wide corridor, musty and air-conned and flanked by a series of rooms. A sign on the beige wall indicated left for rooms 30–34 and straight ahead for 35–39. So, the fifth door. Forty metres, end of the corridor, next to the lift.

Gill was standing outside room 39. His left hand rested on the door knob. In his right was a Glock 9mm pistol, a Gemtech Tundra suppressor fixed to the end of the barrel and a GTL-22 tactical light attached to the underside, shining a white-hot spotlight on the carpet. The bang of the crash bar had alerted him. His head shot up. His face did a flip book of emotions as Gardner unhooked the P228 from his jeans.

Thirty-five metres and closing. Gill raised the Glock. Gardner knew he had to peel off a shot before the Glock was fully level: the tactical light acted as a powerful flashlight to disorientate targets, and would blind him when he fired.

Twenty-five metres. Gardner went for the shot.

Ca-rack!

Clink!

Gill hissed as the bullet pinged his Glock, knocking it from his hand. He gripped his wrist with his left hand.

'What the fuck?'

'Step away, Terry.'

'Fuck it. Get it over with then.'

Gardner would have happily pulled the trigger. But first he wanted to find out the link between Gill and Hands. Killen's waffle about the blood-diamond gig didn't ring true, because Hands had been blacklisted on the Circuit for a good few years. He was more likely to be down the bookies' in Dagenham than in some African hellhole.

'How the fuck did you find me?'

'I met Johnny and Eddie. On a fishing trip.'

Gill grunted. Time hadn't been kind to the ex-Para. His muscles were flabby, his pecs drooping halfway to man-boobs. Love handles sloped out at his sides. His ginger hair was thinning, the whites of his eyes grey and dull.

'Who hooked you up with Dave Hands?' Gardner asked. 'Killen and Stone reckoned you met on some diamond job, but them boys talk such shit.'

'Fucking do one.'

Gill glimpsed the Glock lying two metres behind him. He has any bright ideas, the walls get a fresh lick of paint.

A *click* to Gardner's six o'clock. The noise distracted him and he half-turned, spotting a woman in his peripheral vision as she ran out of her room. 'He's got a gun!' she screamed.

Gill shoulder-barged the walnut door of room 39. Busted it and lunged through the gap.

Gardner hesitated. John can't know you're alive, he told himself. But if you don't stop Gill, John's a dead man.

He had no choice, and dived inside with the Sig close to his chest, the elbow of his shooting arm tucked in at his side.

He expected to find Gill. But the room was pitch-black. A strip of light from the bathroom outlined the bed, desk, wardrobe. Then he saw movement ahead. He steadied himself, depressed the trigger a little, and as his eyes adjusted he made out net curtains flapping like a dress above an air vent. The doors leading on to the balcony were open.

Gardner stilled his breath. Heard blood rushing in his ears. Stepped deeper into the hotel room. It looked for all the world like Bald had jumped.

He felt a pressure in his right ear. The horizon slid like a boat on its beam ends and next thing he knew, his head was crashing into the wardrobe. Gill.

The fucker stood in the bathroom doorway. He swung a boot at Gardner's torso. Something cracked. He felt a rush of air shoot up his windpipe, and, shit, everything hurt.

Gill gave it everything he had and then some. He stomped on Gardner's right hand, grinding the knuckles under his heel.

He then started to aim a kick at Gardner's gut. But the slow backlift gave Gardner enough time to expel the air in his body. He pushed out his abs, honed by years of crunches, creating a rock-solid wall between his stomach and Gill's Caterpillar. The blow was painful, steel toecaps meeting hard flesh, but it didn't knock him for six.

Gardner took a hold of the leg pressing down on his gut, flung it high into the air, shoulder and forearm muscles working overtime. Gill unbalanced. Fell flat on his arsehole.

In for the kill.

Gill had his fingers on the brass threshold in the bathroom doorway when Gardner gave him the good news, grabbing hold of a clump of his thinning hair and yanking his head up. Then he brought it down to the floor. Hard. Again. Three, four, five times. Six, seven. Until the carpet was a sangria stain.

Gill launched a hand at Gardner's face, fingers crawling over his neck and mouth like angry spiders. Then Gardner saw he had something in his other hand – a four-inch Sebenza blade. He crunched Gill's wrist with his Timberland, forcing him to release the knife.

'Stupid cunt,' he breathed into the guy's face.

But he's not going to give up, a voice warned him. It's him or you.

He kicked Gill in the face to daze him, then hauled his body into the bathroom, the fucker clawing at his legs. A year of being forced to rely on his right arm for heavy lifting had strengthened Gardner's biceps, triceps and flexors on that side, but he still found Gill a heavy load. Steroid-pumped muscles surrounded by several inches of boozy fat made it feel like dragging a two-ton truck. Gardner was breathless by the time he dumped Gill by the toilet. As he sucked in air he felt the entire valley of his ribcage sting.

Gill wasn't stupid: the old Para could see what was coming as Gardner stunned him with an elbow to the jaw. Lifting the toilet seat, Gardner thrust him head first into the can. Forced him down far enough that his face was submerged in piss water. Pressed a boot to the nape of his neck and nailed his head in place. Gill thrashed about. But Gardner's control was total. He held his stance and listened to the life gurgle out of the man's mouth.

Gill's hands flapped wildly in mid-air. His legs kicked back and forth. Gardner stayed firm. The bowl water reddened.

After a minute, Gill shit his pants.

Gardner was getting impatient.

'Fucking die,' he shouted.

Gill gargled furiously.

Two minutes and his arms flopped by his side. His legs slowed.

At the three-minute mark, Gill was dead.

Gardner hoisted his leg clear from the toilet. Hit the flush button. His foot was drenched with piss and bloodied water, and the air stank of shit and citrus. For a moment he stood numb in the bathroom, staring at the corpse as a torrent of water splashed over the back of his head. By now the stinging pain in Gardner's ribcage was sounding a high-pitched note that drilled holes in the sides of his skull.

No time to waste. You've got to follow John. He's got – what? – four minutes' head start on you? Maybe more. Got to find him.

Then something caught his eye. Across his right shoulder he noticed the shower cubicle for the first time. The frosted-glass door was closed, but a pink blotch lingered behind, like a cut of stained glass.

Gardner opened the door. Fought the urge to vomit.

He'd seen his fair share of dead bodies in his time. The Wren in the cubicle, however, was worse than anything the Taliban or insurgents did to their women. A cavity existed where her face was supposed to be. A gorge of bones, torn lips and eyeballs sunk in the middle. Her neck, chest and arms were branded with purple bruises. Dried blood on her wrists like wax seals. The woman squatted in an inch of her own blood; the plughole blocked with clumps of hair ripped from her scalp.

Fucking hell, John. *What have you done?*

He had no time to be shocked. Police sirens carried through the open balcony. You need to bug out, and fast.

Bald must have jumped, he figured. That meant he was out in the streets. Exposed. And what, another voice said, if Bald *hadn't* survived? They were on the third floor, a good sixty metres off the ground on a steep slope.

Get downstairs now. If you're quick, you might be able to trace him.

He scooped up the Sig, nabbed Gill's Glock for good measure and tucked it into his jeans, then made a beeline for the emergency exit.

No time to lose.

The door opened before he got to it.

A figure thrust out from the stairwell.

thirty-five

2300 hours.

Gardner reckoned the guy was the hotel manager. Well over six foot tall, blue-suited and with carefully managed stubble and rimless glasses, he looked every inch the officious thirty-something with a corporate pension plan shoved up his arse.

Then Gardner's eyes scrolled down from the single-breasted black jacket and clocked the crowbar in his right hand.

The bar was on a one-way trip to his face.

His fighting instincts took control as he jerked his left arm up to protect his face. The crowbar connected with prosthetic tissue and, though he had no sensation in the myoelectric limb, Gardner felt a sort of shudder in his elbow on impact.

Shudder – but no pain. Mr Crowbar's face lit up like a distress flare at the sight of Gardner remaining upright. No agonized cry. No recoil.

No second chance. With his fake hand Gardner swept the crowbar aside. He shaped to give the guy a Glasgow kiss, arched his head back, tensing his neck muscles, tucking his chin into his neck – and flicked his head forward and up. The forehead nearest his hairline presented the thickest bone on his skull and made for a fearsome weapon. He directed it up towards the tip of the guy's nose, a prime spot to land a knockout blow.

He heard the *snap* of a branch being wrenched from a tree. The guy's nose looked as if he'd snorted a spark plug. He stumbled sideways, backwards.

But Mr Crowbar returned with a vengeance, nailing Gardner with a flat-handed strike to his face. It felt like someone had clipped a couple of jump leads to his cheeks as he stumbled backwards with the force of the punch and crashed into room 36. The door shrieked as it swung back on its hinges, and in the belly of the room a naked woman jumped out of the bed. Both men had dropped their weapons in the struggle. The Sig and Glock were now five metres away, well out of reach of the combatants. The woman reeled away from the guns in horror, as if they were pythons.

A bloated, hairy-backed boyfriend took in Gardner, Mr Crowbar, the two guns – and locked himself in the bathroom, leaving his screaming girlfriend raging at the door.

Mr Crowbar shoved Gardner back, sending him on a collision course with a dinner tray. Glasses, knives and forks clattered.

For someone so tall, Mr Crowbar had agility to spare. He rushed forward in a stretched blur. Gardner had no time to protect himself.

Above the woman's scream, Mr Crowbar's counterattack was deadly swift. He delivered a groin kick to Gardner's balls. Fists hard as kettlebells unleashed in an unbroken stream – a chisel punch to the trench of Gardner's throat, a low blow to his knees. It seemed as if he were fighting an endless riptide.

But the guy seemed anxious about moving in too close. He encircled Gardner, kicking his knees. Lowered a straightened leg down on to his chest like the blade of an axe. Mr Crowbar's heel collided with his ribcage.

Another kick. This time Gardner was ready. He chopped his right hand across the floor, cutting down his opponent's standing foot. The guy slipped, tripped, fell. Gardner picked himself up and Mr Crowbar was back on his feet too.

Jesus, he's not even broken out in a sweat, Gardner realized.

The guy adopted a defensive stance, protecting his head. That still left the rest of his body exposed, and Gardner wanted to make him pay. He readied himself for a front kick to the guy's stomach, lifting his knee straight forward. Mr Crowbar blocked the move by forming an 'X' across his torso.

But then he lowered his hands, and played into Gardner's.

Gardner went for the jaw. One punch. That's all the opportunity you're going to get, he told himself.

An inch from his face, Mr Crowbar somehow blocked the punch with the inside of his left palm. Gardner was left KO'ing air.

As the guy fired off a torrent of blows, Gardner felt his body weakening. If you go down again, you won't be getting up. He's too strong. You need a weapon.

The room service tray. Yes, he remembered now. The knives and forks. The tray was a metre behind him. He dropped with the next punch. As Mr Crowbar wound up for a kick, he reached behind him. Grabbed the handle of something, couldn't see what, and brought the tool forward – and plunged a serrated steak knife into the guy's knee.

Don't let up. Finish the job.

As pain jarred through the guy's body, Gardner forced his head down and wrapped his left arm around the neck. He locked tight, crushing his opponent's head in his armpit. Placing his right hand on his shoulder, Gardner grabbed the guy's wrist with his left hand. Keeping his legs spaced apart, he leaned forward and forced the guy to topple over, with himself on top. Now he flattened his body out, distributing the weight as evenly as possible to create a suffocating press.

Mr Crowbar squirmed, pushing on Gardner's shoulders, but the contortion of his body meant that struggling increased the pressure on his airway. Gardner had him pinned down in a classic figure-four chokehold. A woman's arse fled the room, her wails carrying down the corridor.

'Tell me your name,' Gardner said.

'Go fuck yourself.'

'Who are you working for?'

'Your mother's a whore.'

'Maybe she is, but I wasn't asking you that.' Gardner contracted his elbows. The guy gritted his teeth. His air passage dwindled to the thickness of a straw. 'Talk.'

'Suck your brother's dick.'

'I don't have one.'

'This conversation . . . is over.'

On the final word, Gardner suddenly felt himself rising. He couldn't believe his eyes. Despite being fucked up and choked halfway to death, Mr Crowbar somehow had the strength to heave him off.

As Gardner flew through the air and hit the door, he saw the guy snatch the Glock. I'm fucked, he thought.

But Mr Crowbar glanced back down the corridor. Gardner could see along the corridor for about twenty metres. A security guard had come to check on the commotion and was shouting at Mr Crowbar to put his hands in the air. He might as well have told gravity to take the day off. Mr Crowbar pulled a five-inch combat knife out from his jacket and sank the blade into the guard's groin. He stared dumbly down at his balls.

The lift rang its arrival just as Mr Crowbar fled down the stairwell. Gardner only had time to get up on one knee when the light of the doorway was blocked out by a scrum of men in uniform.

In an instant hands clamped his arms behind his back and slapped handcuffs on his wrists. Whoever did the cuffing fastened them extra tight. A pair of boots stood in front of him. Gardner was so weak he struggled to lift his head. He found himself eyeballing a portly guy with grey hair and a tan straight out of a home fitness catalogue. A badge on the breast of his immaculately ironed white shirt announced him as Lieutenant Colonel E. López. Doughy fingers rested on his utility belt. A forest of hair fluttered in his nostrils.

'All right, easy on him,' he said to the officer doing the cuffing. 'This boy's done giving grief. Look at the state of him.'

'You should see the other guy,' Gardner rasped.

'I'm sure you've both got a story to tell. Been through the wars, my friend?'

'A few of 'em.'

Two officers hoisted him to his feet, into the stationary police wagon.

thirty-six

Time passed like kidney stones in Interrogation Room 3. López grilled Gardner in a voice that sounded as if he had loose gravel in his lungs. One thing was clear from the moment his deputy, Carlos Guerrero, cuffed Gardner to the metal table: they believed he was responsible for *both* corpses in room 39. López read out the accusations against him like a shopping list. Guerrero pulled faces and made not-so-subtle threats. Made Gardner almost miss the days when capture meant a hot date with crocodile clips and a piece of 2x4.

'What were you doing at the King's Hotel?'

'I was there to protect a man called John Bald. He was the guy in the hotel room.'

'Pull the other one. We've checked the hotel's books. They've no record of anyone by that name staying in the hotel.'

'He was there.'

'We found her body, friend. You know who we're talking about, don't you?'

'No comment.'

'*You* headed to the apartment, where you found her sleeping with another man. *You* raped her, choked her, beat her to death and then slashed her wrists to make it look like a suicide. Then *you* killed her lover. That's an evil thing to do, friend. Any jury in the world is going to send you to the prison up

Windmill Road and tell us to throw away the key. You'll be living on rats and maggoty rice for the rest of your days.'

'No comment.'

Gardner had been batting away their questions for an hour or more when an officer barged in and breathlessly announced an urgent call. López and Guerrero left. The deputy flashed Gardner a smile, his small eyes disappearing into the fleshy folds of his face.

Thirty minutes passed. Neither man returned. Gardner could do nothing about his own predicament until he got a lawyer, so he tried to figure one or two things out.

Aside from the murders, the police had him on an assault charge and possession of a firearm. López sounded bullish about pressing charges. Gardner had his doubts. For starters, he hadn't laid a finger on the Wren's body. If she had been raped, DNA testing would also prove it wasn't his semen. Gill's death was harder to explain. His handiwork was all over that body.

He doubted the Firm would come riding to the rescue. Shit, he thought, they're probably covering up their tracks at this very moment.

Gardner turned his attention to Mr Crowbar. He had seen that fighting style elsewhere. In the Regiment he'd received instructions in the way of the fist and the sweet science. Won medals in both tae kwon do and boxing and studied other techniques to become a master of close combat. He loved its focus on individual skill in an age when the Yanks preferred to conquer entire countries from thousands of feet above.

So Gardner knew a fellow expert fighter when he saw one. And the guy at the King's Hotel was one of the best he'd ever traded blows with.

The door was unlocked. Gardner looked at the table like it was the most interesting thing in the fucking world.

He heard the scrape of a chair opposite him, then:

'Cheer up, old chap. It's not every day a man kills someone in a busy hotel and gets to walk away scot-free.'

Gardner looked up.

He should have been relieved to see Land, taken it as a sign that the Firm were coming to his rescue. Instead, he was pissed off. A rage took hold of his body.

'You lied to me.'

Land smiled at the floor. 'I see. No "thank you" for pulling strings that didn't need to be pulled. Just wild accusations. You can be quite an ungrateful little shit when you put your mind to it.'

'You told me there were three men looking to rob John. I don't remember you saying anything about a fourth guy.'

'That's because I didn't know,' said Land, brushing dirt off the shoulders of his cream jacket. 'You don't believe me? Too bad. A lot of time and money have been pumped into this mission and it's no secret that they're two things in short supply in Whitehall. Present climate being what it is. Do you honestly think I'd undo all our hard work by selling you a pack of lies? Not to mention endangering both your life and John Bald's. I'm sorry, but that's not the way things work around here, my good man.'

Gardner looked Land in the eye.

'Maybe that's true. But don't tell me you were in the dark about Killen and his mates doing jobs on the Circuit,' he said. 'I know how the Firm operates. You would have access to our files and have joined up the dots.'

'I had to withhold certain information from you. Who knows how you might have reacted if you'd been aware of their identities? That was a risk I couldn't afford to take.' Land frowned at his shoes. 'Besides, I thought it might be to your advantage that you chaps had a bit of previous. Better the devil you know, and all that.'

'The next time you decide to *withhold* something from me, your face goes through the wall.'

'God, you're infuriating. I had to make a call. Whether you think it was right or wrong is frankly beside the point. Don't get all hung up about it.'

'Your bad call almost got me killed,' Gardner said calmly. 'Matter of fact, considering I'm sitting here on murder raps and with a set of broken ribs, I think I'm handling it pretty well.'

Land stood up, massaged his back.

'Bloody uncomfortable chairs.'

'They think I killed the girl. I wasted that bag-of-shit Gill, but the Wren was dead by the time I got there. Reckon John filled her in to cover his tracks.'

'Yes, well. We didn't see that coming. But the good news is this. I spoke to my boss, he spoke to his boss, and someone very high up had a quiet word in the Governor's ear. He's ordered the police to drop all charges. Much to Lieutenant Colonel López's dismay, I hasten to add. Probably a good idea not to bump into him on the way out.'

'And the Wren?'

'Recorded as suicide,' Land said, nodding sagely.

'I left Stone and Killen at the villa.'

Land stared through the small, wire-mesh-covered window in the door. 'We already had our man down there. No luck. We think your two friends fled across the border to La Concepción sometime in the last hour.' He rapped his knuckles on the window.

'The guy at the hotel,' Gardner said, closing his eyes, searching his memory for something. 'He knew Krav Maga.'

'Say what?' Land asked, distracted.

'It means "close combat". Krav Maga was a fighting technique developed by the Israelis for their Special Forces. Nowadays they teach it to the Regiment. I'm saying he must have a background in the military.'

'We can't locate him,' Land said. 'But we did pull his image from the security tapes and cross-referenced it with our database. I'm afraid we drew a virtual blank. His name is Shai Golan. He was born in Haifa. It appears his father was an entrepreneur who made his fortune in the construction business. Worked closely with the IDF, I'm told. Apart from that, our intel on this chap is thinner than Chinese tea.'

'So he could still be out there?'

'Don't worry. Every police officer on the Rock is tracking him down. We'll soon know all about him.' The door opened. Guerrero entered and unlocked the braces, scowling like he had a mouthful of cow shit. Gardner winked a 'fuck you' at him as he followed Land out of the station.

'What about John?' he asked as they walked down the road. Victorian street lights were scattered along the coastline like landing beacons for the coming dawn.

'Let's just say you owe him. If Bald wasn't pressing ahead with his mission, it would've been rather hard for me to spring you.'

'John's a big boy. He once defended an OP against a hundred Taliban for eight hours. You've got to have brass balls to survive those kinds of odds.'

Land lit a cancer stick. 'Or maybe he's just keen on the money?'

'The John I knew, money never came into it.'

'"Knew" being the operative word, I suppose. You've seen what he did to that girl?'

Land checked a message on his phone. 'The frigate's due to sail in a couple of hours. Minus one Wren. I've put a tail on Bald while he plots his next move. You'd better hurry.'

Gardner shook his head. 'Forget it, mate.'

'I beg your pardon?' Land said, the cigarette limp on his lips.

'I trusted you and nearly paid with my life. I'm not playing your game any longer. If the Firm want to sort this one out, they can take all the risks themselves. Far as I'm concerned, you can take your mission and shove it up your arse.'

'How very kind. But if you walk away now, I'm warning you. This is British territory, Joseph James Gardner. I'm an agent acting for Her Majesty's best interests. Things can happen. People can go missing.'

'Fucking try it.'

He gave Land his back and paced off towards the Charlatan.

'No one quits on the Firm.'

Gardner walked on. In a few hours the sun would be up. New day, new life, he told himself.

thirty-seven

I should have killed him when I had the chance. Golan berated himself as he hobbled over a patch of ground on the Upper Rock. A rusting artillery unit was fixed to a concrete platform a hundred metres away, covered by a chicken-wire fence to make it hard for vandals. He was nearly there.

He stopped to catch his breath. His temple pounded. He lifted a hand to his head. A sticky mixture, red and black, spread over his palm.

Sirens screamed in the distance. Gibraltar Defence Police, turning the Rock upside down in the hunt for him. Going back to the Bristol Hotel was out of the question. They'd find the laptop, of course. Golan could do nothing about that. But he could stop them from discovering the cameras.

The leg wound caused him the greater difficulty. He'd not had time to stop and properly examine it, but ever since that British shit plunged the steak knife into his knee, mobility in his leg had been severely constricted. Maybe you've ruptured your quadriceps tendon? he thought. He tried to flex it. The patella popped.

You really ought to have killed him in the corridor.

He stumbled ten metres further, and came to the spot. There he found the thermal-imaging camera exactly as he'd left it, fixed atop the cleft tree trunk. Its reflective eye gazed past him towards the dockyard. He yanked the camera off the mount and pulled the remote network card out of the back. Did the same to the second camera. Flies buzzed around the dead macaque. He smashed the camera lenses and chucked the remains into the woodland. The network cards he buried, careful to cover over the coffee-coloured undersoil.

Job done. No one would ever make the link between the cameras and his presence here.

Golan was running on empty. He had to rest, if only for a minute. He closed his eyes, settled his breathing into a slow, hypnotic pattern. Felt his blood surge with fresh oxygen. Remembered his training. The past is past. Concern yourself with the present.

OK. Tend to your injury. Then figure out what to do about John Bald.

He perched himself on the tree stump and rolled up his left trouser leg to the knee. Tricky: the blood was like warm glue, thick and sticky. The knife wound was three inches long and an inch wide. White pus seeped out of the hole, smelling of rotten fish.

Lacking water to clean the wound, Golan did the next best thing: he pissed on it. He didn't bother to suture the wound, despite its rank smell. Better to let the pus drain away naturally.

He tore off the lower parts of his shirtsleeves and used the cotton material as a dressing. He wrapped it loosely around his knee, giving the wound plenty of air. Despite the basic first aid, Golan felt his temperature rising. Knew that if he didn't get to a doctor soon, the injury might turn gangrenous.

But I still have the gun, he reminded himself, reaching for the Glock inside his jacket. A gift from God – and a message. Don't make the same mistake twice.

As a teenager and young man, his ways of killing had become ever more adventurous. He thrived on the diversity of death.

Once he'd read about how bamboo grew at a rapid rate and reached heights of several metres. So he nurtured a patch of young bamboo plants in a secluded forest. There he tied a man flat to the ground using stakes, having first sliced off the tops of the bamboo shoots, leaving the sharp ends piercing his flesh. When he returned several days later, the tips had speared his victim right through the chest, neck and arms.

Later Golan's father discovered his secret. He sought the advice of powerful friends, the kind who could keep a secret. He told them his son had a special skill – one that few people had – and wondered whether such a rare talent was in demand. The word came back: we always need such men.

Golan plugged a fresh chip into his BlackBerry. Dialled the number.

'You messed up,' the man said.

'I had things under control, and then—' He was too angry with himself to go on.

'Forget it.'

His forehead throbbed a little less. 'Is the target—?'

'Alive? Yes. We've a satellite fix on him now.'

'Then the mission is not a failure.' Golan's heart jumped ahead of him. He had never failed before.

'Not yet,' the man said, letting two words do the work of ten.

'Just tell me what I have to do.'

'You don't have long. He's making a break for it.' The man paused. 'Hurry.'

thirty-eight

Gardner walked back to the Charlatan and showered. He thought about his next move. His mind was made up: Land and MI6 could go fuck themselves. There were thousands of drug smugglers higher up the food chain than Bald. Gardner had spent fifteen years doing the dirty work for suits, and he had nothing to show for it except a lump of carbon-fibre where his hand was supposed to be. If the Firm wanted to nail John Bald, fine. They were welcome to him. But they'd have to do it without using Gardner as cannon fodder.

He slipped on a fresh pair of Gap combats and a dark-green, short-sleeved shirt. The combats felt a little loose around the waist. Seven days of working for the Firm had its bonuses.

Gardner sipped on a Diet Coke from the mini-bar and carb-loaded with four slices of yesterday's pizza. It tasted like salted leather, but his stomach didn't seem to mind and rumbled its contentment. He switched on the fourteen-inch TV resting on the tattered desk. Flicked over to BBC News 24. Generally Gardner had little time for the media. Back in the line of duty he'd witnessed first-hand how much of the real action went unreported. Journalists instead were spoon-fed bullshit by the head shed and repeated every word to Joe Public.

Between the stories of teenage rape and cancer scares, one item caught his attention.

A dilapidated Arab street at dusk. Onlookers stared at a smoking black object in the road. Ambulance lights illuminated a twisted metal wreckage. Stretcher-bearers rushed across the scene. Men and women hollered at the sky.

A blonde journalist in a shawl gave the lowdown.

'This is the scene tonight in Herat, Afghanistan, near the border with Iran. Eyewitnesses described a loud bang jolting the street at around 9pm local time. The target, it appears, was former Iranian general Mahmoud Reza.'

Gardner tossed the pizza to one side. Reza. The name clawed at his guts. He remembered Iraq at the height of the insurgency. He remembered two mates of his, good Blades by the names of Luke Williamson and Loke Snuka, a Fijian who ate bullets with his oatmeal.

He remembered the pictures of Williamson and Snuka, their torsos charred and dismembered, swinging from Baghdad lampposts.

'Authorities claim Reza, a former cadet in the Iranian military who rose through the ranks, is responsible for a series of cross-border attacks against coalition forces in Iraq. Tehran strongly denies these claims.'

The blonde was replaced by a parade shot of Reza, thick-bearded and flour-faced. He looked like he needed to relax, a night out on the tiles.

'It is thought that Reza, who received drill training in the US, was planning to launch a series of raids on NATO targets in northern Afghanistan. Unconfirmed reports suggest US special forces carried out a long-range air strike on Reza.'

Gardner hoped to fuck the Yanks had slotted Reza.

He killed the TV and fetched his belongings from the safe. Fake passport, credit card and three hundred euros. Gardner figured Land would have already cancelled the Amex, but the passport and cash ought to be good to ferry him back to Blighty. And then? Gardner wasn't quite sure. He'd be going home with nothing – *to* nothing. In a weird way, that's how he liked it. He lived an honest life. Maybe it wasn't glamorous. It was certainly hard. But as long as it kept him away from two-faced pricks like Land, it was a life that suited him down to the ground.

He zipped up his backpack and cast a final look around the room.

Felt a circle of cool air on his back.

Gardner didn't turn around. He already knew who was standing in the doorway.

'Packing your bags already? Looks like we got here just in time.'

Killen.

'What the fuck do you want?'

'To say goodbye, mate.'

thirty-nine

'Give us a smile then, lad,' Killen said. 'Thought you'd be pleased to see me.'

Killen had a Glock in his hands. Stainless steel, 17 edition. The Glock eyefucked Gardner.

'Shut the door, Eddie.'

Stone obeyed, a task that required him to move several tons of muscle bulk. He slipped the 'Do Not Disturb' sign over the knob and clicked the lock on the opposite side. Stone's head leached sweat. He gasped for breath. Gardner figured walking took it out of a guy when he had basketballs for biceps.

'We heard what you did to Terry,' Killen said.

'He had it coming.'

'Just like you. I'm a big believer in an eye for an eye. You do something to a mate of mine, you can fucking expect the same shit done to you.' Killen gave Gardner a screw-face served with a side order of sneers. 'Think you're so smart, don't you? Well, guess what: I never liked you. Told Terry as much, but he rated anyone who'd done their time in the Regiment. Me, I reckon you're a bunch of wankers. Us Para boys were always first into the action, clearing up the shit so you Blades had it nice and easy and took all the glory.'

'Just keep telling yourself that, mate.'

'Nah,' Killen said, peering down the Glock's ramped front sights. 'I'll just kill you instead. Let's see how your fucking SAS skills pull you out of this one. *Mate.*'

'Slot me and you'll regret it.'

'What, your ghost's gonna come back and haunt me?'

Gardner had to go for broke. He was a dead man, unless he gave Killen a reason not to blow his brains out.

'You're after John, right? But here's the thing. There are people involved way above my pay grade, and they watch my every move.'

Killen hesitated, but it was impossible to read the black dots passing themselves off as eyes.

'Nice try, kiddo,' he said, shaking his head, a smirk on his sunburned mug. 'I'm not a fucking idiot. Not like Terry. You couldn't lie your way out of a Frenchman's pocket.'

'I'm telling the truth.'

'There you fucking go again,' he went on, ignoring Gardner's protest. 'Always thinking you're smarter than the pack. Not this time you ain't.'

Gardner braced himself for the bullet. Pictured the hollow-point Parabellum round penetrating his skull and bouncing around his head like a supersonic squash ball. Shockwaves from it tearing chunks out of his face, neck and shoulders. Dying in a seedy hotel at the hands of a two-bob ex-soldier. Shitty way to go. Five minutes ago he'd been contemplating the next five years of his life. Now I don't have five fucking seconds, he thought.

'Boom,' Killen said, gesturing as if he'd popped a round. 'You don't get off that easy. You made Terry suffer. It wouldn't be fair unless me and Eddie here repaid the compliment.'

Training the pistol at Gardner, he nodded at Stone.

'All right, I'll give you a choice. Balls or face.'

'I don't need to hear the story of how your mum and dad met.'

'Funny fucking man,' Stone said. Either he'd stepped towards Gardner, or a solar eclipse was happening right there in the hotel room.

He socked Gardner in the bollocks.

Gardner keeled over, his balls registering a million different types of pain. As Stone laughed the upper half of his body jogged on the spot.

Killen lifted Gardner's head up by the chin.

'Eye for an eye, Joe.'

Stone shoved him towards the bathroom. It was a cramped space, hardly big enough for two people to stand, let alone a third guy the size of a small planet. Killen sat on the toilet, Glock on his lap. Stone squeezed past and ran the bath taps. Water splashed against the porcelain tub.

'They found Terry face down in a toilet. Drowned, they say.'

'Maybe he slipped.'

He watched the water slowly rise. An inch, then two.

'In about thirty seconds you're going to know exactly how Terry felt.'

His mind raced through escape plans. Strike Stone on his solar plexus and throw him into the bath.

Yeah, and meanwhile Killen puts one through your head.

Or grab Killen's gun, slot him and worry about Stone later.

But soon as you make a move on Killen, Stone'll crush you.

Whichever way he looked at it, he was fucked.

The bathwater hit seven inches.

Stone forced Gardner's head over the side of the tub. 'This is where it ends, motherfucker.'

Eight inches.

Nine.

Gardner flung himself backwards at Killen, using his muscle mass to slam him against the wall. His elbow dug into Killen's chest, then jabbed him in the gut. Killen released the

Glock, which zipped along the cracked tiles. This was it! His big chance to bug out. Both guys were stunned. If he could just reach the door . . .

A force tugged at him like a bungee rope. Two bloated hands clamped on his shoulders. Stone wiped phlegm from his face and kicked Gardner in the ribcage. He tried to get up but that fat fuck lashed out at him. The pain in his ribs peaked. Breathing was like swallowing razor blades. He had nothing left in the tank.

'My fucking nose!' Killen shrieked. 'Shit. Get this over with.'

Stone grabbed Gardner by his shirt and plunged his head into the bathwater. He fought back. Thrust his right hand out of the water and searched in vain for the guy's face.

He felt his lungs compress. A pressure formed behind his eyeballs. He thought they might explode any second. His muscles were dead weight, as if parts of his body had already surrendered. He shook his head from side to side to try to loosen Stone's grip. No good. The prick had him on lock-down. Struggling only wasted more precious oxygen.

His world darkened. Killen's voice, distant and distorted:

'Game over, Joe.'

Game over.

The water shaded dark red, and Gardner was sure he was going to die.

forty

A second later Gardner realized he wasn't being held underwater any more. The blood in the water didn't belong to him. He jerked his head up, and out. Precious air burned his lungs.

Stone was face down in the tub, the back of his head like an island.

An island with a bullet hole.

Gardner hocked up bathwater. He turned around, clocked Killen on his feet. Glock hanging by his side, looking daggers to his left. Gardner followed his gaze. Land stood in the doorway holding the smallest handgun he'd ever seen, a Ruger LCP .380. Lightweight and less than three inches from stock to barrel, it was the kind of firearm a female spy might conceal in her purse.

'Don't move,' Land shouted at Killen, his voice wavering.

'Or what? You'll shoot me with that fucking peashooter of yours?' Killen's eyes drifted to the corpse in the bathtub. 'Then again, Eddie always did have shit for brains.'

Gardner felt his energy returning. He focused on Killen. Disarm the fucker. Put that son of a bitch down once and for all.

'This is your last warning,' Land said.

Killen chuckled. He glanced at Gardner. 'You're a fucking disgrace, Joe. Betraying your own kind with these backstabbing nonces.'

Then Killen drew his pistol faster than Wyatt Earp on speed and fired a single shot. The bullet struck the light fitting, plunging the room into darkness. Gardner made a leap for Killen and found thin air. Then he felt himself collide with Land, knocking him aside. The front door slammed. Gardner skipped past the MI6 man's prone body – and backtracked as the Glock punched holes in the door.

Killen's stifled voice carried through the door. 'Come after me and I'll fill you in like a fucking survey.'

Gardner counted to ten. Risked approaching the door, coming at it from the side. Sliding up next to the frame, he rested his hand on the knob, then flung the door open.

The corridor was empty.

Killen had fucked off.

He retreated inside the room. Found Land on the bathroom floor.

'Damn monster butted me with his pistol,' Land said. Gardner peeled Land's hand away from his head, revealing a four-inch cut from his temple to the bridge of his nose.

'Needs a few stitches but otherwise you'll be fine.' Gardner pressed a wet towel to the wound and ordered Land to hold it in place.

'What did I tell you back in Rio, old chap?' asked Land.

'My memory's kind of fuzzy.'

'I said I might be the last friend you'd ever have.' Land frowned at Stone's corpse, as if he'd trodden in dog shit, and nodded.

'Give me a hand,' Gardner said, pulling out the bath plug. The hole slurped the slick red water. Gardner heaved one of Stone's legs over the side, Land tentatively working the other. The legs felt as if they were weighed down with sandbags. Once they'd laid Stone flat in the tub, they pulled the shower curtain across.

'Gonna need more than a bottle of Cilit Bang to clean this up,' said Gardner.

'The Firm will take care of it.'

'You boys must be experts at cleaning up your own shit.'

'Admit it. You had me down as the type of chap who didn't like to get his hands dirty. Leo's too posh to muck in, you thought. Am I right?'

'I didn't think you'd be riding to the rescue.'

'Yet here I am. So what does that tell you?'

'That you're more bent than a boy band.'

Land scraped brain matter off the sole of his shoe. 'You and I aren't so different, you know. We might come from different camps, but we're fighting a common enemy. And we're both taught that killing is only acceptable when it achieves a goal. Call it necessary murder.'

Gardner shook his head. 'I've seen my fair share of dead people. Mates coming home in body bags. Wives and kids breaking down in tears. Killing's never a good thing.'

'War is different.'

'So they say.'

Land rested the peashooter on the bathroom counter. 'John Bald's the enemy. He must be stopped.'

Gardner's mind drifted over the shower curtain. Six months ago he'd been on the piss with Stone, swapping old war stories and jokes about the Kabul nightlife. Allegiances used to count for something. Now he was lying dead in a bathtub, and it seemed like the whole world didn't give a fuck about loyalty or honour.

So where does that leave John? he wondered. Bottom line, John betrayed me. He's no more honourable than Killen. Than a fucking snake.

'I just saved your life,' Land said. 'The least you can do is see through the mission to tail Bald. If you want to walk away from the Firm afterwards, that's up to you. You don't have to take up the job offer; dammit, I'll even sort an alternative position. Perhaps something not as glamorous. A desk job. Or guard duty for a lesser-known royal maybe.'

Gardner quit the bathroom. The smell was making him nauseous. Land hovered in the doorway.

'What's it to be?'

Gardner's rucksack sat on the bed. He wanted to pick it up, flip Land the bird and bug out of the Rock. Out of this nightmare.

'We don't have much time,' Land continued. 'Killen's out there. That bastard's going to try to intercept Bald by hook or by crook, and we can't let that happen.'

'Bald's in hiding. How will Killen know where to look for him?'

Land snooped out of the hotel window. Main Street was quiet.

'That plunge in the water has dulled your senses a tad, mmm? Think about it: Gibraltar is crawling with police. The border with Spain is on high alert for a crazed gunman on the loose, namely Shai Golan – the man whose acquaintance you made at the King's Hotel. Given that kind of police presence, Bald isn't going to risk smuggling the cocaine across the border. And he'd never get the stuff past airport security. So that leaves only one way off.'

'By boat.'

Land clicked his fingers. 'He *has* to leave via the marina. Our sources indicate that a man matching Bald's description reserved a cruiser yacht called the *Defiant* two days ago. All Killen has to do is show at the marina and wait for his chance.'

Gardner recalled something from Rio.

'John can't pilot a boat. That's why he called me to Brazil.'

'Either he was telling fibs, or he's got help. Whichever it is, Bald simply has no choice but to go old-school and ship out his drugs. And MI6 needs him to succeed. Once he's on the boat we've got him red-handed and your mission will be over. This is it, Joe. One more step.'

Gardner searched his eyelids. Just this last job. 'If I do this,' he said, 'I want be back in the Regiment one hundred per cent.'

'Impossible. I told you so a week ago.'

'I'll do whatever undercover work needs doing, but I'm fucked if I have to report back up to some rich prick in a suit with a semi-detached in Fulham. No offence.'

'Plenty taken. But no one can do what you're asking.'

'Talk to Major Josh Oliver.'

'I hardly think the new Commander of 22 SAS is going to be a sympathetic ear.'

'Just talk to him.'

Major Oliver. Just plain old Josh back when he and Gardner fought alongside each other. Worked his way up the old-fashioned way, with grit and determination. Promoted to Staff Sergeant, 2iC and then D Squadron's OC before taking the top job. An old friend and, in Gardner's eyes, the only decent rupert in the business.

'All right. A quiet word, once this is over. But I'm making no promises.'

'Deal.'

'Then it's settled. I suggest you head down to the marina immediately if you're to stop Killen from taking down Bald.'

'The *Defiant*, you say?'

Land nodded.

'Topped up and ready to sail, according to the owner.' Land handed Gardner a photo.

'I'm going to need firepower. And no offence, mate, but that thing you're packing is about as useful as a one-legged man at an arse-kicking contest.'

Then Gardner had an idea. He went to the bath, dragged back the curtain and patted the pockets on Stone's 44-waist jeans. Found a polymer pistol grip jutting out of his back pocket. The grip was attached to a Kel-Tec PMR-30 semi-automatic. It was a newcomer to the weapons block but Gardner had heard a lot of buzz about its capabilities. He snatched the pistol out of Stone's pocket and held it as if shaking hands with an old friend.

'You won't be needing this,' he said to the back of Stone's head.

'Now, you have my permission to do whatever it takes to protect Bald's safe passage. But for God's sake try to keep it covert. I can cover your tracks to a certain extent, but if you go shooting up half the town my job becomes a lot more difficult.'

'Where's John at the moment?'

'We've had eyes on the marina for the past few hours. He hasn't yet shown there. Leaving it until the very last minute, I presume.'

Gardner made for the door. Pistol in his jeans, Bald on his mind.

'You'd better be telling me everything you know,' he said, then slammed the bullet-riddled door before Land could reply.

forty-one

Gardner hit Queensway and circled south around the marina's edge. Nearly four o'clock and night was surrendering to dawn. The sky was a cobalt dome. Whitewashed apartment blocks shaded violet. He banged a right into Queensway Quay, passing a row of five villas and a giant lead anchor slanted over a manicured lawn.

The moon spotlighted the quay. West of his position the quay abruptly ended, giving way to the Strait. Three hundred metres to the south, across his left shoulder, stood the dockyard where HMS *Lizard* would be going through her final checks and repairs before setting sail. He thought about the Wren, about her mashed-up face.

He paced for two hundred metres to the western edge of the quay, where the road arrowed north and nine apartment buildings stood on a rectangle of reclaimed land, bordered by a rocky shoreline.

Gardner paused and scoped out the marina.

There's got to be a hundred boats in dock, he thought. He counted two-seater cruisettes, fifty-foot luxury cruisers and commercial fishing ships, tied up at three concrete piers. He looked at the shot of the *Defiant*. She was a sizeable beast, thirty-eight feet, with a distinctive blue-and-white striped hull and a stern sleek as an arrowhead. Suddenly he spotted the cruiser yacht at the far end of the middle pier. But he didn't move in just yet. He was waiting for Bald or Killen to show. So far, no sign of either.

Four in the morning and Gibraltar was a ghost town. Two until four was Gardner's favoured time of attack. Soldiers called that period the dead hours – when most people were in a deep sleep.

He scanned the apartment blocks. Every window and balcony bay was encased in darkness. He imagined people tucked up in their nice beds, while he knuckled down to the business of killing men.

A thought gnawed at him. While Stone and Gill were dumb as shit sandwiches minus the bread, Killen was different. Cunning. No doubt he'd be figuring out the best approach to the *Defiant*. So Gardner had to be alert.

He backtracked east along the quay, resolving to patrol the larger marina a hundred metres to the north.

A silhouette shifted along the middle pier, thirty metres from the *Defiant*.

Gardner froze. The dark could play havoc with an operator's vision, conjuring up shapes and movement where there were none. He ran his eyes around the silhouette, putting a distance equivalent to the size of his fist between the object and his line of sight. He looked away from it for several seconds, and let his eyes return to the shape. It had moved. His brain wasn't tricking him.

He retreated up the quayside towards Queensway. Between each block of flats he risked a brief glance down to the water-front, where he spied the figure shuffling along the pier. He was slow and deliberate, wanting only to keep an eye on Bald and assessing the surrounding area for threats. Any sudden noise might alert Bald to his presence.

Past the anchor again, Gardner hurried north. Two hundred metres further along the deserted Queensway, he turned left past a large Genoese-style development, all turquoise shutters and terracotta roofs. The pavement coughed him up at the northern pier. Palm trees and cannons lined the walkway. The middle pier was eighty metres south, and the silhouette was nearing the *Defiant*. Closer up, it took on definition. A man, tall, solid build. It had to be Bald. He held a torch in his right hand. His left gripped a black object. A pistol, Gardner guessed.

But where was Killen? If he planned to jump Bald at the marina this was his prime opportunity. And yet there was no sign of him.

Instinct – not even instinct, more like a clotting fear that fired from the base of his spine to the back of his skull – told him to glance back inland. He scanned the blanket of darkness swirling over the foliage. Shit! That's it. He'd assumed Killen would be going for the up-close and personal approach. In doing so he'd ignored the widest vantage point of all. *That's fucking it.*

The Upper Rock. The steep, jagged rock dominated the Gibraltar skyline.

Gardner surged towards the middle pier. John Bald was walking into the ideal spot for a sniper on the Upper Rock.

I've got to get John out of the line of fire, Gardner thought. But your cover will be blown.

If I don't, he'll be killed.

The hollow sound of Gardner's feet pounding hard on the planks alerted Bald, who had stopped at the *Defiant*.

Twenty metres, and Bald was spinning around, torchlight searching the pier. Gardner fixed on the black object in his right hand. Bulky-looking thing, some kind of a gun. He had time enough to think how shit it would be to die at the hands of the corrupt ex-Blade he was trying to protect.

Ten. Gardner ducked like a sprinter at the finish line. The Upper Rock was eight hundred metres away. Clear night, full moon. No wind to distort the shot. If Killen got his shot off, it was all over.

Five, and Gardner caught the faint *crack* of a rifle. He lunged at Bald. The torch blinded him. Gardner knocked them both to the pier floor, the torch dropped into the water and the *Defiant* reeled with the smack of a bullet into her hull.

Gardner blindly grappled with Bald. He couldn't see shit. He dragged Bald away from the boat. Bald struggled. Gardner brought an elbow down against his skull. Jesus fucking Christ, John, he thought. Bald's grip was stronger than he remembered.

Scarcely able to see ahead of him, Gardner moved as quickly as his legs and Bald's weight allowed. Another *crack* and the plank in front of him exploded. Splinters speared his forehead.

He ducked behind the remnants of an old fort. Weathered stonework now shielded them from the Upper Rock. Gardner gathered his breath and peered around the corner of the fort. The Upper Rock was jagged and dark as a lump of charcoal. *Fuck*, he told himself. Without a viewing aid, he had no way of getting a fix on Killen's location.

Bald tried standing. He was unsteady on his feet. He reached into his jacket pocket.

'Not this time you don't, mate,' Gardner said, smacking him in the middle of his back with the butt of the PMR-30. Bald grunted, dropped and rolled on to his back.

Then Gardner noticed a dull, sticky stain on his knee.

Moonlight splashed across his face. He stared at Gardner from behind a pair of black Ray-Bans. Blood gleamed out of a fresh gash on his jaw, where Gardner had struck him on the pier. The man's features were coated in the grainy film of night, but they were clear enough.

'You're not John,' he said

Mr fucking Crowbar.

forty-two

'Where the fuck is John Bald?' Gardner said, aiming the PMR-30 at the big man's chest.

'I would think carefully about your next move, if I were you,' Golan, aka Mr Crowbar, said. His accent was foreign, the bastard offspring of French and German.

'Only you're not me. You're the fucker with the gun in his face.'

Gardner noticed the elbows of the guy's jacket were smeared with blood and dirt. Wherever he been in the five hours since Gardner had introduced him to a steak knife, it wasn't the local A&E.

'You've got about six seconds to tell me who you are and what you know.'

'Kill me and you'll upset a lot of very important people.'

'Fucking talk,' Gardner said as he pushed the PMR-30 hard to Golan's temple. The polymer housing dug into his flesh. One click, he was thinking, and a .22 Magnum cartridge, powered by two hundred joules of muzzle energy, would carve open his skull. Like a boot through soft snow.

Golan must have sensed that Gardner was ready to back up his threat because he gritted his teeth and glowered, as if steeling himself for the bullet. Gardner couldn't see his eyes through the shades, but he got the impression that Golan was an unflappable son of a bitch.

'What the fuck are you doing here?'

'My mission is simple,' Golan said, talking to the barrel of the PMR-30. 'My people instructed me that no harm must come to the mark.'

'The *mark*? What are you on about?'

'The man I was sent here to protect.'

Gardner burned up like diesel. 'Terry Gill?'

'That is not the name I was given.'

The realization struck Gardner like a boomerang.

'John.'

'John Bald,' Golan said. 'Yes. He is the one.'

Gardner inched closer to his face. He wanted to tear off his shades and go eyeball to eyeball with this arsehole. He had the sense he was only dimly aware of the full story surrounding his old Regiment mucker.

'Who sent you?'

'That I cannot say.'

'Mossad?' His finger tensed on the trigger. 'You're Israeli, I know that much.'

Golan grinned at the barrel, like he was fucking flirting with it. 'If I told you who sent me – well, I'd have to kill you.' He laughed, then went on:

'Oh yes, your superiors gave you weak information. They told you Bald would be departing from the marina. On the *Defiant*, yes? They are badly mistaken.'

'Tell me where John is.'

'Why? So you can kill him?'

Gardner shook his head. 'I'm here to protect John.'

Golan frowned.

'The shots fired just now were intended for John. It's an ambush,' Gardner said. 'Looks like it's not just my intelligence that's full of holes.'

'You're lying.'

'Nah, mate. Hate to break it to you but the only reason I saved your arse back there is because I thought *you* were John.'

Golan looked sceptically at Gardner.

'You remember the King's Hotel?' Gardner said. 'The guy who turned up there to slot Bald—'

'An MI6 agent,' Golan cut in.

'No, he was a bloody cowboy. Out to slot John and rob him. The sniper on the Upper Rock is a cowboy mate of his. Name of Killen. And if we fuck about much longer, John's going to end up very dead.'

Golan weighed up the words.

'It seems to me we're on different ends of the same boat,' Gardner said. 'Either we work together to find John and get him out of the line of fire – or we're both going to end up on the losing team.'

Gardner glanced over the fort wall. Queensway was deserted. Not a fucking soul about.

Golan took off his shades, unveiling a swollen right eye socket, a battle scar of their earlier fight. 'OK,' he finally said. 'We help each other.' He reached for something inside his jacket. Gardner's right hand shot up, PMR-30 level with Golan's mug. His finger tensed on the trigger mechanism.

'Keep your hands where I can see them.'

'I have a handheld tracker. It will lead us to the mark.'

Gardner recalled the black object Golan had been holding on the pier. He'd assumed it was a gun, but perhaps it really was a tracking device. Gardner had no choice but to trust the Israeli. Since Land had sold him dud intelligence, Golan was his only hope of getting a lock on Bald.

'Do it.'

Golan quickly dipped a hand into his jacket.

'Slowly.'

The Israeli produced a sleek black device the size and thickness of an iPhone, except this one featured five buttons at the bottom and an extended aerial on top.

Gardner lowered the PMR-30. He leaned in as Golan entered a pin code on the touch screen and was presented with a thermal satellite map of Queensway, with one centimetre representing a hundred metres. A red icon blinked in the middle of the map.

'The Navy woman who was supplying cocaine to Bald,' Golan explained. 'I put a transponder into one of the packages before she completed the delivery. It emits a signal to a satellite in near-orbit and relays the position directly to me. Simple – but effective.'

Gardner nodded. 'So . . . where is he?'

Golan brushed his index finger over the screen. He tilted the device and looked over his shoulders, trying to establish his bearings.

'We don't have much time.'

'He's very close,' Golan said. 'And still on dry land, it seems. Rosia Road.'

'That's to the south.' Gardner scanned the screen. 'Fifty metres beyond the Botanic Gardens. That means he's just over three hundred metres away. Maybe he's winging his way up here. To the boat.'

'Then we can intercept him.' Golan was scrambling to his feet.

Gardner blocked his route with an outstretched arm. 'The sniper's still out there.'

'But Rosia Road is highly exposed,' Golan said. 'If the sniper spots Bald, he has an easy shot.'

'Let's keep low. We can move behind cover to John's position.'

'Agreed.'

'You lead the way.'

If he tries anything, I'll get the first shot off, Gardner thought.

Golan paced south, hugging the hotels' walls and pausing at the gap after each hotel. Gardner looked ahead for any sign of

Bald, but his eyes had not yet fully adjusted to the dark. It took an hour for the average person's eyes to adapt to seeing in the dark as the brain switched from retinal day cells to night. He'd left Land at 0350, less than forty-five minutes ago.

Golan moved with surprising ease, Gardner thought, considering the state of his left knee. Gardner kept up the pace to the rear, hoping to fuck that they reached Bald before Killen could zero in.

'This sniper—'

'Killen.'

'Is he a good shot?'

Gardner considered the question as they passed the plush villas with the giant anchor staked out front. 'He qualified top of the class in the sniper cadre of 1st Battalion, Parachute Regiment.'

'I'm not familiar with that school.'

'Put it this way. To pass out of the cadre, the sniper's got to achieve a first-round kill on a man-sized target at nine hundred metres. Killen could do that blindfolded.'

Golan was silent as they approached the Ragged Staff Gates, an eight-metre-tall wall of eroded concrete originally built by the Moors and later used as a defensive perimeter during the Siege. The gates provided them with cover as the marina ended and Queensway became Rosia Road. They were now just one hundred and twenty metres from Bald's position.

'What made you think I was MI6?' Gardner asked.

'I have my sources.'

'Well, you're fucking wrong. I don't work for anyone but myself.'

'Spoken like a true government man.'

Golan passed the Botanic Gardens. Then he slowed his step. Gardner halted in his shadow. They crouched down behind a cargo container parked beside the road and adjacent to the industrial park. A hundred metres due south Rosia Road curved to the right, rolling around the fringe of the industrial park and the dockyard. Gardner cocked his eyes. His vision had improved in the last few minutes, but he was troubled by what he saw. Or rather what he didn't see.

'Where's John?'

Golan consulted his tracker. 'According to the transponder, he should be here.'

'This is a built-up area,' Gardner said. 'There's any number of locations he might be. Inside a building, hiding in a hotel room, maybe parked up in a car somewhere ... We need a pinpoint fix.'

'When I said "here" I meant right on this very spot.'

Gardner darted his head left and right. Not a sniff of Bald in any direction.

'So where the *fuck* is he?'

forty-three

Craning his neck around the edge of the container, Gardner scoped out the scene. Street lamps poured orange light over a vacant road. The pavements were deserted, save for a macàque rummaging through a rubbish bin.

'I don't see him,' said Gardner, running his eyes over the Upper Rock. 'Something's wrong. Maybe your transponder signal's fucked.'

'Impossible.'

'It's either that, or John's turned into the invisible man—'

Golan had tuned out. He was scrolling down on the tracker, shifting his position and glancing down at the industrial park. He looked confused.

'What is it?' Gardner asked.

'The signal's moving.'

'Bullshit. He's not here. There must be some kind of problem with the hardware on that thing.'

'There is not, I can assure you.'

For fuck's sake! Gardner thought. Two spies tracking the same man on a slab of land of less than three square miles, and neither of us can find him. Anger lodged in his throat. He was mad at Golan's tracker, mad at Land's dodgy int.

The transponder blinked Bald's location: the industrial park. Gardner scanned the docks and the berthed *Lizard*. The sun was rising in the east, mottling the blackness. Seagulls flapped. No trace of Bald.

'What the fuck's going on?'

The dot shifted further south.

Gardner dug out his mobile to call Land.

He got nothing. Not even a dial tone. The signal displayed no bars.

'My phone's down . . . something's wrong.'

'Your phone isn't the problem.'

'What do you mean?'

'Communication countermeasures.'

Golan looked up at the sky and the paling stars. 'We wanted to make sure MI6 was not in a position to compromise the mark's safety. Until 0530 all foreign satellite and radio comms in a mile radius are disabled.'

Gardner's skin burned like hot rubber. He sensed everything was going pear-shaped fast. His shot at redemption – at being a soldier – was disappearing quicker than a Scouser into the nearest William Hill.

Fuck it! All this way. The shit I survived in Rio, the fucking cowboys, and now—

A throbbing, purring noise drilled his mind.

The two men exchanged a look.

'Sounds like—' said Golan.

'A boat engine!'

In a flurry they darted into the industrial yard.

'There's no boats coming in or out. I don't understand,' Golan said.

'The noise – it's coming from further down the way,' said Gardner. Then he remembered something he'd spotted earlier when spying on the Wren. He raced down Rosia Road, legs pumping so hard he could feel the burning in his calves, as if someone was holding matchsticks to them. His breathing was short, fitful.

After fifty metres he rested by the side of the artillery place-ment. It stood on the edge of a cliff face, the surrounding banks dotted with unfinished apartment blocks. He kneeled beside the reinforced armour plating fixed to the metre-long cannon. Below lay an isolated inlet.

'Earlier I remembered spotting a cove,' Gardner said. 'There was a small opening at the bottom. A tunnel.' His eyes searched the inky sea. 'It stuck in my mind because I'd read somewhere that smugglers used it back in the day, to hide contraband.'

Surf white as soap suds bobbed on the surface leading out from the tunnel, like a jet stream that had fallen from the sky. Gardner's eyes ran along the surf trail. And there! Barely a hundred metres beyond the cove, a cruiser yacht rose and dipped as it skimmed across the waves at a high speed. Had to be doing eighteen, twenty knots an hour, he figured.

'No,' Golan said, a trace of disgust in his tone. 'I do not believe it. All this time the signal was true.'

'John was *under* us. Under the fucking Rock.'

That's John all right, Gardner thought: hanging over the rails and puffing on a fucking victory cigar. Bald faced away from Gibraltar, looking out across the vista of Algeciras on the Spanish coastline.

'He is not alone,' said Golan.

'Figured as much,' said Gardner. Bald couldn't pilot a boat for all the money in the world. Someone else had to be manning the controls. As if on cue, a second face presented itself. This one was rounder and redder than Bald's, and his fleece and tracksuit bottoms hung loose from his portly frame. But he moved with the speed and balance of a man who'd spent many years honing his sea legs. He exited the wheelhouse and scaled the ladder down to the deck, gathering up the ropes.

'Pete Maston,' Gardner said.

'You know this man?'

'He taught me everything I know.' Gardner suddenly recalled how he'd respected Maston as the Major of his squadron in the Regiment. How Maston had taught him how to pilot a ship one day and survive sub-zero temperatures the next. Maston had moulded him into an expert in the art of warfare. A graduate in death and destruction.

Gardner watched the boat shrink down the Strait.

'What about the sniper?' Golan asked.

'Once he realizes that the target has escaped, he'll be worry-ing about getting the fuck off Gibraltar. Matter of fact, he's probably already quit the Upper Rock.'

'That is good.'

A cold spot formed at the back of Gardner's neck.

'Son of a bitch,' he hissed, and felt Golan press the barrel of his pistol harder against his flesh. Should've disarmed him back at the pier, when I had the fucking chance.

'For a man who claims his job is to protect the mark, you seem to know a lot of John Bald's enemies,' said Golan.

'What can I say?' The sun was lightening the sky to gunmetal grey. Waves crashed against the coast, spraying salt water into his face. 'It's a small world.'

'How about I make it one man smaller?'

'You sure that's a wise move – killing an MI6 operator?'

'But you said you weren't with the government.'

'And you believed me?' Gardner replied, trying to mask his fear by giving it some lip.

He waited for a reply that never came. The circle on his neck warmed. Then above him he heard a pulsating din, fast and furious and devastating. A carriage of cold air hit him like a fist, almost knocking him over the edge of the cliff. He clung on to the cannon to stabilize himself. Felt as if the world's biggest fan was blasting in his direction.

Gardner managed to swivel around on the battery mount. Sixty metres out from the coast a UH-60 Black Hawk helicopter hovered over a patch of water. Its four main blades whirled frantically, whipping up the waves into an electric swell. One of the crew lowered a rope ladder, bridging the forty-metre drop between the chopper and the sea.

Out of the waves, a long, sturdy hand grabbed hold of the final rung. Golan steadily climbed the rope ladder. He paused near the top. The Black Hawk banked south. Wrapping his left hand fully around the width of the ladder, Golan turned and grinned at Gardner, waving his right hand like a president at his inauguration.

Gardner watched as the chopper powered into the breaking dawn.

Who the fuck is that guy? he wondered. To be able to call upon an emergency evac with a Black Hawk told Gardner that Golan had to be a top-level operator. More than that, it also meant protecting Bald was high on someone else's agenda.

He stumbled back up Rosia Road. His mobile squawked. The comms systems were back up and running. Then he heard the nasal voice on the other end of the line.

'Where are you? Where the devil is Bald?'

'He escaped.'

Land breathed his relief, heavily. 'Meet me at Europa Point. I'm at Harding's Observation Post, next to the rather charming lighthouse. Do hurry along. It's important.'

forty-four

Europa Point lay at the southernmost tip of Gibraltar. Morocco's Atlas Mountains were a faint wash in the distance. Gardner passed the Ibrahim al-Ibrahim mosque to his left, cricket field to his right, the crease a strip of grass surrounded by sand.

At the very edge of the cliffs stood the lighthouse. Below it, three chimneys protruded like blocks of salt. And east of the lighthouse stood Harding's Observation Post.

Land stared down at a shiny metal plaque fixed to the ground that indicated the direction of North Africa across the Strait. He didn't turn to greet Gardner as he strode up the concrete path fixed between the cricket ground and the mosque.

'So,' Land said to the sea. 'You made it.'

'No thanks to you,' Gardner replied, hanging back a few feet from the agent.

'Oh? How so?'

'That intelligence you had about Bald escaping on the *Defiant* down at the marina? Bullshit. He'd hidden a boat in the smugglers' tunnel. If it wasn't for the Israeli and his transponder, I'd never have found him.'

Land tapped a cigarette from his pack. He rolled it in his hands mournfully.

'We gave you the best information we had available to us at the time, old boy.'

'Well, your so-called best stank the place out.'

Land spun round and walked towards Gardner. For the first time, Gardner saw aggression in his face. 'Look, I've already apologized to you. What more do you want from me? Christ, even when we did eventually work out Bald's escape plan, we had no way of reaching you. All of our radio and mobile systems were down.'

'Golan mentioned that. Speaking of which, any more news on this guy?'

Land shrugged as he put the cigarette between his lips. The breeze rolling up from the cliffs conspired to extinguish his lighter.

'We're getting nowhere. All of our enquiries have hit a dead end. Our best guess is he's a criminal freelancer.'

'Could be Mossad.'

'Not a chance,' Land said, striking a match and cupping the flame around his cigarette. 'I spoke to their chief earlier. He assures me that Golan is not one of their people. I'm inclined to believe him. We have a good relationship with the Israelis, you know.'

'Golan – he got away too. A Black Hawk lifted him out. That's no criminal.'

'Well, you might be right,' he shrugged.

'They haven't caught Killen yet?'

'Matter of time.'

Land stubbed out his half-smoked cigarette on the plaque.

'There's another thing—' Gardner began.

'You saw a familiar face on the boat.'

Gardner angled his head at Land.

'How did you know?'

'One of our SIGINT listening posts intercepted an exchange two days ago between Bald and Major Pete Maston. Or *ex*-Major, I should say. Old mentor of yours, I believe?'

'And you didn't think to let me know?'

'The identity of the driver of the boat doesn't affect your mission directly.' Land inspected his shoes. 'And anyway, Maston suffered a bad fall from grace. The head shed had to let him go. Afghanistan did, shall we say, odd things to his mind. He drowned his dog in the bath. Then he tried to do the same to his pregnant girlfriend.'

Gardner said nothing. All Special Forces soldiers were trained in first aid, and every patrol had its specialist medic. Gardner knew of more than one guy who could take out a dozen armed men but struggled to come to terms with his own mind. Some topped themselves. Others destroyed their own lives, or the lives of their loved ones.

'After he got the old heave-ho, Maston went looking for answers in the bottom of a whisky bottle. He was declared bankrupt late last year and a few months ago the bailiffs seized his house. Been sleeping on friends' floors since, apparently.'

'So you're saying Maston's doing this for the money?'

'I'm saying, Joe, the man's broke. I imagine Bald offered him a cut in exchange for his help.'

Out of the corner of his eye, Gardner noticed a figure sitting on a bench sixty metres to his right, by the cricket clubhouse. The man was tearing chunks off a white loaf. He threw the chunks to the seagulls. Paused, glanced across his shoulder and carried on feeding the birds. He had hair the colour of volcano ash and a hangdog expression. His face, dappled with liver spots, was more creased than an old shirt. Gardner guessed he could be anything from sixty to ninety.

Gardner looked back at Land.

'So it's all over? I can go home now?'

Land smiled.

No more Bald, no more fucking Firm. You'll be back in the line of duty, Gardner thought. Away from the politics and the lies and the mind games.

'Certainly. But first I would like you to meet someone.'

Land gestured to the old man feeding the birds. He nodded at Land. His large hands gently placed the remainder of the loaf by his side on the bench. The seagulls flocked to the bread as he walked over to the two men, his crisp suit rustling in the breeze, his blank eyes staring right through Gardner.

'This is Massimo,' Land said. 'And he's here to make you an offer you can't refuse.'

forty-five

Massimo Macca rubbed a hand over his jaw. He had a thin veil of stubble that ran black at the chin, flour-grey higher up the sides. His eyes scanned the foot of the cliff face. He was grizzled and fat and Joe Gardner doubted the guy had ever seen the inside of a gym, but he was sure he'd been in his fair share of scraps.

'This is Signor Bald's friend?'

'He's no friend of mine,' snapped Gardner.

Macca suppressed a laugh. 'Then maybe you are Bald's *consigliere*?' His voice was gruff. 'You worked together, no?'

'Not any more we don't. Look, I don't know who the hell you are, but I'm warning you.'

'The *signore* is a man of violence. That's good. Nowadays people are so sensitive. They don't understand that some people are created bad, and bad people have to be crushed.' He crumbled an imaginary rock in his fist.

'If you say so.'

'And which side are you on? Good, or bad?'

'Massimo, please,' Leo Land said. He rested a manicured hand on Macca's shoulder. 'Joe's on our side. Lately he's been of great help to our investigation. Indeed, if it wasn't for Joe, Bald would be dead by now, along with any hopes we have of bringing some of these bastards to book.'

Macca yawned. He had nostrils so wide he could hide a tank up there.

'Forgive me, signor. I am afraid trust does not come very easily to a man in my position.'

'I'd say that depends,' said Gardner.

'On what?'

'Whether your job title is Chief Dickhead.'

Macca shot Gardner a sour look. 'The men I put behind bars would kill you for less.'

'Massimo is a prosecutor for the region of Calabria in southern Italy,' Land said. 'He's been chasing the Mafia down in those parts for some twenty-five years. A tiring job, I imagine.' Land frowned at the sun. 'We should talk somewhere more private.'

Macca nodded. They gave Africa their backs and left Harding's Observation Post. Gardner noticed that a navy-blue Mercedes CLK Coupé was parked up on the verge of Europa Road. Land offered to drive. Gardner sat in the back, Macca in the front passenger seat.

The car had a milky smell to it, which is to say it smelled exactly how Gardner imagined a car driven by Leo Land would. The dashboard was varnished walnut, the windows at least sixty per cent tinted.

Land fired up the Mercedes and reversed north out of Europa Road, tracing a route west then north on the same stretch of asphalt.

'The old Mafia – the *Cosa Nostra* – is history these days,' said Macca. 'Today the real danger comes from a new source. The 'Ndrangheta. "The Honoured Society".'

'Imagine an organization more powerful and secretive than anything in the history of the Mafia,' Land added.

'The original 'Ndrangheta,' Macca resumed, 'was formed a hundred years ago by Calabrian peasants to protect themselves against the landed gentry. For many years they practised extortion and bribery. Then the leaders made a deal with the Colombians. Tonnes of cocaine poured into the docks at

Gioia Tauro. Now they have soldiers across the world: Europe, America, Australia. Each *picciotto d'onore* – or foot soldier – is sworn to a blood oath. They control the cocaine. The heroin. Arms trading. Human trafficking. The construction business. It's endless.'

Macca shook his head, then went on: 'I lost my wife to the cancer two years ago. The tumours, they consumed her body. Until there was nothing left of her to give, you understand? This is what the 'Ndrangheta are. A tumour that does not stop.'

They rolled back up past the dockyard.

'I still don't see what this has to do with me.'

'Your friend, Signor Bald—'

'He's *not* my friend.'

'He will strike a deal with the 'Ndrangheta for his cocaine—'

'Bully for him.'

'And you are going to witness it.'

'Yeah? And at what point did you became my fucking boss?'

Gardner then directed his rage at Land. 'We had a deal, and I've more than fulfilled my end of the bargain.'

The MI6 man's face crinkled in the rear-view mirror like a wet rag. 'You brought this on yourself, Joe. The incident at the King's Hotel, the business with Killen – because of you things got a tad too noisy. As a result Bald fears for his life, and he's changing plans.'

Land nudged the Mercedes up Winston Churchill Avenue and into the parking lot next to the Victoria Stadium. The lot was empty.

'Our original aim had been to simply detain Bald once he docked in Gioia Tauro in western Calabria – Massimo's back yard. Now it appears Bald isn't happy about meeting the Italians on their own soil. We've picked up communications which indicate that Bald is rearranging the venue for neutral turf.'

'Communications? I thought all your systems were down?'

'The land-based ones, yes. But we've had a Navy submarine tapping into the optic fibres running along the seabed. You know, the ones that carry all that internet and landline chitter-chatter back and forth. It's more common than the public and media would have you believe. Our SIGINT chaps listened in to a conversation between Bald and a fellow he refers to as the Pallbearer. We believe this is code for Gianni Petruzzi. His nickname is known only to his immediate family – or so he thinks.'

'This Petruzzi bloke – he's 'Ndrangheta?'

'A *capo crimini*,' Macca said, passing Gardner a black-and-white snap of the man himself. Whatever ideas he had about the style of a Mafia head honcho, the photograph quickly dispelled. Here was a bloated, flabby man, loose jowls and drooping eyelids. The only young thing about him was the twentysomething bimbo hanging from his arm.

'He is the chief of a local clan. He and his brothers once carried a coffin through the streets of San Luca. A coffin filled with cocaine. That's where his name comes from. Now it has an additional layer of meaning: when people owe him money, Petruzzi buries them alive.'

'Bald said that he felt someone was watching him,' said Land.

'So where is he now?'

'Currently making his way along the Alboran Sea heading east. He's en route to Algeria. The 'Ndrangheta have contacts there, established through the human trafficking network. We believe a private jet awaits Bald in Algiers.'

Gardner nodded, soaking up the int. 'And the jet's taking him where?'

'Belgrade,' Land said, patting himself down for his cigarettes.

'Serbia has strong links to the 'Ndrangheta,' Macca put in.

'So go to the fucking Serbs for help,' Gardner said.

Macca shook his head. 'You cannot ask rats to hunt other rats.'

'Then ask Interpol. Or the fucking A-Team, I don't care.'

'We need someone who knows Bald, who can track him. Face it, Joe. You're the man for the job.'

Gardner weighed it up. As much as he felt like taking a hot shower every time he spoke to Land, he had unfinished business with John. Gardner was the kind of guy who liked to see things through. He'd never been one for quitting halfway into a job.

'My government,' said Macca, 'wishes to recognize your, how do you say, courage in waging war against the scum of the 'Ndrangheta. Anyone who helps to kill this cancer is a good friend of Italia.'

Land found his smokes, rolled down his window. He sucked on the unlit tab in the left corner of his mouth and spoke with his right. 'What Massimo is saying is that you'll be amply rewarded for the mission.'

'Half a million euros,' Macca said.

'Fuck you.'

'Don't be a bloody fool,' Land said. 'With that money you can buy all the women and lagers you want. Or spend it on whatever else you Regiment people do in your free time. Take the money, Joe.'

'If I do this one last mission for you, I want my old job back – fucking end of.'

'Stubborn as well as a fool, eh?' Land lit his cigarette. The smoke tickled Gardner's nostrils and settled like fog in his empty stomach. He suddenly felt painfully hungry.

Land unlocked the Merc's doors.

'Massimo, my dear chap. It is time for us to part.'

Macca climbed out of the car with difficulty, without another word. Back problems, old face, despairing eyes: that old bastard time hadn't been kind to him. A Porsche pulled into the parking lot and drew up alongside the stooping Italian.

'Fun guy,' Gardner said as the Porsche gobbled Macca up.

'He's quite a nut in his own way. Legend has it he killed more than two hundred Mafiosi.' Land frowned. 'Now, a quick word. My chiefs are very upset at the damage Bald has caused so far.'

'Scared of any mud sticking?'

'Not at all. But they feel it would be better if perhaps he wasn't given any public exposure.' Land spoke slowly, emphasizing each word like a primary school teacher. 'If he were arrested, that might bring some unwanted coverage in the news. Not the kind of thing HMG needs at this point in time.'

'You want him dead?'

'Only if he actually makes the exchange. If he pulls out, even if it's the last minute, then we'll have to think of something else. But if Bald hands them the coke, and gets his prize in exchange, he'll have gone too far, and you have permission to engage.'

'To kill, you mean?'

'Do you have a problem with that?'

Gardner thought about it. Revenge had been on his mind ever since Bald had double-crossed him in Rio. Sure as shit he wouldn't hesitate to fill Gardner with lead if the chance presented.

'None at all.'

'Good man. I want you – the Firm wants you – to do whatever it takes.'

Land removed a cream envelope from the breast pocket of his shirt. Gardner wondered how an agent who spent his life living out of suitcases managed to keep his shirts and jackets so neatly ironed. Like the guy was a fucking walking steam press.

The envelope was unsealed. A flick of the thumb and forefinger and it popped open. Inside: ticket to Belgrade, one way; new passport, name of Gary Dutch; American Express, black, same name; pay-as-you-go mobile. He could be getting ready for his stag weekend.

'You do right by us on this one, Joseph, and I can personally assure you that it will be worth your while.'

'Let's just get it over with.'

Land flicked his lights. The police car moved on and two minutes later the Mercedes exited the stadium lot. As it dropped Gardner at the airport, the same bobby in a fancy uniform was mincing about outside.

Gardner climbed out of the car.

'When you get to Belgrade, call me. There's a local contact who'll sort you out,' said Land, then fucked off.

Gardner was left standing there, wondering if he hadn't just made the worst decision of his life.

forty-six

You can always spot a first-timer, thought Aleksandr Nikolai Sotov as he surveyed the private military airfield at Sobransk, some twenty kilometres south of Yakutsk, in north-east Siberia. However tough a man's constitution, however thick his skin or thin his blood, nothing could prepare him for the cold.

Sotov recognized straight away the man climbing down the steps from the plane. The bug eyes, the bent nose. The swollen cheeks. As if his head had been compressed in a vice.

The man looked lost. The old saying of the English came to mind: like a rabbit caught in the headlights. Only you didn't get rabbits in Siberia. Not in conditions up to minus fifty.

Sotov exited the black Lexus and approached the runway. The cold pierced his skin like salt in an open wound.

'Maxim, Maxim, my good friend! So glad you could make it.'

'What a miserable journey,' replied Maxim Ledinsky, the chief of the Military Counterintelligence Directorate of the Federal Security Service of the Russian Federation (FSB). 'The plane was held up for two hours at Moscow. Then we had the worst turbulence I've ever experienced. In the old days we would report back and have the pilot killed,' he said, slitting his throat and winking in a manner which suggested to Sotov that he was only half-joking.

'You are here now.'

'And prepared!' waving to his clothes. Padded jeans, Gore-Tex boots, woolly scarf, hat, gloves and winter coat. Concealing underneath, Sotov was certain, several layers of thermal garments.

'That's very good, Maxim. But please, take off your glasses.'

Ledinsky blinked his confusion.

'In this weather the metal will stick to your skin and when you remove them you'll tear off chunks of flesh.'

'Yes, yes, of course,' Ledinsky said, fumbling at the frames with his heavily gloved hands.

'And the package?'

'In the back of her,' said Ledinsky, thumbing the Hercules.

'Show me,' Sotov said.

Ledinsky grumbled as he escorted Sotov around to the rear of the aircraft. The turbines whirled out streams of air so fast and so cold that to look directly ahead was like being jabbed in the eyes with cocktail sticks.

The ramp lowered. Sotov moved forward. The Herc's cargo area was a tangle of cables and ropes. Crates were stacked to the rear. Emergency lights flashed.

'Where is it?'

'There,' Ledinsky signalled to a wooden crate marked with the Red Cross symbol. The crate was a metre wide and about the same high.

'Open it,' Sotov said.

'I can't feel my fingers,' Ledinsky protested.

'Maxim, I need to see it.'

Ledinsky hollered at the crew. Two men in overalls scaled the ramp and used the stocks of their AK-47s to prise open the lid. It took them three tries before the crate began to split open.

'Quickly, my nose hurts,' Ledinsky urged them.

'Be patient,' he was told.

Sotov peered into the crate. It doesn't look like much, he thought. No. It really seems like hardly anything at all. A lot of fuss for something so – he reached for the right word – ordinary. Yes, that was it.

'You sure this is everything, Maxim?'

'Yes, yes.'

'OK, I'm satisfied. Now we can leave.'

Sotov marched towards the Lexus, full of renewed vigour. Only Ledinsky's constant bitching threatened to bring him down from his high. 'Shit, this weather. They warned me in Moscow, but I didn't think it would be this bad. I mean . . . I don't know how you people survive.'

You people, Sotov thought. His parents had been part of the migration from the west, which is why he stood out from the native Siberians. Where they had dark features and ruddy cheeks, Sotov sported blue eyes, sandblasted hair and pale skin.

'It's warmer in the car,' he said.

'Yes?'

'Well, perhaps only minus ten.' Sotov was smiling to himself.

His chauffeur, Denis Popov, six-two with a long, thin neck and silver hair the colour of a knife edge, manoeuvred around the Lexus and opened a door for Ledinsky. The Lexus was just one of a fleet of luxury cars. Sotov's official title was the CEO of Russia's leading diamond-mining outfit, Strelka Corporation. But Sotov was also *Mafya*.

The engine was already running when Sotov and Ledinsky took their seats in the back of the Lexus.

'I take it you've covered your tracks?' said Sotov.

'Of course,' Ledinsky replied. 'I'm taking a big risk too, you know. If this thing goes missing—'

'It won't.'

Sotov pointed to a black truck reversing towards the Herc's ramp. Strelka guards stood either side of the truck. Overhead one of the Sikorsky helicopters belonging to Sotov's private fleet patrolled the surrounding area.

'I didn't realize you had so many men,' said Ledinsky.

'Here, in Yakutsk, I'm the only law there is. The people around here joke that when Aleksandr Sotov shrugs, the whole of Siberia shakes.'

'How many—?'

'Men in my force? I forget the exact number. Eight thousand? Enough to get things done.'

'What kind of—?'

'Vodka?' Sotov produced a bottle of Russian Standard and two shot glasses from a fold-away cabinet.

Ledinsky eyed the bottle suspiciously. 'I don't drink.'

'Nonsense! A man cannot do business in Yakutsk without vodka warming his belly.'

Sotov poured Ledinsky a generous shot. Knocked back his own and *aaahed*.

Popov steered the Lexus out on to the highway. The icy road was flecked with black spots: frozen corpses of the millions of midges and mosquitoes that had swarmed over Yakutsk in the brief summer respite. Only three weeks ago temperatures had been a mild fifteen degrees. Seemed like history now.

'What about my payment?' said Ledinsky, looking down at his still-full glass.

'I've decided to kill you instead.'

Ledinsky froze.

'I'm joking, Maxim. We're on our way to collect it now.'

They drove through what an outsider would have mistaken for a ghost town. No cars were on the roads, just a few trucks shipping in vital supplies of petrol and food. Streets devoid of people. Only the fish market showed any signs of activity. It was where, decades earlier, Sotov had set up his first business, crushing his competitors by poisoning their catches with diesel fuel.

The Lexus slowed to fifty kilometres an hour as they headed north-west, Yakutsk in the rear-view mirror, the banks of the

River Lena to their right. Now and then the car jumped and sank from the holes in the road.

Heading west, they passed a radar installation and a pyramid-roofed church. The chauffeur turned on to a gravel path and, half a kilometre down, stopped at a checkpoint. An imposing yellow sign warned that intruders would be shot. Guards, armed with A-91M bullpup assault rifles and with the company's Siberian husky logo sewn to their lapels, peered inside and nodded sombrely at Sotov. The gates opened; the guards waved them through.

The road continued for another couple of kilometres until it reached the mouth of a low cave. Foot patrols with sniffer dogs cleared the Lexus to proceed. At the cave's mouth four guards stood to attention, two on each side of a solid-lead vault door.

Golden statues of snow leopards were perched on the pillars either side of the door. Sotov exited the Lexus and took a keycard from his pocket. One of the guards also removed a keycard. They inserted their cards simultaneously into their slots. A series of clicks followed, then the door cranked open.

'Come, I have something to show you,' said Sotov.

Ledinsky hesitated. 'What's inside?'

'Why, your reward.'

'Good. And please, let's make it quick,' Ledinsky said, the blood draining from his face. 'I'm a busy man.'

'Of course.'

The cave was cool and dark. Ledinsky took off his hat to reveal a comb-over. Steam wafted from his bald patch like cigar smoke. Another guard directed them towards a lift. They entered. The guard slammed the cage door shut, and the lift rattled as it descended three hundred feet below the surface. Ledinsky wiped sweat from his pate.

'I was not aware you had another facility.'

'We needed somewhere to store a few things.'

'What things?'

'Secrets, Maxim. Secrets.'

The lift screeched to a halt. Brilliant light flooded the black of the shaft. A guard cranked the door open. Sotov gestured for Ledinsky to exit first. The FSB chief scrunched up his eyes, as if staring directly at the sun. Sotov handed him a pair of sunglasses.

'We're in the only place in Siberia where a man needs these,' he grinned.

Ledinsky's jaw slackened.

'In Yakutsk we like to say, there's a lake or river for every person who lives here,' Sotov said. 'But the truth is that we have more diamonds than people. Here, comrade, diamonds are as common as snowflakes.'

'It's incredible . . . I've never seen—'

'Quite a sight, isn't it?'

They were standing in a dome-shaped underground mine. Searchlights fired powerful blue rays at the ceiling, fifty feet above. Sotov lowered his eyes to the ground, to an area the size of six football pitches. Filled with mountains of polished diamonds.

Ledinsky picked up a handful. Each gleaming stone hypnotized him. He managed to peel his eyes away. Looked quizzically at Sotov.

'These must be worth billions.'

Sotov shrugged.

'But . . . why are you hiding them underground?'

The *Mafya* man kneeled beside a small mound of diamonds. A stone the size of his fist rested on top. Four times as large as the Cullinan diamond in the English Crown Jewels, the rock in front of him, he reckoned, was the largest rough diamond in the world. And it was kept underground, gathering dust.

'Some things are more valuable when they are not seen,' he said.

'You're not making any sense.'

'Do you know that one diamond merchant controls fifty per cent of the global market? That's an impressive figure, no? It means they have the power to raise the price of rough diamonds or lower it, however they see fit.'

Ledinsky frowned.

'They say diamonds are rare,' Sotov continued. 'It's a myth. We keep the stones down here, in the mine, because it benefits this particular merchant to have fewer organic diamonds on the market. They pay us *not* to supply them. It works for both of us. They keep the price of diamonds artificially high, and we get paid for doing nothing.'

'That's preposterous.'

Sotov rose to his feet. He scooped up the fist-sized diamond and offered it to Ledinsky.

'Accept this as your payment,' he said, lighting up a black Ziganov. 'Take as many as you want, or need. Take some for your wife, your children. Take some as bribes for your colleagues. Take all you want, Maxim, but remember this: each diamond in your pocket is a promise from you to me. Cigarette?'

Ledinsky shook his head, rolled the sparkling stone in his hands like a ball. 'What kind of a promise?'

'Simply that we both agree to keep silent about our arrangement.'

Sotov waited for an answer that did not come. He turned to look at Ledinsky, and found the much-respected FSB director plunging his hands, joyously, into a pile of diamonds.

'I'll take that as a yes,' Sotov said.

forty-seven

Gardner parked his rented Toyota Avensis two blocks from the Tiger Bar, slap bang in the heart of Silicon Valley. The district got its name from the number of artificially enhanced women who prowled its streets. A few days ago Gardner would have been tempted to check out the scenery. But he had come to Belgrade to settle a score and bury an old friendship. The Page Three girls of Silicon Valley would have to sit this one out.

Land had instructed him to hit the Tiger Bar at precisely six-forty the evening he arrived.

'Who am I looking for?' Gardner had asked.

'Don't worry, my boy – they'll find you,' Land had assured him.

Now Gardner's eyelids felt heavy, as if someone had sewn hockey pucks into them. Just three hours' sleep in more than forty-eight hours, and it had finally caught up with him. He'd taken a British Airways flight from Gibraltar to Heathrow. Passed the two hours waiting for his flight at a chain restaurant, drinking sugary coffee and grazing on a ham-and-cheese sandwich that gave him £2.50 change from a tenner. From there he boarded a Swiss Airlines plane bound for Zurich. He drank a pint of Guinness at a bar and watched Sky Sports News for an hour before taking an onward flight to Nikolai Tesla Airport.

Belgrade. It was twelve years since Gardner had set foot in the city. He felt like a murderer returning to the scene of the crime. A lot of fucked-up shit had gone down there during the Kosovo War, and the Regiment had played a right royal part. Dispatched to the capital, their mission had been to cripple the Milosevic state machinery by whatever means necessary.

As the troop's designated demolitions expert, Gardner had been part of a four-man patrol charged with silencing Milosevic's personal mouthpiece, the state radio. At sun-up he had rigged the station with enough plastique to tear the ozone a new arsehole. Intel had indicated the building was empty. But the int turned out to be wrong. At the moment Gardner pressed the clicker, twenty-eight civilians were inside. No one survived.

He never saw any bodies. Didn't hear their screams above the explosion. But their shadows still haunted him, shadows without arms and legs, limp as rag dolls.

Twelve years later and the city had been given a fresh lick of paint. Snazzy new shopping centres, casinos and mobile-phone shops jostled for attention. Gardner saw that hints of the old Belgrade remained: the Communist architecture tucked away in dilapidated backstreets, and the frothing nationalist graffiti on underpasses and bridges.

It was cooler than Gibraltar, hovering around ten degrees. Gardner wore navy combats, a white V-neck T-shirt and a grey hoodie. He'd snapped up all three from a duty-free shop at Heathrow. And he had something else slapped around his wrist.

'I'm concerned about your personal safety on this mission,' Land had said in Gibraltar. 'Now Bald's more cautious than ever before and is working with some bad apples, there's a fair chance they might suss you out. If that happens, you're in trouble. Wear this.' He'd given Gardner a red bracelet. The bracelet was fitted with a radio-frequency identification chip which sent out a signal on UHF passive frequency, triangulated via the Firm's GIS computers to produce a real-time fix on the bracelet's location.

'If you press this button,' Land had told him, tapping a small metal circle attached to the plastic, 'it will send an emergency relay directly to MI6 HQ. That's your signal that you're in extreme danger and wish to be extracted. I can't give any guarantees, but in normal circumstances we should be able to extract you within an hour of your pressing the button.'

Now, as Gardner approached the Tiger Bar, he clocked a photograph taped to the door. Some mean-looking guy in military uniform stood in front of a tank, surrounded by his militia mates. He had an AK-47 in his right hand but in his left was a curious thing: a baby tiger, held up by the scruff of its neck.

He pushed through the door. It was like crossing into another dimension, a place where smoking bans didn't exist and Lady Gaga hadn't yet been invented. Accordion music bleated out of a single speaker. About a dozen men huddled in groups of two and three at booze-soaked tables, drinking brandy, smoking foul-smelling tabs. They eyed him suspiciously as he made his way to the bar. He ordered a pint of the local lager from a barman with a face like a pig's arse. Fuck me, he thought. It's like I'm in Yates's, minus the slappers.

Gardner pulled up a chair. He sipped his beer; it tasted watered down and glowed green beneath the bleary lights. His eyes adjusted and he realized there was a single female in the bar, a woman smiling a broad smile at him.

She had coffee-brown hair, brushed back behind small, elf-like ears, to fall in teasing strands at her neck. Her lips were delicate in the middle and curved up at the corners. She wore a three-quarter-sleeve flame top and a pair of indigo jeans, and had the kind of body that could look good in a shell suit.

She was by herself. Her eyes, black as a winter sky, searched his. I might be in here, Gardner decided. He glanced away, then stole another look at her figure, legs like a catwalk model. He had a strong urge to jump her bones.

The woman seemed to ignore him for several seconds. Then she stood up and walked over.

'You must be Joe Gardner,' she said in a soft and light voice that confused him. He'd assumed she was Serbian but the local women all seemed to have deep, full voices. He couldn't quite place her accent.

She drew up the seat opposite him and placed a half-full glass of red on the metal table. Rested a black purse beside it.

'And you are?' he said.

The woman arched one of her elegant eyebrows at him. 'You don't need to know my name.'

'No, but I guess I'm a bit old-fashioned like that.'

As a smile spread across her lips Gardner felt a hot wave of air push against the wall of his chest.

'Leo warned me about you,' she said.

'Really? What—?'

'Just that trouble follows you around like a bad smell and you've got some anger-management issues.'

Gardner drank some more cheap lager and reflected.

'Pretty accurate, I'd say.'

The woman laughed, the smile full-on now, stars sparkling in her soft eyes. 'Leo's telling the truth for once?'

'But I still don't know your name.'

She sipped her wine, and the corners of her lips coloured dark red. 'Aimée Milana,' she said. 'Pleased to meet you.'

'Likewise, Aimée. I'm guessing you're not local.'

She shook her head. 'Strictly speaking, I'm only half-Serbian. My father's from Belgrade, my mother's from Paris. I grew up here but moved to France to study when the war broke out.'

'And now you work for the Firm?'

Aimée's eyebrows met at the bridge of her nose. They were arched and alluring. 'Not for. With. If your government wants to stop people using my country as a drugs market, that is a good enough reason for me.'

'You know why I'm here?'

'Yes . . . back to business?' Her smile crawled back into its hole.

He nodded. 'Leo said you might be able to show me around.'

'It seems your friend is mixed up with some very bad people,' she said. 'Come, I'll take you there.'

Gladly leaving behind the filmy gunk in his glass, Gardner followed Aimée out of the bar. He was wondering what kind of shitstorm John Bald was stirring up in their old stomping ground.

forty-eight

The Zira Hotel stood on Ruzveltova Street in old Belgrade, a concrete maze east of the River Sava. Gardner and Aimée were sitting in the Toyota on a side street opposite the hotel. He could see all the way to the other side of the river, where the tall buildings of new Belgrade dominated the skyline.

'This is where your friend is staying,' Aimée said.

'He likes to travel in comfort.'

Aimée popped a stick of chewing gum in her mouth. 'He checked in under an assumed name. Let me see,' she said, checking her phone. 'Gary McAllister.'

Gardner laughed.

'What's so funny?' Aimée demanded.

'Too hard to explain,' said Gardner, reflecting on the striking similarity between Bald and the old Liverpool midfielder.

At that moment Bald emerged from the hotel lobby. Gardner thought he looked tired. Bald climbed into a Mitsubishi Shogun 4x4 parked out front. The windscreen wipers swiped at drizzle as iron-grey skies leaked rain. Throw in a bunch of hoodies setting fire to a BT phone box, Gardner reckoned, and you could almost be in Moss Side.

The Shogun lunged forward.

'Let's follow him,' said Aimée.

Gardner pulled out into traffic three vehicles behind the Shogun. Bald powered south-west down Ruzveltova for about a kilometre, then turned right into Aleksandra Boulevard. Gardner followed the Shogun past baroque libraries and museums. The old gave way to the new: porno shops and fast-food joints. Men slept on park benches in the mid-afternoon sun. The Shogun headed south. New apartment blocks lined the road: Belgrade was demolishing its old quarters, eager to join the twenty-first-century rat race.

Gardner gripped the wheel hard, fighting to keep his emotions in check. Been a hell of a ride, he told himself. Halfway across the fucking world. He dared to think he might be nearing the end of his mission. The thought dripped like acid in his stomach.

Less than ten kilometres south and the city receded like a politician's hairline.

'I know this place,' Gardner said. 'Belgrade's slummy end.'

'Used to be.'

They rolled past swish new penthouses. Parks, a gym, tennis courts, an outdoor swimming pool. Each of them carried the same bold message: Belgrade's going places.

Bald parked up outside a two-storey villa. Gardner brought the Toyota to a rest a hundred metres back, next to a bus stop. He reached for his Nikon D3.

The digital camera was a specially modified unit cour-tesy of the Firm. Instead of Gardner saving images to a flash memory card, a secure network adapter transmitted the images in encoded format back to Vauxhall via a near-space satellite. The 12.1-megapixel snaps were hitting Land's desk in the time it took to microwave a Pot Noodle. That way, if Gardner lost the camera or it was damaged, MI6 already had the photographs of everyone involved in the smuggling ring.

The front door of the villa opened and a man came out and shook Bald's hand. His eyes scanned the street and, at one point, seemed to bore holes right through Gardner.

He had pockmarked cheeks like weathered marble. Pierced eyebrows and mangled ears that looked as if a Rottweiler had chewed on them. He was decked out in a tattered leather jacket with a Ferrari logo on the breast, turtleneck sweater and scuffed white sneakers.

'Klint Valon,' Gardner said.

'You know him?' Aimée asked. 'He's one of the most feared criminals in Belgrade.'

'Fucking right I do. Albanian. He played both sides in the war, Albanian and Serbian. Eventually NATO got wise to him and he turned snitch. Actually helped the Regiment bust an arms-trafficking movement involving the Russian *Mafya* and NATO soldiers.'

'I had no idea he helped NATO.'

'He gave Grade A int to hunt down the traffickers and put a stop to the ethnic cleansing. Trouble is, soon as the war was over Valon did a vanishing act. Probably shit-scared that the mates he'd dobbed in would be hungry for revenge.'

'Never famous for his loyalty.'

'The only loyalty Valon knows is to his wallet.'

Bald paced back to the Shogun, clutching a brown paper bag. Gardner figured it wasn't a can of Special Brew in the bag – more likely a pistol for his personal protection.

Gardner revved up the Toyota once the Shogun had pulled off again.

'Why would your friend be dealing with Valon?'

'Maybe he's looking for a little backup before he goes ahead with the exchange,' said Gardner, waiting for a goat to cross the road.

'Valon would perform such a service?'

Gardner nodded. 'For a slice of the profits he'd whore out his gran and post the video on YouTube.'

Their conversation was interrupted by his squawking phone. He answered.

'So you've met our local contact then?' Land said. 'Quite the siren, isn't she?'

'Helping me get the low-down,' Gardner said. He filled Land in on the presence of Klint Valon.

'I suppose it makes sense. I've just got off the phone to Massimo. His undercover man in Calabria says that Petruzzi is going to arrive in Belgrade at nine o'clock tomorrow morning.'

'Figure the deal's not going to happen without Petruzzi present.'

'Just to be on the safe side, we'll have Bald's hotel under surveillance. I'll alert you the moment he leaves his room. But first we need to sort you out with some goodies ahead of the meeting. Aimée should come in handy, I think you'll find.'

forty-nine

The drive north to downtown Belgrade was a quiet one. Gardner thought about Valon. He recalled a story that did the rounds during the war. Rumours that Valon once drove a school bus through a village and offered to take the ethnic Albanians living there to a safe house. The villagers were crammed on the bus. Men, women, children. Then Valon drove them straight into a Serbian militia camp. The militiamen paid him a handsome reward. Valon counted his money while the soldiers ordered the Albanians on to their knees and shot them in turn in the back of the head.

The Toyota crawled up Topcider Hill, south-east of the city centre. On the northern slope of the hill Gardner noted Hajd Park, named after Hyde Park. Down the other side of Topcider Hill, from where Aimée directed him towards a low-rise block of flats with a red-brick front, French windows and ornamental railings. The cars parked outside were all BMWs and Mercedes.

'Bloody hell,' said Gardner as Aimée searched for her keys. 'The Firm obviously pay you good money.'

'I do this work for my country. Not to buy myself a luxury sofa.'

They climbed wooden stairs, treads groaning like an old woman on her deathbed. On the third floor Aimée approached the door to flat 7 and twisted her keys in a series of locks.

Inside, she had an alarm. This woman takes her security seriously, Gardner thought.

Aimée punched in a code number. The alarm cut short. She led him down a narrow hallway. Lino floors, framed newspaper articles that he noticed carried her name on the byline. He couldn't read them, but he knew they were in French.

'You used to be a journalist?'

The back of her head nodded. Gardner found himself staring at the smooth nape of her neck. 'I worked as a crime reporter for *Le Figaro* for five years. It was fun, but crime in France is petty compared to what happens in Serbia.'

Past a kitchen on their left, a bathroom on their right, and at the end of the hallway she opened a door to the left, flicked a switch.

The room was bare. No furniture, no decorations. Just a single lightbulb hanging from the ceiling like a burning fuse. Gardner wondered for a split second what he was supposed to be looking at. Then he ran his eyes across the walls and wondered no more.

Weapons were racked on the walls. Gardner recognized a bewildering variety of guns. Some he'd used many times before: Heckler & Koch Mark 23 semi-automatics, Benelli M4 Super 90 shotguns and Glock 9mms. Then there were the obscure guns procured from Russia and the Far East. A GM-94 grenade launcher and a PP-19 Bison 2 machine-gun. Weapons so rare that even the Regiment had a tough time getting hold of them.

'Leo said for you to take what you need.'

'Jesus,' Gardner said, approaching one wall and understanding why Aimée needed so much security. He turned to her. 'You're an arms dealer?'

'Nothing quite so grand. I'm just helping people fight the criminals who are trying to ruin Serbia. You're welcome to whatever you want.'

Gardner selected a long, sleek black piece.

'This is—'

'The Sako TRG-22.'

'You know your guns.'

'In my family it was impossible to grow up and not know them.'

Gardner ran a hand over the sniper rifle. He'd used the TRG-22 on combat missions in the Regiment. While the rest of the Armed Forces swore by the Accuracy International L96, SAS operators had a degree of freedom when it came to selecting weapons and gear. Gardner favoured the TRG because it came with a muzzle break that reduced recoil and kickback, and the .308 Winchester rounds were lethally effective up to eight hundred metres. You couldn't ask for more from a sniper rifle.

I'll be targeting John from long range, Gardner reasoned. I need a gun that's going to be surgical from distance. The TRG-22 fitted the bill perfectly.

'I'll take it,' Gardner said.

'What's the business between you and the target?' Aimée asked.

'He used to be a good friend. Not any more.'

'Are you going to kill him?'

'What kind of a question is that?' He kept a tight face. Her eyes hung on him. Gardner felt air freeze in his throat. They stood in silence for several seconds.

'Would you like a drink?' Aimée said.

'That sounds good.'

She led him out to the hallway and into the bedroom opposite. There he sat on the edge of the bed while she popped into the kitchen. The knots in his leg muscles slackened. He heard the clinking of glass and the sticky shuffle of feet on lino.

Aimée returned clutching a bottle of wine in one hand and two glasses in the other. As she put the glasses on her bedside table and poured, Gardner studied her. Her eyes were soft and sharp at the same time, like teardrops on their sides. There were no hard lines on her face and she radiated a kind of inner strength.

'Been a while since I had a glass of Serbian red,' Gardner said. The wine tasted good. It uncorked the pressure building between his ears.

'You've been here before?' she asked him.

'A long time ago.' Images like talons dug deep in the sides of his skull. Burning houses, streets littered with shrapnel.

'Many people have suffered,' she said. 'I have to help take the fight to the enemy. People think a war ends when the soldiers leave. They're wrong.'

'You're preaching to the converted, Aimée.'

She sat on the bed, resting her back against the pillows, her long, smooth legs almost touching Gardner. He noticed the white strap of her bra low on her shoulder. As she adjusted herself the flame top tightened into a knot at her back, pulling the fabric over the curves of her chest.

Gardner drank more wine. Two gulps and he'd almost finished the glass. A pleasant mist settled behind his eyes.

'So, how did you go from being a journalist to helping MI6?'

'It's complicated,' she said, curling a rogue strand of hair around her index finger. 'My father was part of the under-ground resistance to Milosevic's rule. To begin with he fought with words: pamphlets, newspapers, that kind of thing. After Milosevic killed our mother he decided to carry on the strug-gle with guns.'

'I always thought shoot first, ask later was the best policy.'

Aimée smiled.

'My father had one rule for himself, another for everyone else. He was like you.'

She topped up Gardner's glass. The logical part of his mind told him to refuse. He needed to stay alert. He was behind enemy lines. But Land had said the deal would be happening tomorrow noon, and he was grateful for a moment's respite from the stress of his mission. He necked more wine. The alcohol burned cobwebs inside him.

'My father killed many of Milosevic's biggest, baddest thugs,' Aimée went on. 'He even tried to assassinate Milosevic himself. But they caught him, tore off his fingernails and toenails, cut off his nose and threw him over a cliff, leaving him for dead. I was seven years old.' Her breath escaped in spurts. 'My father's friends made me see his body. *So I could never forget*, they told me.' The smile took on worried curves. 'It worked.'

'I'm very sorry to hear that.'

'It was many years ago now. But thank you.'

'And you decided to follow in your father's footsteps?'

'Not exactly. I mean, I respected his work, and his devotion to the cause of a free and liberal Serbia. But, you know, times have changed. In this country there is a big divide between the older people and the young. Those who remember the war don't want to forget or forgive, and their first choice is the gun. The rest of us, the young, all have an iPod. We live in a different world. Today wars are waged on TV screens and newspapers.'

'But the weapons racks—?'

'Yes, Joe?'

'I'm not here to cause a riot, Aimée. I want to stop an old friend from doing bad things.'

Her smile evened out and her eyes sighed at him. 'I think Leo was wrong. You're a good man.'

'I don't really know.'

'You are. I see it in your eyes.'

'Sometimes I don't think there are good people any more,' Gardner said. 'Just some people who do something and other people who do nothing.'

'And what does that make you?'

He shrugged. 'Guess I've never really been the type to sit back and let things happen.'

'You're always in control?'

'I try to be.'

An awkward silence passed between them. Gardner fixed his eyes on his wine glass. Rain rapped on the windows.

'And what about if you lost control?'

He raised his eyes and saw Aimée was sitting up straight. She let her gaze trace around the edges of Gardner's face. She placed her glass on the floor next to the sofa. Licked her lips and pushed herself across the coffee table, wrapping her arms tight around his neck. He leaned in and let her kiss him across the divide. She kissed him hard. Gardner pulled her close and saw that her eyes were clamped shut, as if she was fighting not to wake up from a powerful dream.

fifty

Sotov was carving a dollar sign into the whore's face when the call came.

Bad fucking timing.

He paused, the knife point suspended above her left eyebrow. Blood trickled into a carmine river above her brow and streamed down her nose. Droplets fell from the tip and on to her trembling lips. Each drop made her shiver.

Sotov was torn between taking the call and telling the assistant to say he was busy. It had become increasingly hard for him to source good women. Russian girls were out of the question. They aroused too much suspicion. So he had resorted to flying them in from the old satellite states, and some from further afield. China, Venezuela, Vietnam. They were cheaper, and so was their silence.

You have to take the call, he was thinking. The girl can wait.

The Lithuanian prostitute gave a muted cry. Her eyes rested on the knife grip wrapped around his pale fingers. The two other prostitutes, a couple of black-haired Chinese, were being paid to watch. The Lithuanian was a redhead with such a perfectly symmetrical face that it almost felt scandalous to mark her in such a way. Almost.

His assistant handed him his mobile.

'Someone's watching Bald,' the voice said.

'Shit,' Sotov growled. 'Who? No one knows about this. I've paid the FSB off, for fuck's sake.'

There was a pause at the other end of the line. Sotov knew the man used an iridium-powered satellite phone for security purposes. He found the time delay maddening.

'Forgive me,' the man said. 'I'm not sure how he learned of Bald's intentions.' Another pause. 'I think he might be an old friend.'

'When I want your opinion,' Sotov replied, 'I'll fucking well ask you for it.' His rage shot down the line. 'Do we even have a name for this cunt?'

'Joe Gardner,' the man's voice quietening. 'I understand he's a former soldier.'

Sotov's right hand twitched. The blade sank a quarter of an inch into the girl's forehead and a scream pierced the walls.

He motioned for the two Chinese girls to suck each other's tits. They climbed on to the ornamental four-poster bed once owned by the Romanovs, now enjoying pride of place in the private bedroom of Sotov's twenty-room mansion in Moscow. He always came to the capital for this sort of thing. You couldn't very well ask girls to fly to Siberia. And somehow it seemed more appropriate amid the decadence of Moscow, where the bankers paid to watch their wives fuck other men and the noble politicians of the Duma buried truths and people in equal abundance.

Sotov watched the Chinese girls as one nibbled at the other. The girls moaned, like they were genuinely having a good time.

'What would you like me to do, Aleks?'

'Kill him,' Sotov said.

'He's with a girl. Kill her too?'

Sotov sipped from a glass of finest-grain Scotch malt whisky. 'No. I want the girl.'

Call over, Sotov went back to work. Anger boiled in his veins. He wanted to make the redhead cry. She whimpered as he cleaned the blade on a napkin and pressed the serrated tip against the warm, doughy flesh of her breast. Her breathing was fitful. Forget this soldier: he's a fucking small fish in a very big pond, he told himself.

fifty-one

Gardner woke early. He watched the light from the street lamp, crisp and bright as sulphur, decanting through the inch-wide gap between the curtains. The light coloured in the faces on the holiday and family snaps lining the wall. Every square milli-metre of space was devoted to pictures and press cuttings, old birthday cards and poems. Gardner lived without a past and not much of a present. He didn't have a Facebook profile or Twitter page and, as far as he knew, no photos of him existed since he was a teenager. It wasn't a lifestyle choice. It was the only way he knew. But, looking at Aimée's wall of friends and fond memories, he felt a little hollow at his core.

He sensed the bracelet on his wrist. Hated the feel of the plastic against the hairs on his skin. Tagged like a fucking paedophile, he thought. Suddenly he hungered for freedom. Manoeuvring his body so he didn't wake Aimée, he brought his wrist to his mouth. Snagged the lock between his teeth and yanked at the bracelet. Something snapped. It came loose. He tossed the bracelet to the floor. It landed somewhere amid the sea of clothes.

Aimée stirred. Her head rested on his chest, the flat of her nose using the curved ridge of his pectoral muscles as a pillow. When he peered down at her he saw only a head of ruffled hair. But Gardner felt her breath rise up his chest and stream on to his chin. She kissed his chest, then the side of his neck, working her way up muscle by muscle. Finally she kissed him on the lips and rubbed her nose against his stubbled cheek. Her face – fifty per cent sleepy and fifty per cent smiley – pronounced her happiness.

'It's early,' she said.

'You can go back to sleep.'

'Are you kidding? I'm not sleepy at all.'

'Me neither,' said Gardner. He swung his legs over the side of the bed, rubbed sleep from his eyes. In the Regiment he got by on two or three hours' sleep a night. These days it was more like five or six. He was getting slack.

'I have to go,' he said.

'Already?' Aimée made a noise in the base of her throat, like a poorly dog. 'Damn it, and there I was thinking you could wait just a few more hours before killing evil drug dealers.'

'I might be persuaded to leave a few minutes late.'

'Persuaded – how?'

'Surprise me.'

The noise in her throat came again, now a note higher. She squeezed his right bicep. Her fingers traced the route of his bluish veins, visible on the surface like steel cables. 'They're so soft and smooth,' she said. 'I thought they'd be harder.'

Her left hand slid under the thin white sheet that covered them from the waist down. He felt her fingers against the inside of his leg. Her fingertips were warm and he felt a pang of electricity course through his body when she touched him.

'People think muscle's rock hard, but that's not the truth.'

'*Every* muscle?' Aimée said.

'Well, maybe one exception.'

Half an hour later Gardner was woken by the revving of an engine and the screech of wet brakes in the street below. He checked his watch. Not yet five. Now the violent slamming of car doors and the urgent pitter-patter of feet on the pavement made him suspicious.

Leaving Aimée to bury her head under the pillows, he slid out of bed, rushed across to the bedroom window, pulled the curtains a little way apart and stared down. He spied a black Land Rover behind his Toyota.

Three figures had debussed from the Land Rover. Two guys Gardner didn't recognize. One was no more than five foot five and shaped like a giant testicle with arms. Gardner spotted a crucifix the size of a GI Joe hanging on the end of a necklace.

The second guy, a lot taller, had a mouthful of gold teeth and a shaved head covered in tattoos: swastikas, skulls, crucifixes. He was decked out in a dark-green Puffa jacket, white vest and black trousers with toe-capped boots.

The third was Valon.

Son of a fucking bitch, Gardner thought.

'What's going on?' Aimée was awake, arching her head up towards him, the outline of her face imprinted on the pillow.

Gardner spun around. 'Grab some clothes. We're leaving.'

'Not before you tell me who's outside.'

'There's no time. Trust me, Aimée. Get up.'

The urgency in his voice spooked her. She threw on a pair of tight jeans and a Nike T-shirt while Gardner went to grab the TRG-22.

A crash stole Gardner's attention as he stepped across the hallway. The sound of wood splitting, metal buckling. He froze. The goons were at the periphery of his vision, the door busted open. Valon stood between them. He held up his hands. He was toting a gun. Testicle squeezed past Tattoo and marched down the hallway.

At three metres' distance, Gardner dropped his right shoulder, faking to swing with his left. Then he dug his fingertips into his palm to form a sharp ridge with the first knuckle joints. Testicle moved to cover his face with his enormous arms, leaving his stomach exposed. Gardner set his sights on a gut shot, hoping to knock the wind out of his sails. He rammed his knuckles into the guy's abdomen.

Pain gnawed at his hand. His fingers burned. What he'd figured was a fleshy gut was in fact a hard wall of muscle. Testicle's abs were swollen up like sandbags.

The goon chuckled. His fat fingers clamped themselves tight around Gardner's head and wrenched his neck back. Gardner's chin was level with Testicle's forehead.

As Testicle punched him on the jaw, Gardner felt his body defy gravity. He was on the ground one second, airborne the next. Testicle shrank from view as the force of the punch flung Gardner several metres down the hallway. His back smacked against the lino floor. Pain sprang up in clusters along his spine.

'Fuck you, man,' roared Testicle, shaking his wrist.

Tattoo trained the business end of a Sig Sauer P229 on Gardner. In his enormous hand the big fuck-off pistol looked like a joke gun-lighter.

'Take her and you'll fucking pay,' Gardner said. 'When I'm done with you, there won't be anything left to identify you, except for your tiny fucking dick.'

'Sure, man,' said Tattoo, stepping closer to Gardner. 'Whatever makes you feel better.' On the last word he pistol-whipped Gardner in the face, stunning him. Gardner's head rang with pain, and the next thing he knew, Tattoo had yanked his hands behind his back, restraining him.

Testicle walked into the bedroom. A moment later Gardner heard Aimée scream and the slap of a hand against flesh. 'Fucking bitch,' rasped Testicle as he dragged Aimée out into the hallway.

'I'm sorry, Aimée,' Gardner said.

'Get this bastard off me!'

'I'm going to get you free. Don't worry. Everything's going to be OK.'

'Yeah, listen to your boyfriend,' said Testicle. 'You remember his words while we're raping the shit out of your pussy.'

Testicle manhandled Aimée out of the flat. Tattoo followed, nudged past Valon, Aimée's squeals echoing up and down the stairwell. Valon said something that Gardner couldn't quite catch. Next thing he knew, Valon was directing the pistol at his temple.

Gardner squinted at the black hole of the muzzle. Frost spread from his spine down to his hands and feet. He couldn't move: the gun had him in a trance. So this is how it ends, he thought. Killed by a fucking chancer.

A flash, a sound so loud it seemed as if a grenade had kicked off inside his skull. Blood leaking from his nose, his eardrum throbbing. Taste of burnt gas on his lips, the smell of it in the air. To his left, a neat bullet hole burned into the lino floor.

And the realization that he wasn't dead.

He looked up. Valon was running down the hallway.

How did he miss me from that range? Gardner wondered.

Petrol fumes stung his throat. He watched in a daze as Testicle slopped a jerrycan of the stuff around the hallway. On the floor, over the walls. Petrol dripped from Aimée's framed newspaper clippings. When he'd fully doused the hallway, Testicle paced to the front door, turned and removed a thick roll of paper from his back pocket. With his cigarette lighter he torched the end of the paper and chucked it towards the petrol.

The fire spread spontaneously, fast. Flames licked at the walls. Glass cracked. Plastic blackened. Smoke thick and grey as charcoal rapidly filled the hallway. Gardner's eyes reddened.

He choked on the fumes.

Get out of here – before you die.

fifty-two

Gardner ran to the end of the hallway and ducked into the room on his left, smoke and burning plastic stinging his throat. Slinging the TRG-22 sniper rifle over his shoulder and grabbing a Glock 9mm as a secondary firearm, he retraced his steps to the bedroom and made a beeline for the window looking down on to the street. Testicle was slamming the door of a black Land Rover, Tattoo jumping in the other side. Valon behind the wheel.

Flames hissed at the bedroom door. He felt the heat on his back, smelled the melting paint. Gardner yanked at the window. Fucking fastened shut! He tugged at the rusted brass lock. No dice.

Grabbing the butt of the TRG-22, he swung it like a base-ball bat against the glass. He was grateful for single glazing as the two large panes smashed with one clean swing. He raked the remaining shards with the muzzle of the sniper rifle. Fresh air hit him and he sucked in hungry breaths. Then he climbed through the gap head first, the balls of his feet balancing on the window ledge.

The drop to the pavement was about fifteen metres. High enough to be dangerous, low enough to be Gardner's only realistic way of escaping the fire. He might break a leg, or he might walk away unharmed. The jump was a lottery. But with the fire eating up the hallway, he had to buy a ticket.

Gardner pushed himself off the ledge as the Land Rover raced off. He extended his arms at his sides like wings to balance his body as it dropped. The wind gushed over him. The pavement grew larger and larger until he could see nothing else.

He closed his eyes as he hit the concrete shoulder first. A dull throb swam from his ankle joint right up to his shoulder blade. He felt as if someone had clubbed him on his right side.

Picking himself off the ground and checking himself for injuries, Gardner rifled through his pockets. My car keys. I can still stop them. They can't have gone far.

The Toyota was ten metres away. As Gardner beat a path to it he hocked up cloying, blackened phlegm. He chucked the TRG-22 and the Glock on the passenger seat, shoved the key into the ignition and pulled out into the main street, swerving to avoid an approaching fire engine. Looking back, he saw the flames engulf the entire third floor of the apartment block.

Soon hitting 110 in a forty-kilometre zone, Gardner wrenched the steering wheel hard left. Matchsticks lit under his wrists. The Toyota slalomed left at the end of Gavrilo Principa. He'd studied the layout of Belgrade for months in advance of the Kosovo War and knew that Gavrilo Principa was one-way. The only way out was left.

At 0525 the roads were deserted. Gardner throttled the Toyota, reaching 130. He spotted the Land Rover sixty metres ahead as it banged a right. Gardner jerked the wheel to his right, the Toyota screeching under the pressure. He eased off and at the apex of the turn he hit the accelerator again and levelled out. He'd reduced the distance to the Land Rover to thirty metres.

Clink!

A bullet starred the windscreen. One, two, three rounds cracked the glass. Then Gardner heard the clunk of hot lead thwacking against hard leather as the rounds ripped into the passenger seat. He swerved left, then right, in a zigzag manoeuvre.

Sparks bounced off the bonnet. The shooter couldn't get a fix, he reckoned, loosing off shots in the hope one would strike lucky.

Gardner urged the Toyota up to 145. He was gaining on the Land Rover. Fifteen metres now. Close enough to see Aimée's tinted-grey outline in the back seat.

They were heading out of the city.

Crack!

Another round. This one missed the windscreen and the bonnet. Gardner thought the trajectory might have sent it high into the air. But an angry hiss set the record straight. The bullet had punched a hole in one of his tyres.

He had no time to react. No time to think. The Toyota wobbled. He was fucked. He felt the motor shudder under the pressure. Shudder, then slide. He wrestled with the wheel. No fucking use. He could feel the lack of friction. The Toyota swapped the road for the fence of a small park. The fence beckoned. Gardner applied maximum force to the brakes. Braced himself for impact.

The crash damn near threw him out of his seat, but his arms were locked tight around the wheel. G-force kicked his arse, smashing his forehead against the dashboard and unleashing waves of pain across his skull. His jawbone tremored, as if someone had taken a defibrillator to the sides of his face. *Rat-rat-rat* went the Toyota's engine in its death throes. Steam fluttered out of the grille.

Gardner gathered his senses. He mopped blood from his nose and looked to his right. Forty metres ahead, the Land Rover had stopped at a deserted junction. A single lamppost gave the asphalt a spit and polish; a wire fence sealed off naked farmland. In the distance he could see a cottage, lights off.

A white Ford Transit pulled up smartly alongside the Land Rover, breaking the silence. Testicle and Tattoo bundled

Aimée into the back of the van while Valon looked on approvingly. He watched the Transit head off into the distance, the two heavies and the girl with it.

Now Valon began to walk over to Gardner. He was wielding an AK-47.

Gardner kicked open the driver-side door. The TRG-22 was lying on the passenger seat, the Glock 9mm on the floor. Seizing both, he climbed out of the wreckage. He still felt disoriented. The world jarred. A shrill sound perforated his left eardrum, as if mice were crawling inside. Every muscle in his body ached.

Then came the shots. A maddening volley of them, metal shredding metal, the contorted Toyota shell lighting up like it was fucking bonfire night. Bullets whirred into the chassis. Gardner heard leather tear, the wheezing of tyres. Any one of the rounds could bounce off a hard metal front, deflect into the path of his brain like a squash ball. That's all it would take, he thought, as he ducked for cover behind the chassis.

Valon's going to finish you off.

No. I won't let that happen.

He steadied himself. Christ, his body was in bad nick. But he had to forget about the pain. He closed his eyes and silenced it. Opened them and saw Valon, twenty metres away, inserting a fresh clip into the AK.

More bounds chopped up the Toyota. Gardner placed the TRG-22 on the ground and grabbed the Glock. It felt light and cold in his hands. He chambered a round of 9x19 Parabellum ammunition. He was counting Valon's shots like a kid memorizing his times table.

Seven, eight, nine . . .

On the twentieth and final round, Gardner risked a peek over the Toyota. Valon was eight metres off, reaching for a third clip. The Toyota had more holes in it than a political manifesto. Gardner crept around to the boot. On a three-count he shot to his feet.

'Drop it, or I'll drop you like a fucking bad habit,' he said, his voice firm and steady as the Glock pointed at Valon's mug.

The guy's right hand held the AK by the underside of the barrel. His left was suspended by his side, like a gunslinger in a shoot-out. Gardner had caught him about to reload. Valon beamed a bad-toothed smile, opening his arms in a bear hug.

'The fucking rifle, Klint.'

Valon laid the AK on the ground like a mourner laying flowers at a memorial. 'Shit, OK, bro. OK. See? I'm not armed now.' He was still smiling. 'What the fuck's this, man? This is how you greet an old friend?'

Gardner edged out from the shelter of the Toyota. 'Yeah, next time I see a mate I'll lock him in a burning flat, then shoot the shit out of his car.'

'We had to take the girl. Orders are orders. You're a soldier. You know how this shit works.'

'You're no soldier, Klint.'

'Harsh, bro. And after all we've been through.'

The sun crept above Valon's back. Gardner didn't fancy hanging about in the sticks. First law of any firefight – always displace. He waved the pistol towards the Land Rover. Valon got the message: *move.* When they reached the vehicle Gardner nudged Valon into the driver's seat. Sat in the back himself, the Glock resting between his knees, eyeballing Valon's seat.

'Try any funny business and I'll put one through your spine.'

Valon turned the engine on. The Land Rover growled.

'Where to, man?'

'Where's the girl?' asked Gardner.

'You don't want to know.'

'Think so?' He tightened his face into a scowl. 'You and me are gonna have a little chat.'

fifty-three

Blame the synthetics, Sotov liked to say. Beautiful, man-made rocks produced using chemical vapour deposition in American laboratories, burning carbon at temperatures in excess of 800°C. They looked exactly like the real thing. Even to the expert eye, distinguishing synthetic from real diamonds was increasingly hard.

They flooded the market, the synthetic diamonds, lowering the cost of organically harvested rocks and eating into the profits of mining operations like Sotov's. Then there were the arseholes in suits who demanded he line their pockets. The state officials, the meddling politicians in the Duma. Everyone took their cut.

To be sure, there was not much money in diamonds these days. Drugs were the real cash-spinner. Always had been. He could make more in a single drugs deal than in a month of dealings with the corrupt diamond merchants. Although it benefited Sotov to have a legitimate business empire – made him look respectable. If it wasn't for that single benefit, he would have sold up the diamond business a long time ago.

The fifty kilos of cocaine he was acquiring was worth $30 million in America, but he intended to sell the coke on to contacts he'd acquired through his years of service in the *Mafya*. Contacts that had taken a lifetime to build up, ever since his early days as a *vor v zakone*, a thief-in-law. Thanks to his influence, in less than twenty-four hours he'd be rich once more. Thirty million could buy a lot of hookers.

Sotov paused at the edge of the forest clearing and lit a Ziganov. He allowed his body a moment to acclimatize. Compared to Yakutsk, Serbia in the early autumn was positively tropical. Warm air swirled in his nostrils. His mouth was dry, a severe case of cotton mouth, and the cigarette did not taste good. He took three drags on the cigarette before stubbing it out on a rock. Then he paced briskly back down towards the clearing, where a Lincoln Navigator was parked up.

A dirt track led from the clearing into the main road some two hundred metres away. Popov the chauffeur leaned against the hood of the Lincoln and ran a hand through his silver hair. The four-man team under Sotov's command was equipped with OTS-33 automatic pistols he'd acquired by bribing an army officer. Popov himself was ex-Spetsnaz – Sotov considered it wise to travel with a guy who could shoot as well as drive – and had an AK-47 as his primary weapon, a virtually indestructible assault rifle that could be burned, frozen and buried and still work perfectly.

The greatest legacy of our Soviet Union, thought Sotov. A brutally effective gun.

These men – Popov and the other four – were Sotov's finest soldiers, the ones he could rely on when he needed something done and done right. Popov watched as the others diligently performed last-minute checks on their firearms, going through their paces. Sotov knew there was no room for error. The exchange had to be quick and smooth, and he didn't trust the Italians an inch.

Sotov checked his Rolex. Ten-fifteen.

Not long to go now.

He turned back to Popov.

'It's time.'

Popov nodded; his phone rang. He showed Sotov the text message. 'We're in place,' it said. 'Awaiting further orders.'

Popov looked at Sotov. 'Something on your mind?' he asked.

'The first fire team is already at the site,' Sotov replied.

'That's good.' Sensing that Sotov was still not satisfied, Popov added, 'I have a good feeling about this operation, Aleks.'

'I hear from Valon that Petruzzi – the man they call the Pallbearer – is a greedy fuck.' He felt a laugh ripple in his lungs, didn't quite make it to the surface.

'When are the Italians ever anything else?'

Sotov laughed out loud now. 'You're right. As always, Denis.' He smiled at Popov. 'That's why I trust you so much. Other *vory v zakone* are like crows. Their only interest is to line their own pockets. They speak of loyalty. Bullshit. They know nothing of the word. But you—' Sotov patted Popov on the back. The chauffeur went to say something, cut himself short.

fifty-four

They drove in silence for several minutes, due west along Route 19, until Gardner indicated for Valon to take a left turn. As they headed south the motorway corkscrewed past an old farm, its overgrown fields populated by mangy goats and starved sheep, an early nineties Nissan Firebird out front. A minute later they came to an abandoned depot west of the Makis freight station. Gardner ordered Valon to stop the car.

They got out, Gardner keeping the Glock on Valon. The earth was reclaiming the train tracks, grass shoots clawing at the old iron path. Three hundred metres to the north-east stood the functioning Lokomotiv depot. Just after eight o'clock in the morning and the mechanical grunts of trains stopping and starting carried on the chill air. Gardner and Valon were too far away for the rail workers to spot them. He led the Albanian towards the carcass of an old train carriage, its rusting frame dumped at the end of the line. Gardner recalled this spot from his operations here as a Blade. They'd settled on the disused depot as an RV point in the event of the op going tits up.

Once they reached the depot, Gardner got down to business.

He brought his pistol hand down hard on to the dip between Valon's shoulders, heard the crunch of the grip connecting with bone. Valon dropped like shit out of a dog's arse. His body made unnatural sounds as Gardner smothered him with body blows. The guy writhed this way and that. Gardner booted him in the ribcage, then the gut. Then the balls. He eased off, allowing Valon to catch his breath. The guy was on his hands and knees, scrambling to catch his breath. His mouth open, he sucked at the ground.

'Where'd you take her?'

'*Fuck*—' Valon angled his head up at Gardner, his voice no more than a cancerous rasp.

'Wrong answer, mate.'

Gardner raised the Glock parallel with his elbow – then swung it in an arc. The pistol swept down and smashed into Valon's face. His hands gave way; his knees buckled. The front of Gardner's T-shirt was flecked with red dots. Something dark and sticky clung to the end of the Glock's barrel.

Getting down on one knee, Gardner lifted Valon's head. He was fucked. A three-inch dent stretched like an oversized leech from his ear to his jaw. His forehead and nose were freckled with blood, and snot around his mouth had mixed with dirt from the ground to form a sort of sandy paste covering his chin.

'I fucking swear, mate, the next one is a bullet in your head. Do you understand?' Valon gave a battered nod. 'Now, where the fuck is Aimée?'

'Is that her name? Very cute.' He slurred his words. 'Forget her, Joe. She's better off dead. And she soon will be.'

The fury crescendoed from Gardner's stomach to the small of his throat.

'So where is she?'

Valon's silence answered for him.

'What are you doing working with John Bald?'

'Fuck your mother.'

'When's the exchange happening?'

'Shit, brother. You kill me and you'll never see Bald or the girl again.' Gardner pressed the Glock against Valon's temple.

Do it, he was thinking. One shot. That's all it'd take. Put a hole in his noggin that you could drive a cattle rod through.

No. I can't kill him. Not with Aimée out there, not with Bald on the verge of making his deal.

He pulled the gun away.

'Give me your hand, brother,' he said.

Valon obeyed. Stubborn cunt, Gardner thought as he directed the muzzle at Valon's balls. The Albanian offered up his left hand instead of his right. Gardner fished the red bracelet from his pocket and clicked it around his bony wrist.

'Hey, what the fuck is this?'

'This bracelet's loaded with bang-bang powder,' Gardner said, making up a spot of bullshit. This guy's a sly cunt, he thought, but he ain't exactly clever.

'It operates on a remote-control detonator. One press of the clicker and you won't be doing any hand shandies for a long time. Try and take it off, you'll short the circuit – boom. See, you're going to lead me to John Bald, mate. And I'm going to put the drop on him.'

Valon eyed the bracelet, his pupils bulging like white poker chips. He'd clearly bought Gardner's line about the explosives. 'You're fucking crazy, brother. Bald will notice this.'

'Then tell him you're trying to make poverty history, I don't give a fuck. But you'd better come clean, or I'll blow your arm to fucking mush.'

'Shit. OK, OK.' Valon snatched at air. Sweat trickled down the sides of his head. 'The meeting is at a place called the Presevo Valley. It's about 320 kilometres south of Belgrade, maybe a bit further.'

'I know it,' Gardner said. The valley, near the border with Macedonia, had been a hotbed of ethnic violence in the war. In the years since then it had become the site of conflict between the Kosovo Liberation Army and Serbian security forces.

'Where in the valley?'

'On the E-75. Near the village of Brezovan.'

'What time?' Gardner said.

'Noon today,' Valon said back.

'And you're John's bodyguard?'

'Fuck no, man. Don't insult me, I'm more important than that,' Valon snorted, bringing up phlegm. 'I'm here to make the introduction between Bald and the Russian.'

'The Russian?'

'A *Mafya* guy, name of Sotov.' He flashed a look at Gardner. 'He's the one who told me to kidnap the bitch. They call him the Grey Wolf.'

'Some kind of a joke?'

'Don't you get it, bro? He's *Mafya*. He's got this big diamond company, lots of money, and he's a stone-cold killer. Fuck, man, you don't mess with this guy. I'm fucking serious. He's a real player.'

Daybreak announced itself in harsh, unforgiving rays. We'll be visible to the depot workers if we stick around much longer, Gardner realized. He watched Valon wipe his nose with the sleeve of his coat, then ordered him to his feet.

'Tell me about your plan,' he said.

Valon struggled to stand upright. His legs wobbled, he remained unsteady. 'I'm supposed to rendezvous with Bald at nine o'clock on the dot. We run through a checklist, get our shit together and head out to the meet.'

'At Presevo?'

Valon nodded, eyes on his sleeve.

'In the car,' Gardner said. 'Head to your get-together with Bald. I want you to pretend like nothing's happened. You go to the drug swap. When the deal's done and dusted, you pretend you lost the car keys. Search the ground and stay the fuck away from Bald. And if you say a word about me, I'll blow your bloody arm off.'

'You're gonna kill him, aren't you?' Valon ran his hands over the ugly wound on the side of his face. The flesh had coloured a kind of oily black, as if his cheeks were made out of rubber.

'I'm here to bring him in, that's all.'

'Nah, brother. I see it in your eyes.'

'Just get a fucking move on.'

After Valon left in the Land Rover, Gardner handrailed the road north, back to the 19 motorway. He kept fifteen metres between himself and the road, manoeuvring along a parallel path a metre lower than the road and blanketed by trees. He passed dead animals: rotting cats and rats. Took him twelve minutes to reach the same farm he'd passed on the trip down with Valon.

Gardner walked eighty metres beyond the farm, then turned around and retraced his route. His eyes were alert for any sign of movement or activity. The farm seemed to be empty, the road likewise. He unhooked the wooden gate at the front of the property. Goats chewed cud and blinked at him as he approached the old Nissan Firebird. It was a clapped-out motor, but easy to jack. No hi-tech alarms or locking mechanisms to piss about with.

He broke the driver's window with the Glock and opened the door from the inside. Then he hot-wired the engine and reversed out of the drive.

It was now 0840 hours, leaving Gardner barely enough time to hit Presevo Valley. He estimated the driving time at three hours clean if he kept his foot to the pedal. He'd rock up to the meeting point twenty minutes before the meeting.

But you can't leave Aimée, he agonized.

Right now, I don't have a fucking choice. I'm out of time.

His ultimate objective – the termination of John Bald – loomed in his mind. Unlike action heroes in the movies, Regiment operators took the business of killing seriously. Gardner liked to say that no man could understand the power of one man over another, the power to take his life, until he'd held a Glock 9mm in his hands and pointed it at another man's head. Taking the life of a friend he'd known for fifteen years wasn't something he relished. He reconciled himself to the fact that Bald had taken a path he himself couldn't agree with. The drugs, the money, luring Gardner to Rio. He'd betrayed the Regiment code.

When he was about a hundred kilometres from his destination, Gardner put a call in to Land.

'Christ, man,' Land said. 'I've been trying to contact you for *hours*. What the devil is going on down there?'

'That streak of piss Valon. He ambushed Aimée's apartment.'

'Good God.' A curious pause had followed. 'What – what the hell were you doing at Aimée's place all that time?'

Gardner ignored him. 'Valon took Aimée hostage. Handed her over to some bloke called Sotov. He's *Mafya*.'

He waited for Land to say something, but the Firm man stayed silent.

'You stitched me up,' Gardner said, finally.

'Nonsense,' Land snapped. 'I warned you that he was in with a bad crowd. You went into this mission with your eyes wide open, Joe. Just because it's getting a bit uncomfortable doesn't mean you can start bandying accusations about.'

'Spare me the bollocks,' Gardner said. 'There's more than the 'Ndrangheta and the Serbs involved here. You didn't say anything about the fucking Russian *Mafya* sticking their hands in the pie.'

Gardner heard people talking near to Land. 'The Russians were a source,' Land said. 'But we couldn't confirm their attachment to the deal one away or the other. Your work has proved that they are indeed involved.' He sniffed. 'You might think you're one step ahead of the Firm, dear chap. But in truth you're just another soldier doing exactly what we tell him to do. No more – and no less.'

'There's one thing you and your mate Macca definitely called wrong,' Gardner said. 'John Bald's not selling to the Italians. He's doing business with the Russians.'

'Yes,' said Land impatiently. 'And the 'Ndrangheta are the protection for him, in return for receiving a cut of the profits. We know. The Firm's been aware of this development since last night. That's why I tried to call you. But from the sounds of it, you were . . . preoccupied?'

'Fuck off!'

'Now, now, Joe—'

'I take John down, this cunt's next on the list.'

'You will do no such thing.' Land sighed. 'If you start taking down Russian *Mafya* – particularly those with links to the government – then you'll cause a diplomatic incident. And if that happens, you're on your own.'

Gardner felt something scratch at his throat.

'I'm not abandoning Aimée.'

'And I'm not asking you to. Look, bring Valon in alive after you've killed Bald. He knows Sotov. I'm certain Valon can lead us to your woman friend, given a little encouragement.'

'Fuck it,' Gardner said. 'I'm on my way to Presevo now. I can just make it ahead of time. Valon gave me the location. I'm going to get there before John—'

And then you're going to kill him, he thought.

A pause.

'Stop him, Joe,' said Land quietly. 'Whatever it takes.'

fifty-five

The E-75 motorway cut through Europe like a scimitar. It ran from Vardo in Norway down to Sitia at the fag end of Greece. It coursed like a river through the basin of the Presevo Valley, straddling the five-kilometre buffer zone separating Serbia from Kosovo. The land was harsh and fallow. Grey dew on the tips of the rotten-brown valley grass. The few towns dotted about the spruce-stippled slopes of the valley looked as if the NATO bombing campaign had taken place the previous night. If Belgrade was the modern face of Serbia, Presevo was an ugly reminder of its past.

The past, Gardner wondered. They say history's written by the victors. Well, I'm going to write John Bald's history. I'll write it in fucking bullets and blood.

He noticed a sign indicating a turn-off eight kilometres ahead for the village of Brezovan.

Gardner had raced at 130 kilometres an hour almost the entire distance to Presevo and was arriving in good time. Along the way he'd stopped at a café, gorged himself on a fatty burek filled with hot cheese and spinach, and a generous serving of coffee. The caffeine was working its magic. Energy gushed through his body, like someone had turned on a tap inside him, and he could feel his lungs expand and compress in his chest.

Five kilometres now.

He ran through the plan one more time in his mind. Valon would lead John to the meeting point and the Italians as backup. The deal would take place. Once the Russians had fucked off, he would line Bald up in his sights and pop a round clean through his head. Valon wouldn't back out of the plan. Mainly because he believed the bracelet attached to his wrist was riddled with explosive det cord.

But that still leaves Aimée, he realized.

The cynical part of his brain figured that she was just another in a long line of women who meant less and less the longer he spent with them. But another part asked, why was he so desperate to rescue her?

Because it's your fault she got snatched in the first place. If you hadn't got involved, she would never have been a target. But thinking about her isn't going to help right now, he decided. I need to focus on the mission. I put Bald six feet under, then I worry about saving Aimée.

He flexed the muscles in his neck. They hardened.

Two kilometres.

Suddenly the valley plateaued. Traffic thinned. He came to the Brezovan turn-off, took the slip road. Gardner went easy on the pedal. Down to eighty, sixty, forty . . .

Gardner scanned the rest stop two hundred metres down the slip road. The road was vacant. The rest stop was a sixty-metre strip of rocky asphalt. A barbed-wire fence ran parallel to the stop on the valley side, backing on to a tired, weather-beaten field, home to a couple of diseased-looking cows.

The meeting point.

Perfect location, Gardner thought. No secret hiding places, right out in the open and with a quick avenue of escape – the E-75 – if things didn't go according to plan.

That left him with the problem of where to ditch his wheels and observe unseen. The old banger had one advantage: it came with a worn atlas of Serbia. He studied the arterial roads and turn-offs on the motorway either side of the Brezovan exit and drew up a mental list of possible vantage points.

He took the slip road. There was no traffic in front or behind him. Brezovan wasn't the kind of place people visited. More like escaped from. It was a village in the loosest possible sense of the word.

A hundred and fifty metres ahead of the rest stop, Gardner spotted a ramshackle petrol station. The map had marked out the station as closed since the Albanian insurgency in 2001. No shit, he thought. The forecourt concrete was split open with weeds, the pumps rusted and the signage AWOL.

Gardner brought the Nissan to a halt next to the station. He glanced in his rear-view mirror. Eleven forty-five and no sign of the Shogun.

Grabbing the TRG-22, Gardner hurried ten metres across the forecourt. He knelt by a crumbling, three-metre-high pillar to the south-west of the rest stop. The pillar, combined with the bank of old pumps, obscured him from passing vehicles. From here he had a good view of the asphalt strip. A horse chestnut tree towered over the scrubland beyond the rest stop, and behind it a bank of spruces helped muffle the noise from the motorway. A hundred metres west of the chestnut sloped a gentle hill scattered with rocks. Gardner had considered the hill as an alternative vantage point. But, unlike the petrol station, it lacked an easy access road, and eventually he'd decided against it.

Gardner assembled the bipod and rested the TRG-22 on top. He rested on his belly in a prone firing position beside the pillar. He piled a few stray lumps of concrete around his position, further concealing his body. Then he adjusted the optics. And waited.

He didn't have to wait long.

fifty-six

The Shogun arrived bang on time. Gardner knew Bald would hit the meeting point a few minutes early. He figured that he had probably scouted out this area two or three times ahead of the meeting, assessing threat scenarios. Like the highly trained operator he was. Or once was, he thought.

The two men debussed. Bald scanned the horizon, Valon fighting to light a cigarette, the breeze blowing out the flame like a candle on a birthday cake. To Gardner's eyes, Bald seemed tetchy. Gardner adjusted his shoulder muscles, and hoped that Valon had kept his fucking piehole shut.

A few minutes later the Italians rocked up.

Valon managed to light his cigarette as the Italians pulled up behind the Shogun at the rest stop. The amber end of his fag oozed smoke.

The 'Ndrangheta fronted in style, three ants disgorging from a silver Bentley Continental Flying Spur. Gardner pressed his eye to the TRG-22 optics and the ants became guys in black trim-cut suits and police shades. A fourth figure took a while longer to emerge. His flaccid cheeks, rotund belly and white hair told Gardner that the guy was the wrong side of seventy. He recalled the photograph Macca had shown him. There was no doubt in his mind that he was looking at the Pallbearer, Gianni Petruzzi.

The *capo crimini* embraced Bald. Brief handshake with Valon. His three goons scoped out the area. One of them was shaven-headed and his shades sat below the steep hill of his temple. He seemed to be in command of the other two men. Gardner caught his breath in his throat as the goon ran his eyes over the petrol station. Gardner was sure he wasn't visible, but the human eye is prone to spot sudden or sharp movements, and the slightest twitch of an elbow, he knew, might alert the guy to his presence.

Finally the goon turned away.

Gardner parted his lips, exhaled.

Petruzzi nodded to the Bentley. The shaven-headed guy paced round to the rear doors, motioned for someone to come out. A figure emerged. Unsteady on his feet, his hands bound behind his back, his face badly fucked up.

At first Gardner didn't recognize the figure staggering towards Bald. His features were swollen and bulged black and blue. His mouth was split open, the right side of his bottom lip sagging and bloody.

Something about his rickety gait buzzed Gardner's memory. *Maston.*

I'm looking at my old fucking Regiment Major.

The shaven-headed *picciotto d'onore* swung his boot at Maston. The ex-Blade stumbled and sank to his knees in the shadow of the horse chestnut. The tree suffered from bleeding cankers, its leaves prematurely shedding, the bark peeling away like orange skin. The spruce trees shivered like mourners at a funeral.

Gardner watched with a grim feeling in his guts. What the fuck are the Italians doing with Maston? He guessed he was just about to find out.

Maston maintained a look of defiance. He stared ahead and past his captors as Bald pointed an accusing finger at the 'Ndrangheta men. For a split second Gardner sympathized with his old mucker. No soldier deserved to be treated like a fucking dog, especially one who'd sacrificed so much for his country.

One of the goons produced a Beretta 92 semi-automatic pistol, beefy and cool as shit. Its stainless-steel barrel winked in the sun's rays. The goon screwed on a suppressor. Coolly lifted the Beretta to the top of Maston's skull. Bald tried to move forward to protect Maston but the three other goons forcibly restrained him.

Gardner couldn't hear the shot, but Maston spasmed as the bullet speared the parietal section at the back of his skull. Blood sprayed out, like a spurt of hot lava. Then his eyes rolled into the back of his head. He keeled over and died.

Bald was ranting at the Italians. If they'd hoped to intimidate Bald by slotting Maston, their scheme had obviously backfired. He went into meltdown. Gardner could see the situation was getting out of control.

Petruzzi gave an order. The shaven-headed guy held his Beretta 92 to the roof of Bald's skull – like he'd done with Maston – and shoved him towards Petruzzi. The *capo crimini* exchanged words with Bald, the Scotsman neither nodding nor shaking his head, his eyes rooted on the fallen body of his old Regiment Major. The Beretta was still aimed at his head.

It was clear what Petruzzi was telling him. Do as we say, or you'll end up like your friend. Each second mixed with the sweat on Gardner's back, running over his knotted muscles. Then the shaven-headed goon spotted something approaching from the slip road to the north and waved to his *amici*.

Gardner took a long draw of breath.

Two more vehicles pulled into the rest stop. A black Lincoln Town Car and, behind it, a Mercedes-Benz eighteen-tonne sleeper truck with a trailer hooked to the back. The trailer was small – Gardner put its capacity at four or five cubic metres, the truck at sixteen – and carried an advert for some sort of frozen-foods company. He recognized the words as Russian.

Italian leather shoes ground cigarette butts into the asphalt. Italian guns were stowed back inside jackets.

I'm ready, Gardner thought. He had plenty of experience using the TRG-22. Unlike most other so-called sniper rifles, the Finnish-designed TRG-22 was developed specifically for long-range target-acquisition ops. He tugged on the bolt and felt the heart of the weapon beat. Shifted his body weight to the right side, nestling the polyurethane stock against his shoulder. The barrel didn't glisten; the last user had painted it black to mask the metallic sheen underneath.

Fourth men got out of the Lincoln, one from the sleeper truck. They were all dressed in sweaters and jeans instead of suits. But to Gardner's eye they looked the real deal. Each man wore a bulletproof vest over his sweater, and rugged Gore-Tex boots. They moved with a swagger.

Gardner saw no weapons.

A fourth Russian, sporting a shock of silver hair and dressed in a grey suit, emerged from the driver's side of the Lincoln. The chauffeur, Gardner figured. The man walked to the rear door while his three mates approached the Italians. They stood four metres from the 'Ndrangheta. No warm hugs or firm handshakes or backslapping. Gardner felt as if he was watching a Mexican stand-off.

The rear window of the Lincoln lowered. The man with the silver hair bent forward, propped an elbow against the window frame and swapped words with a guy in the back seat. He was sitting on the left side, just out of Gardner's view. Gardner saw an arm reclining on leather upholstery, thin and long.

Bald veered between edgy and pissed off. His fists clenched by his sides, he practically blanked the Russians, fixing his dead-eye gaze on Petruzzi. He's no longer in control of the deal, Gardner figured. The Italians were using him to get the money from the Russians – and would waste the Scot for sure as soon as the *Mafya* were out of sight.

On the word from old man Petruzzi, one of the 'Ndrangheta goons fetched a large black suitcase from the boot of the Bentley.

The guy struggled with the weight of it. He dumped the suitcase on the ground, between the Italians and the Russians.

Silver Hair exchanged glances with his mates. He stooped down beside the suitcase gracefully, like he was bowing before royalty. Then he unzipped the suitcase. From Gardner's position he couldn't identify the contents. But Silver Hair's big old smile gave the game away. The coke was all there.

Then Silver Hair clicked his fingers. Another of the Russians zipped up the case, started to lug it towards the back of the Lincoln. The Lincoln sagged a little with the weight of the cocaine. At the same time the driver of the sleeper truck tossed a set of car keys to Bald.

A sonic boom at Gardner's nine o'clock, a shriek fast on its heels. He spotted a second Bentley, this one black, racing into view. An ambush! The car skidded to a halt by its silver cousin, tyres flinging dust clouds into the air. Four men launched out of the car, decked out in identical suits to the 'Ndrangheta. Except for one small detail – they were all brandishing their Beretta 92s in full view. On cue, the three original goons standing beside Petruzzi brandished their own Berettas.

Russian hands slowly pushed skywards in unison. Surrendering. And confirming Gardner's guess that the Italians were making a play for the cash as well as relieving Bald of the cocaine. Sneaky bastards. He expected Silver Hair to be venting his spleen. But the Russian wore an intractable mask.

Petruzzi gestured angrily for Silver Hair to retrieve the suitcase from the Lincoln. Outnumbered, with seven guns trained on them, the Russian was left with little choice but to comply. He calmly relayed the order, and the Lincoln exhaled as another *Mafya* guy removed the suitcase from the boot. Heaved it back towards the 'Ndrangheta. He dumped it beside Silver Hair's feet.

Then Gardner clocked movement on the hill west of the spruce trees.

The shapes were indistinct at first, and an untrained eye would not have spotted them. They moved in a ragged line three-quarters of the way up the hill, so their silhouettes did not stand out against the smooth, undulating background. The spaces between the men – Gardner had counted a dozen of them – were irregular. They moved in among the shadows cast by the scattered rocks. Settled between several large rocks and propped the black-painted barrels of their guns on top.

Who the fuck are these guys? Gardner wondered. More 'Ndrangheta?

But the 'Ndrangheta were oblivious to the men on the hill. Petruzzi's goons forced Bald to hand over the keys to the sleeper truck. Bald chucked them to the ground. Petruzzi bent to scoop them up and, when he stooped, Bald gobbed in his face. The Italian didn't flinch. Instead he produced a spotless-white handkerchief, dabbed it on his forehead and motioned to his goons.

One of the 'Ndrangheta stepped forward and booted Bald in the crotch. The Scot yelped, grabbed his aching nuts and sank to his knees. Petruzzi made a beeline for the sleeper truck, his crippled, weary body carrying him as fast as it would allow.

Gardner turned his attention back to the hill. The twelve-man fire team produced their weapons: fuck-off big FN F2000 bullpup assault rifles, sixty-four centimetres long, with telescopic sights and 40mm FN EGLM grenade launchers attached to the underslung Picatinny rail systems. The F2000 was a hi-tech piece of kit and Gardner had heard all about its lethal rate of fire – 850 rounds a minute – and its bullseye accuracy. The grenade launcher came with a single round of 40x46mm High Explosive ammo. It packed a mean punch: the kind of grenade that could tear a target limb from limb and leave fuck-all for the vultures.

Gardner's bowels constricted.

Then the throats of the F2000s barked.

fifty-seven

1218 hours.

Vicious bursts of rimless brass bullets fractured the air. Through his optics, Gardner could see the cartridge cases ejecting out of a tube running along the side of the hammer-forged barrel. Cases tumbled; bodies soon imitated.

The 'Ndrangheta went over to the dark side. Their bodies jerked as each successive round yawed through their tissue. The F2000 used 5.56x45mm NATO ammo, bullets that fragmented on impact, creating wounds the size of glass tumblers. Chunks of flesh were torn from the goons. Ten seconds in and the seven goons had been razed. Petruzzi, the *capo crimini*, was the last to fall. Several rounds struck him in the back of the head, the cartridges making a strange tinny sound, brass bouncing off his crooked spine.

Beyond the punctured corpses, Silver Hair stood his ground impassively. The Russians weren't fleeing. They weren't targets. So the fire team on the hill must be with Sotov and the *Mafya*, Gardner figured. They'd planned on being backstabbed by the 'Ndrangheta the whole time, and prepared an ambush of their own accordingly.

At the first sound of gunfire, Bald looked to bug the fuck out. He picked up one of the goons' Beretta 92s, forward-rolled towards the cover of the horse chestnut and dropped the nearest *Mafya* guy. Silver Hair and the other two *Mafya* retreated behind the sleeper truck.

Valon had broken into a sprint towards the fields. Bullets zipped around him, his legs breaking the long grass. His run was doomed. The only available cover was a ditch three hundred metres away.

No way he's gonna make it, Gardner thought, then ran his scope over the men on the hills. He needed to protect Valon, because he was the only link to Sotov – and Aimée. He latched on to the nearest target in his optical sights. Breathed out. And . . .

Something inside him froze. He didn't pull the trigger.

Start shooting now, his training voice lectured him, and the Russians will target you next. Eight armed-to-the-teeth *Mafya* against you, in exposed territory? That's a fucking suicide note.

Valon ran for his life. He made it halfway to the ditch, bullets slapping into the dirt around him, scything grass and mud. Finally one of the men on the hill switched tactics. He pressed a breech-release button on the left side of the launcher body and peered down the optics. Tilting the rifle upwards to align the grenade trajectory with the target, he then squeezed the grenade launcher's trigger, located underneath the F2000's standard trigger mechanism.

The EGLM launcher belched. The round whizzed through the air, *crumped* on impact, and Valon disappeared behind a hurricane swirl of smoke. Shrapnel and charred soil showered the grass in a fifteen-metre radius, splashes of blood in the mixer, and Gardner knew the Albanian was shredded.

The Italians are slotted. Valon is down. John's the last man standing.

Swinging his rifle back to the rest stop, Gardner spotted him at the tree. The Scot emptied the last of the Beretta 92's Parabellum rounds at the fire team on the hill. He kept on firing even after the *click-click* of the empty chamber. Never John Bald's way, to admit defeat. Not even in the face of insurmountable odds. Not even now, when he was cornered on both sides.

Seeing Bald was out of ammo, the team on the hill ceased fire. Silver Hair and his two mates edged out from behind the truck. Both groups began to march towards Bald's position. The Scot was slumped against the horse chestnut's trunk. He shot glances at his three o'clock and nine, then crawled around the tree. His eyes flicked towards the Shogun, as if he still believed there was a way out.

Gardner swallowed his spit. He wasn't going to shoot Bald and give up his position. The thought briefly crossed his mind that he could take down the fire team, save Bald's arse. He dismissed it.

I've repaid what he did for me in Afghanistan ten times over.

Bald rested his head against the tree trunk's bleeding cankers. His chest heaved, his head arched skywards, his eyes closed. The fire team were fifty metres from him; Silver Hair and his mates less than half that distance. Bald seemed to whisper something to himself, but his lips hardly moved and Gardner couldn't make out any of what he was saying.

Opening his eyes, Bald snarled at the pistol on his lap. Cast it aside, as if disgusted that it had let him down in his hour of need.

'There's nothing to save you now, John,' Gardner found himself saying under his breath. Part of him wanted to be the one to kill Bald. Having come so far, and with the history they shared, it seemed only right that he should take Bald's life. Instead some greasy Russian fucks were going to do the job for him.

End of the fucking line.

A few steps closer and Silver Hair was almost at the tree. To the west, the twelve angry men on the hill kept their F2000s directed at Bald. The rifles were intimidating in their size: each man looked like he was wrestling with a shark.

Bald reached for something at his ankle. A knife, strapped in place with black masking tape. He tore the four-inch blade free. Sprang to his feet. Charged at Silver Hair, one last act of defiance.

Got to within ten metres.

The F2000s boomed.

Bald jolted as rounds thrust into his torso. Bullets ripped out clods of flesh. Dozens of shots tore into him. His arms and legs twitched. After three or four seconds the shooting stopped. Bald raised an arm to his chest, trying to plug holes the size of coffee mugs dotted along his front. Blood fountained out of his wounds. He staggered for a moment, his arms hanging loose. The knife dropped from his hand, stabbed the soil.

Silver Hair placed a cigarette between his lips and flicked open a Zippo lighter. He took a long drag on the tab, eyes never veering from Bald. The Scot managed a limp step further towards the *Mafya* man. Silver Hair spared him the effort by walking right up to Bald. Blew smoke in his face.

Bald collapsed, and Gardner was left looking at a bloody pile of clothes.

fifty-eight

Silver Hair smoked the rest of his cigarette while the fire team dispersed beyond the crest of the hill. He heard the hoarse throttle of an engine some two hundred metres distant. He took the car keys from Petruzzi's corpse. Done with his cigarette, he tossed the butt into the pool of blood laking around Bald, turned on his heels and strolled back to the Lincoln.

Gardner spied Silver Hair jumping into the front seat. He tossed the car keys to one of the *Mafya* goons, who promptly stowed the suitcase in the boot and climbed into the sleeper truck's driving seat. The engine sputtered. He reversed into the main road, the Lincoln following.

Gardner was alone. Just him, eleven corpses and the caustic stench of spent ammo.

When he was sure the Russians were out of sight, he picked himself up and made his way across the field towards the rest stop.

Bald was a smeared-red heap on the ground. His body was contorted, arms splayed to his left, legs to his right. There wasn't much left of his limbs, and the bullets to his core had almost severed him in half. Gardner rested his eyes on his old mucker for a moment. This is what you get, John, he thought. Staring at the fag butts in the blood, the holes in his face, he experienced both hate and relief in his stomach. They mixed in his throat, formed a bitter taste in his mouth.

'Stupid bastard,' he said to the dead Scot.

The silence was broken by a faint dribbling noise to his nine o'clock. He glanced across his shoulder and spied a body lying in the field, fifty metres distant.

Surely not, he said to himself.

Valon was still alive when Gardner came upon him, his chest swelling and retracting in an erratic beat. Nearer to Valon, Gardner saw that his right arm was missing from the bicep down. Strips of flesh flapped against his bone. The HE grenade had mashed him up but failed to kill him. Gardner figured the round had landed a couple of metres short of the target. Anything inside a three-metre kill zone and Valon would have been dust.

Sad twists of his entrails seeped out of the guy's abdomen. Flaps of skin, hard black chips, protruded from the wound. The stench of burned human flesh hit Gardner. He retched in the back of his throat. Knelt down beside Valon.

The Albanian spoke in childish gurgles. His one good lung fought to fill his body with air. The right side of his face looked as though someone had roasted it on a barbecue. Warts and boils on his skin crackled like pork fat. His eyes were scorched opaque.

Gardner spotted something red on his right wrist. Too bright and plasticky to be blood. He bent forward for a closer look.

And did a double-take.

Valon wore a bracelet identical to the one Gardner had been given by Land and had put on the Albanian's left wrist. Not quite believing what he was seeing, Gardner reached for Valon's left arm. The same fucking tag, and the same fucking question: what's Valon doing with two MI6 bracelets?

'I'm with the Firm,' Valon said, answering Gardner's curious face. 'I work . . . have been for years . . . Since the war.' His facial muscles convulsed. Valon took a deep breath.

'Back at Aimée's flat,' Gardner said. 'You deliberately missed your shot, didn't you?'

Valon nodded, his mouth emitting a guttural murmur. Some new and hidden pain was making itself heard inside his mutilated body. 'Jesus, I . . . couldn't give up my cover. They wanted . . . you dead. I had to make it look like . . . you were.'

He examined his wounds, his mouth ajar in horror. The skin around the right eyeball had been blown away. Gardner could almost make out the connective cords at the back of his eye.

'You must stop the Russians . . . They're going to a rendez-vous in . . . shit!'

Gardner closed his eyes for a second. He'd seen a lot of trauma wounds in his time, but nothing as messed up as Valon's. His were gopping.

'Drobny, on the border,' Valon continued, drawing in breath and choking on it like glass. 'The church. Two o'clock. It is very important you get to the truck. Before it continues its journey and—'

'And Aimée? You told me she was nabbed by the Grey Wolf. Is that a lie?'

Valon was delirious. 'Sotov. He has her.' He gulped. Made a gargling noise in his throat.

The words gnawed at Gardner's stomach. He pushed Aimée to the back of his mind.

'What's in the truck?' he said.

He detected a soft, flopping sound inside the other man's chest.

'Talk to me, Klint. The fucking truck.'

But Valon was on the brink. His breath stilled like frost in his mouth.

Gardner watched him pass over.

He dug out his mobile, called Land. Needed to give him the heads-up on how the drug exchange had gone fubar.

Six rings, seven – and no fucking answer.

An automated female voice asked him to leave a message after the bleep.

Gardner declined. He knew that the Russians were transporting the truck and Sotov had followed directly behind it in the Lincoln. The odds on him accompanying the truck all the way to Drobny were more than reasonable.

So that's what you'll do. Get to the village of Drobny in the hour. That'll give you just under thirty minutes to intercept whatever the fuck's in the truck. Time-wise it's tighter than a Jock at a Poundstretcher, but since when you did roll any other way?

He raced back towards the Nissan.

fifty-nine

'That was crazy,' Popov said, laughing, as he drove through the factory gates. The site had once been the pride of Serbian industry, building cars and motorbikes for the West. Now it was a barren pit, the machinery rusted brown, stockpiles of spare motor parts.

'I mean, those Italian shitheads. They got what they had coming to them. But that Scottish guy was out of his fucking mind. Trying to run at you with a fucking knife, Aleks. I've never seen anything like it.' Popov beat his palms against the wheel, shaking his head.

'The Scot used to be an SAS soldier,' Sotov said. 'They're taught never to give up.'

They parked inside the excavated shell of a factory building. Sotov ordered his two surviving henchmen to leave the vehicle and perform a perimeter search. The Grey Wolf waited by the Lincoln, Popov next to him and staring in the direction of the two men.

'The Englishman this morning,' Popov said. 'The one who died in the fire. He was SAS too?'

Sotov nodded.

'Two SAS soldiers murdered in a single day.' He laughed, but the sound came out like he was having a seizure.

A white Ford Transit shuttled into the factory entrance. Sotov watched the van draw up alongside the Lincoln. Two men, big as grizzly bears and equally as dumb, got out. One sported a tacky gold necklace. Bulgarians have no taste, Sotov thought. But at least they come cheap. The man with the necklace opened the Transit's rear doors. Sotov smiled.

The bitch was inside.

'In the boot,' Sotov ordered the Bulgarians.

'Let me go!' the girl yelled, backing deep inside the van. 'Please!'

Sotov watched her the way a visitor might look at a creature in the zoo. He lit a Ziganov, his nostrils venting smoke into the van. 'Does she have a name?'

'Aimée,' said Necklace Guy.

He liked the name. Had a nice ring to it.

'My sweet Aimée, there's no point blaming me for the situation you find yourself in. We know you were with the English soldier. We know he told you certain things.'

Her face hardened. The Bulgarians disappeared out the front of the factory.

'I believe,' Sotov directed his gaze at Aimée, 'his name was Joe Gardner.'

He waited for the words to sink in. Aimée paused for a beat.

'He'll make you pay for this, he'll—'

'But he's dead, my dear.'

Aimée stared blankly back at Sotov. As though she didn't understand – didn't *want* to understand – the words coming out of his mouth.

'The fire at your flat this morning. He was trapped inside.' Sotov suppressed a laugh. It tried to push free at the corners of his lips. 'Burning is a terrible way to go. The flames take a long time to kill a man. There is much suffering.'

Tears slipped down Aimée's cheeks. Her lips trembled.

'You're lying,' she said, her voice breaking, weak.

'I'm afraid not. No one is coming to save you, Aimée. It's just you and me.' Sotov leaned into the van. He pinched her teary cheek. 'You and me,' he whispered, reeling in his finger. A teardrop plinked on to his fingertip. He tasted it. Salty, and yet somehow sweet.

'Now, the problem with the SAS,' he went on, 'with people like Joe Gardner, is that they don't give up very easy. A Russian man – you beat him once, he runs like a fucking dog. Not the same with the British. Gardner can't have been operating by himself. There must be other soldiers working with him, yes?'

'I don't know what you're talking about.'

'Come on, my sweet. You slept with Gardner; you fucking stink of sex. And a man will tell a woman anything, even his most closely guarded secrets, to get her into bed. He will have said things to you. Plans, numbers, names.'

'He didn't, I swear!'

The cold light of day punctured Aimée's beauty. She had a bruised eye, a bloodied nose. Some marks on her wrists. As if she'd been trapped in the van with a wild dog. Yet with a bit of work and a few days to let her wounds heal, she could be a model.

'I do hope you're not claustrophobic, my dear,' Sotov said. 'We're going for a little ride.'

The Bulgarians had returned. Necklace Guy stashed a silencer pistol into his jacket pocket. Popov glared daggers at them, but they stared ahead, small eyes rooted to the van. They grappled with the bitch. She flailed. Necklace Guy wrapped his substantial arms around her chest and transported her to the Lincoln, his bloated legs waddling from side to side.

Popov went to the car and reached inside. Pushed a button on the dashboard. The boot yawned.

'Joe's still alive. I'm sure of it,' Aimée said.

'Yes, yes,' Sotov chuckled. 'Of course he is. Don't worry. Soon the reality of your situation will hit you, and you'll talk.'

'I told you, I don't know about any plans.'

Sotov considered the sky. 'That's too bad. Because if you don't tell me what I want to know, I'll have to do things to you.

Things that will make you cry. Things that will make you wish you had never been born.' He turned to face her. 'Think about it now, why don't you?'

The Bulgarians chucked the girl in like she was a rolled-up carpet. Sotov heard a dull thump as the boot locked shut, the Lincoln rocking on its rear wheels. Her shouts seeped through the exterior, muffled and distant. Yes, she was a wild one all right. Sotov looked forward to having fun with her. It was so much more exciting when they fought back.

'Thank you, Denis.'

Popov rubbed his hands. They were smeared with blood. 'No problem.'

Sotov laughed with his mouth closed. 'No, I mean – for everything.'

Popov's hands abruptly stopped. He stared at something on the ground. 'I'm afraid I don't understand, Aleks.'

'I'm afraid you do.'

Popov suddenly became aware of the Bulgarians closing in on him. He backed off, edging closer to his shadow cast against the wall. Popov's eyes flicked from the two men to Sotov. The Grey Wolf and his chauffeur stared at each other for a brief moment.

'Why—?' Popov's voice was ghostly, as if his soul had already left his body.

'You know why, Denis. No more games.'

Popov was quiet. He stared at the pickaxe in Necklace Guy's hand.

'Make it slow,' Sotov told the Bulgarian. Then he walked outside for a cigarette. Caught the squelching sound the pick-axe made as it gored Popov's face. Sotov emerged from the factory, and the door shut on Popov's feeble groans.

sixty

1334 hours.

Drobny was forty-five minutes' drive along the border with Macedonia. Gardner gunned the accelerator. The speedometer on the Nissan hit 140. The chassis felt like it was stuck together with Scotch tape. A question whizzed across the pulsing surface of his brain. What's in the truck? And another question: did John know he wasn't going to be paid in cash?

The road rose, then lulled, then flattened as he drove deeper into the Serbian badlands.

Gardner had been to Drobny once before. Back in 1999, he and John Bald had been given orders to man an observation post on a hill overlooking an Orthodox church. When the militia arrived they'd rounded up every ethnic Albanian suspected of collusion with the Kosovo Liberation Army and imprisoned them inside the school. They were being held captive there, and the NATO gin merchants wanted to verify reports about ethnic cleansing. Gardner and Bald were given strict instructions not to intervene.

They had moved in at night, tasked to recce what the head shed, in their fancy language, called 'suspicious activity'. What the two of them found in Drobny wasn't suspicious. It was paid-in-full murder.

A chilly November dawn, the cold scraping Gardner's lungs. The fourth day of their mission. Bald had shaken him awake. They'd been on a hard stag routine, each man taking the watch in four-hour turns while the other ate ration packs, rested and operated the radio.

'Look, Joe,' Bald had whispered as ten militiamen frog-marched eighty civilians into the cemetery. He'd handed the binos to Gardner and he had looked on as the civilians were lined up against the church wall.

The sergeant counted to three. Then his men opened fire. Bald and Gardner gritted their teeth as they grimly watched the wall spatter with the guts and brains of innocent men, women and children. Smoke was still issuing from the militiamen's overheating muzzles when Bald reported to the head shed asking for permission to engage. The request was denied.

'Bloody cowards,' Bald said on hearing the news. 'Come on, Joe. What do you say we show these fuckers the meaning of a turkey shoot?'

They had loaded their Colt Commandos and put rounds down on the militia. Wiped out all ten of the evil cunts, filling their bodies with so much brass they could be sure they were dead. It was a blatant breach of orders, but it had felt the right thing to do and Major Maston, if he had ever known, had let it slide. It was hard for Gardner to believe that John Bald was now dead, a no-good criminal.

Modern-day Drobny wasn't some sort of memorial to the massacre, more like an abandoned, lawless patch of shit that someone had forgotten to clear up. Gardner saw precious few people in the streets. The faces he did see had more lines than a Shakespeare play and the distant, glazed expressions of a people who'd lost everything. Burned-out windows stared back at him like black teeth. The roofs of most houses had caved in. Mangy dogs roaming the rutted roads, sniffing at dead birds and crushed Coca-Cola cans.

The church, Valon had said. That's where he told Gardner he would find the sleeper truck. Gardner felt he was colliding with the past. Ghosts everywhere, the filmy residue of night-mares he'd tried to bury at the bottom of a pint glass.

He checked his watch. One forty-two. A little over fifteen minutes before, according to Valon, the truck would move on to a new, unknown location. You've got to get to the truck, he thought. Find out what the fuck's inside. Then track down Sotov and find Aimée.

Gardner made a few turns west then south, the village seeming to disintegrate in front of him. He came to a particularly desolate place. Shabby homes, ragtag cars, roads that wouldn't have looked out of place on a rally course. He passed a police station fallen into disrepair, the walls swamped with graffiti denouncing Milosevic, Arkan and Karadzic. Heard something up ahead. The low rumble of an engine. He killed the Nissan.

Land called him back. Took his fucking time, Gardner thought.

'Christ, Joe,' Land snapped, 'where the—?'

'You didn't tell me Valon was working for you.'

Gardner heard Land cough down the line. 'Klint Valon's cover was on a strictly need-to-know basis. A man like Valon walks a tightrope. With every person who knows his true identity, his position becomes increasingly perilous. I can't afford to lose him.'

'You already have,' Gardner said.

A pause stretched out, like rope tensing.

'The meet was a colossal fuck-up,' Gardner continued. 'Valon's dead. John too. The Italians tried to hijack the whole deal, take the coke and the money. Soon as they made their play, the Russians wiped the fucking floor with them. They spared no one.'

Another pause. 'You mean—?'

'No one,' Gardner replied flatly. 'They killed the Italians, then they went for Bald and Valon. They're all fucking dead.'

Land muttered something; it came down the line as a static hiss. Three seconds of silence, then he regained his composure. 'What about the cocaine? And the money?'

'The Russians took both. But Valon said there was no money, the Russians were swapping something else for the drugs.'

'And what—?'

The line crackled and fizzed. Land's voice distorted like a badly tuned radio station. And suddenly he was gone. Gardner tried calling him back, but his mobile couldn't get a signal. He checked the time again. One forty-seven.

This is it. Do – or fucking die.

He stepped out into the street, Glock in his hand, looking for trouble.

A couple of locals glowered at him, two knurled men with skin like worn sandpaper and greasy hair. An elderly woman trundled past, knuckle-joint nose and eyes the colour of dirty net curtains. Gardner had been on the receiving end of a million evil-eyes in Iraq and Afghanistan and he came to understand that the only language these people understood was made in a munitions factory. The men saw the Glock and swiftly looked in the other direction. No one else around to bother him.

Forty metres ahead he clocked the sleeper truck from the rest stop. The truck was in front of the old church gates. He crept forward, his knees bent, making sure he didn't cause any noise.

To his nine a road peeled off between several vacant properties to the left and the ruins of a library church to the right. Thirty metres down the road Gardner noted three vehicles parked in a column. The front and rear ones were Toyota Hilux 4x4s, each with black canvas draped over the open section. The middle vehicle appeared to be a bulletproof van with blacked-out windows and a secure compartment with double doors at the back.

Three men came into view. Two looked like guards: tan tops, dark-green trousers, black boots, AK-47 straps tight around their chests. Their faces seemed too dark and smooth to hail from this neck of the woods. The third man was chubbier, older. He had a beard thick as a clenched fist.

The third man shouted at the guards. Gardner hid behind the police station. The guards heaved something out of the sleeper truck's trailer. The third man was shouting at them. Gardner thought he sounded Arabic. Carrying their load as if it were an expensive piece of furniture, one man gripping it at either end, they headed west down the street. Gardner followed, stopping behind a wrecked Skoda ditched next to a stone house at the eastern edge of the street. Weeds had reclaimed the car's tyres and much of its shell. The two guards flipped open the doors of the secure van and wheezed as they placed the object on its floor.

The doors slammed. The third man headed up the road in the opposite direction to Gardner. The two guards walked towards Gardner, but they hadn't seen him. They were thirty metres from his position. Then twenty. One of the guards, a lanky teenager with a bumfluff moustache, then made a right and walked south down an adjacent street, out of sight. The other, a short and stocky guy with teak skin, was now ten metres away.

Sweat percolated down Gardner's spine.

Five metres.

He hoped the guy would walk straight past and continue on his patrol.

Gardner hunkered behind the Skoda. As the guard's shadow loomed, he caught his breath in the back of his mouth.

The guard was now a metre beyond the Skoda.

The shadow stopped. Hovered over Gardner.

The guard spun around. Clocked Gardner. His mouth opened wide. Poised to sound the alarm.

Gardner leapt to his feet and in one smooth movement fastened his arms around the guard's neck, fixing him in a headlock. He slapped his right hand tight over the guy's mouth. The kid with the tache was out of sight, but Gardner had to assume he'd return soon. He dragged the guard out of sight and pushed his elbows out until he could feel the rubbery tunnel of the guy's air passage crushing from the force. The man kicked at the dirt with his feet, hands pawing at Gardner's face. Gardner squeezed harder. Then something warm and chunky seeped through his fingers. The guy had vomited.

Gardner didn't let go. He held and held, squeezed and squeezed. After two minutes the legs stopped thrashing about. Gardner dragged the body to the side of the Skoda and filched a set of keys from the guy's pocket. Checking that the coast was clear of other guards, he moved diagonally forward until he was behind the rear Hilux. The black canvas seemed to be covering some kind of a mini-gun.

Peering over the pickup, Gardner scanned the streets to his nine, six and one o'clock. A guard was patrolling away from him to the left. Twenty metres away now, Gardner broke out from behind the Hilux and scrambled towards the van. Reached it in eight quick strides. He inserted the key in the lock. A red light glared above the locking mechanism. He heard the shifting of cogs within. Then the light turned green, and the doors at the rear were open.

A single object was lying on the floor of the van. It was half a metre tall and half as wide and its cylindrical shape reminded Gardner of a forty-gallon drum. Sealed inside a protective camouflaged case, it looked like the kind of thing a guy could carry as a backpack. A rectangular grey box was strapped to the object's waist. Between loose rope ends at the top of the object, Gardner noted a battery cell, an LCD display and a key-operated panel.

Jesus fucking Christ, he whispered to himself.

He had seen pictures of this thing before. It was a miniature armed warhead – what they called a suitcase or backpack nuke – modelled on the Special Atomic Demolition Munitions system developed by the US and the Soviets at the height of the Cold War. Devices of this kind were designed to be parachuted into Soviet territory if the Russians ever invaded the West. They had, Gardner knew, a yield equivalent to several kilotons of TNT, and packed enough radioactive uranium to make Chernobyl look like fucking Disneyland.

Jesus, John, Gardner thought. What the fuck were you going to do with a backpack nuke?

Cold spread across Gardner's back. Then he realized it was coming from a muzzle tip digging into the top of his spinal column.

'Drop the weapon.'

Gardner released the Glock from his hand.

'So finally you arrived,' a voice said. 'That is good. Now I can do what I couldn't do before.'

Gardner didn't turn around. He knew who was holding the gun to his neck. Could tell by the way his voice jolted and jarred, an accent that sounded like no other.

Shai Golan.

sixty-one

1418 hours.

'I knew you would come,' Golan said as he jabbed Gardner with the tip of his pistol.

'Don't tell me,' Gardner said. 'You're a mind-reader as well as a cunt.'

'Instinct,' Golan answered, ignoring the jibe. 'You strike me as the type of man who cannot resist the big prize. This way,' he said, tilting his head towards the church. 'And please, no noise. If you alert the guards, they'll only kill us both. Neither of us wants that now, do we?'

Gardner didn't respond. The coast was clear. Golan led him through the imposing wooden doors of the church. The building was empty and retained little of its former splendour. The pews were layered in decades-thick dust, the altar was naked and muddy light filtered through the cracks in the stained-glass windows.

'Bald's dead,' Gardner's voice echoed.

'I know.'

Golan was behind him, but Gardner could feel the Israeli's finger tugging back on the trigger. He imagined the gases primed to flood the chamber and propel the hollow-cased bullet out of the muzzle and into his head.

'Now you've seen the bomb, I will have to kill you,' said Golan.

'You can't kill me,' Gardner said. He felt the pressure of the muzzle, as if it was drilling through to his brain.

'Give me one good reason.'

'Right now, there's a dozen other MI6 agents in this area alone. Many more in Belgrade. If you kill me, they'll fucking hunt you down like a dog.'

Golan didn't reply.

He believes me, Gardner thought. I've bought myself some time—

He felt a shockwave of pain as Golan bashed the pistol butt against his temple. Gardner dropped to his knees, screams inside his head.

'Son of a bitch!'

'On your feet,' Golan said. 'This way.'

Gardner stood. His hair was sticky and warm.

He staggered into a dim room behind the altar, eight metres by six. The room was sparsely furnished: a wooden table on the left, a bricked-up fireplace at the far wall, a small statue of the Virgin Mary on the mantelpiece. A wooden chair in the middle of the room, a length of parachute cord on the floor by the chair legs.

Gardner went to open his mouth, then felt a boot connect with the small of his back. Golan grabbed him by the arms, dragged his knackered body to the chair, then bound his arms behind his back with the nylon cord. He stood in front of Gardner, wiping the lenses of his glasses with his shirt-sleeve.

'Those fucking idiots at MI6 –' he spat out the last word like mouthwash '– are they aware of the nuclear weapon too? Or is their so-called intelligence as inadequate as ever?'

'You knew about the nuke?' Gardner's mouth was dry as sawdust.

'Of course. Since the very beginning.'

The upper part of Gardner's chest was tight like a belt. His head suddenly felt heavy as Golan approached the table. On it Gardner could see a number of implements. Screwdrivers, hammers, scalpels, ice picks, crocodile clips. Golan inspected them.

'You're fucking insane,' Gardner said.

'Insanity means to be illogical,' Golan replied. 'But I'm perfectly logical.'

He picked up a scalpel, examined its sharp blade in the harsh light.

'So, how about you begin by telling me where these agent friends of yours are?'

'Fuck you!'

'If you knew who I worked for, you wouldn't say that.'

'You're not Mossad, I know that much.'

'I work for a special division of Mossad that is secret even to the rest of the organization. Our codename is Shiloh. We draw out men from Mossad's Collections and Research Departments. Only the top men and women are recruited. They have to be willing to kill, poison, maim and terrorize the enemies of Israel. No one is aware of our activities,' he said, by now laughing heartily, 'especially not MI6.'

His long hands settled on a pair of crocodile clips. Gardner felt his guts twist.

'Shiloh learned of a plot by your friend to trade cocaine with the Russians for an easily transportable nuclear weapon. Some call it a suitcase nuke. According to ex-KGB chiefs, hundreds of these devices have gone missing in Russia. Some in old depots. Others on the black market. Your friend John Bald intended to sell this weapon on for a substantial profit.' Golan paused. 'To Mahmoud Reza.'

Gardner remembered the third man at the convoy. A memory hit him like a rush of blood to the head. That man was Reza, the outlawed Iranian general!

Golan went on, 'The media reported he was killed. In Afghanistan, they said. They are fools. The Americans killed a lookalike. Reza is alive and well, and as we speak Reza is preparing the convoy for its journey. He does so with the blessing of the Iranian state.'

'You stood back and let a nuke get into the hands of your worst enemy?'

'Madness, yes. On the surface. But in Shiloh we look at the bigger picture. How to turn our enemies' actions to our advantage. Most people would try to stop this deal from ever taking place. We are not most people.'

Golan brought the crocodile clips and a power unit over to Gardner. Plugged the clips into the unit and flicked a switch.

'Give me one name,' he said. 'Just to begin with. One name, and then I'll go easy on you. I promise.'

Gardner swallowed his fear. It tasted sickly in his throat.

'Suck a dick.'

The pain's coming, pal, he said to himself. You need to think of an exit strategy, and you need to do it fucking yesterday.

Golan shrugged, as if he expected nothing more from the man.

'Why let the ragheads get their grubby mitts on the nuke?' Gardner asked.

'The Iranians are celebrating because they have a nuclear power plant,' Golan said. 'The truth is, the station at Bushehr is nothing. The technology is old, the uranium barely enriched, the parts supplied by the Russians, who themselves are unreliable. If Israel's government perceived the station to be a threat, they would have bombed it long ago. As we did in Syria.'

Golan attached the clips to Gardner's pecs. Gardner concentrated on steeling his body for the pain. He took deep breaths, trying to fill his red blood cells with as much oxygen as possible. He felt the cold bite of the clips as their teeth pinched his muscles.

'What is most important,' Golan went on, 'is that the Iranians do not proceed further with an enrichment programme. For that to happen, we need more than mere sanctions and tough words from your Prime Minister and the United States. We need a catastrophe.'

Gardner squirmed in the chair. The air in the room was muggy. Oily sweat slithered down his chin and on to his groin like a dripping tap. Better rustle up a plan quick, soldier. Because Golan's in the mood to fucking kill me.

'You mean . . . an accident?'

Golan snorted. 'I think *you* read *my* mind, friend.'

He held the power unit in his hands, his fingers skimming along the bank of dials.

'If Iran was caught trying to acquire nuclear weapons of a much higher grade of uranium, and there was to be a tragic accident in, say, Istanbul, well. That would shock the world into action. International pressure from the UN and NATO would force Iran's hand. Russia would have to dismantle the Bushehr plant, and a blanket ban on nuclear materials to Iran would soon follow. Its ability to develop nuclear weapons destroyed for ever.'

'So you were going to let the nuke get as far as Istanbul—?'

'And detonate the device early? Yes.'

'But for that you'd need to set the timer, the codes—'

'Obtained from the Russians.'

Gardner's head throbbed. He felt fluid draining from his brain. His mind was filled with noise. Questions, anger, denial. He shut his eyes, trying to blot everything out.

'Why would Bald do something like that?' Gardner asked. 'We launched incursions into Iran during the Iraq War. And suddenly he does business with them?'

'Your friend was interested in profit, nothing else. One hundred million dollars,' Golan said, and Gardner's heart skipped a beat. 'That's why the 'Ndrangheta tried to hijack the deal. They knew the price Bald had received from Mahmoud Reza. Hard for any man to resist that kind of money, especially Italian Mafia.'

'But why Istanbul? Why not Tehran, or anywhere else?' Gardner figured that the longer he could keep Golan boasting about his master plan, the more he could delay his torture. In the dark recesses of his mind he busied himself with his escape. The table presented several weapons. Get free of the ropes and you've got a fighting chance, he told himself.

'Relations with Turkey are very low,' Golan said. 'Because of the embargo, and the fact that the ruling Turkish AK Party is run by a pro-Islamist who freely admits he wishes for Turkey to usurp Egypt as the leader of the Muslim world. We used to be close to the Turks. They were a moderating force in our negotiations with the Palestinians. Politics and the embargo changed that for ever.'

'When Bald died,' said Gardner, recalling the chaotic aftermath of Brezovan, 'the Russian *Mafya* took the nuke. Why didn't they just deal directly with the Iranians, rather than selling it at a cut-price figure to Bald?'

'The *Mafya* have close links to the Russian government. Senior figures advised them not to sell directly to Reza. If anyone did link them to the nuke, the international outcry would turn Russia into a pariah state. But the *Mafya* couldn't leave the nuke at the exchange, not once they'd killed everyone else. They had no choice but to deliver it here, to Reza.'

This is crazy, Gardner thought. I've got to warn Land. Before it's too late.

'They know about the plan to detonate it?' he asked.

Golan shook his head.

'It's a secret. Until eight o'clock tonight, at the Bosporus Bridge in Istanbul, when the whole world will get a chance to see nuclear horror with their own eyes.'

He stepped back until he was four metres from Gardner.

'Now,' he said. 'This is your last chance. Where are the other agents?'

In a flash Golan's right hand rotated the voltage dial clock-wise, and Gardner felt his bones jump out of his skin. The pain was unlike anything he'd ever experienced. It started on his skin and burned through to his inside, like acid. The first jolt was light. The second fried his stomach, as if someone was pulling out stitches. Then the jolt abruptly stopped, and his stomach was sewn up.

'I appreciate American innovations,' Golan said. 'They turned execution into an art form. The electric chair is my favourite. Such a long and painful way to die. They say the average victim takes five minutes to expire. Sometimes the current cooks their body to a temperature that melts their eyeballs.'

'Fuck you,' Gardner wanted to say. But his jaw felt loose, as if it was hanging on by a thread.

A third charge, this one more intense than the last. The screams inside him grated, like a saw cutting metal. The hairs on his arms and chest began to burn. The smell was bitter. He felt as if he was being skinned alive.

'Tell me,' said Golan. 'How long do you think it will be before *you* die?'

Fighting the pain was hopeless. His training in the Regiment simulated torture, but nothing had prepared him for this. The tactical part of his brain told him that Golan was a psychotic fuck who took pleasure in seeing him writhe in agony. So there's going to be breaks between the shocks. You can use those—

The fourth wave hit. Pain ricocheted beneath his skin. Needles stabbed his bones. He clenched his jaw.

'Come on, friend. Give me a little yell. It must hurt, no?'

A smell drifted to Gardner's nose. Burning latex. He wondered what the hell it was. A second later he understood that he had a way out.

My prosthetic hand. It's come loose.

He glanced up at Golan. The Israeli hadn't latched on. Gardner hunched up his shoulders. The join between the nub of his forearm and his artificial hand was melting. Half of the lower limb had detached. He shook his elbow. Golan went to administer a fifth charge.

The next charge is the killer, Gardner thought. He buzzes you again, there's no way back.

Then he caught a snap, and the thud of his hand against the floor.

He was free.

sixty-two

Gardner went in fast, and he went in hard. He'd learned his lesson from his previous dust-up with Golan. The Israeli was an expert in Krav Maga. And the only way to fuck up someone trained in the world's dirtiest and most effective martial art was to beat them at their own game.

He raised his left thigh until his knee crunched against Golan's balls. Air gusted out of the Israeli's mouth as he lowered his hands to his squashed gonads. Gardner exploited his shoddy defence with a palm-strike to the bridge of his nose. The flat of his hand shattered the frame and lenses of Golan's glasses, and the man howled as plastic splinters darted into the corners of his eyes.

With just the one functioning hand, Gardner was fucked if Golan unleashed a torrent of blows upon him. His muscles were zapped, fried, distended. But the taste of freedom and the early scores against Golan gave him a second wind. Energy flowed through his veins.

Gardner kicked Golan in the knee. The same right foot then swung down like a hammer on Golan's left foot. The Israeli faltered. Gardner dealt him a two-fingered jab in the eyes. The jab became a combo attack as he followed through with an elbow to his ear and smashed his face into his left knee. Golan's legs caved in.

Golan fell to the floor. Fucking poleaxed. Gardner delivered a succession of boots that swung into every crevice of Golan's crumpled body. His legs, back, face, arms.

Then Golan was still. Gardner saw the pistol grip in the back of his trousers. He dug it out. A Sig Sauer P228. The stainless-steel handgun felt good in his hand. Catching his breath, Gardner drilled the muzzle against Golan's dazed skull.

'I know where Aimée is,' Golan said.

Gardner felt something catch fire within his chest. 'Don't fuck with me, pal.'

'I know . . . because Shiloh have been tracking Sotov's every move.'

'Bullshit.'

'It's the truth,' Golan said. 'Israel has a lot of friends in Russia. We have a man on the inside. Denis Popov, he . . . he works as Sotov's chauffeur. He's the one who originally alerted us to the sale of the nuke.'

'Where's Sotov now?'

Golan shook his head and chuckled wearily. 'It does not work like that. If I tell you now, you'll kill me.'

Gardner lowered the Sig.

'What do you want?'

Golan tended his sore balls. 'Immunity. And safe passage back to Tel Aviv – tonight.'

'Forget it, mate. The Firm will never agree to your demands.'

'Time is ticking, my friend. The convoy has already left. Check outside if you don't believe me. If you want to stop the bomb, you need to play by my rules.'

Gardner shoved Golan to one side and drew up Land's number on his mobile. One, two, three rings. Pick up, pick up! Land answered on the fifth ring. He was breathless.

'Where are you? Did you find the nuke?'

'Yeah—'

'Great work, old chap, there's a real future for you—'

'The convoy's already left.'

Land went quiet.

'It's headed for the Bosporus Bridge in Istanbul,' Gardner said, then heard a flurry of swear words rasping down the line.

He caught a bang and pictured Land thumping his desk. For several seconds the connection was quiet. Then Land said, 'Right. This is what we're going to do. I'll alert the Turks. Get them to set up a blockade at the bridge. A Black Hawk will transport you onward to Istanbul.'

'Fuck off,' Gardner said. 'Send a specialist team to disarm the nuke.'

'There isn't one. We'd have to locate engineers, call them back from operations, brief them, transport them . . . There's not the time. You're only a couple of hours away by helicopter. And I do recall' – Gardner heard the rustling of paper – 'that you have experience in detonations.'

The radio station in Belgrade. The shadows, and the bodies.

'Golan says the suitcase bomb is due to detonate at eight o'clock tonight, yes?' Land continued. 'So that leaves us with a shade over four hours to get you on-site and deactivate it. You're the best man for the job, Joe.'

'What about Aimée? She doesn't deserve to die.'

'She won't. Soon as Golan calls his informant she'll be granted a stay of execution.'

Gardner sighed. Each passing minute revealed strange new pains along the crescent of his chest. This one last step. Then it's over.

For ever.

'Just make sure you get Aimée away from the fucking Russians,' he said.

'You worry about your job, old boy, and I'll worry about mine,' Land replied, then hung up.

'OK,' Gardner told Golan. 'You'll get your safe passage. But first you give us Sotov's location.'

'How do I know you won't backtrack on your promise after finding her?'

'If Aimée is where you say she is, you'll be sent home. You have my word.'

Golan chewed on it for several seconds.

'OK,' he said. 'We have a deal.'

The word spiked Gardner's stomach. The nausea returned.

'Get a fucking move on,' he said to Golan.

They made their way down the aisle and out of the church. The sun had packed its bags and pissed off, replaced by a continuous grey curtain that seethed rain. Puddles plopped with raindrops in the pitted streets. Gardner felt the rain on his head, cool and refreshing. He let Golan walk in front as they passed around the side of the church.

The rain washed wet heat into Gardner's mouth. He tasted salt on his tongue; felt his stomach unstitching again. He'd asked a lot of his body the past seven days. There wasn't much left in the tank.

He stopped dead in his tracks.

The sky blackened. Steel-grey clouds seemed to oscillate like the vibrations of heavy machinery. Gardner peered into the distance. A fleet of eight UH-60 Black Hawks surfaced on the horizon, their four main rotor blades flickering above the long main profiles of the choppers. They were small as distant birds. The vibrating intensified and the Black Hawks grew and grew until they blocked out the clouds. Two of them hovered over a clearing to the south of the church, a field that had perhaps once belonged to a farm but now stood neglected. The wild grass and weeds parted like waves, shimmering as the two helicopters began their descent.

The choppers set down. Soldiers immediately debussed from both Black Hawks. Six men raced over to Golan and dragged him to the chopper to the right. Last I'll ever see of that cunt, thought Gardner.

Two men approached Gardner from the other Black Hawk. The nearest man offered his hand. A face Gardner didn't recognize, but the cold stare and grizzled expression told Gardner that he had yomped up the Pen-y-Fan mountain more than once in his life.

'Let's go,' the man said. He had a Brummie accent thick as old boots, bulbous nose, brown eyes and ears that were doing a good impression of cauliflower buds. Gardner approached the Black Hawk with the two men, climbed inside and strapped himself into a seat. The second guy sat opposite him. Gardner studied him. He was scraggy, with a curly black beard that covered his jaw like webbing. His face had the hard lines and gritty texture of a man who lived his life in hard terrain. His muscles were toned rather than large. Gardner noted the CAR-15 Colt Commando assault rifle between his legs, the Benelli shotgun and spare 5.56x45mm NATO ammo clips on the spare passenger seat.

'Name's Weston,' said the Brummie as the Black Hawk lifted off. It was a bumpy ride and Gardner felt his guts lurch. 'This is Dooley,' the pilot said, nodding at the bearded guy.

'Gardner. You lads are Regiment?'

'Twenty-three SAS, G Squadron,' replied Dooley. The whirr of the rotor blades, like rolling thunder, meant he had to shout to be heard. 'I'm told you used to be a Blade?'

'Discharged two years ago.'

Dooley glanced at the nub where Gardner's fake hand used to be.

'Fucking hard luck, mate,' he said in a cockney accent. He grinned, revealing the worst teeth in Britain. A lot of Regiment lads sported awful gnashers, a result of months spent in the field with only basic hygiene. 'But you're back on the front line now.'

Gardner's heart pulsed. He felt the tension winding up in his spine as his body overdosed on adrenalin.

'You picked a bad day for it.'

Too fucking right. Gardner kept the thought to himself.

They flew on to Istanbul.

sixty-three

The Bosporus Bridge lit up like a glowstick across the sea. On the European side, glass-fronted towers clustered together in the Levent financial quarter. Sleek, shiny wet pebbles that looked down on the other side of the bridge. The Asian side was a tapestry of shabby mosques, slum dwellings and rickety roads.

The size of the city left Gardner breathless. It seemed to unfold into the horizon.

No time to enjoy the view. He ran his right hand over the newly attached prosthetic limb attached to his left arm. An on-board medic had patched up Gardner's wounds and fitted him with a temporary limb, but it lacked the nerve sensors and control of his old hand. Nothing more than a fancy-looking club.

At a cruising speed of 150 knots, equivalent to 173 mph, the Black Hawk had taken a little over two and a half hours to clear the 650 kilometres to Istanbul, flying at an altitude of 8000 metres.

Seven thirty-four and Gardner was first to rappel down from the Black Hawk, using a Marlow rope connected to a figure-eight descender to slow his fall. He couldn't fast-rope, not while he was essentially one-handed – he'd slam into the ground at speed and fuck his legs up.

His stomach muscles cramped on the drop. Twenty-four hours ago his V-neck shirt had been pristine white. Now it was grubby, black and brown-red. It chafed against his chest.

He dropped on to Camlica Hill, the highest point in Istanbul. Touched down on a clipped grass plain criss-crossed with several walking paths and hemmed in by pine forests and beds of tulips. A smattering of tea gardens and restaurants stood empty, cleared by the army to provide a suitable LZ. The hill stood some 250 metres above sea level and afforded Gardner an excellent view of the Bosporus Bridge in the distance.

Dooley and Weston were next to touch down. The Black Hawk scuttled away into the skyline. A man approached Gardner. From his Turkish military colours, Gardner placed him as an NCO. Narrow black eyes, pallid lips and bronzed skin. Gardner couldn't make up his mind which bits of him hailed from the Mediterranean and which had fallen off Genghis Khan's family tree.

'Colonel Deniz Sahin, Ozel Jandarma Komando,' said the Colonel, referring to the elite Turkish Special Forces unit. He didn't offer his hand. 'You're the Brits who are going to stop the bomb?'

'Something like that,' Gardner replied. He got the impression that Colonel Sahin wasn't exactly thrilled about a bunch of foreigners coming to save the day.

'Do your fucking job, Englishmen. Then get out of my country.'

Sahin waved Gardner, Dooley and Weston towards a waiting army Jeep.

'Get in,' Sahin said. 'The convoy is almost at the bridge. My men have set up an ambush. We will take care of the Iranians. When we have finished annihilating the enemy, we'll give you a signal to come forward and disarm the bomb.' Sahin glared at all three men. 'You are not to take part in the engagement unless I give permission.'

'We understand,' Weston said. Fair play, Gardner thought. This was Sahin's turf. He'd feel exactly the same if a bunch of Turkish operators rocked up in London in the middle of a crisis.

Weston and Dooley sat in the back of the Jeep. Gardner rode shotgun alongside Sahin. They raced out of Camlica Hill and skidded through the chaotic traffic linking the sideroads to the four-lane O-1 motorway, which ran across the bridge and continued on the Asian side of the city.

The Jeep shuddered as Sahin cut up a motorbike. The Bosporus Bridge loomed, its huge zigzagging steel cables spanning the river. A bottleneck of traffic had formed on the bridge, and any other day Gardner would have stopped to admire the stylish towers brightly lit in shades of purple, green and red at intervals along its fifteen-hundred-metre length.

'We've shut down the toll-booth computers,' Sahin explained. 'To stop anyone getting through.'

Gardner spotted the van, in the outside lane, a hundred metres from the bridge itself. Identical silver Toyota Hiluxes were positioned to its immediate front and rear. It was the convoy from Drobny.

'Our assault team is ready,' Sahin said.

No more needed to be said. Hard men getting ready to do a hard job. They didn't have time for fucking dinner-party conversation.

A clock on the Jeep dashboard read 19.45. A little further on and Sahin slammed on the brakes, stopping the Jeep fifty metres from the convoy. Traffic, clogged thicker than a smoker's arteries, prevented them from getting any closer.

'Wait for the signal,' Sahin said.

Gardner snatched at his breath. His right hand was shaking.

Seven forty-eight.

A shot cracked. A tyre burst.

'That's it!'

At the signal, Sahin flew out of the car, M16 assault rifle in his hands. Up ahead the doors on a lorry sixty metres ahead of the furthest Toyota Hilux swung open and dozens of Turkish soldiers and attack dogs poured out. More sprang out from nearby cars and vans. Must have been a hundred in total. Enough firepower to start a fucking war, Gardner was thinking as he looked on.

Sahin was twenty-five metres from the convoy when the shooter in the first Hilux returned fire. The NCO hit the ground, bullets cracking the tarmac around him. More shots rang out. Electric *ca-racks* of sniper fire filled the air. Gardner counted sixteen Turkish snipers based on the rooftops of the flanking apartment blocks. They rained down rounds, their bullets streaking the Hilux. A soldier on a loudspeaker ordered civilians to remain in their cars, but most didn't listen and legged it. Amateur mistake, Gardner thought. They should have sealed off the road a couple of kilometres in either direction, made sure no innocents got zapped in the crossfire.

Another *ca-rack* and this one hit the jackpot. The shooter gasped as a round put a hole through his throat the size of a two-pence coin.

Meanwhile two figures emerged from the rear Hilux. Thirty Turkish soldiers beat a path towards them. They worked in a fire-and-move formation in pairs, one man putting rounds down while the other shifted forward. Faced with a continuous stream of bullets, the two men who'd debussed from the Hilux didn't stand a fucking chance. The Turks slotted them both at close range, fifteen metres. The second guy took so many rounds in his guts that his legs were severed from his torso.

Mahmoud Reza was the last to emerge, from the van between the Hiluxes. He looked more emaciated than ever, and his thick beard glistened with the blood of his fallen comrades. Clutching an Uzi, he sprayed rounds at the soldiers in a wild arc, forcing them to take cover behind the rear Hilux. Stray rounds struck a middle-aged woman in a white suit as she fled from her Ford Focus. The poor woman didn't make a sound. Just crumbled in the middle of the road. Her right leg trembled. Then it stopped.

Reza made a run for it, heading for the bridge. Sahin lined up the retreating Iranian from a distance of fifty metres and unloaded four rounds into his back. Reza dropped. The Komando containment team, thirty men decked out in fire-proof riot gear, surrounded Reza. Ten or more attack dogs snarled on their leashes.

Sahin motioned to Gardner and his mates to hurry up.

Climbing out of the Jeep, Gardner moved towards the van. Spent cartridges littered the road twenty-five metres from both the front and rear Hiluxes. The windows were starred, the rubber on the tyres peeled off the rims. He saw two dead guys at the back of the rear vehicle. Their heads were obliter-ated, brain matter speckled along the greasy tarmac in a star-burst pattern.

'Good fucking work,' he said, impressed.

'They got what they deserved,' Sahin said coldly.

Gardner glanced over Sahin's shoulder and saw the attack dogs hungrily biting off flaps of flesh from Reza's corpse.

Turning back to Sahin, he said, 'I thought you were best friends with the Iranians these days?'

Sahin shook his head, tucked his thumbs between his utility belt and his army-issue combats. 'We don't trust anybody.'

Gardner eyed the van. Swore he could hear the faint tick-tock of a timer device. His muscles were sapped of energy. He bit his bottom lip, drier than a fig leaf, and tried to shut out the background noise.

'Got the hazmat suit?' he asked Weston.

Dooley sprinted to the Jeep. Returned with a Level A reflective suit. He helped ease Gardner into it, then slipped the glove over his right hand. Popped an earpiece into his right ear and put the helmet over his head.

'Toolbox?' Gardner's breath steamed on the helmet visor.

Dooley handed him a metal box. Gardner gripped its handle.

'Good luck,' Dooley said.

Gardner turned and took the long walk towards the van. The suit constricted his movements and after forty metres he'd worked up a sweat that poured down his forehead and on to his eyelids. The heat and discomfort seemed to reflect the grinding in his skull.

You've got one shot at this, he told himself. Get it wrong, Istanbul gets vaporized.

He tried not to think about what would happen if the nuke detonated. The first explosion was the conventional one. That would fry him, turn him to dust. The explosion would in turn activate a neutron trigger, a small disc of highly radioactive material that would cause widespread damage with a death toll of anything between thirty and fifty thousand. And that wouldn't be the end of it. A nuclear cloud would drift across the fallout zone, endangering hundreds of thousands of people with exposure to massively high doses of radiation poisoning.

Gardner stopped at the van. He looked towards the Bosporus, dark and slick as a whale's back. Might be the last thing you ever see, he thought.

Static crackled in his right ear.

'Joe, can you hear me?' Land said.

'Loud and clear.'

'This is a three-way line with Lieutenant Steve White. Steve's an engineer on the Trident submarine the HSM *Vigilant*. He's going to talk you through the disarming process.'

'Don't worry about a thing, mate,' White said in an accent so Welsh you could bottle it and sell it as Taff Valley water. 'This is a bloody tough gig, but Leo here tells me you've got demolitions experience, so you've got the basic skill set in place. It's just a matter of guiding you through the interesting bit.'

'I'll be fine, mate. Let's get this over with and then we can share a pint in Hereford. First round's on me.'

The doors of the van were open. Gardner placed the tool-box just inside on the floor. He prised it open and removed a torch. The van lit up like a cave. Placing his right hand on the floor, he slid up into the van.

Inside, the heat rose again. Gardner felt his clothes clinging to his legs and torso. He was soaked through.

Once again an image of the radio station flashed across the surface of his mind. The way the building toppled, the smoke plume billowing into the bright blue sky, a dozen small fires breaking out among the mountain of concrete and steel, slab and cable. All that death, all of it unseen in the fury of the explosion. He thought about how the nuke would be like that – except a million times bigger.

'Can you see the top of the device?' White asked him.

'Looking at it now.'

'What's the timer say?'

Gardner angled his head. The LCD display was a blur through the steam and sweat. 'Zero-zero-three.' *Three fucking minutes.*

'OKaaay,' said White. He sounded like he was talking more to himself than Gardner. 'This type of nuke should be battery-operated. You should see a red or black cable connecting the timer to the battery attached to the side of the actual nuke.'

'I see it,' Gardner said. 'It's a red wire.' The glossy wire was a quarter of an inch thick and ran from the timer to the canvas box strapped to the back of the nuke.

'I'm going to need you to cut that wire.'

Gardner fumbled inside the toolbox for the wire cutters. He secured the wire between its teeth.

'But' – White's voice was rushed, unsteady – 'before you cut it. These types of nuke aren't highly evolved, but the Soviets liked to booby-trap their devices.'

Fuck! Gardner thought. He held the cutters in place, his hand a second away from plunging Istanbul into a nuclear holocaust.

'I want you to look down the back of the device,' White said.

'What am I looking for?'

'Something beneath the battery. It will have been concealed from view.'

Gardner ran his eyes up and down the battery. He was feeling dizzy. The heat, the exhaustion, the dehydration – a perfect physiological storm. Spittle collected at the corners of his mouth. He thought about that cold pint in Hereford.

He found a small black box taped to the underside of the battery. Gardner described it to White, who said, 'Here's what you've got to do – what's the timer read, Joe?'

'One minute.'

'Plenty, plenty of time.' White's voice sounded artificially calm. 'You need to cut the booby trap.'

Gardner paused with the wire cutters. He didn't want any more nasty surprises from White. 'And then?'

'Once the trap is cut, it will automatically short-circuit the timer. There's nothing you can do to prevent that. Soon as you cut the booby trap, you'll have about three seconds to cut the red wire.'

'What do you mean, "about three seconds"?'

'Well, it depends how efficiently the lads have wired the trap.'

Thirty seconds.

Gardner reached down with the wire cutters to the booby trap. A single grey wire snaked up from the grey box and fed into the timer. The awkward angle and the dim lighting made it difficult for him to get at the cable.

Twenty seconds.

Sweat dripped on to his visor. His vision was deteriorating. He felt his heart pulse, and his hand spasmed. He dropped the wire cutters on the floor.

'Shit!'

'What is it?'

Gardner fumbled on the dark floor for the cutters. His hand touched something bumpy. He found them. He straightened his back – and could barely see a thing. His visor misted up and the booby trap was no more than a blur underneath a much bigger grey blur.

Ten.

He felt the wire cutters grip something hard. The cable.

A deep breath. The visor cleared.

Gardner squeezed the handles.

He heard a light click as the cutters sliced through the wire of the booby trap.

A fraction of a second behind it came a buzzing noise, followed by an incessant beeping. The lights on the LCD panel flashed, illuminating the van. Gardner rushed up to the screen. He searched for the red wire. One second had gone, he knew that much. Got to find it, got to—

His eyes located the red wire. He brought the cutters to the wire. Squeezed again.

The red lights continued to go batshit. The LCD presented a single word: 'ARMED'.

Fuck!

Gardner closed his eyes and waited for the world to swallow him up.

After a second, the beeping and buzzing noises stopped.

Nothing happened.

He opened his eyes.

'What's going on, Joe?' White asked.

'I cut the wire, but the timer kept going,' Gardner said.

'Yeah, it'll do that. But without the battery pack to activate the neutron trigger of the bomb, the nuke can't initiate the conventional explosion. Or the uranium isotopes. You've done it, mate.'

On hearing the words Gardner crawled out of the van. He wasn't euphoric. He didn't feel a sense of victory. He just ripped off the helmet and felt like a drowning man coming up for air. He breathed, and his whole body sighed. Dooley and Weston came running over, grinning like the fucking Chuckle Brothers. Sahin tossed him a begrudging nod.

'Water,' Gardner said.

Weston produced a canteen. Gardner thought about drinking it. Instead he poured it over his head. Felt the cool shower of it washing away the thick heat. He let the water rinse the salty taste out of his mouth. And dear God, it was finally over.

Dooley handed him a mobile.

'That pen-pushing wanker at the Firm wants to talk to you,' he said. 'Probably got a gerbil shoved up his arse that he needs unplugging.'

Gardner laughed. It felt good to be back among Blades. He loved the sense of brotherhood, a special bond that some jumped-up posh prick like Leo Land would never understand.

'Bloody good work, Joe,' said Land. 'Really, I'm speechless. I thought we were done for.'

'*We?*' Gardner sputtered. 'If I'd fucked up, you'd still be sitting in your ivory tower.'

'The consequences would have reached much further than the atom cloud,' Land replied sternly.

'I don't give a shit. Where's Aimée?'

'Golan's providing us with her location now. He promises that she won't have come to any harm.'

'He'd best not be lying.'

'Relax. It's under control.'

But Gardner wasn't listening. He looked around for Dooley and Weston, hoping to shoot the shit with them for a while. Nowhere to be seen.

They'd already bugged out.

sixty-four

Maxim Ledinsky watched the news and sipped his mineral water. His office was frugal and lacked the furnishings of his peers. Not because of any firmly held Communist dogma, but simply because he hadn't yet shared the affluence of the others at the FSB. He was relatively young, thirty-eight, and had come to the game late. By the time he'd entered the organization his peers had already rubbed shoulders with the plutocrats and the oligarchs. They'd acquired shares in oil and gas companies, forged links with the *Mafya*.

All that was about to change.

On the TV, the journalist excitedly pointed to the van. The camera zoomed in on it. The van was bathed in spotlights, a security cordon establishing a ten-metre perimeter around it. Ledinsky spoke good English and preferred the BBC to the Russian channels. You learned more and, ridiculously, they even told the truth. The man on his screen, fat and wavy-haired, seemed pleased with himself.

'Nuclear engineers on their way . . . to dispose—'

'Fools,' Ledinsky muttered under his breath. He glanced at his watch. His soon-to-be-replaced watch. He'd get a Rolex, studded with diamonds.

Any second now.

Each nuke came with a killswitch code. A timer override.

Ledinsky walked over to his window. His mind was lost for a moment. Then he snapped out of it and returned to his desk. He propped himself on the corner of it and sipped more water. He liked the dink of ice against the glass.

The killswitch was in place. The orders were simple.

His phone rang. Ledinsky blanked it. He watched the screen whiten as the nuke detonated, then faded to black. Finally the TV returned to the BBC news desk and two presenters with quizzical expressions on their faces, wondering why their colleagues' reports had cut out.

Why indeed? Ledinsky thought, and afforded himself a smile. It was so good when things went according to plan.

sixty-five

Colonel Deniz Sahin looked on as the medics zipped up the last of the body bags. The black plastic sheet consumed the bullet-riddled body of Mahmoud Reza like a snake devouring its victim. Eight bodies. They were running out of body bags and had squeezed two of the five Iranians into a single bag. The death toll also included a single Turkish civilian. The other two, his own men.

There was still a lot of blood on the road, still a swirl of gun smoke that stung his eyes. Still a ringing in his ears. The sound amplified when he closed his eyes. But Sahin didn't want to leave the scene of the shoot-out. At the security cordon perimeter a clutch of politicians were lapping up the attention. Sahin had never been one for the limelight. He preferred to stay in the shadows.

Besides, the deaths of two of his men gnawed at him. Sahin, commanding officer of the Ozel Jandarma Komando, ran a tight ship and he felt their loss keenly. The feeling was familiar yet cold, like gathered dust.

Lieutenant Colonel Umit Bulent, Sahin's 2iC, drew up alongside him. Bulent's face was locked in a permanently blank expression. Never happy, never sad. Except today. Except now. He wore a smile so wide it that could outrun the Bosporus. He lit a cigarette. The brand, Sahin noted, was Russian. Sobranie.

'That was close, boss,' Bulent said.

'I thought you gave up.'

Bulent made a big-deal gesture. 'I'm celebrating. We're allowed to celebrate, boss. We just stopped the fucking city from being blown to pieces.' He sighed smoke. 'Something on your mind?'

Sahin shook his head. 'Look at these idiots,' he growled, nodding at the politicians. 'Acting as if they saved the day.'

'I don't—'

'Someone will pay for this,' Sahin said.

Bulent tilted his head at the departing ambulance. 'Someone already did, boss.'

The 2iC stubbed out his cigarette and left to join in the revelry with the rest of the soldiers. A group of them shook hands and slapped each other on the back. Sahin wished he could share their happiness. That sense of satisfaction. Of a job well done.

Sahin spat on the ground and turned away. Found himself staring at the van containing the nuke fifty metres away, framed by the smooth expanse of the Bosporus Bridge and the blackness of the Strait beneath. Lights crackled and popped on the banks of the Asian side of Istanbul.

Half a dozen forensic experts were scouring the van. Sahin stood still for a moment, then decided he would have a look at this suitcase bomb for himself. After all, it wasn't every day a man got to see a nuclear weapon and lived to tell the story.

Helicopters zipped overhead as he approached. In the distance he could make out the damp blare of car horns. Istanbul was already itching to get moving again. Sahin liked that resilience. He was looking forward to going home to Izmir. To his wife and his two surviving sons.

That was his last-but-one thought.

He was twenty-five metres away when the van seemed to

rock. White heat gushed out of the rear doors in an angry torrent. Something rumbled. In a split second the heat was overwhelming Sahin. And his last thought, as the heat peeled off his skin and burned his hair and nails, was simply: *God, no*.

sixty-six

The cabin shuddered. At first Gardner thought it was turbulence. Then he remembered that the Black Hawk was cruising at 6000 feet – well below its service ceiling of 19,000. Too high up to be affected by wind turbulence from the ground. Too low for mountain turbulence to come into play. Gardner looked out of the open fuselage door and clocked a rinsed-blue basin. Cloudless, which ruled out storm turbulence.

Then Gardner saw something in the distance. Ballooning up from the ground, like a bubble rising to the surface of a body of water.

The bubble burst over the Istanbul skyline fifty miles away. Opaque rings rippled out from the bubble's nucleus and spread across the Bosporus Strait. The rings broke free from the Strait and hit the Sea of Marmara.

The rings kept coming. The waves kept rising. Then the centre of the bubble erupted. Blinding light. Gardner screwed his eyes up. The other guys in the helicopter, the support team of seven MI6 field agents who'd travelled to Istanbul, shielded their faces. Then came a powerful high-pitched note that pealed like a hummingbird inside his skull.

First a fireball rose from the bubble like a gas flare on a giant oil rig, its surface swirling violently as it soared. A stem of smoke pushed the fireball higher into the sky until it hit 3000 feet. At that point the fireball seemed to pause. Then it pulsed a wave of white-hot energy. Gardner braced himself for impact.

The wave moved at a supersonic pace. It blasted everything on the horizon: planes, helicopters, birds – all were blown aside like snowflakes in a blizzard.

Shit. It's coming right this way, Gardner thought. He felt as if he was rocketing towards the belly of an angry volcano. The wave was less than ten miles away. Another second and a half and it would be on top of them. If it hits, he was thinking, it's going to put the chopper into a deadly spin.

The other guys on board should have been burying their heads between their thighs and holding on to their straps for dear life. But every man was transfixed.

A mile away now and the wave turned almost translucent. It was burning up, rapidly losing more energy. He figured that since the wave was dying, maybe the contact wouldn't be so bad.

Then the wave hit, and he knew he'd figured wrong.

Christ, the heat. It blazed his facial hair, seared his eyelids.

The Black Hawk shook violently, lurching this way and that. Gardner felt the G-force of 7000 kg of out-of-control melted steel yank his head from side to side. He could feel the pilot wrestling with the controls, trying to keep the chopper on an even keel. It didn't seem to be fucking working. The Black Hawk spun into a swift descent. Gardner heard the chopper's engine grunt. The extra power and pitch the pilot was applying only forced them down faster. The chopper descended through its downwash. The view out of the fuselage door was sky and sea. Then it was just sea. Charred black water.

Gardner felt his stomach jump, his kidney and liver and bowels playing musical chairs. They were at 3000 feet. Now 2000. Now 1000. The sea became a grid of surging waves. The Black Hawk was so close that Gardner could make out individual dead birds, white petals on the surface.

Less than 500 feet from the sea, and the descent slowed. At 300 Gardner reckoned it was touch and go. At 200 he thought it was just go. One of the agents leaned forward, puked up milky white shit. Around the 150-feet mark the Black Hawk snarled, wobbled and – a breakthrough. It began to lurch forward rather than down. The pilot was fighting hard against the downwash. The chopper bounced like a truck racing over speed bumps.

The engine stopped screaming. Meaning, Gardner knew, the pilot had regained control. Sure enough they began a slow ascent, the men silent, not even able to look each other in the eye. Lost in their thoughts. Only one guy gave the thoughts a voice.

'That was fucking close,' he said.

And then Gardner looked out of the door as the Black Hawk climbed to 2000 feet, and he saw Istanbul. Or rather, what was left of it. Which wasn't much – a shredded land-scape. As far as Gardner could see, not a single building was left standing.

'No,' Gardner replied. '*That* was fucking close.'

He watched the mushroom cloud frozen in the sky. He'd seen a lot of shit in his time. A lot. Seen men maimed, others tortured, still others shot so many times there was literally nothing left but rags and bones. But nothing prepared him for the sight of a nuke totalling a fucking city. He closed his eyes. It must be fucking hell on earth down there, he thought.

'Get us out of here,' he told the pilot. 'Before that big fuck-off radiation cloud starts blowing in our direction.'

The pilot banked right, and right was west. West was Canakkale, and the Strait feeding into the Aegean Sea. West was away from the nuclear holocaust currently taking place in downtown Istanbul. West sounded fucking good to Gardner.

They left the Sea of Marmara behind them. The mushroom cloud shrank. The agents stared back at it. Gardner realized he was actually fucking praying.

They skated south down the Aegean, breezing low past the island of Kos. A signal finally kicked in on Gardner's mobile. He figured the nuke's radioactive rays had interfered with nearby comms systems. He put a call in to Land.

'Jesus, did you see that?' Land's voice was stripped and raw like he had never heard it.

'See? We had fucking front-row seats.'

'It's chaos here, Joe –' the line fizzed with static '– absolute pandemonium.'

'Suitcase nukes were designed for remote detonation,' Gardner replied. Land said nothing, so he went on: 'One guy plants the nuke on foot. Then he retreats to a safe distance and activates it. The idea is they can work even without timers. Think of it as an override. Even after the timer's been disabled, the right person, with access to the right equipment, can still trigger the bomb.'

'Yes, yes, I know all this. What's your point?'

'So who pushed the red button?'

He heard Land scratching something, then say, 'Most likely the Israelis. Publicly they're pinning the blame on the Iranians.'

Gardner took a deep breath. The air circulated around the cave of his chest. 'How many?'

Land was quiet for a beat. Gardner wondered if he'd lost his signal.

'I asked, how many?'

'Heard you the first time, old boy. Best-case scenario is ten thousand dead, twice that number wounded. Factor in those affected by radiation in the medium term and God knows.'

Gardner felt the cold air rise in his chest. He found it difficult to speak. 'And the worst?'

'Fifty thousand. Two hundred thousand wounded.' Land sniffed. 'There was no way you, or I, or anyone could know that someone else was waiting to activate the bomb.'

'Maybe.'

Land was right. But Gardner knew the nightmares would be waiting for him all the same. The women with no legs, the kids burned to charcoal skeletons. He already saw their accusing stares. Asking him why he didn't save them.

Gardner gripped the overhead rails as the Black Hawk pitched to the left. The waves on the Aegean glinted like a million knife edges in the sun. He refocused his mind.

'Where's Aimée?'

'I beg your pardon?'

'We had a deal,' Gardner said.

Land laughed bitterly. 'In case you didn't notice, Joe, a bomb has just gone off. A nuclear bomb. If you're asking me to commit valuable men and resources to picking her up, forget it.'

'But you know where she is?'

'I really don't have time for this,' fumed Land. 'Of course I bloody well know. Thanks to your chum Shai Golan.'

'And?'

'And what, Joe? The base is an old meat-packing factory in the industrial part of Athens. That city's a stinking mess. Worse than bloody Naples.'

Gardner had never been to Naples, or Athens. But he'd operated in some of the most dangerous corners of the earth and ignored Land's bitching. The MI6 man struck Gardner as the kind of guy who'd have a panic attack if he flew economy class.

All Gardner wanted to do was find Aimée and give Land and the Firm his middle finger. He was of a mind to tell Land to shove his job offer up his fucking arsehole. Then again, he figured it was already pretty crammed up there.

'The factory's on Sissi Street in the Votanikos neighbourhood,' Land continued. 'Now if you'll excuse me. Half of Istanbul's blown to smithereens.'

Land hung up.

Gardner was left looking out of the fuselage door. Greece rolled out to the west, parched and rocky. Seven days since I flew to Rio. Feels like a lifetime ago.

sixty-seven

The corn-yellow taxi was stuck in a seemingly endless traffic jam. Sweat on Gardner's palms. Not the sweat of perspiration, but of anticipation. He looked at his palms and realized he was looking forward to seeing Aimée again more than he'd thought. Her face had taken root in his mind. Her voice too. Once we're out of Athens, he decided, we'll go travelling. Mauritius maybe. Or Bali.

Land was right, Gardner reflected as the taxi coughed him up on the corner of Patsi Street and Aigaleo. Athens was a dump. The bits that were old were falling apart, and the bits that were new were falling apart. Gardner had the sense of being caught in a Greenpeacenik's worst nightmare. Every building was crumbling, every street lined with rubbish. A thin, greasy smog wafted through the city. It covered cars, window sills and pavements in soot.

He took €40 from a roll of €700 he'd withdrawn on the Firm's credit card, pressed the notes into the driver's wrinkled palm. Twenty for the fare and twenty for forgetting his face. The driver grunted his agreement.

To the east worn-down neo-classical houses were squeezed between peeling apartment blocks. Stray cats and dogs knocked about the streets, sniffing at bins overflowing with rubbish. Two hundred metres to his north stood the Agricultural University of Athens. Its blocks, white and flat as cake icing, stared out at the Iera Odos Road jammed with restless traffic. Westwards the houses were replaced by a sweeping industrial landscape of creaking factories and warehouses.

Gardner took the left from Patsi Street and walked up Aigaleo for a hundred and forty metres, then hit Agiou Polykarpou Street and paced north-west for five hundred metres. He passed milk-processing plants. It was dark – a few dim street lamps seemed to have been added as an afterthought.

Sissi Street was a left midway down Agiou Polykarpou. The factories carried some security deterrents. Fat padlocks wrapped around the gates, CCTV cameras mounted to the fence posts and Rottweilers snarling and yapping the other side of the chain-link. He found the meat-packing factory; hanging from the gates was an old metal sign with a jokey image of a pig giving a thumbs-up painted on it.

Gardner inspected the gates. No padlock. The place must have been disused for a while, he figured. Then he prised them apart, the metal frame scraping against the tarmac. He made his way across the empty car park towards the factory doors fifty metres away. The windows revealed a neon-blue light humming inside, radiating like a fly trap.

The padlock on the double doors to the building was nothing more than a gesture and covered in ginger-coloured rust. Gardner targeted it with the butt of the Glock 17 9mm pistol he'd retained from the Presevo Valley. Had a full clip, seventeen rounds, felt fucking good to be going in armed. A single swing followed by a satisfying *clank* and the padlock broke loose. He gave the metal door a tug. It gave way without a fight.

This is bloody easy, he thought.

Too easy.

He found himself facing a huge room some forty metres wide and fourteen high. It was maybe sixty metres long, but so dark inside that he could make out less than nothing at the far end. Metal hooks on a looping rail system hung from the ceiling, spaced at eight-metre intervals. The tips of each hook were coated in dried blood from where slabs of cow and pig meat had once hung. Gardner could taste pig fat in the air. In between the rails were long, thin pipes. Lightbulbs dangled from the pipes. They were all dead.

Gardner took a step inside. Needles of cold air pricked his skin and bored down all the way to his bones. He shivered and looked at his feet. The ground was covered in a generation of caked blood and cow shit mixed into a dried, oily-brown paste. I'm in what used to be the meat-processing facility, he thought. Now it was barren.

Except when he looked up, he saw that it wasn't.

In roughly the middle of the room he made out a pair of blue lights fixed to the overhead pipes, glowing softly. The light Gardner had seen outside. They spotlighted something on the floor below. A silhouette of a standing man. Gardner took a few steps deeper into the room and, still some twenty-five metres away, the lights picked out the features on the silhouette's face.

The man's face was pale as a pint of milk, and he had wide, arctic-blue eyes that bulged in their socket. His face displayed the hungry grin of a guy at a dog fight.

'You must be the one with the pretty girlfriend,' he called out.

Sotov, Gardner realized.

'Where is she?'

'I was quite disappointed to learn you didn't die in the fire in Belgrade,' Sotov said. 'But then I always believe in looking on the bright side. And the bright side is – now I get to kill you myself.'

Gardner's right hand gripped the Glock 17. He felt the spring pressure on the trigger mechanism.

'It's Aimée, isn't it? A nice name. And a very attractive face, to go with it, you know.' His lower lip jutted out in agreement. 'A good choice, if I may say so.'

'If you've fucking hurt her, I swear—'

'Please, spare me your machismo.' Sotov waved a hand dismissively. 'Anyway you should try to forget her, my friend. You have far more important things to worry about.'

The sound of boots scraping against the floor made Gardner spin round. He'd been half-expecting an ambush. Two figures were powering towards him from the doorway. T-shirts two sizes too small or biceps two sizes too big, he couldn't quite decide. Eyes grey and blank as rivets nailed into their sockets. The guy on the left had a scar that ran from his upper lip to his eye. The other one had a chinstrap goatee and plasticky skin. Serious-looking, probably ex-Spetsnaz.

And both were packing weapons. Scarface wielded an aluminium baseball bat. Goatee had a Remington Model 870 pump-action shotgun, the barrel sawn down from half a metre to a quarter. Scarface charged ahead of his mate. The tip of the bat was ten metres from Gardner, Scarface storming forward, angling his shoulder muscles, the bat in a two-handed grip. Winding up for a powerful swing.

Seven metres.

The Glock 17 was by Gardner's side. The average human running speed is about four metres per second and he figured Scarface's bulky frame put him a little bit slower than that. So he had just over two seconds to react. Enough time to raise the Glock, but not to aim his shot. By the time he'd centred his sights, Gardner's head would be winging its way to Beijing.

Five metres, and he had his counterattack ready.

At four metres Scarface locked his elbows and flexed his forearms and the bat came crashing down, then horizontally in a swiping manoeuvre. Gardner observed its arc unfolding. Less than a second till it connected with his jaw.

Scarface is a big fucker, Gardner thought. Big – and slow. He had signposted his attack, and Gardner was going to make him pay.

Midway through the guy's swing, with the bat's sweet spot an arm's length from his skull, Gardner dropped his shoulders, bent forward and tucked his chin tight to the base of his neck so that his ears were level with his shoulder blades. He felt the hairs on the back of his head flutter as the bat breezed millimetres overhead.

A half-second and the bat completed its arc. Gardner's eyes centred on Scarface's feet. They were lurching to the left, thrown off balance by the momentum of the swing. One second, maybe two, Gardner told himself. That's all you've got.

It's all I need.

Now he sprang up like a jack-in-the-box, launched himself at Scarface. He wrapped his left arm around the guy's head and pulled it tight against his chest. Scarface was caught unawares; he still had both hands clasped around the handle and couldn't free himself from the headlock. Gardner raised the Glock 17. Drove the muzzle into Scarface's left ear. The big guy saw what was coming and ditched the bat. Too little too fucking late. Gardner depressed the trigger. No safety switch on the Glock. It used a triple integrated safety mechanism. The mechanism was automatically deactivated when the right pressure was applied to the trigger.

Gardner applied the pressure. The trigger clicked.

A bright flash followed by a hollow *ca-rack* bouncing off the factory walls. Scarface howled. His ear was blackened with burn marks from the discharge. Gardner felt blood and brain drenching his left arm. He had to engage all his core and leg muscles to hold Scarface up. Gardner figured he weighed north of twenty stone. But he fought to keep him vertical, because ten metres away Goatee was targeting him with the sawn-off Remington.

The shotgun's muzzle roared. Scarface's body spasmed, the 12-gauge cartridge slamming into his back with such force that Gardner nearly toppled over. His calf muscles burned with the effort. As he fought to regain his balance, blood slopped out of Scarface's lower back and drip-dripped to the floor. Past the dead guy's shoulder Gardner spotted Goatee's left arm sliding the tube magazine beneath the barrel and unloading one, two, three, four rounds of 12-gauge ammo. Each round tore lumps out of Scarface's back and skull. Gardner was thankful that Scarface was so fucking big. He absorbed each bullet like a HESCO block.

On the fifth round, as he grew accustomed to absorbing the shock of the blasts, Gardner managed to nudge the Glock over Scarface's shoulder and direct it at Goatee. He put down three rounds in quick succession. *Tap-tap-tap.* On the first shot Goatee howled and dropped the shotgun. Blood squirted out of his bulging forearm. On the second shot he pawed at the gaping hole torn into his cheek, bits of his teeth blown out of the cavity. Then the third dropped him like a bomb over Baghdad.

Gardner let go of Scarface. Then he spun around, Glock level with his shoulders, primed to finish Sotov. His finger was halfway depressed on the trigger.

Sotov wasn't there.

Gardner became dimly aware of a door at the southern wall. He paced towards it. Twenty metres off he saw it was metal. The door was ajar.

Then he heard the voice. Muffled and frantic. Like someone being smothered with a pillow. Gardner broke into a jog. Scarface's blood ran down his left arm and onto his prosthetic hand. Ten metres to the door and the scream became even more high-pitched. A woman's voice.

Gardner aimed a boot at the rusted lock and kicked it hard. It smashed apart and the door buckled on its hinges and swung open. A battery of ceiling-panel lights glared at him. He scrunched up his eyes, shielded his face and scoped his surroundings. He was in some kind of a storage room. Metal shelf units ran for twenty metres to the other end of the room, and between them a column of storage boxes, more than thirty in total. On the shelves were stacks of computers and hard disks.

Lying amid the boxes was Aimée.

She was bound at the ankles and wrists with nylon cord. A gag was tied around her mouth. The gag was tight; it dug deep into the corners of her mouth. Aimée's eyes widened at the sight of Gardner. She shook her head furiously. She was drenched in sweat. He ran his eyes over her body for injuries. No bloodstains on her shirt or jeans.

Gardner knelt beside Aimée and unknotted the gag.

'It's a trap,' she gasped.

Her eyes were fixed at a spot beyond Gardner's left shoulder. He followed her gaze and saw a small black box the size of a webcam at waist height on the left shelf. A red laser beam projected from the black eye of the box. It cut a path across the room – until it hit Gardner's left shoulder.

A network of wires ran out of the box and coiled up the wall and along the length of the ceiling. At the far end they descended into bulky plastic packets, each the size of a brick and off-white in colour, fixed to the walls. C4 plastique, Gardner realized.

Factory's primed with enough of the stuff to flatten a fucking village.

The dread set in a fraction of a second later.

Gardner hoisted Aimée to her feet. She grabbed his shoulders. Her soft fingertips pressed against his muscles and sparked up something warm inside the cave of his chest. The warmth trickled down to his stomach. He blocked it out.

'We have to get out of here,' he said.

Aimée was on her feet, hesitating.

'Right the fuck now!'

In Gardner's experience sensor-trigged explosives had a time delay of around twelve seconds from the shorting of the circuit to the ignition of the primary detonator. Gardner put them at ninety metres from the factory doors.

'Wait,' Aimée said. She lunged at the shelf on the right and scooped up an Apple MacBook Pro laptop and two USB flash drives, each attached to a loop of cord.

'We don't have time!'

'That's it,' she said, putting the loops over her head like a couple of necklaces. Gardner was already at the door leading into the processing room. He seized her hand and hauled her through the doorway, her feet lifting half an inch off the ground. Eight seconds.

They sprinted down the meat-processing room, Gardner's eyes unsettled by the shift from light to dark. He stumbled once, twice; regained his balance. Thirty metres from the door, he figured they had four seconds at a push. Aimée was straggling behind him. Her breathing had more ups and downs in it than a Wall Street stock graph. Ten metres from the door and her breathing stopped altogether. Gardner turned. Aimée had tripped up. He grabbed her. Three seconds.

Pushed Aimée through the doors.

Two seconds.

'The laptop!' she shouted.

One.

Gardner burst through the opening. He had the laptop in his right hand. He felt the ground buckle and grind. A rush of hot wind whipped his back, a wind that bent metal and blasted mortar and broke glass, the mass of it swirling out from the epicentre, unstoppable. Debris rained over him. He was three metres outside the building, then five. Aimée was still running ahead. He increased his running speed, fighting hard not to lose his balance, and reached Aimée as she pushed through the chain-link gates. Behind them, the factory was crumbling, great fists of smoke pounding on its roof.

'I thought' – Aimée's hands were on her knees – 'you were dead.'

Gardner wiped smoke from his eyes. 'You OK?'

Aimée nodded.

'Come on,' he said, holding out his hand, 'it's not safe here.'

Not with Sotov still on the loose.

sixty-eight

2352 hours.

They fled down Iera Odos and hailed a taxi. Gardner told the driver to take them to any hotel where they could get a room at a quarter to midnight. The driver was slow and had a lazy manner. Gardner told him to step on it. He ferried them down the road, fire engines and police cars speeding down the opposite lane. Then he took a left at the end of the road and after six hundred metres a right at the Acropolis. Another six hundred south and they came to the Palace Hotel on Constitution Square.

The receptionist was a guy in his forties with a permanently arched left eyebrow. One look at Gardner and Aimée, head to toe in dust, blood and bruises, and the right eyebrow was soon challenging the left for top spot. But he said nothing as Gardner parted with the better part of €400, cash, for one of the better rooms, then slipped another €100 into the receptionist's breast pocket.

'Anyone asks after us – you don't have to lie,' he said. 'Just call our room and give us a warning.'

The receptionist thought about it for a long second. His eyes drifted to his breast pocket. Drifted to Gardner's chest. He nodded.

The room was luxurious in the old European style. King-size bed with Egyptian silk covers, an antique wooden dresser, overhead fan and a view overlooking a courtyard. In other circumstances Gardner would have been tempted to jump Aimée's bones. But now he was curious about the items she'd insisted on recovering from the factory. Aimée paced over to the dresser, cleared away the welcome packs and tourist maps and fired up the MacBook Pro. Removing the flash drives from around her neck, she inserted them in the slots on the side of the laptop. Gardner went into the bathroom. He ran the taps and scrubbed off Scarface's blood.

'Mind telling me what's on the memory sticks?' he called from the bathroom. No answer. He sloshed more cold water over his face. Wiped his hands and face with a towel soft as Aimée's arse.

'Aimée?'

'I don't know.'

He stepped back into the bedroom. A knock at the door. He frowned at Aimée, gestured for her to stay put. The Glock was lying on the bed. Gardner grabbed it and slipped it behind his back. He peered through the spyhole. Spied a Greek guy in his late fifties to early sixties, dressed in a butler's outfit. Not the assassin type. He rested his hands on a dining tray in front of him. The old man looked dog-tired.

Gardner opened the door.

'Wine and canapés,' said the butler, wheeling the trolley in, Gardner rotating so that the Glock remained hidden from view. 'Compliments of the hotel.'

The butler parked the trolley in the centre of the room. Tucking the Glock into the waistband of his combats, Gardner gave the butler a €10 tip. Guy didn't even bother to smile or say thanks as he left.

'Our lucky night,' Gardner said.

Aimée returned to the MacBook. She double-clicked on the flash drive's icon and a series of twelve folders displayed. They seemed to be in sequence. The first folder was labelled ML_0001, the second ML_0002, and so on, with the last folder labelled ML_0012.

'I overhead Sotov talking on the phone,' Aimée explained. 'He shouted for a long time. When the call was over he ordered his men to rig explosives up to the whole building. I remember him saying to one of the men, "Nothing must survive." Then he looked at me with this . . . this grin on his face. "That includes you," he said.' Aimée turned back to the screen.

Gardner turned to the canapés. The tray was filled with asparagus spears layered with Parma ham, smoked salmon roulades and mozzarella, cherry tomato and basil skewers. He poured two glasses of Katnook Estate 2002. He gulped some of the fruity red as Aimée opened the first folder.

It held several Word documents. Gardner leaned in while Aimée opened the first file.

Reams of seemingly random characters ran across the screen. Like hieroglyphics. Aimée scrolled down. Two pages in, the gibberish turned into some kind of a script. Gardner ran his eyes down the text. It was in Cyrillic.

'Transcripts of mobile-phone conversations,' Aimée said. She pointed to a row of numbers above the first line of dialogue. 'This is the encrypted GPRS data being transmitted from the mobile to the carrier.' Gardner studied the numbers.

'They all begin with a seven,' he said.

'The international dialling code for Russia,' Aimée said.

'Do you speak Russian?'

She feigned surprise. 'I investigate the *Mafya*. In Serbia. Both of which have strong links to Russia. Seriously, what do you think?'

Shrugging, he said, 'Just asking.'

'I need a few minutes to read through and get my head around what we're looking at.'

Gardner left Aimée to it. He munched on a couple more canapés and decided that finger food was fucking overrated. The grub hadn't filled a divot, let alone the hole, in his stomach. He ditched the wine glass and scoped the courtyard. It looked quiet outside. More than quiet: dead. The air was hot, but a mild breeze blew through the cypresses lining the court-yard. His mind wandered back to Aimée and the way their breaths mixed in the warm space between her lips and his. He liked the thought.

'OK,' Aimée said, her breath shaky. 'I think I got it.'

Gardner stared away from the window. 'What does it say?'

'It's a conversation between two men. One of them is Aleksandr Sotov—'

'The *Mafya* guy.'

'The other's Maxim Ledinsky.' Seeing Gardner's blank expression, she went on, 'Ledinsky heads up the Military Counterintelligence office at the FSB.'

Gardner sat down on the edge of the bed. His muscles ached for a time-out. FSB. Federal Security Services in Russia. Shit was getting deep. 'What are they talking about?'

Aimée scanned the lines again, mouthing strange words. 'They're discussing the delivery of a package. Here, this conversation is from three weeks ago. Ledinsky says, "Everything is under control, but it will have to be a suitcase device rather than something bigger." Sotov says, "Why? The Iranians expect a full-sized delivery. We give them something this small, they'll think we're fobbing them off." Ledinsky says, "If something that big goes missing, it makes us all look stupid. A suitcase device – anyone can lose one of those. Besides, Reza will be glad just to get his hands on anything."' Aimée scrolled down.

'They're talking about the nuke,' Gardner said. 'Mahmoud Reza was the army guy trying to smuggle the suitcase bomb across the border to Iran.' He rubbed his brow. 'Who is this Ledinsky guy again? FSB?'

Aimée nodded. She opened another file and browsed through it. 'There must be fifty transcripts here,' she said. 'Maybe more.'

'All between Ledinsky and Sotov?'

'Some are encrypted. I can't decode them.' She smiled apologetically at Gardner. 'My skills don't extend to decrypting stuff, I'm afraid.'

'We'll find someone,' Gardner said. He ran a hand over his stubble. It felt greasy. 'From what you've just told me, it sounds like Sotov and Ledinsky – the Russian *Mafya* and government – *knew*.'

'I'd go further than "sounds". I'd say "one hundred per cent proves".'

'But Russia's a close ally of Iran,' Gardner said. 'It built their nuclear power station, for fuck's sake. Screwing them over doesn't make sense.'

Aimée gently rested her fingers on the keyboard. 'You know, these files might be the only evidence of Russia actively taking part in the attack.' She opened another file and furrowed her brow. 'Look!'

'What is it?'

'There are some pictures on the drives too.'

Gardner knelt beside Aimée for a closer look. His hand brushed against her thigh and he felt something warm expand and contract in his chest.

'They don't exactly look like Sotov's holiday snaps,' he said, looking at the thumbnails of a dozen pixellated images in the folder. Aimée blew one up to full-screen. Just a mess of colours, kind of thing a five-year-old would bring home from school.

'They don't look like anything at all,' Aimée said.

'Whatever they are, someone doesn't want other people looking.'

Gardner stood up and dug out his mobile. He hit dial on Land's contact details.

Athens was an hour behind London, which made it 23.19 wherever the fuck Land was. Probably still in his office,

Gardner guessed from the sound of his voice. 'Yes?' He croaked his words. They were strung out like guitar strings.

'You'll want to hear this,' Gardner said.

A pause. 'Make it quick.'

Gardner told Land about the factory, about the *Mafya* lying in wait for him and the explosion. When he was finished, Land said simply, 'Is that it? You've got Aimée.'

'There's one other thing,' Gardner said. 'We pulled some files out of the factory right before it turned into a giant fucking firework.'

'Oh yes? What kind of files?'

'Transcripts, mainly. Some of them are encrypted, but the general picture is clear enough. The Russians knew about the Israeli plot. In fact, it seems like they even helped make it happen.'

'Impossible,' Land chuckled.

'I'm looking at the transcripts right now,' Gardner told him. 'If it hadn't been for Aimée, these would've been destroyed back at the factory. They don't want this information to get out.'

Land was quiet for a long while. Gardner heard the gaslight crackle of a cigarette end lighting up.

'Right,' he said finally. 'Where are you right now?'

'The Palace Hotel.'

'Stay where you are,' Land exhaled smoke. 'I'm coming to get you.'

sixty-nine

Fifty-four minutes later Gardner's phone sparked into life. Land.

'I've got you a way out of there,' he said.

'Go on.'

Aimée was lying asleep on the bed. Gardner stayed awake. One of them had to. But he wouldn't have slept anyway. His mind was jumping through hoops, trying to figure out what the Russians' fucking game was. Tension tied his back muscles into figure-of-eight knots. He paced up and down, intermittently sitting on the desk chair opposite the bed. Red Bull from the mini-bar on the desk, Glock 17 in his lap, eyes on the door.

'There's an airstrip just outside Malakassa, about forty kilometres north-east of Athens. Be there in an hour. I've arranged for one of our private planes to escort you both back to London.'

Land killed the call. Gardner placed his right hand on Aimée's shoulder, gently nudged her. She moaned. Her breath tickled the locks of her hair lying across her lips. He rubbed her arm. This time she woke up.

'Time to bug out.'

'If you're going to wake a girl up at this time, you really should have a cup of hot chocolate ready,' she said, rubbing her eyes.

'Sorry, love, no time. You'll have to make do with cold water.'

'The attractions of your lifestyle are endless.'

Aimée carried the MacBook and flash drives, Gardner stuffing the Glock under his shirt. He'd weighed up their exit strategy and decided not to risk leaving through the front door. The same receptionist was likely to be on duty and if anyone came asking questions, he'd have the exact time of Gardner and Aimée's departure noted on the computer system. So at the end of the corridor they turned right instead of left and down a marble staircase that led into the court-yard. From their room Gardner had spotted at the other end of the courtyard an ornamental gate which led to an alley-way adorned with overhanging vines and murals. At the far end the alley opened onto a busy main street. They headed towards a 24/7 car-rental joint. It was dark in the streets, save for the Parthenon lit up on top of the Acropolis.

The rental place was a local business. Gardner parted with €90 for a black BMW E46 sedan, 325i model, 2.5-litre engine. He was left with the short end of €60. Aimée kept the laptop and flash drives with her in the front seat. Gardner whacked the air con on full blast.

Four kilometres north of the Acropolis, Gardner hit the toll road onto the same E75 motorway he'd driven on from Belgrade to Brezovan. In Serbia the road had been fairly busy, but, in Greece at nearly one in the morning, their BMW was the only vehicle on the road. Aimée checked more files on the second flash drive.

Gardner chewed up thirty-three kilometres of motor-way flanked by half-constructed villas and run-down hotels, cordoned-off ruins and ramshackle farms. He spotted the Malakassa turn-off and felt a band tighten around his core.

Malakassa was a dot-on-a-map kind of place and had a half-arsed feel to it, as if the builders had given up partway through. They entered from the south, which seemed to be the centre of town. A couple of kilometres north and the bare-knuckle range of Mount Parnitha loomed. Gardner felt the knots on his back begin to loosen. At fucking last. We'll get home and be done with the Firm. Gardner wasn't exactly a romantic type of guy, but he imagined spending the night with Aimée in a cottage somewhere in the Cotswolds, wrapped up on a sofa, flames crackling in the fireplace while droplets of rain tap-tapped on the old window panes.

The airstrip was a ribbon of smoothed-out clay about two kilometres long in the middle of a grassy field. A farmhouse to the east of the airstrip looked abandoned. A Gulfstream 100 private jet was waiting at the strip's southern edge.

Gardner switched off the headlights and hit the brakes. The BMW halted a hundred metres from the airstrip.

'What are we waiting for?' Aimée asked.

'Something's not right.'

Aimée scrunched her eyes up.

'The soil on the airstrip,' Gardner said. 'It's undisturbed. And the whole place is dead. This look like a plane that just landed to you?'

'Maybe the plane was already waiting here.'

'A luxury jet just happens to be lying dormant a kilometre north of nowheresville in Greece?' Gardner reached for the Glock he'd dumped in the side pocket of the door. Thirteen rounds left and no spare clips.

'I'm going ahead on foot. Wait here till I signal,' he said, stepping out into the night. The Glock felt cold in his hand. The full moon cast a thin wash of light over the landscape.

Sixty metres from the airstrip Gardner checked out the terrain around the Gulfstream. Christ's thorn bushes and bundles of rocks were scattered parallel to the airstrip. The farmhouse looked abandoned: black holes for windows and worn car tyres dumped by the front door. A Grand Cherokee

Jeep was parked by the farmhouse. Tinted windows, engine off.

So where the fuck's everyone?

He looked back to the BMW. Saw the faint glow of the MacBook screen refleced on Aimée's face.

Ca-rack!

The first shot seemed to come from nowhere, like a quake rolling under the valley floor. Soil burst up a few inches ahead of Gardner. Dirt sprayed his face. He couldn't place the shot. His first instinct was to hit the ground, but his training told him that he had to reach proper cover, fucking immediately.

A second shot, this one ripping into the ground an inch from his feet. Now he had a bearing on the sound. He looked to his west. Towards the farmhouse. The Jeep. The headlights pushed out tubes of light, and between the rifle cracks the bass note of its engine revving up.

A third flash now. The round whizzed past Gardner close enough that he could feel the heat coming off the cartridge. Fifty metres separated him from the BMW. Too far to go back.

The Gulfstream's wheels, he thought. At ten metres, that was the closest protection. He broke into a low run, scrambling forward on the rugged surface. White flashes from the Jeep, one after the other.

Five urgent strides and Gardner was at the wheels, midway down the underside of the jet and directly beneath the wing canopies. Each wheel was about half a metre wide and half as tall. He hunkered behind the wheel. A triple volley of rounds slammed into the rubber. The Jeep picked up speed and headed away from the Gulfstream and towards the BMW. Gardner knew that if he stayed behind cover, Aimée would be exposed. But he didn't have a choice; if he broke free from cover now, he'd be fucking toast.

Cursing, he hustled round the side of the wheel to avoid the Jeep's shifting line of fire. The shots came in a staccato rush which made him think there was more than one shooter in the Jeep. Semi-automatic weapons had a smooth rate of fire, and the space between discharges on a single-shot trigger selector tended to be even. Some of the shots came on top of each other. Definitely more than one shooter, he figured.

Gardner returned fire, putting four rounds down in quick succession. The maximum effective range for the 9x19mm Luger rounds chambered in his Glock 17 was about a hundred metres. In the hazy blur of daylight he'd halve that number, but on a crisp night like this the rounds travelled clean and they travelled true. Each round lit up the Gulfstream's bodywork.

Nine rounds left.

Sixty metres from the airstrip the Jeep slowed next to the BMW.

A shadow emerged from the Jeep's front passenger door and approached the car. He could see Aimée inside the BMW. She was shutting the MacBook and reaching for the door lock selector. Gardner shaped to race out from behind his cover. The shooters inside the Jeep had other ideas. Bullets sounded and pinned him down. He crawled around to the rear of the wheel, his body heavy with sweat and failure.

A break in the gunfire and the growl of the engine. Gardner rolled out from the wheel and adopted a kneeling firing position, Glock held in a sturdy firing position, his left arm bent at a ninety-degree angle at the elbow and across his chest, his fake hand acting as a firing platform beneath the tensile wrist of his right hand. He saw the shadow dragging Aimée back into the Jeep. Now the Jeep was growling again, ready to race away.

Ninety metres, he reckoned. Nearly a hundred. Nearly out of range.

He took a deep breath, relaxed his shoulder muscles, tensed his wrist. Put down two rounds at the shadow, who was now trying to shoot up the BMW's tyres. The bullets cracked both ways through the cold sky. He missed the shadow each time but as he was about to loose a third round, two brilliant-white flashes spat out the rear of the Jeep. The first slapped into the Gulfstream's wheel, puncturing the rubber. The second hit Gardner's right arm. He recoiled. The shadow was back inside the Jeep. The Glock fell away from Gardner's hand.

When he looked up, the Jeep was gone.

Gardner dragged himself to the BMW. He slumped in the driver's seat and felt the searing hot pain screaming on his right arm. Aimée's scent was still in the air. Then it was overwhelmed by the cordite on his body.

He put a call in to Land. The line stammered with a series of clicks as it struggled to establish a connection. Then he got a shrill beeping tone. He hung up, waited a minute and dialled again. Still engaged, so he turned his attention to his wound.

A graze ran the length of Gardner's good arm. Up close it was worse than he'd first assumed. A five-millimetre-deep trench of necrotic tissue began just below the short head of his bicep, carved up into his rotator cuff and signed off at the clavicle bone at his shoulder. There was blackened skin at the frayed edges of the trench. It looked like he'd grown impatient with a slow-healing wound and ripped out the stitches.

Still, could've been worse, Gardner told himself. If the bullet had penetrated the flesh, you'd be haemorrhaging blood and miles from the nearest doctor.

Gardner U-turned the BMW and headed back to Athens.

I need to speak to Land. I need answers.

And I need to find out who the fuck's snatched Aimée.

seventy

The Panthers Gym was located down a nothing backstreet in the fashionable quarter of Hamburg's Schanzenviertel. Spitting distance from the boutique shops and the free-trade coffee houses and the students in tight jeans and scruffy haircuts, it was open twenty-four hours a day, which indicated that the manager knew his customers well. Specifically, career-minded guys in their mid-thirties to early fifties who needed to cram in forty minutes of stress-busting weights and cardio whenever their schedules permitted. So, 24/7 opening hours. But no staff at the desk at five-fifteen in the morning, to save money.

So it was easy for Charles Kruger II to enter the place and locate the target.

Kruger didn't do gyms any more. He had the overall definition to show for twenty-five years of crunching abs and hacking squats, the classic X-shaped figure. But his chiselled body was offset by his face. Untrimmed beard that looked like a rat had lain down and died on his jaw. Roman nose that lost its way halfway down his face and wound up somewhere approximate to his right cheek. About the only thing that was perfect about Kruger's face were his teeth.

The gym was practically empty. He made his way past the rows of dormant treadmills and exercise bikes and hit the weights area. Dumb-bells were lined up on a rack to his right.

In front of him several exercise benches and a cable-crossover machine.

The target was to the left.

Kruger had spent the past seven days monitoring the guy, looking for a pattern. Like most guys in his position, the target tried to avoid having any semblance of a routine. He took a different route to his workplace each morning, slept in a different hotel every night of the week. He was careful, Kruger conceded.

But not careful enough.

The target was grunting his way through a set of wide-grip bench presses. His back was arched against the bench and his feet planted firmly on the floor as he strained to push up the bar. Kruger counted three 20kg weight plates and a 10kg plate on each side. The bar counted for another 20kg by itself. The guy was pressing a total of 160kg, or twice the weight of the average man. That was another thing, Kruger thought: his employers had told him that the target was a big guy and would present a formidable opponent. Big as an ox and twice as fucking dumb, they said.

Didn't bother Kruger none.

After all, the bigger they come ... Well, let's just say you ain't met the guy who could beat you, Kruger told himself.

'Need a spot?' he said.

'I got it,' the target grunted. Then his elbows seemed to lock and his grip on the barbell wavered. The guy shut his eyes and gave it everything he had.

'Here, let me help you out,' Kruger said. The guy couldn't talk. His disc-shaped face bloated like a pig's bladder as he fought to keep the barbell suspended eight inches from his chest.

Kruger paced around to the back of the bench press. The only other gym user, a wafer-thin strip of a guy busting out 10kg dumb-bell curls in front of the mirror, glanced over.

Kruger shot him a nod that said, Get the fuck out of here. The guy ditched the weights. Bugged out. Kruger tended to have that effect on people.

'OK, I got it,' Kruger said to the target.

The target breathed a sigh of relief as Kruger clasped his hands around the grip.

Then the target opened his eyes, and the relief washed away. 'What the fuck—?'

He eyeballed Kruger's right arm. The entire lower portion of his arm beneath the elbow was prosthetic.

Kruger released his left hand. He held the barbell's full weight in his right hand but despite the heavy burden, he displayed no sign of stress. Indeed the opposite was true. Kruger seemed as if he could hold onto that barbell all day long.

'Your name is Stefan Margitz, correct?' said Kruger, his voice finally betraying his Texan drawl.

'I don't understand—'

Kruger eased his grip on the barbell a little. It dropped five centimetres, fifteen from the target's chest.

'Shit. OK, I'm Margitz,' the guy said. He stared at the barbell. His eyes leaked pure, unfiltered fear.

'I have a message from a mutual friend. Dmitri wants his money.'

'I don't have it with me.'

Kruger dropped the bar two more inches. Margitz's lungs filled with terror.

'Choose your words carefully, pal.'

Snatching at air, the target said, 'Please, just give me two more days.'

'You got two more seconds.'

'Shit, shit . . .'

Kruger shook his head. 'Last chance.'

Margitz's face tightened up like a screw in a hole. He seemed to find courage from somewhere. 'Fuck it, I don't have it. I'm warning you, asshole. You'd better lose the fucking weight.'

'Or what?'

'I'll grab that hand of yours and shove it so far up your ass you'll be tickling your fucking tongue.'

This last comment made Kruger laugh. Not because it was funny, but because Margitz had made the mistake of so many others. He saw a false limb and assumed weakness. Whereas the opposite was true.

Kruger's was no ordinary limb. While the standard-issue prosthetic was designed to look like and perform the tasks of the one that had originally been lost – essentially a replacement – Kruger's arm actually enhanced his capabilities.

Three years earlier he'd been the subject of a cutting-edge Pentagon programme. Targeted Muscle Reinnervation (TMR) involved connecting his prosthetic limb directly to the nervous system and motor cortex of his brain, using a cyberware gateway implanted in his spinal column. This cyberware allowed Kruger to control any network or machine that used a computer processor. He could remotely operate machinery, drive cars from a kilometre away and even access the internet *just by thinking about it.*

The geeks at the Pentagon's Defense Advanced Research Projects Agency (DARPA) didn't stop there. They built him an arm that was practically indestructible. His arm was bulletproof, flameproof and fitted with special bionic muscles that had fifty times the force and stopping power of a human arm. Kruger could crush a man's neck with one quick clip.

So Kruger laughed, because really, Margitz didn't know shit.

'What's so funny?' Margitz asked.

'This,' Kruger said.

He let go of the barbell.

The barbell crashed down ten centimetres onto Margitz's chest. Then it drove several more into his pectorals. His ribs cracked, splintered, snapped. His diaphragm made a dull squelching sound as the bar squashed it. Kruger heard the hiss of air escaping. Which was appropriate, he reckoned, because his chest looked like a fucking punctured American football. Blood gurgled in Margitz's mouth as he pawed at the barbell.

His face turned a shade of frozen blue.

Then he stopped pawing.

Kruger quit the gym.

Out on the backstreet, he lit a cigarillo. Kruger wasn't a cigar kind of guy. Used to be. Until the ban. But fucked if he was going to spend thirty minutes outside working his way through a Cohiba. Cigarillos were smaller, lighter, quicker to smoke.

He was tapping through his contacts list when the guy called him. Not the guy on the Margitz assignment; someone else. A job he was sitting on. Kruger smiled. He liked these periods when work was easy to come by.

'We have the girl,' said the voice. He spoke slowly and mauled his words. They all did. It was a Russian thing.

'Sweet,' Kruger said.

'She will be at the premises in three hours.'

He checked his watch. It was five-thirty, exactly an hour behind Greece. 'Sweet.'

'The soldier – the Englishman,' the Russian sneered, 'he thinks he can save the bitch.'

'Aww,' said Kruger, puffing on his cigarillo. 'Sweet.'

seventy-one

Athens. 0556 hours.

Four hours and no fucking word from Land. Gardner tried getting through for the fourth time in forty minutes. Engaged. Again. He threw the phone against the dashboard and swore at the windshield.

Back to Athens. Back to streets of unfinished buildings and empty store units, a legacy of the tanked economy.

Gardner rested the BMW on a side street in the Plaka district, in the centre of the city. While driving he'd thought about renting a cheap hotel room but decided against it. He was down to his last €60. He might need that money for an emergency. And whoever had waited in ambush at the airstrip would surely be looking for him. Besides, it was a hell of a lot easier to ring around hotels and get a name than chase a guy in a car.

He had to clean his wound. Regiment operators were required to have a better understanding of treatment and medicine than the average squaddie. They were expected to survive months in hostile terrain with no recourse to professional medical care, with the result that Gardner knew pretty much everything there was to know about bullets and the damage they caused. For a start, bullets were not sterilized, nor were the guns they were fired from. Ditto the air they travelled through. Which meant they carried bacteria into the flesh. Clothing fabric was also riddled with bacteria. And Gardner's flesh had been exposed to a large dose of both.

He rooted around the BMW. Found what he was looking for in the glove compartment. A bottle of fresh mineral water. Gardner unscrewed the cap on the bottle with his right hand. Then he gripped the bottle in his fake left, awkwardly tipping the contents over the open wound. The water was lukewarm. It flowed through the gouge of his wound, carrying bits of grit and dirt with it. When he was done, Gardner chucked the bottle and tried moving his arm. Stung like fuck, and the smell was rotten. But at least he could flex it.

Then he tried Land again.

This time he answered.

'Call you back,' he said before Gardner could get a word out.

Gardner waited for several minutes. His heart was beating fast. He felt its beat fluttering at the top of his throat. Whoever's snatched Aimée, he swore to himself, they're going to pay. With their fucking lives.

Ten minutes later his phone sparked into life.

'Yes?' Land said.

'It was an ambush. We got attacked at the plane, we—'

'I heard. The pilots have both turned up dead in a hotel room in Kalamos. Had their throats slit.'

'Someone was waiting there for us,' Gardner replied. 'They shot at me and nabbed Aimée.'

'I'm sorry to hear that.'

'Spare me the bullshit, Land. Who the fuck were those people?'

'Calm down, Joe.' Land's voice was steadying now. 'And listen carefully. I've this very moment come out of a meeting with our top field agents. You say they took Aimée?'

'I couldn't get to her.'

'It was the Russians.'

'Sotov?'

'This goes higher than Sotov. The Russian government is involved.'

'What about Aimée?'

'One of our agents in Moscow says two particularly unpleasant individuals have been hired to take care of her.'

Matchsticks lit under Gardner's chin.

'Who are they?'

'They're called the Kazan Twins. A man and a woman; brother and sister, allegedly. They specialize in torture for the *Mafya* and the federal security services. The man skins people alive.'

Gardner's world shrank. You promised, he reminded himself. You said you'd protect her.

And now this.

'But what do they need to torture Aimée for?' Gardner wondered aloud. 'They've got the laptop and the flash drives.'

'That's not the way Russians think, Joe.'

Gardner rang his tongue over his teeth. They were stained with dirt. 'Where is she?'

'An apartment block on Kapsis Square, in the Marousi district. About twenty minutes from your present location.'

'How long until these fucking torturers get there?'

'Spot of bad news for you, I'm sorry to say,' Land said, his voice now sibilating with stress. 'Our agent says the Kazan Twins boarded a private flight to Athens nearly three hours ago. It takes around three hours from Moscow by plane. Say another thirty minutes to reach Aimée.' Land paused. 'If you hurry, you can just about make it. You have to stop them, Joe—'

The mobile lost its signal. Gardner removed the battery pack, gave it ten seconds and reinserted it. When he turned the phone on, he had a weak signal. One measly bar. But he also had a new message. A brief video clip. No more than five seconds. It was grainy and heavily pixellated. A face was set against a grey-brown background. The expression was fear. The person's lip was cut and one eye bruised.

Aimée.

seventy-two

Gardner thundered east down Alexandras Avenue for five kilometres, then banged a left on the dual-lane and shuttled north along Kifisalas Avenue and past the graffitied shell of the old Panathinaikos football stadium. The fuel gauge indicated that the tank was half empty. The tachometer needle was in the red zone. Gardner put the BMW into fourth gear and watched the speedometer climb to ninety-five.

The Marousi neighbourhood was moneyed up and extravagant. It housed the financial district and the Olympic Stadium was visible in the distance. Kapsis Square was sandwiched between two small hills. Gardner pulled into the side of the road, killed the engine and rested his hands on the wheel. Daybreak in Athens and the wild dogs were retreating.

He double-checked the address Land had given him: 10 Kapsis Square. He scoped the square. Hotel to the right, a three-star job trying to front up as a five-star and falling way short. High-rise building on the left, apartments stacked on top of each other, each floor smaller than the one below it, like a mountain of shot glasses. Half the apartments had 'For Sale' signs tacked to the balconies. The road was slick from a burst of rainfall at three o'clock that morning. Gardner's eyes settled on the offices at the bottom of the apartment block.

That's where they are, he thought. His pulse quickened.

Torture was a fucking speciality dish in Russia, and the Kazan Twins were about to make Aimée the main course.

Gardner climbed out of the BMW. The grain of the Glock 17's stippled grip pressed into the small of his back. The square was deserted. He noticed a Mercedes-Benz E550, arsenic black, outside the apartments. A car that swish looked out of place here. Raindrops on the bonnet and windshield told Gardner the car had been sat there since at least three that morning.

He paced the thirty metres to the building, scanning his peripheral vision. At the main door he pressed the handyman button. There was a buzzing, then a click. He was in.

The corridor was empty. Gardner dug the Glock 17 out of his jeans, gripped it by his side. The lino floor smelled of bleach. His footsteps echoed in the cool corridor.

He climbed two flights of stairs, his shoes squeaking on the polished lino treads. At the door to apartment 10, Gardner raised his right leg, dragged his foot back and delivered a front-kick directly onto the lock. People only shot door locks in the movies. In real life the shooter was more likely to blind himself from the metal splinters flying off the lock plate, or even have the round rebound on him, than actually bust it open. A simple kick was twice as effective and half as loud.

The lock cracked. The door swung open. Gardner hoisted the Glock to shoulder level and edged into the hallway. Three doors ahead. Two on the left, one on the right. Doors on the left closed, door on the right open, sunlight spilling like honey into the hallway from an unseen window. He felt his bowels constricting. His breathing was fast and light.

Gardner smelled cigarette smoke.

He heard the slam of a door and the shudder of a wall. Coming from your ten o'clock. From beyond the open doorway, twelve metres away.

Now he was inside the room, Glock nosing ahead of him.

He was hyper-alert. The room was L-shaped. He arced the pistol in a clockwise direction. The room was bare. Totally fucking spartan. No furniture to speak of – just an ashtray on the floor, thin smoke rising from a dozen filter tips. Next to the ashtray was a box of crumpled Mayfairs. Who the fuck smokes Mayfairs in Greece?

Then he spied movement at his three o'clock.

At the far wall.

The wall had a door that led out onto the northern face of the apartment block. As Gardner walked towards it he caught the hurried *clank-clank* of shoes treading on metal. He burst through the door and found himself on the platform of a fire escape. He scanned the area below. A metal staircase spiralled down into an alleyway that was a universal shade of brown. Two figures were sprinting out of the alley and into the square. A man and a woman. Too far away and too grainy still to make out their faces. All he could see was that the woman's hair was ginger. The guy was scrawny, had a bald patch and wore a grey suit.

The fucking Kazans.

He thought about firing off a shot. Decided against it. The twins didn't have Aimée with them. He needed to capture them alive and find out where she was being held.

He cleared the bottom step of the fire escape five seconds after the pair had disappeared from view.

Back in the square, he clocked his BMW. The chassis was sitting a few inches lower than normal. They'd slashed his fucking tyres before hightailing it. Gardner figured they could have only gone one way out of the square, and thundered into a street backing on to an American-style mall. And there was the woman, the guy just ahead, both sprinting hard.

Gardner's own running style was pretty solid. He had a lot of calf and quad muscles to compensate for his average stride, and his lungs put the average guy's to shame. But the Kazans were tall and skinny, with long legs, and for every stride they took Gardner needed to take two to stop them widening the gap.

If I can just get to her, he thought. He was thirty metres from her. Thirty-five to the guy. He felt an elevator of pain shoot up from his right oblique to his ribcage. Don't lose the pace, he urged himself. Beads of sweat dripped into his eyes, salting his vision.

The street ended where the mall ended, and there the twins took a right into a narrow side street that served the backs of restaurants on both sides. Outdoor chairs and tables were stacked up against the walls on either side of the road. Waste food formed a sludge river that flowed from one end of the street to the other.

Twenty metres to the woman.

Then she tripped on her ankle.

Gardner dug deeper. The pain took a return route down his left side, but now he was just ten metres from the woman. She was scraping herself off the pavement. He glanced ahead towards the man as he hit the end of the street. The guy paused, head darting back and forth, uncertain whether to leave her or come back.

The woman spared him the choice. She shot to her feet with a renewed agility that caught Gardner off guard. She grabbed the leg of the bottom chair in a tall column and pulled hard on it. The chairs toppled, their metal frames clattering against the ground. Then she ran off. Gardner kicked the chairs aside.

The man, then the woman, catching up with him, spun left, out of view.

Gardner hit the corner and saw them racing down a gentle slope. Pigeons squawked and flapped as they fled. The road flattened out forty metres down and led into a junction. Gardner saw the nose of a car shoot out like a spear across the junction, thought it was going to slam into the twins.

The car, a Focus, stopped dead, but the bumper hit the man's legs and he fell onto the bonnet. The woman grabbed him by the lapels and pulled him upright and they took off again.

Gardner sprinted down the slope. He passed the junction, where drivers were yelling at the guy in the Focus for braking so hard. He chased the twins as they ran past a row of kebab houses and souvenir shops and up a set of concrete steps.

The steps led into a ticket office, and Gardner saw a sign on the outside: they were heading into a suburban railway station.

He was just ten metres from them now, his superior stamina and strength kicking in. In a sprint, Gardner didn't have the pace, but put him in for the long haul and he'd hunt down anyone, eventually.

The twins vaulted over the ticket barriers. Gardner likewise. A train pulled into the adjacent platform, shining grey, all moulded plastic and futuristic design. An announcement on the Tannoy. A dozen people got off; plenty more boarded. Gardner searched among the throng for the pair. Couldn't fucking see either of them. Maybe they're not on the train, he thought.

The doors beeped. They were about to close.

You need to call it. On or off?

Gardner ducked into the corridor of the nearest carriage. He scanned the platform through the window as the train gently eased forward, got a long, hard look at the faces bobbing towards the station exit. There were twenty humdrum faces, bored faces, angry faces, the kind he'd seen on the Tube a million fucking times. Commuters who looked like their lives needed a reboot. Twenty faces, but none of them matched the man or the woman.

That means they're on this train.

The platform shrank from view.

An automatic door slid open and he dipped his head and steamed through the doorway into the carriage itself.

seventy-three

0700 hours.

Cool air greeted Gardner as he made his way along the carriage. The train was packed. Men and women, most of them middle-aged and stressed, sat and fiddled with their BlackBerrys and iPhones. Others stared out of the window at the ticker-tape landscape: trees, roads, cars, houses, fusing into a granite blur.

At each seat Gardner checked out the faces. The commuters either ignored him or eyed him suspiciously. Hardly surprising: he looked like shit. His T-shirt was torn at the sleeve and his right arm emitted a pungent aroma. He didn't exactly blend in. At least my Glock's hidden away, he thought. He'd stuffed it back into his jeans, covering the pistol grip with the bottom of his T-shirt.

He cleared the first carriage. No luck. He paused at the next sliding door separating the carriages. A soft female voice made a pre-recorded announcement just before the train slowed and pulled into the next station.

Gardner peered through the window of the automatic door. Saw a couple of guys dragging themselves out of their seats, going through the same rituals as workers the world over: straightening the tie, pin-locking the mobile, reaching for the briefcase from the overhead storage rack.

One of the guys shuffled down the aisle.

Gardner spotted a knot of ginger hair at the next seat.

He hung by the door, waiting for the right moment. The train eased into the platform. Some place called Pallini. Then the train stopped. As soon as the lights blinked and the doors slid back like some kind of robotic curtain call, Gardner stepped through the automatic door and used the departing crowd to obscure his profile from the Kazans. The ginger-haired woman remained seated. They weren't getting off. The guy was on his feet and making his way to the toilet at Gardner's end of the carriage. He hadn't spotted him in the throng.

Gardner retreated into the previous carriage and peered back through the window. The man slipped into the toilet. Now Gardner rushed back into the next carriage and in a second he was blocking the closing toilet door with his left arm and using the force in his shoulder muscles to push it back. The door whirred, clicked, conceded defeat.

The guy was standing at the toilet, primed to take a leak. He'd heard the whirring and was turning around to see what the fuck was going on behind him. Gardner raised his right leg at the knee and put his foot level with the lower part of the guy's back.

Knocked forward by the blow, the guy seized hold of the cistern just as the door closed. There was piss all over the floor. Gardner grabbed him by his hair. The guy yelped. Then Gardner smashed his face into the mirror above the basin, and the yelp fizzled out to a low wheeze. But Gardner didn't stop. He drove the guy's head repeatedly into the mirror. Spiderweb cracks formed with every impact. Blood spots painted the glass.

Now he smashed the guy's head against the porcelain edge of the basin. Gooey blood and snot streamed out of his nose. Now he wasn't making any sound at all. His arms hung limply by his side.

Gardner spun him around and shoved him onto the toilet seat. The toilet stank of piss and sweat. The guy's dick dangled out of his zip. The ash grey of his trousers was a much darker colour on the inside thigh of both legs. The guy cupped his nose between his hands. Tiny shards of glass were embedded in his forehead. Before he had a chance to react, Gardner whipped out the Glock and nestled the cold muzzle between his balls.

'Tell me where Aimée is.'

'Please—' the guy said.

Gardner swiped the guy's hands away from his face. His nose was purple and swollen. His lips were purple and swollen. His whole face was a mass of purple putty.

'Please, don't—'

The voice hit Gardner like a piece of two by four.

'What did you just say?'

The guy stammered, 'Please, please, don't kill me.'

Each syllable throbbed inside Gardner's skull. Not because Gardner recognized the voice. He didn't. But the accent was unmistakable. The guy spoke with a London accent. He swallowed his Ts and made his double Ls a W.

'Who the fuck are you?'

'We're on your side,' the man said.

'Your fucking name,' Gardner shoving the Glock harder into his groin. The man squirmed.

'Peter Stokes.'

'You were on your way to kill Aimée.'

'No, I swear.'

'Bullshit.'

'I don't know anyone called that!'

'Then who the fuck are you?'

The guy's face twisted with pain. Snot dribbled down his nose and formed a slithery tache around his mouth. He stared at the broken mirror for the longest while, then directed his gaze at Gardner.

'I'm with MI6,' he said.

seventy-four

Gardner kept the Glock pressed against Stokes's balls. His first reaction was that the guy was full of shit. But then he considered the accent. It was as English as beating the shit out of someone in the town centre on a Friday night. And under-cover spies, even ones who practised the accent for years with such discipline that they avoided ever talking in their native tones, still betrayed occasional traces of an accent. Especially when someone had a Glock in their face.

And then he thought about Stokes's appearance. The guy looked more like an accountant than a crazed killer. He had a doughy jawline and the slack body shape of someone who spent his nine-to-five hunched in front of a computer. He probably moisturized first thing in the morning and ironed his shirts last thing at night.

But part of Gardner didn't want to believe Stokes.

Because if he really was MI6, then he had no lead on Aimée.

The silence lasted for several seconds. Then Stokes broke it.

'I'm telling you the truth. My colleague's name is Rachel Salvago. We're agents with the counterintelligence division at the Ministry.' He frowned at the Glock. 'Look, why don't you put the gun away and we can talk about this?'

'The gun stays where it is,' Gardner said. 'Who's your boss?'

'Leo Land.'

'Land sent me to kill you.'

'How well do you know Land? And who the hell are you anyway?' said Stokes, eyeing Gardner's frame.

'Don't worry about me, mate,' Gardner said. 'Tell me your story.'

'All this is about Istanbul.'

Gardner loosened the grip on the pistol. 'I'm listening.'

'Land *knows*,' Stokes said.

'Knows what?'

Stokes shook his head at the piss-streaked floor. He took a deep breath. 'Like I said, me and Salvago work for Land. We just get on with our jobs and look the other way. But—'

Gardner was staring hard at Stokes. What the fuck was he talking about? Every minute without a lead made it less and less likely he'd find Aimée.

Stokes went on: 'About a month ago Salvago picked up a string of mobile calls made between Moscow and the Firm. They were made late at night, and always to the same number in Russia. We did some digging, and found out that the Russian number belonged to a guy in the *Mafya*. His name was Aleksandr Sotov.'

Gardner felt invisible hands Chinese-burn his neck. He knew what was coming next, but he had to ask the question. 'Who was he talking to at the Firm?'

Stokes's face hardened. 'Take a wild guess.'

'Shit!' Gardner said.

The train slowed once more. The doped-up female voice informed them they were pulling into the next stop: Kantza.

'What were they talking about?' Gardner asked.

Someone rapped their knuckles on the toilet door and shouted angrily in Greek. Once, twice, three times.

'Be out in a minute,' Gardner called out. He looked back to Stokes and gestured for him to answer.

'Land knew that the Russians intended to sell a nuke to somebody and blow it up in Turkey. And not only that, he played his part too.'

'How so?'

'Land recruited an ex-SAS soldier to take delivery of the bomb.'

Gardner felt his guts stretch, like someone was pulling him in either direction. 'Land made me track Bald.'

Stokes just looked blank. He clearly had no idea who the fuck Bald was.

'Did you try and confront Land?' Gardner asked.

'You're kidding? Land is one of the most powerful mandarins in Whitehall.'

Stokes touched his jaw and winced. 'We didn't say anything, but somehow Land must have cottoned on that we knew.'

'How?'

The train was now gathering speed again.

'Because the day before the bomb exploded, he suddenly dispatched both me and Salvago to Athens. I mean, like that,' he said, snapping his fingers. 'Told us to head to an address and await further instructions.'

'Number ten Kapsis Square.'

'Then we heard about the bomb.'

'And then you saw me coming.'

'And we knew he wanted us out of the way for good. So we ran.'

Gardner tore a fistful of paper towels out of the dispenser and chucked them at Stokes.

'Clean yourself up. Then you're going to introduce me to Salvago.'

'Why?'

'Because I want to see if her story matches yours. If it does, maybe I'll start believing what you're saying.'

'There's something you should know,' said Stokes, dabbing at his bleeding nose. He pulled the towel away and examined the red splodges. 'A friend inside the building sent me a message last night. Our offices were ransacked. Computers taken away. Mobiles too.'

Gardner thought back to Aimée. She was carrying the MacBook and the flash drives. 'All right, let's meet Salvago,' he said.

One hand holding a tissue under his nose, Stokes unlocked the toilet door and walked down the aisle. The carriage was mostly empty now. The ginger girl was at a table seat. Steam wafted from a cup of coffee in front of her. She took one look at Stokes's face and made to stand up, but he put her at her ease. She slid back down into her seat. Gardner thought he saw something in her eyes when she looked at Stokes. Something that said they were maybe more than just colleagues.

There were two seats either side of the table. Stokes sat next to Salvago, Gardner opposite them.

'Who are you?' Salvago said in a warm and husky voice. Gardner didn't much rate redheads but a bit more time spent around her might make him change his mind. She had eyes the colour of summer grass, high cheekbones and a ten-out-of-ten rack. She had left two buttons undone on her white blouse, revealing cleavage that would make a grown man punch a hole in a wall. If Salvago and Stokes were getting it on, fair play to the lad.

Gardner looked at her and told her, 'Land sent me to kill you.'

'It's true,' Stokes said. The bruises on his face said the rest.

The woman leaned as far back from Gardner as the seat allowed and exchanged a look with Stokes.

'It's OK,' Stokes said.

'Land told me you were a couple of Russian torturers,' Gardner went on. 'He said you were holding a friend of mine hostage.'

Salvago arched an eyebrow. 'What friend?'

'Her name's Aimée. We worked together in Serbia. She was freelancing for the Firm.'

Salvago bit her lower lip. 'This Aimée, does she know stuff?'

'She knows all right. Transcripts of conversations between Sotov and a guy by the name of Maxim Ledinsky, a director in the FSB.' Salvago nodded on hearing the guy's name. 'Other files were encrypted. We didn't have time to crack them.'

Salvago said, 'I'll bet my mortgage those files name and shame Leo bloody Land. Where'd you find them?'

'Pulled them from a factory the other side of the city. Sotov had some kind of a storage facility there.'

'What happened to the rest?'

'Up in smoke.'

'Damn,' Salvago muttered. She struck Gardner as the sort of girl whose swear-scale stopped at 'bloody hell'. 'Then we can't prove the link between Land and the Russians.'

'Aimée had some of the files with her.'

'Where is she?' Stokes asked.

'I don't know. Land arranged a flight home for us. It was an ambush. They took her,' said Gardner, then fished out his mobile and played them the clip. Salvago and Stokes squinted at the grainy images.

'Jesus,' said Stokes. Salvago was quiet. Gardner was left alone with his thoughts. If Land was involved with the nuke, that would explain why Land had asked him to kill Bald only *after* the exchange had been made.

'Give me your phone,' Salvago said. Gardner pressed it into her palm. She dug out an outdated Nokia notebook from the front pocket of her jeans and tapped away on a few keys. 'My expertise is e-crime and communications,' she said. 'The Nokia is a specially modified handset. It bypasses the security encryptions and protocols on networks and gives me the raw data direct from the satellite. Basically I can track the GPS details of any mobile, anywhere in the world, just by plugging this into it. Like so.'

'Fucking hell.' Despite himself, Gardner was impressed.

Salvago tapped some more. Then she unplugged the Nokia from Gardner's mobile and took a sip of her coffee.

'I know where your friend is,' she said.

Gardner and Stokes flashed quizzical looks.

'Rotterdam.'

seventy-five

Rotterdam, Holland. 0930 hours.

It was exactly nine-thirty in the morning in Hamburg, an hour behind Athens, and Kruger debarked from a VLM plane splayed on the gun-metal runway at Rotterdam Airport. Kruger hated flying but his employers insisted he come to Holland immediately. They explained that the Brit and his two friends would be in-country soon. Kruger had checked out the train route, his preferred mode of transport. It would have taken him something like twelve hours and five stopovers: Hamburg to Bremen, Bremen to Leer on the Dutch border, Leer to Groningen, yada fucking yada. The journey was just over an hour by plane, so he bit the bullet and flew.

Kruger had no baggage. In his opinion a man needed only three things in the world: protein, water and the ability to hunt and kill.

She'll be at the premises in three hours, the Russian had said. That was at five o'clock. The woman would be there already. Knowing the Russians, she probably wouldn't be in mint condition. No big deal. She was fucking dead either way.

The Chevrolet Avalanche was nestled among the people carriers and the Golfs in the long-stay car park. Kruger hit the A13 south towards Rotterdam and curled his lip at the flat skyline. He hated Holland. Despised the fucking place. Dirty, grey, flat as day-old cola.

Fuck it, he told himself as he neared the premises.

The targets will be here in a couple of hours. Deal with them, you could be out of the country by nightfall. He lit a cigarillo and tightened his grip on the wheel.

seventy-six

Fifty-nine minutes after Kruger's VLM touched down, a Boeing 737-700 landed at Rotterdam and taxied into the same parking spot the VLM craft had occupied. Gardner, Stokes and Salvago briskly moved through passport control and made their way through arrivals. The airport was a ghost town. Ditto the flight. The nuke seemed to have put a lot of people off flying.

Salvago checked something on the Nokia.

'How accurate is that thing?' Gardner asked her.

'It picks up on the broadcast signals from satellites, the same ones that phones link with to get a reading on their longitude, latitude and altitude. Normally a phone receives radio signals from at least three satellites. This *thing*,' Salvago said, 'receives its signals from twenty-four. So yeah, pretty damn accurate.'

Salvago turned her attention back to the Nokia. Stokes and Gardner had ditched their phones in Athens in case Land tried to trace their signals. Once word reached Land that Salvago and Stokes were still alive, he'd do everything in his power to track them down and slot them. Gardner was sure of it. He'd also had to dump his gun. Somehow he figured airport security wouldn't approve.

'Stop,' Salvago said as Gardner reached the main doors. 'Step outside those doors and Land will see you.'

Gardner frowned. 'How come?'

'Latest satellite tracking technology.'

'Spies in the sky?'

'Years ago satellites were pretty poor at tracking human beings. All you could see from space was a head of hair. Not exactly a lot to go on when you're looking for one person among six billion. But there's new software that maps out someone's gait. See, everybody has their own way of walking. The software matches your shadow, gets an instant lock on you wherever you are.'

'So how do we get out of here?'

'We wait for a black spot.'

'Like when the satellite's not over us?'

'Exactly. You see, there's only a few satellites that have this software installed. So there are periods when the sky is clear. Twenty minutes at a time. And the next one is in' – she consulted the Nokia – 'fifteen minutes.'

To pass the time they sat at a café in the arrivals area. Stokes took a coffee, black. Salvago ordered a decaf. Gardner went with a Diet Coke, sipping at it as he watched Sky News on a big plasma TV hooked to the wall. The he-and-she presenter team looked stern-faced. The camera cut to a shot of a guy in a dark-grey suit. He was standing in front of a lectern, a bank of microphones in front of him.

'This was the damning response from the Israeli Prime Minister Lev Yalom to last night's atrocity,' a reporter announced over the images. Yalom spoke aggressively, his right hand formed into a chubby fist. He thumped the lectern, disrupting his notes. 'No more broken promises,' Yalom said. The voice-over said, 'Here in Jerusalem it's become increasingly clear that Israel sees the Iranians' attempt to smuggle nuclear arms into Tehran as a declaration of war.'

There was footage of an Israeli F-15I Ra'am fighter plane, followed by a shot of the Knesset. The chamber was packed.

'This morning Prime Minister Yalom issued an ultimatum to Tehran: either Iran unconditionally agrees to dismantle its nuclear programme within the next twenty-four hours, or Israel will do it for them. Even as he spoke, the Israeli Air Force was making preparations for retaliatory attacks against key military and civilian targets in Iran, believed to include the civilian Bushehr nuclear facility.'

The report cut back to the news desk. Breaking news scrolled across the bottom of the screen. A defence expert was introduced. Gardner had seen dozens of these experts on TV and never rated their opinions. They were all retired ruperts or Whitehall pen-pushers. He looked away.

'It's starting,' he said.

Stokes tore open a sachet and tipped sugar into his cup. 'Israel's bluffing. They won't dare bomb Iran.'

'You sure about that?'

'Joe's right,' Salvago said.

'They *want* this to happen,' said Gardner. 'Blaming the Iranians for the nuke gives them licence to shoot up whoever they please for the sake of national security. They'll bomb Iran back into the fucking Stone Age.'

Gardner finished his Coke and licked his lips. He felt the sugar and caffeine ease the pressure behind his temples. A bus pulled up outside the airport. Salvago took a last gulp of coffee.

'It's time,' Gardner said. 'We need to go.'

They shuffled through the exit and ran the twenty metres to the bus stop. Hopped on board the number 33 bus and purchased three one-way tickets to Rotterdam Centraal station.

'Where exactly are we headed?' asked Gardner, sitting opposite the other two.

'An address on Van Brakelstraat,' Salvago told him.

'Any idea what kind of place?'

'Nope.'

Great, Gardner thought. We're going in half-cocked to face an enemy we know nothing about. He prayed that Aimée was there. He prayed she was OK. He hoped the guys who snatched her were saying their prayers too. Because when Gardner came face to face with them, they were going to the dark side.

All of them.

seventy-seven

1111 hours.

Van Brakelstraat was a narrow street off the arterial road
snaking its way alongside Rotterdam's docks. The turning
was signposted by a Russian Orthodox church on the left, a
crucifix planted like a flag atop the cupola, its golden surface
turned a muddy bronze by the clouds.

They walked down the street, sticking to the shadows cast
by the three-storey buildings, hunched and Gothic. After two
hundred metres they came to a residential block with a brown
façade like someone had coated it in old carpet. It had rusting
gates and neo-Nazi graffiti sprayed over the walls. Some kind
of shop occupied the ground floor. There was no sign, just a
paper notice taped to the reverse of the glass upper part of the
door that read: 'DISCREET SHOP. BY APPOINTMENT
ONLY.'

Stokes finished reading the notice and said, 'Weird.'

'No,' Gardner said. 'It's a porn store.'

Stokes lifted his hand to his forehead and peered through
the grime-coated glass. 'Well, whatever it is, there's nobody
home. Maybe those GPS coordinates weren't spot-on.'

'No, it's definitely here,' Salvago said, irritated.

Gardner settled the lovers' tiff with a boot to the door.
The glass pane shattered. Then he raked away the remaining
shards with his prosthetic hand. *At least there's one use for
this fucking thing*, he thought, reaching through the hole with

his left hand and unhooking the latch. He twisted the door-knob and gestured to Salvago and Stokes.

The shop was dingy and dark. A musty, stale aroma hung in the air. There were rows of ancient DVDs, porn titles ranging from softcore to extreme. Most of the covers were coated with greying dust. Gardner clocked security cameras fixed to each corner of the ceiling. He headed past a rack of sex dolls and plastic vaginas towards the counter, to the top of which were taped faded posters advertising local prostitutes and massage parlours. There was no cash register. Behind the counter was an unlocked door, and Gardner opened it. Fluorescent tubes mounted on the ceiling flashed on like paparazzi. They lit up a staircase leading into a basement. Gardner started down the stairs, trying to get a bearing on the room below. Stokes and Salvago followed close behind. Gardner felt the temperature drop with every step. It was cooler and felt damp in the base-ment. By the time he'd reached the bottom step, the bristles on his right forearm were standing on end.

His first thought was that it didn't look like a standard base-ment. The walls were lined with metal sheets, the floor tiled. The ceiling was divided into solid-looking panels. Overall it resembled an underground bunker.

The space was also a lot bigger than he expected. It stretched for forty metres, was roughly the same width and seemed to be divided into three distinct areas. This place is fucking huge, Gardner thought. It must stretch underneath several build-ings. He'd seen smaller underground car parks back home.

In the nearest section stood a group of metal drums marked with hazard labels and giving off a toxic smell.

'Piperonyl methyl ketone,' Salvago said at his shoulder. 'PMK. It's synthesized from sassafras tree. They use it in perfumes.'

'In porn-shop basements?'

'They also use it to make something else.'

'Like what?'

'Take a look,' Salvago said, nodding towards the next section.

Four benches almost filled the basement's middle area. They were cluttered with portable heaters, fans, distillation flasks and funnels, packets of surgical gloves and breathing masks, plus a large waste pipe that ran the length of the place. A tablet-pressing machine was connected to a mobile power generator to the left. The machine had a wide metal base shaped like a tree trunk with a sequence of punches aligned above and below the die plate that chemical compounds were fed into. Rotating turrets were screwed like shoulders to each side of the unit and at the top a piston connected the turrets along its horizontal plane. A solid-metal punch was suspended above the die at the top of the machine. The head of the punch was about ten centimetres across and the sharp tip about a centimetre. At the bottom of the machine a silver slide collected the pills as the die spat them out. A few lay in the bottom of the tray and Gardner picked one up. They were eggshell white with a blue smiley face on them.

Gardner looked to the far end of the room, where a third area had been established. Clear plastic bin liners were filled with tens of thousands of the same small white pills. A ladder on the back wall led up to a metal cellar hatch that opened upwards in the middle, like horizontal double doors. Gardner figured they fed the pills up the ladder and into the street, where they were loaded into a disguised lorry.

'Jesus Christ,' Stokes said.

'There must be fifty thousand pills in those bags,' Gardner said.

Salvago examined the table apparatus. 'At least. And it's not surprising. The Russian *Mafya* play a major role in Ecstasy production. The chemicals are smuggled in from China to Russia, then shipped here where they make the pills and then put them into lorry containers to ship via the North Sea to England.'

'I thought Amsterdam was where the drug action is?' Stokes said.

'Amsterdam has the rep, but Rotterdam is the real drug capital of Europe. About six thousand people are employed by the drugs industry round here.'

'This doesn't feel right,' Gardner said. 'The *Mafya* don't use big developments like this to produce drugs. It's too clunky. Nowadays they have mobile vans for that kind of stuff. And you can practically turn a toilet cubicle into an Ecstasy factory. Why go to the risk of having such a large processing plant – and then have no kind of security on the door? It makes no sense.'

'And I don't see Sotov anywhere,' Salvago said.

Gardner was drawn to a light coming from the far end of the basement. It glowed green and bright, like a cathode ray. As he neared it, Gardner realized the light was coming from a separate room, a laboratory of some kind. He signalled for Salvago and Stokes to stay back. He stepped inside and ran his eyes over the equipment. Computer servers, scales, navigation charts, what appeared to be a radar monitor, and a pile of chunky old mobiles with aerials sticking out of them. Cables snaked from the devices along the ground to the generator.

Gardner didn't see anyone. But he heard rapid, shallow breathing. At his four o'clock.

He stilled.

'Joe? Is that you?'

She was hiding the other side of the doorway. She held a spanner in both hands. She had a look in her eyes – not fear, Gardner thought. More like anger. But that look drained from her face as she dropped the spanner and pounced on Gardner and hugged him and held him tight.

'You're warm,' Aimée said. 'Your hands are warm.'

Gardner felt a bubble rise in his stomach and burst in his chest.

'What happened to you?'

Aimée sighed into his shoulder. 'They put a bag over my head. We were in a car, then on a plane. Then they took me here.' She paused. 'I heard other voices with you—'

Salvago and Stokes stood in the doorway. He introduced them to Aimée and said, 'They believe Land is involved in the nuke plot.'

Aimée said nothing. She peeled away from Gardner and made her way to the computers. 'They trashed the MacBook, but they weren't clever enough to find the flash drives.'

She tapped away at the keyboard. Gardner noticed that one of the memory sticks was plugged into the front of the computer tower. Aimée drew up several Word files on the screen.

'I still can't break the encryptions,' she said.

Salvago stepped forward. 'Mind if I have a go?'

Aimée waved a hand at the screen, as if to say, Be my guest. Salvago took Aimée's place and typed ultra-fast while Aimée looked on beside her. Gardner left them to it. He went to check on the basement. He was mindful that the owners of the Ecstasy plant might return at any moment. The presser drew his attention. It was a large-scale industrial machine and Gardner reckoned the *Mafya* must be pumping out a million pills a day using it. Enough to keep London happy for a weekend. Fresh chemical dust covered the floor around the presser. It's been used recently, Gardner thought. So where the hell did the *Mafya* fuckers go? He was no closer to answering that question when Salvago announced that she had cracked the encryptions.

'Already?' Gardner asked, returning to the lab.

'Told you she was good,' Stokes said, crossing his arms and nodding at the computer.

Gardner, Aimée and Stokes drew close to the screen. Gardner read the transcript. Aleksandr Sotov was explicitly talking about the nake and the plan to blow it up in Istanbul.

Except Sotov wasn't shooting the shit with some FSB bigwig.

He was talking to Leo Land.

Stokes flashed an I-told-you-so look at Gardner. Salvago gave him a slight nod and said, 'We need to get these files public.'

The pressure behind Gardner's eyes was red-hot. From the neck down his body tightened up, like a rope bearing a heavy load. Land had betrayed the Firm. He'd participated in the deaths of tens of thousands of people. And he'd betrayed Gardner too.

No, he corrected himself. He played me like a fucking drum kit.

'Land is going to fucking pay,' Gardner said.

'Pay how?' Salvago asked.

'The old-fashioned way. With a bullet.'

'I've got a better idea,' said Aimée.

'Which is?'

'We gather the media at Parliament Square and tell them the truth.'

'And Israel will have to call off its attack,' said Salvago.

'Then we'll need to act quickly,' said Stokes. 'Yalom was saying the bombings would start in twenty-four hours.'

If that happens, Gardner thought, there won't be any going back. He made a silent promise to himself. Once the truth is exposed, Land is mine. And I won't show that cunt a grain of mercy.

'OK, let's get a move on,' he said.

Aimée unplugged the flash drives from the computer and tucked them into her knickers. So that's her secret place, Gardner told himself. Aimée gave him a dirty look as they followed Salvago and Stokes up the stairs and out of the basement. They lingered at the shop door, Stokes scoping out the street.

Salvago glanced at her Nokia. 'We're in a black spot. OK, let's go.'

Gardner was first outside. He glanced across his shoulders in both directions. Force of habit. He could see no movement to his right. A white-diamond Chevrolet Avalanche was parked up eighty metres to the left. Gardner noticed the windows weren't tinted. He had a clear view of the interior. He saw the leather seats and the dark cashmere dash. No one behind the wheel.

Satisfied the coast was clear, Gardner began pacing down the street. Movement the other side of the road. He glanced over his left shoulder, saw a figure standing opposite. The guy was built like a tank and dressed like a wrestler. He wore a threadbare army-green vest beneath a mid-length trench coat and black combats. The guy's right arm was tucked into his coat pocket. And he was wearing heavily tinted shades. But Gardner sensed the guy was eyeballing him.

Then the guy called out to him. 'Hey, buddy.' His accent was thick and slow as roofing tar. American, Gardner figured. From the South.

Gardner walked on.

'I fucking said, hey buddy.'

Gardner stopped.

'Come get some,' the guy said.

Gardner stood by the side of the road and asked himself who the fuck this guy was. But then he countered that it didn't matter. The chances of some random guy heckling them in the street were low. This guy has something to do with the basement, Gardner thought. He was of a mind to ask the Yank a few questions.

'Yo, I'll fuck you up,' the guy said.

Gardner was quiet. But he began to pace across the street.

The guy opened his mouth again, lips like a knife-slit beneath the thickness of his beard. A sound came out like a swarm of angry bees.

Then Gardner realized the sound was coming from up the street. A motor being gunned. He angled his head and saw the Avalanche bombing forward.

Heading straight for him.

seventy-eight

1203 hours.

The car hit him like a fist, and he felt ribs crack as the front bumper knuckled his midriff. His entire front was a wall of pain. His arm thumped against the bonnet and dented the aluminium base. Then the Avalanche braked, the chassis rocked on its wheelbase and Gardner fell to the ground, face smacking against the tarmac. Between the bulbs of pain behind his eyes, a distant voice in his head asked, Who the fuck is driving the thing? Because he hadn't seen a driver behind the wheel.

His thought was interrupted by the growl of the Avalanche revving for round two.

It had reversed twenty metres back from Gardner's position, building itself up for another run at him. He tried to pick himself up off the floor. It hurt like fuck but he willed himself to raise himself to a knee. Couldn't stand. He spat blood and heard a kind of garbled laugh from his three o'clock. The Yank.

'Fucking idiot,' the guy said.

The Avalanche thundered towards Gardner.

He was bang in the middle of the road. The Avalanche was almost on him.

At five metres, the car suddenly swerved to his left. Stokes was making a run for it down the street. Salvago was in tow, Aimée further behind, her outline shaded by the interior of the porn shop. Gardner realized the Avalanche was beating a direct route towards Stokes. It slammed into him and crushed his body beneath the tyres. Gardner heard something snap, like an axe splitting hardwood. He glimpsed arms and legs beneath the tyres' grinding weight.

Salvago shrieked. The Avalanche continued on up the street. Gardner was sure it was going to turn round up ahead and hurtle back down the street to finish them off. But Salvago seemed oblivious. She was rushing over to Stokes.

Gardner couldn't see Aimée. He sprinted after the Avalanche.

The car slowed as it came to the end of the street, then skidded into a U-turn. As it cleared the apex of the turn, Gardner reached the driver's door. He flung it open as the vehicle completed the turn and began to pick up speed again. Gardner had a clear view of the street. He couldn't see the Yank anywhere.

With the door open and his feet off the ground, Gardner planted his left foot on the driver's seat. The sudden forward motion acted like a wind against the open door and began to swing it shut. Gardner grabbed hold of the door frame and felt the door bang against his back.

The impact pushed him inside head first. Gardner landed on his front, the gear shift winding him, but he looked up and saw Salvago six metres from the windscreen, her face bewitched by the onrushing Avalanche.

It was heading straight for her.

Gardner clasped his right hand on the wheel. It didn't roll easy, not like a steering wheel ought to. There was a counter-force working to keep the wheel straight. But Gardner had strength and muscle mass to burn. He broke the pressure and the wheel loosened like a defeated contestant in an arm wrestle. Gardner yanked it all the way to the right.

He saw Salvago's face sweep past the driver-side window, and relief washed down his back. The Avalanche had narrowly avoided her.

And crashed straight into a parked VW Passat.

Gardner jolted in his seat. His wrist muscles absorbed the shock of the crash, stayed clamped around the wheel, but he reeled and banged the back of his head against the headrest. The pain echoed around his skull, mixing with the Passat's alarm, its scream blotting out every other sound. The Passat went through a symphony of alarm sounds, each one more annoying than the last.

A banging sound on the Avalanche's roof. Its body rocked, as if it was caught up in the middle of a real fucking avalanche. What the fuck's that? Gardner wondered. He moved a hand to the door . . .

The roof above his head was ripped open, the metal torn apart like wet paper. Gardner's eyes flicked up. He saw the downward plunge of a balled fist, knuckles forming a jagged line that was on a trajectory straight for his face, fast and deadly.

Gardner was faster. His reactions engaged in a split second. He dodged the hand and shifted all his weight to his left and forward, reached across and shunted the shift into reverse. Then he accelerated and jerked the wheel clockwise, the Avalanche quickly gaining speed. But now the hand gripped Gardner's neck. The fingers seemed unnatural. Cold and plastic.

Like my own.

When he'd reversed about twenty metres, Gardner stamped on the brakes. Now he shifted into first gear and trod down, making the Avalanche lurch forward. Gardner watched the arm shoot up through the hole in the roof like an upside-down periscope. Next thing he knew, a figure was tumbling down the windscreen and rolling across the bonnet before disappearing behind the front bumper.

The Yank.

Gardner scrambled out after him.

The guy was already up and charged at him.

Gardner was knocked off his feet and landed on his back. The guy was on top of him and shaped to punch with his right hand. Gardner clenched both his hands around the guy's wrists. They were locked in a stalemate on the ground. That fucking arm.

The Yank's strength overwhelmed Gardner. His forearms burned. The guy was halfway to pinning him down when Gardner got a second wind. He headbutted the guy on the slope of his nose. The guy winced and the force on Gardner lessened. Now Gardner slammed his left hand against the Avalanche's open door, sandwiching the Yank's head between the door and the frame. He felt the head being pulped, and the Yank dropped. Gardner shot to his feet and called to Salvago.

'Where's Aimée?'

'I . . . I don't . . .'

Salvago's big, moist eyes glanced towards the porn shop. Aimée was back inside.

'Let's get out of here,' Gardner said, offering Salvago his hand. She looked at it, then back at Stokes.

Fuck this, Gardner thought. He hauled Salvago with him back into the shop, and found Aimée crouched behind the counter.

'We're leaving,' he said.

'That guy . . . he's still out there.'

'He's finished.'

Aimée nodded and stood up. Her eyes were warm and bright. Then they clouded grey and rested on a spot past his right shoulder. Gardner slowly turned around and saw the Yank. He was alive. His face looked like someone had worked on him with a mallet, purple blotches on his forehead, his nose bloody. But he was most definitely fucking alive.

Pounding down the street. Towards the shop.

The Yank was a few metres from the door when the shop's windows rattled. Inside, daylight dimmed as a hefty metal shutter tumbled down over the front of the shop. Gardner glimpsed the Yank standing out in the street, the top half of his body cut off from view. There was a terrific clattering as the shutter sealed up the shop, like a million snare drums sounding at once. Light crept in between gaps in the metal. The only exit route was blocked.

'We're trapped,' Aimée said.

Gardner had an idea. 'Maybe not.'

Aimée asked what he meant. Gardner didn't reply. He was heading down into the basement, beckoning the two women to follow him.

seventy-nine

The fluorescent lights guided them down the stairs. Gardner's left hand trailed and Aimée held on to it. He couldn't feel her fingers on the plastic, but he felt her breath, warm packets of it stroking his shoulder blade. Salvago was a couple of paces further behind. When he reached the bottom, Gardner's eyes had adjusted to the gloom. They focused on the hatch in the ceiling at the far end of the basement.

'We'll use those overhead doors to get out to the street,' he said.

'But he'll be waiting for us—' said Aimée.

'I'm going to take care of this guy.'

'His arm—'

'I've read about them,' Gardner said. 'They were designed to help people with wasting diseases, so they could control their limbs. Give them their quality of life back. Then the Pentagon got hold of the idea and decided to test them on wounded US soldiers. Used them as fucking guinea pigs.'

'That's how he was controlling the car?' The question was from Salvago.

Gardner didn't reply because the basement suddenly sank into a smothering darkness. Like a hessian sack pulled over his head. Everything switched off: the fluorescent lights, the computers, the lamps on the work tables. Tiny hammers seemed to tap against the generator as it powered down. Gardner couldn't see a metre ahead of him.

The blackness was silent and cold.

'I can't see you,' Aimée said.

'Keep a hold of my hand,' Gardner said, then to Salvago, 'Hold on to Aimée.'

Neither replied. Gardner pushed forward. His steps had to be cautious, had to be slow. He had no way of orientating himself. Walking in a straight line in the pitch-darkness was easier said than done. He heard an electrical whirring sound which lasted for several seconds. It ended with a deliberate, dull thud at his eight o'clock.

He saw something in the blackness. Nothing distinct. A soft patch of light lingered at ceiling height. What little there was of it came from the porn shop. One of the panels in the ceiling was lowering. Atop the panel was a lift, and as it touched the basement floor the Yank stepped quickly out of it and into the shadows.

Gardner froze.

'What is it?' Aimée whispered.

Gardner steered Aimée and Salvago in the direction where he imagined the cellar hatch in the ceiling to be. 'Walk that way and don't stop. When you hit the ladder, open the doors if you can and get the hell out of here.'

'I'm not leaving you,' Aimée said.

'No one's leaving anybody. I'll see you outside. Now go.'

Aimée's breathing grew fainter as she and Salvago made their way through the basement.

Listening to the Yank's footsteps, Gardner braced himself.

The footsteps stopped.

Gardner cocked his ears and held his breath in his throat. He suddenly felt very vulnerable.

A gust of wind whooshed over Gardner's face.

At the end of the gust was a fist.

The fist drove hard into his solar plexus. Gardner felt the knuckles connect with his flesh, each one digging in like the handle head of a screwdriver. His bowels spasmed. He couldn't breathe. He still made an effort to fight back, slugged his right arm into the blackness in front of him even as he doubled up in agony. He punched cold air.

The wind swirled around him. Then it seemed to settle at his back and drop-kicked his lower spine. Gardner dropped to his hands and knees. He felt a string of spit dangling from his lower lip.

He's fucking found me. Even though it's pitch-black.

Gardner was powerless to stop the onslaught. The blows kept on coming, a three-sixty melee attack that left his senses scattered like marbles on the floor. He tried to push himself to his feet and felt the hard surface of a rubber sole stamp on him. The underside of a tactical boot crushed his right fingers. The joints cracked and grated. The pain went through the fucking roof. He was dragged this way and that, until he had no idea which way was up or down.

The lights flickered on. The overhead panels cast shadows on the sheet-metal walls. Gardner squinted. The guy was standing over him.

They were next to the tablet presser.

The Yank appeared to turn it on just by looking at it. A hundred moving parts clanked and whirred inside the machine. Gardner saw the punch come to life. It began to stamp up and down on the die plate, up and down, up and down. The Yank gripped Gardner's right arm, his good one, and thrust it towards the die hole. Gardner struggled but his body had taken a fuck of a beating and he had nothing left to give.

His fingertips were under the punch. He imagined it piercing holes in his hand like it was a fucking power drill. Could feel the punch driving through his flesh and bone.

He tensed.

The machine stopped suddenly. Then it started again suddenly. The grip around Gardner's fist weakened. He was able to shake his arm free. The Yank's arm was level with Gardner's face. He shaped to block, but knew that if the arm was anywhere near as powerful as he reckoned, no amount of blocking would save his arse. His face would be reduced to pulp.

The guy's fist drove forward. And down instead of straight. Eight inches from Gardner's face, the hand curled sharply inward and smacked clean into the Yank's own knee. He gasped.

Gardner rolled onto his side and sprang to his feet. He saw Salvago sitting at a computer, typing furiously. Aimée was next to her. Aimée ran towards Gardner. She shouted to Salvago to hurry up.

The building was going haywire. The lights flicked on and off like the basement was having an epileptic fit. The double doors at the top of the stairs opened and slammed. The lift jerked two-thirds of the way up to the ceiling, then crashed back to the floor. Everything seemed beyond Kruger's control. His arm punched the wall, leaving a giant fucking crater in a metal panel. Kruger himself looked unconscious, as if the arm was the only part of him alive.

'Let's get the fuck out of here,' said Gardner.

The three of them ran towards the ladder. They could see the heavy double doors flapping open and shut, seemingly of their own accord. First to the top of the ladder, Gardner applied maximum force to the doors, pushing them apart. Aimée squeezed past him and hauled herself out into the street.

Salvago was still on the first rung. She raised her hand for a gimme. Gardner stretched down as far as he could with his good hand.

'Come on, you can make it,' he said.

She clasped his hand with both of hers.

Gardner clocked Kruger charging up behind her.

'Get up!' he yelled.

He was having one fuck of a job holding the heavy doors open with his left arm.

Salvago was halfway up the ladder when Kruger grabbed at her. He tore her from Gardner's grip, spun her round and hit her full in the face.

The punch was hard and true. Like a torpedo.

There wasn't much of a head left.

With a last huge shove Gardner pushed the doors back far enough to be able to climb out through the opening. He let them slam behind him. The last thing he saw was the Yank furiously staring up from the bottom of the ladder.

Aimée was waiting for Gardner. They had emerged onto a backstreet. Pubs with dark windows. Tatty apartment blocks with darker ones. A North African family of six – mum, dad, four kids in traditional garb except for the teenage daughter – across the narrow street eyeballing him. Gardner held Aimée's hand and walked up the street fast, eyes forward.

'What did Salvago do back there?' he asked.

'She figured the man had to be controlling the car and the lights with a type of neural interface.'

'Which is why the Avalanche was unmanned.'

'He has to have control over the network using his arm. But networks work two ways. You control them but they leave you exposed to attack from the outside.'

Gardner said, 'You got a phone on you?'

Aimée shook her head.

'Then our next job is to find a payphone and put calls into those media pals of yours,' Gardner said.

'I hope you've got lots of change. When this breaks, it's going to be a hell of a story.'

eighty

St James's Park in the autumn was preferable to the summer months, Leo Land reflected as he drew up on a bench and crossed his legs. Summer meant tourists, all manner of unpleasant types with their curry smells and loud voices and cameras clicking. He sat with his hands in his lap and watched the ducks bobbing along the lead-coloured lake, listened to the songbirds chirping in the shrubbery. Up from the lake was a children's playground. Autumn sun flicked sparks off the metal swing bars and slide. A dozen or so children, newly liberated from school, ran around in circles and screamed notes of excitement that even the songbirds were at a loss to match. Parents looked on, their faces etched with caution. Caution about paedophiles, the fear uppermost in the minds of every parent in the country these days, Land thought. One young girl hung back from the throng and tugged pleadingly at her mother's leg.

Land realized his hands were shaking. He was used to the shakes. Had them for years. To begin with they'd come and gone. There was no rhyme or reason to them. But for the past two weeks he'd suffered from them every single day. He extended his left hand, palm down. He tried to still his hand. It didn't work.

Stress, Land told himself. He looked at the children and felt a pang of relief. It did not last for long.

Another man was approaching the bench, a few sad streaks of white hair brushed across his liver-spotted pate. He wore a classic navy-blue single-breasted suit that had Savile Row written all over it. White shirt, conservative-blue tie. As he sat down Land noticed tufts of hair in the man's ears. He had never studied the man's profile before.

The man unfolded his copy of the *Evening Standard*, browsed through the news section and harrumphed. Then he too looked at the children. Seemed a bit preoccupied with them.

'Leo,' he said.

'Milton,' Leo answered.

Sir Milton Pierce, the Foreign Secretary, went to speak. But somewhere between his throat and his mouth he changed his mind, and there was only a short intake of breath. Then he lowered his head, his brow furrowed, and Land felt the onus was on him to talk first.

'Someone is mounting a smear campaign against me,' he said.

Again Pierce said nothing.

'They're preparing to spread lies about me, Pierce. Outright, blatant and scandalous lies.'

Pierce said nothing.

'They have friends in the media. They'll print these lies and bury me.'

'Do they have "evidence" to support these rumours?' Pierce asked.

Land shifted uncomfortably on the bench. 'You know how it is. Technology these days means people create whatever truth they damn well please.'

'Indeed.' Pierce shook his head. Land suddenly felt sick. 'I'm afraid I can't help you, Leo. My hands are fully tied trying to keep our European chums onside. The bomb's ruffled a few feathers.'

Bastard, Land thought. 'This isn't my problem exclusively,' he said.

Pierce shrugged.

Land stood up from the bench. Pierce continued to stare at the children.

'I'm not the only person they will spread rumours about,' Land said.

Cracks appeared at the corners of Pierce's eyes.

Land said, 'These people have access to all sorts of nonsense.' He smiled. 'All unsubstantiated, of course.'

'What do you need?' Pierce said through gritted teeth.

Land sat down again and leaned towards Pierce. 'A Europe-wide alert on these individuals. A man and a woman. Domestic forces on high alert too. I know that's not technically your ground, but you have the Home Secretary's ear.'

Pierce said nothing more. Spent two minutes looking at the playground, sharing the silence with Land. Then he stood up and left the bench. No goodbye or even a look. Land didn't care if they never spoke again.

He checked his watch. Three-thirty. In less than eighteen hours the Middle East would be thrown into conflict once more.

eighty-one

They spent forty minutes working their way through the streets before reaching Rotterdam Centraal. There Gardner took to patrolling the station's platforms and exits, looking out for anything suspicious, while Aimée spent the last of their euros in the public phone box. On his third circuit Gardner grabbed a Mars Duo and a Diet Coke from a vendor. The soft drink and the chocolate woke him up a little.

With the last of the euros gone, they were out of cash and in need of a way home. Land would have blocked the credit card, and Aimée didn't have a penny on her. Gardner ran through options for getting hold of some quick cash.

Aimée hung up the phone and returned.

'It's ready,' she said. 'Nine o'clock tomorrow morning. Parliament Square. Everyone's going to be there.'

Gardner wasn't listening. He was staring past Aimée at a giant TV screen next to the live timetable. A photofit of a man and then one of a woman filled the screen. The woman's face was like a blown-up version of Aimée's. There was no sound from the TV, but the breaking news along the bottom of the screen read, in English: 'MURDERS IN ROTTERDAM: MAN AND WOMAN WANTED FOR QUESTIONING BY INTERPOL.'

'Joe?'

Aimée noticed the screen. She put a hand to her gaping mouth.

'Land,' Gardner said. He grabbed Aimée and they took a less busy side exit out of the station, emerging into a narrow street.

'They're going to arrest us,' Aimée said.

'No they're not. We're still going to make it to London.'

'But how? The news said the police are looking for us. We can't take a plane or a ferry. Maybe we can drive?'

Gardner shook his head. 'Land's a cunning fucker. He'll have thought of that. The minute we give our details to the rental company, he'll know about it.'

'So what are we going to do?'

'Snakehead,' said Gardner.

'Sorry?'

'Smuggling people to England's big business here. The Chinese and the Africans are all at it. We find a snakehead, pay them and hitch a ride back home.'

'And where do you find . . . snakeheads?'

'They'll have friends and family working on the inside of the port, giving them the heads-up.'

'So we just turn up and say, Hi, can you get us to London?'

'Pretty much.'

'And what if they report us to the police?'

'These are human traffickers. They don't speak to the cops.'

They took a roundabout route to the port, sticking to back-streets. The port was a bewildering network of piers, red and yellow and green shipping containers stacked like giant metal bricks. Ships of all shapes and sizes chugged in and out of each pier. Cargo ships, tankers, fishing trawlers, barges and lighter vessels jostled for space. It took Gardner forty-five minutes to find the right person.

A group of five Chinese workers were huddling from the wind in a semicircle, smoking roll-ups and wearing sombre faces. Gardner approached the guy he took to be the ring-leader. He was taller than the others and a little older and podgier. He was hostile at first. Gardner explained his predicament. The guy listened impassively, brushing greasy black hair away from his face. When Gardner was done, the guy turned away and conferred with the others.

'My brother say he see you on TV,' the guy said, making a throat-slitting gesture. It was difficult to understand whether he disapproved.

'Then you know I'm not bullshitting,' Gardner replied.

'Pay first, then ride later.'

'I lost my credit card. I'll sort you out when we get there,' Gardner said.

The guy snorted. 'Very funny. You funny man. You fucking pay now, or you no go.'

That's us screwed, Gardner thought.

Then Aimée stepped forward. She was holding a plastic baggie filled with pills. In fact the baggie was stuffed. Gardner reckoned there must have been 1000 pills in the bag, street value £6000. The Chinese guy eyed the bag hungrily.

'This enough?'

He nodded and snatched the bag in the same instant. Gardner looked on, stunned.

'Come back here nine o'clock,' the guy said. The others leaned in for a closer look at the bag's contents. He waved their prying faces away.

'You don't understand,' Gardner said. 'We need somewhere to hide out. Otherwise we'll never survive that long.'

The guy finished his roll-up and blew smoke into the air. 'Come with me.'

They followed him into a warehouse. It was big and cold and mostly empty, though a few containers were scattered about the place. The smell of industrial chemicals soured the air. The guy led Gardner and Aimée to an empty container; the doors were shut, a crowbar shoved through the handles. He removed the crowbar and pulled the doors open, the scrape of metal against concrete echoing through the cavernous warehouse. Dull light penetrated the container and Gardner counted nine pairs of desperate eyes attached to nine grubby, pale faces.

'You stay here,' the guy said, spitting on the ground. 'I call you when time is come.'

eighty-two

Three hours later Gardner and Aimée were summoned by the Chinese guy banging on the door. They were escorted out of the container. The other hopeful migrants began to get up at the sight of the man, but he snapped at them. Something Gardner took to mean, Sit the fuck down, because that's what they all did. Gardner and Aimée emerged into the night. The air was crisp and quiet. Searchlights illuminated patches of ground amid an otherwise solid darkness. Aimée yawned; she'd spent the past three hours asleep on his chest, the beat of his heart matching her breathing pattern. Gardner had craved forty winks himself, but he didn't trust the other people in the container. Sleep would have to wait.

'Quick, quick,' the guy said. He ushered them across the pier. They came to the end of the pier. A barge was docked. Next to the barge was a small boat covered in black tarpaulin. The guy glanced across his shoulders at another Chinese man standing watch at the pier entrance. The man gave a thumbs-up. The first guy leaned over the edge of the pier and ripped off the tarpaulin.

'You didn't tell me you took the pills,' Gardner said.

Aimée shrugged. 'Well, I guessed that I had to have some money to pay my way if I escaped and, well, there they were. It seemed kind of stupid not to. Given the circumstances.'

'Without them,' Gardner said, 'we'd be screwed.'

Gardner wasn't sure what he was expecting to see underneath the tarp – maybe a piece-of-shit vessel with a leaking hull and a pair of oars for a motor. Instead he was confronted with a mean-looking speedboat. Twelve metres long and shaped like a traffic cone, the stern four times wider than the bow. The hull was made from glass-reinforced plastic – durable but lightweight. A two-metre-tall wheelhouse stood in the middle of the deck, the size of a Portakabin. It was painted black, like the rest of the boat. Eight 250-horsepower engines were fixed to the stern. That's a fuck of a lot of motors, Gardner told himself. Evidently a bag full of pills bought a great deal more than a spot in a lorry container and a small air vent.

'You go now,' the guy said, shooing them like they were pests at a restaurant. 'No time, no time!'

Another man bounded up the pier and joined them. He was middle-aged, dusty face, rust-belt beard with a greying pony-tail tied at the back of his head and a pair of wraparound Ray-Bans sitting on a peeling nose. He introduced himself as the pilot. Said his name was Peterson. He had a Southern US drawl. Peterson didn't ask after Aimée or their reasons for wanting covert entry into the UK. On a trip like this, the less crew and passengers knew about each other the better.

'This thing will get us to the shore?' Gardner asked.

'Depend on it,' said Peterson, gobbing over the side of the pier. 'We do three or four runs a week with this baby, but not usually with human cargo, if you get my drift. You must've paid Chang here a good service fee?'

Gardner said nothing. He helped Aimée onto the boat. She wobbled, almost lost her balance. One look at her and Gardner realized she wasn't a big fan of the sea.

Peterson said, 'Anyways, we'll be doing sixty knots or there-abouts the whole crossing.'

'Is that fast?' asked Aimée, holding tightly onto the hull with both hands.

'About seventy miles an hour, land terms,' Peterson replied. 'But then you gotta remember we ain't travelling on no flat surface.'

Gardner surveyed the boat. 'Low profile, dark colours, sixty knots . . . You can probably outrun the navy in this.'

'Some fool looks at his radar, I'm just a fucking blur.'

They set off into a night black as a mine shaft, engines chugging as they cut through the dark water. The distance to the English coast from the port of Rotterdam was 132 miles, or 115 nautical miles. At sixty knots they'd reach Felixstowe in two hours. Factor in the time to land undetected and gather their shit, and Gardner was looking at an ETA of midnight, leaving him and Aimée with nine hours to hit the road and wing it down to London. He noticed the deck was scattered with the leftovers from the last drug shipment: spare rope, plastic sheets and buoy markers for dumping product over-board, and Very flare guns used to alert their contacts ashore of their arrival. The flare guns were bright orange, breech-loaded with a single twelve-gauge round.

Twenty minutes into their trip and the speedboat was bounc-ing up and down like a cork in a pan of boiling water. Stars dotted the dome of the sky, brilliant and raw. The smell of diesel fuel and sea salt corralled in Gardner's nose. He saw the lights of ferries and tankers blinking miles away. Reds, greens and yellows strung along the horizon like Christmas tree decorations.

'Wind's picking up,' Peterson said. 'It's gonna get bumpy.'

'And this *isn't*?' Aimée asked. She was ashen-faced already.

'Try to focus on the horizon,' Gardner said.

'*What* horizon?'

Something zipped through the air. Unseen. Like an invis-ible dart. Peterson grunted and flopped to the deck. Aimée screamed. Blood squirted out of a hole in the American's neck. His legs twitched. Then Gardner made out a distinctive noise above the loud whirr of the engines. He killed them to steady the boat and turned to face the stern.

The guy with the prosthetic arm was riding on their coat-tails.

eighty-three

2155 hours.

Kruger burned the engine on the Zodiac rubber raiding craft and drew alongside the Brit and his fucking bitch. It had taken two hours to debug the virus she'd downloaded to the cyberware network. He was looking forward to making that whore pay.

He had chopped down the pilot with a single shot from the Stoner Rifle-25. The rifle was chambered for 7.62x51mm calibre ammunition and accurate up to a distance of 1500 metres. The detachable sound suppressor did its job as the round propelled out of the muzzle. The SR-25 was mounted on top of a Harris bipod. The bipod was connected to the underside of the rifle's barrel along the length of its Picatinny rail system via a hardened aluminium adapter. Inserted into the SR-25 was a small computer chip which allowed Kruger to control the weapon through his arm. Fuck, he only had to think about pulling the trigger and the SR-25 obeyed.

Kruger's employers usually asked for zero collateral damage, but the Zodiac had a max speed of around thirty-five knots and only half a tank of fuel, so killing the pilot had been the only way to catch up.

When the Zodiac was parallel with the speedboat, Kruger stopped the engine and leapt over the void onto its deck. Gardner saw him coming. But Kruger's arm was super-humanly fast, capable of delivering a hundred-mile-per-hour uppercut before he had even finished thinking about it.

But the Brit wasn't slow. He was fucking fast. Slugged a solid fist into Kruger's chest. He had a strong punch on him. But not nearly enough to put Kruger down. He staggered on the deck and mentally directed the SR-25 at Gardner's chest.

But the Brit was now diving at Kruger's legs. The SR-25 kicked up a little as the round was fired and the jacket ejected. There was a half-second's silence, then a raging hiss. Bullet striking the inflatable hull.

This time Kruger was knocked backwards by the Brit. He didn't panic. His arm gave him the tactical advantage and, when it came down to shit, the Brit was going to be on the losing team. Gardner's fingers were searching for Kruger's eye sockets. He wants to fucking gouge me, Kruger thought.

In your dreams, buddy.

Kruger accessed the Zodiac through his mind and fired up the engines. Then he steered it into the speedboat. The bow piled into the hull and rocked the vessel. It felt like the whole world was sliding this way and that. Like they were sitting on top of an angry whale.

The bitch lost her balance.

Woman overboard.

'Aimée!' shouted Gardner.

Kruger thrust his right arm up and clamped his fingers around the Brit's neck. His face blew up like a blowfish as air became trapped in his throat, depriving his brain of vital oxygen. Kruger imagined all those red blood cells inside his skull desperately competing for air. Credit to him, the Brit fought hard. Both of his hands were trying to force apart Kruger's prosthetic digits. But it was a futile act.

Another forty-five seconds and the guy would be dead. That's all it would take. Kruger could hear the girl splashing and screaming in the water, but figured he'd leave her to drown, or freeze. Whichever happened first, he was easy.

Thirty seconds.

The Brit stopped pawing at Kruger's fingers. Looks like he's given up already, he thought. I figured he was a pussy. Came down to it, the SEALs had the beating of the SAS any day of the week.

Twenty seconds.

Then Kruger noticed the Brit dropping his right hand down and to his rear, scrabbling for something on the deck. Kruger tightened his grip and told him to hurry the fuck up and die.

Ten seconds.

Gardner lifted something up in his right hand. Kruger couldn't immediately make it out. It was bright red and clunky. Then, when Gardner brought it level with Kruger's face, he realized he was eyeball-to-eyeball with a Very flare gun.

'Son of a fucking bitch!'

Gardner pulled the trigger.

The flare set fire to Kruger's upper right arm. The part that was real, not fake. The part that could feel pain.

The flare's magnesium and nitrate mix ate into him like acid, burning away skin and flesh. Sparks rained down on his face, scorched his beard and melted the cartilage in his ear lobe. Kruger couldn't see shit. His world was doused a pyrotechnic green. His arm loosened from the Brit's neck as the pain overwhelmed him. Nerve endings fried and sent signals to his brain. It felt as if he was overheating at his core. He reached across with his left hand, trying to pat out the flare. But the heat, sweet Jesus. Too fucking much.

Then he felt movement. Gardner was dragging him across the deck. Kruger went to lunge at his legs, but the flare had turned the whole right side of him into a goddamn spit roast. The smell of burned flesh took him back to Afghanistan. A smell nobody ever forgot. When he lashed out at Gardner, the nerve endings were screwed and the power drained from his arm. If anything, the prosthetic felt super-heavy now.

Still he fought. Because he knew what the Brit was doing. Because Kruger would do exactly the same.

Gardner shoved him halfway overboard. His legs on the deck, his body doubled over the hull, his head pushed just beneath the surface of the water. And in a weird way he was relieved to be underwater, because the flare was extinguished and the chill North Sea cooled the wounds on his face, shoulder and arm.

Then he saw the propellers spinning furiously either side of him, slicing through the water, and he wasn't so relieved.

The Brit was going to start the engines.

Turn my head into fucking chop suey.

He tried to lift his head above the water. Fought and fought and fought. He yelled into the water, 'Fuck you, you fucking English bastard . . . sack of shit,' but the words just came out as bubbles of air that floated to the surface and burst.

The engines sputtered into life.

'Fucking son of a fucking bitch, cunt ass—'

eighty-four

Gardner rowed the last five hundred metres to the port. By switching off the engines he could keep the noise to a minimum. He didn't want to disturb anybody. Least of all some over-zealous copper. Not with his and Aimée's faces splashed all over the evening news.

Aimée sat in the wheelhouse, shivering from her plunge into the sea. Gardner had wrapped her in two thick woollen blankets he discovered in an emergency compartment in the cabin. She'd only been exposed to the water for less than a minute. Get her a brew and a new set of clothes and she'd be OK.

Gardner pulled ashore two hundred metres from the private harbour where the sailing yachts and gin ships slept. He escorted Aimée onto the beach. His mind was on Land and the final act of revenge.

Nine hours to go.

eighty-five

Leo Land paced up and down the Foreign Secretary's office. The room was a tasteless clash of the old and new. Fusty portraits on the walls, antique timepieces and ergonomic sofas, glass coffee tables and an HD TV. Pierce sat in his executive leather chair. The more relaxed he seemed the more Land's mood darkened.

'Try again,' Land said, stopping in front of an antique floor-standing globe carved from solid beechwood. As he ran his eyes over the exotic place names – Niger, Mauritania, Algeria, Egypt, Sudan – he could feel the opportunity slipping away from him. 'I said, why don't you try them again?'

Pierce sighed. 'Because the answer will be the same. If the police had found them, we'd be the first to know about it, and . . . for God's sake, Leo, you can't smoke in here!'

Land left the unlit cigarette dangling from his lips. 'I don't understand.'

'Understand what?'

Land didn't reply. He was turning over scenarios in his head. If they come out with the truth now, he thought, I'm done for. I'll be fed to the bloody dogs.

Think, man, he told himself. There's got to be a way out of this.

'We should talk to the Israelis,' he said.

Pierce raised one of his unruly eyebrows and the liver spots on his forehead were pushed together in a sort of polka-dot pattern. 'Oh, and do tell, Leo, what good would that serve?'

'We could encourage them to strike early. Before these idiots have a chance to sabotage all the hard work.'

'And you really think the Israelis aren't going to suspect foul play, when we come knocking on their door and asking if they wouldn't terribly mind getting stuck into the Iranians?' Pierce tut-tutted.

Land took a deep breath. The smell of polished mahogany filled his nostrils.

'Wherever they are, they can't go far. If they'd made it to the UK, we would've picked them up by now.'

Pierce somehow frowned and smiled at the same time. 'The Border Agency's under dreadful pressure,' he said. 'Thousands of people arrive undetected in Britain every week, you know. And if this chap is ex-Regiment ... What the *hell*—?' Pierce was staring out of his window at the street below. The Secretary's Office backed on to Parliament Street and the Cenotaph. Land paced to the window and cast an eye over proceedings. A media scrum was making its way down Parliament Street heading south, towards the House of Lords, the Treasury and Parliament Square. Land counted satellite vans from all the major news outlets, some reporters in cars, others on foot. They seemed to be in a frightful hurry. Sound booms and video cameras and digital recorders weaved amid the scrum.

'Bloody hundreds of the buggers.'

'I wonder what they're here for?' said Pierce.

'I haven't the foggiest,' said Land. The trembling in his hands had returned.

Pierce called in his assistant and asked him to operate the forty-two-inch flatscreen TV which stood on a stand next to the coffee table. The assistant flicked to Sky News. The feed was live. From Parliament Square. Land saw the figures on screen. He vomited a little in his mouth. Swallowed it. He scooped up his jacket.

'Where the hell are you going, man?'

Land stopped, turned, stared daggers at Pierce. 'I won't let them do this, Milton. There's too much at stake here. For you as well as me.' Pierce's eyes sank to the floor, but he said nothing.

Land stormed out of the room.

eighty-six

They stood on a sodden patch of earth at the eastern tip of Parliament Square. The ground was mulch from the peace protesters whose tents and placards had occupied the square for years.

Gardner and Aimée were side by side and felt their hands brush against each other. The morning was overcast, the sky a patchwork of dirty white sheets. To Gardner's right was the grand fortress of HM Treasury, and to his left the Purbeck marble and flying buttresses of Westminster Abbey. The two buildings stood on opposite sides of the square, like chess pieces on a board. Gardner and Aimée were poised to make their move.

Aimée was back in her comfort zone. She'd spent the two-hour train ride from Felixstowe planning her address. It was short, simple and to the point. She waited for the scrum to settle down, gave time for the photographers to set themselves up and then she spoke.

When she mentioned the involvement of foreign agents in the nuclear disaster at Istanbul, the reporters shouted questions at her ten at a time, left, right and centre. She paused. The voices simmered down.

'We have evidence,' she said, her tone measured and confident, 'that a person within the British establishment was aware of collusion between the Russian and Israeli authorities to detonate the suitcase nuke during its transit to Iran.'

This girl knows how to play a crowd, Gardner thought. He scanned the rooftops and the slow-moving traffic encircling Parliament Square. They were in an area that afforded no protection, and Gardner had to remain vigilant. He had three fears. One was that the police would arrive at the scene and detain Aimée before the truth could out.

The morning was ugly and brought with it a blustery wind that stabbed his cheeks and made his eyes water. When this is over, he thought, maybe I'll move abroad. Maybe with Aimée. Somewhere warm and sunny.

'This person may or may not have been acting alone. What we can say is that he not only neglected to inform the government of the plan, but he actively encouraged that plan to succeed. This man's name is Leo Land.'

His second fear was that one of the reporters might be an undercover agent doing Land's dirty work. He ran his eyes constantly over the journalists. They didn't necessarily have to be carrying a gun on their body. He'd heard of pistols being concealed inside the hollowed-out frames of video cameras.

His third fear was Land himself.

'He is responsible for the deaths of tens of thousands—'

Aimée cut herself short. A group of reporters were shouting at somebody deep in the scrum. Gardner stepped forward. Someone was trying to push to the front.

'Out of my way!'

The voice was unmistakable. Gardner's third fear was being realized.

Leo Land barged through the crowd. He looked flustered. Crumpled shirt, his normally immaculate head of hair ruffled. He cast withering looks at the reporters, smoothed out his tie and pointed a finger at Aimée.

'Stop this nonsense at once,' he said.

Aimée had a look in her eyes that Gardner couldn't place.

Somewhere on the road between pity and loathing. 'We have the evidence,' she replied in a flat voice.

Land walked right up to Aimée. Gardner put a hand between them. Land lashed out at him. 'Get the hell away from me!'

Gardner held his position and said, 'If I were you, I'd be on the phone to a lawyer.'

'You're the one who needs a lawyer.'

Gardner stepped towards Land until he was almost in his face.

'Get the fuck out of here. You're history.'

Land chuckled. 'Who are they going to believe, old boy?'

Land gave Gardner his back and marched to a spot just in front of Aimée, facing the massed cameras and microphones. He tended to his hair, then folded his hands in front of him in a pose of sincerity. 'These two are wanted by Interpol in connection with two murders in Rotterdam,' he said.

'You framed us,' Aimée shouted.

Land toyed with her, half-turning his head. 'Oh, you're innocent, are you? If you didn't kill them, why are you on the run?' He turned back to the reporters. *Fucking unbelievable,* thought Gardner. *They're actually listening to this prick.*

'We have the documents to prove it,' Aimée said quietly.

'Yes, my dear, you have some transcripts which have obviously been doctored. Well done.'

Gardner moved forward to lamp Land. Aimée held him back. He shot her a quizzical look. *As if to say, So we're just going to let him get away with this?*

'These people are traitors to the British government,' Land was lecturing.

'There's more than just transcripts,' Aimée said.

Land stopped. His arms were spread-eagled like a preacher reading from the Bible. 'Oh really? Don't tell me, more fake documents and doctored scripts, my dear?'

'Photographs, actually.' Then Aimée whispered to Gardner, 'I managed to decrypt the rest of the files.'

Land was speechless for a moment. His arms drooped. 'What kind of photographs?'

'I think I'll just show people and let them make up their own minds.'

Gardner wondered what the fuck Aimée was banging on about.

'You little' – Land's lips quivered – '*bitch*.'

Aimée blanked him. She held up a flash drive and looked at the reporters. 'Someone got a laptop we can use? Then we'll see who is really telling the truth.'

Someone approached Aimée and handed over his Dell Inspiron. She plugged the drive in and brought up the file. Reporters huddled around the screen.

'You'll pay for this,' Land said.

Gardner looked up. The clouded sky was clearing, like the tide peeling back from a sandy beach. Sunlight poked through the clearing. Spots of it landed on the square.

Something glinted on the rooftop of Westminster Abbey.

Gardner frowned.

Then he froze.

The glint was from a rifle barrel. From a hundred metres away, Gardner was able to pick out individual details on the shooter's face. He clocked a handlebar moustache and pasty complexion. Clocked the greasy hair.

No.

No fucking way!

Dave Hands was aiming down at him.

Gardner shot a look across to Aimée. She was triumphant as she blew up the first of the photographs. She stepped back, almost presenting herself as a target. A red mil-dot traced its way up her back.

Rested on the back of her head.

GET CLOSER TO THE ACTION

For a first glimpse of the new Chris Ryan Extreme Book, *Night Strike*, turn the page. Night Strike is published in hardback in January 2013 but in the meantime you can buy the *Chris Ryan Extreme: Night Strike* Missions in ebook format from December 2012.

one

His name was Hauser and he moved down the corridor as fast as his bad right leg allowed. The metal toolbox he carried was heavy and exaggerated his limp. He paused in front of the last door on the right. A yellow sign on the door read 'WARNING! AUTHORIZED PERSONNEL ONLY'. He fished a key chain from his paint-flecked trousers and skimmed through the keys until he found the right one. His hand was trembling. He looked across his right shoulder at the bank of lifts ten metres back down the corridor. Satisfied the coast was clear, he inserted the key in the lock and twisted it. There was a sequence of clicks as the pins inside jangled up and down, and then a satisfying *clack* as the lock was released.

Hauser stepped inside the room. It was a four-metre-square jungle of filing cabinets, cardboard boxes and industrial shelves with a tall, dark-panelled window overlooking the street below. Hauser hobbled over to the window. An electric pain shot up his leg with every step, like someone had taped broken glass to his shins. He stopped in front of the window and dumped a roll of black tarpaulin he'd been carrying under his left arm. Then he set the toolbox down next to the tarp and scanned the scene outside. He was on the fourth floor of an office block adjacent to the Lanesborough Hotel at Hyde Park Corner. The current tenants were some kind of marketing agency who, he knew, were badly behind with their rent. They'd have to relocate soon. Shame. From that height Hauser had quite a view. The pavements were packed with commuters and tourists flocking in and out of Hyde Park Corner Tube station. Further in the distance lay the bleached green ribbon of the park itself.

Yep. It was quite a view. Especially if you wanted to shoot somebody.

Hauser was wearing a tearaway paper suit that had been vacuum-packed. The overalls came with a hood. He also wore a pair of surgical gloves. The suit and gloves would both prevent his DNA from contaminating the scene, as well as protecting his body from residue such as gunpowder. Now Hauser knelt down. Slowly, because any sudden movement sent fierce voltages of pain up his right leg, he prised open the toolbox. It was rusty and stiff and he had to force the damn thing apart with both hands. Finally the cantilever trays separated. There were three trays on either side of the central compartment. Each one was filled with tools. Hauser ran his fingers over them. There was a rubber-headed hammer, tacks, putty, bolt-cutters, a pair of suction pads, a large ring of different-sized hexagon keys and a spirit level.

There were two more objects in the bottom of the main compartment of the toolbox. One was a diamond cutter. The other was a featureless black tube ten inches long and three and a half inches wide. Made of carbon-fibre, it weighed just 300 grams, no more than a tennis racquet. Hauser removed the tube. There was a latch on the underside. Hauser flipped this and a pistol grip flipped out, transforming the tube into a short-barrelled rifle.

Hauser cocked the bolt. The whole operation had taken four seconds. Four seconds to set up a selective-fire rifle effective up to 300 metres.

Hauser set the rifle down and took the diamond cutter from the toolbox. Moving with speed now, he ran the cutter around the edges of the window until he had cut out a rectangle of glass as big as a forty-inch TV. Then he took out the suction pads and, with one in either hand, pressed them to the sides of the cut-out sheet. The glass came loose easily. Hauser laid this down on the floor with the suction pads still attached. Then he took the black tarp, hammer and tacks and pinned one end of the material to the ceiling, allowing the rest to drape down over the opening. Seen from the street below, the tarp would give the appearance of reflective glass. If anyone looked up at the window, they wouldn't see shit.

Going down on one knee, Hauser tucked the stock tight into the Y-spot where his shoulder met his chest. His index finger rested on the trigger, then he applied a little pressure. He went through the drill he had practised thousands of times before.

Breathe in. Breathe out.

Keep the target in focus.

Firm shoulder. Left hand supporting the right.

The woman in his sights meant nothing to him. She'd simply been the first person he targeted. She was sitting on a bench and eating a sandwich. The optics were so precise that Hauser could identify the brand. Pret A Manger.

He pulled the trigger.

She was eating a sandwich one second and clutching her guts the next.

The subsonic .22 long rifle rimfire round tore a hole in her stomach big enough to accommodate your middle finger.

And he went for the stomach with the next seven targets too. Unlike head shots, gut shots didn't kill people, and Hauser had been specifically told not to kill. Only maim. He kicked out the rounds in quick succession. Two seconds between each. With each shot the muzzle *phtt-ed* and the barrel jerked.

The bodies dropped.

The crowd was confused by the first two shots. The built-in suppressor guaranteed that the shots didn't sound like the thunderous *ca-rack* of a bullet. But when the third target fell they all knew something terrifying was happening. Panic spread and everyone ran for cover.

Twenty-four seconds. That's how long it had taken Hauser to leave eight civilians sprawled on the pavement soaked in their own blood and pawing at their wounds. The victims were strangely silent. No one else dared approach them. Any sane person would wait for a clear sign that the shooting had stopped.

Hauser stepped back from the window. He was confident no one had seen him. The suppressor had phased out more than ninety per cent of the sound, making it difficult for anyone to clearly understand that they were gunshots, let alone pinpoint their origin. A breeze kicked up. The tarp fluttered. Hauser quickly folded up the weapon and stashed it in the toolbox. He removed the overalls and stuffed them into the toolbox. The overalls he would dispose of shortly, in a nearby public toilet, courtesy of a lit match and some wetted toilet paper to cover and disable the smoke detector. He left the room.

Police sirens in the distance. And now screams from the crowd, as if the sirens gave them permission.

two

He downed it in three long gulps that had the barmaid shaking her head and the three gnarled alcoholics at the other end of the bar nodding welcome to the newest member of their club. Joe Gardner polished off his London Pride and tipped the foamy glass at the barmaid.

'Another,' he said.

The barmaid snatched his empty glass and stood it under the pump. Golden beer flowed out of the nozzle and settled into a dark-bronze column. She cut him a thick head and dumped the glass in front of him.

'Cheers, Kate.' Gardner raised his glass in a toast but she had already turned her back. 'But you're forgetting one thing.'

Kate sighed. 'What's that?'

'Your phone number.'

'The only thing you'll get from me is a slap.' A disgusted expression was plastered over the right side of the girl's face. Gardner doubted her left side was any more pleasant. 'That's your last pint till you settle your tab.'

'Give us a break,' Gardner grunted, rooting around in his jeans pocket for imaginary change.

Then a voice to his left said, 'This one's on me.'

On the edge of his vision Gardner glimpsed a red-knuckled hand slipping the barmaid a pair of crisp twenty-quid notes. She eyed the queen's head suspiciously before accepting it.

'Thanks. This'll about cover it.'

'My pleasure,' the voice said. 'After all, we've got to look after our own.'

The voice was hoarse and the man's breath wafted across Gardner's face and violated his nostrils. It was the smoky, medicinal smell of cheap whisky.

'Didn't I see you on the telly once?'

Gardner didn't turn around.

'Yeah,' the voice went on. 'You're that bloke from the Regiment. The one who was at Parliament Square. You were the big hero of the day.'

The voice swigged his whisky. Ice clinked against the glass.

'You look like a bag of bollocks, mate,' said the voice. 'What the fuck happened?'

Gardner took a sip of his pint. Said nothing.

'No, wait. I can guess what happened. I mean, fucking look at you. You're a joke. You're a right fucking cunt.'

Gardner stood his beer on the bar. Kate was nowhere to be seen. Then he slowly turned to face his new best friend.

'That's right. A complete and utter cunt.'

He looked as ugly as he sounded. Red cheeks hung like sandbags beneath a pair of drill-hole eyes set in a head topped off with a buzzcut. He was a couple of hundred pounds or thereabouts, half of it muscle and the rest fat that had been muscle in a previous life. The glass in front of him was half-full of whisky and ice. The glazed expression in his eyes told Gardner the drink had not been the guy's first of the night, or even his tenth.

'I'm not looking for trouble,' Gardner said quietly.

'But you found it anyway. You know, there's nothing more tragic than a washed-up old Blade.' The man pulled a face at the prismatic bottom of the tumbler. 'Know what? Someone should just put you out of your fucking misery now.'

Gardner attempted to focus on the guy and saw two of him.

Sixteen pints of Pride and a few shots off the top shelf will do that to a man. Rain lightly drum-tapped on the pub windows. The guy leaned in close to Gardner and whispered into his left ear.

'Me, I'm from 3 Para. Real fucking soldier. Real fucking man.' He winked at the barmaid. 'Ain't that right, Kate?' She smiled back flirtatiously. Then the guy turned back to Gardner. 'Now do me a favour and fuck off.'

A shit-eating grin was his parting gift.

Gardner swiftly drank up. Made for the door.

Outside in the deserted car park the rain was lashing down in slanted ice sheets. Gardner zipped up his nylon windcheater to insulate himself against the cold and wet. The Rose in June pub was set on the outskirts of Hereford and the low rent was probably the only reason it hadn't shut down. Gardner made his way down the back streets, snaking towards the Regiment's headquarters. He navigated around the housing estate that used to be the site of the old Regiment camp on Stirling Lane. Now it was all council-owned. The rain picked up, spattering the empty street that edged the estate. Gardner couldn't see more than two or three metres in front of him. A ruthless wind whipped through the street and pricked his skin. Gardner closed his eyes. He heard voices, subdued beneath the bass line of the rain.

When he opened his eyes a fist was colliding with his face.

three

2301 hours.

The fist struck Gardner hard and sudden, like a jet engine
backfiring. He fell backwards, banging his head against the
kerb. A sharp pain speared the base of his skull and it took
a moment to wrench himself together. You're lying on your
back. Your cheek is on fire from a fucking punch. And Para is
towering over you.

Para's hands were at his side and curled into kettlebells.
He hocked up phlegm and spat at Gardner. The gob arced
through the rain like a discus and landed with a plop on his
neck.

'Get up, prick.' Para's voice was barely audible above the
hammering rain.

Gardner wiped away the spittle with the back of his hand.

'I said, get the fuck up.'

Gardner noticed two guys with Para, one at either shoulder.
The guy on the left was shaven-headed with black dull eyes
and the kind of hulking frame that you only get from inject-
ing dodgy Bulgarian 'roids. He wore a grey hoodie and dark
combats. Gardner noticed he was clutching a battery-operated planer. The guy on Para's right stood six-five. A reflective yellow jacket hung like a tent from his scrawny frame.
He smiled and revealed a line of coffee-brown teeth. He was
holding a sledgehammer. Raindrops were cascading off the
tip of its black head.

'Call yourself a Blade,' Para said. 'You're just a washed-up cunt.'

Hoodie and Black Teeth laughed like Para was Ricky Gervais back when he was funny.

Gardner began scraping himself off the pavement. The rain hissed. The guys were crowding around him now. He swayed uneasily on his feet.

Black Teeth was gripping the sledgehammer with both hands. He stood with his feet apart in a golf-swing posture and raised the hammer above his right shoulder. Gardner knew he should be ducking out of the way but the booze had made him woozy. Dumbly he watched as the hammer swung down at him.

Straight into his solar plexus. *Thud!*

A million different pains fired in the wall of his chest. He heard something snap in there. Heard it, then felt it. His ribcage screamed. He dropped to his knees and sucked in air. The valley of his chest exploded. He looked up and saw Black Teeth standing triumphantly over him.

'What a joke,' he said.

Black Teeth went to swipe again but Hoodie came between them, wanted a piece of the action for himself. He'd fired up the planer and was aiming it at Gardner's temple. Gardner managed to climb to his knees. He didn't have the energy to stand on two feet, but he wasn't going to lie down and leave himself defenceless. First rule of combat, he reminded himself: always try to stay on your toes. The planer buzzed angrily. Gardner was alert now, his body flooded with endorphins and adrenaline. In a blur he quickly sidestepped to the left and out of the path of the planer. Momentum carried Hoodie forwards, his forearm brushing Gardner's face, the planer chopping the air.

Then Gardner unclenched his left hand and thrust the open palm into Hoodie's chest. Winded the cunt. Hoodie yelped as he dropped to the ground. The planer flew out of his hands and Gardner reached for it, but Black Teeth was on top of him and bringing the sledgehammer in a downward arc again. Gardner feinted, dropping his shoulder and leaving Black Teeth swiping at nothing. Out of the corner of his eye Gardner spied Para fishing something out of his jacket. Gardner folded his fingers in tightly and jabbed his knuckles at Black Teeth's throat. He could feel the bone denting the soft cartilage rings of the guy's trachea. The sledgehammer rang as it hit the deck.

Para had a knife in his hands now. Gardner recognised the distinctive fine tip of a Gerber Compact.

'Fuck it, you cunt,' said Para. 'Come on then.'

Para lunged at Gardner, angling the Gerber at his neck. Gardner shunted his right hand across and jerked his head the same direction, pushing the blade away. Then he launched an uppercut at Para's face. His face was a stew of blood and bone.

Gardner moved in for the kill. He grabbed the planer and lamped it against the side of Para's face. Para groaned as he fumbled blindly for the Gerber.

Too late.

Gardner yanked Para's right arm. He pinned his right knee against the guy's elbow, trapping his forearm in place. Then he depressed the button to start the planer. The tool whirred above the incessant rain as he slid it along the surface of Para's forearm. The blade tore off strips of flesh. A pinkish-red slush spewed out of the side of the device. Gardner drove the planer further up Para's arm. His scream turned into something animal. The skin below was totally shredded, a gooey mess of veins coiled around whitish bone. It didn't look like an arm any longer. More like something a pack of Staffies had feasted on.

Pleased with his work, Gardner eased off the button and

ditched the planer. It clattered to the ground, sputtered, whined and died.

The rain was now a murmur.

'My arm,' Para said. 'My fucking arm!'

'I see you again, next time it's your face.' Gardner's voice was as sharp as cut glass. 'Are we fucking clear?'

Gardner didn't wait for an answer. He gave his back to the three fucked-up pricks and walked down the road, past the construction site. He had reached a crossroads in his life. Lately he'd been getting into a lot of scraps. And deep down he was afraid of admitting to himself that fighting was all he was good for. The problem was, he was no longer an operator. His injury had reduced him to cleaning rifles and hauling HESCO blocks around Hereford, and the suit did not fit a fucking inch.

He was a couple of hundred metres from the site when his mobile sparked up. A shitty old Nokia. Gardner could afford an iPhone 4, but only in his dreams. The number on the screen wasn't one he recognized. An 0207 number. London. He tapped the answer key.

'Is that Mr Joseph Gardner?'

The voice was female and corporate. The kind of tone that belonged on airport announcements. Pressing the phone closer to his ear, Gardner said, 'Who's this?'

'Nancy Rayner here. I'm calling from Talisman International.'

Gardner rubbed his temples, trying to clear the fog of booze behind his eyeballs. The name sounded vaguely familiar.

'The security consultancy?' the woman went on. 'You submitted a job application . . . let me see . . .' – Gardner heard the shuffle of papers – '. . . two weeks ago.'

Her words jolted his mind. Fucking yes. He did recall applying for a job. He also recalled thinking he had next to no hope of getting it. Talisman were one of the new boys on the security circuit. He'd not heard anything, and figured it was the same better-luck-elsewhere story.

'We'd like to invite you for an interview.'

Gardner fell silent.

'Mr Gardner?'

'Yes?'

'How does tomorrow sound? One o'clock at our offices?'

It sounded better than good. It was fucking great.

He said simply, 'OK.'

'Excellent. So we'll see you tomorrow at one.'

Click.

Gardner was left listening to dead air. Suddenly the drunken mist behind his eyes was lifting. He tucked the mobile away, dug his hands into his jacket pockets and quickened his pace.

Maybe he wouldn't be hauling gravel around Hereford for the rest of his miserable life.

four

London, UK. 1257 hours.

As the First Great Western train slithered into Paddington, the passenger announcement shook Gardner from his slumbers. 'All change.' The doors bleated and opened, and Gardner made his way to the Underground. The concourse was crawling with armed police patrolling around with their Heckler & Koch MP5K submachine guns strapped around their chests. Gardner afforded himself a wry smile. These coppers couldn't shoot their way out of a wet bog roll yet here they were prancing around like fucking Rambo. He parted with six quid for a one-day Travelcard and caught the Bakerloo Line towards Elephant and Castle. Twelve minutes later the Tube coughed him up at Charing Cross.

Life had not been kind to Gardner since he had stopped MI6 agent Leo Land from engineering a conflict between Israel and Iran. Land had been publicly humiliated and war narrowly averted, but the media didn't give Gardner any credit. Not that he wanted it. Aimée Milana, the journalist he had been protecting, had been killed by a sniper's bullet in London's Parliament Square in front of the world's media. The 7.62x51mm NATO round entered her left eye, bored through her brain and exited via her left shoulder. Aimée died immediately, and in death she became both martyr and the intrepid investigator who had uncovered the plot. Gardner hadn't loved her, but he cared enough to let her take the afterlife glory.

He emerged from the Tube into the chaotic embrace of Charing Cross. More coppers. The crowds were thinner than he recalled from his last visit. The shooting at Knightsbridge had put everyone on edge. Copies of *Metro* carpeted the ground, stamped with shoeprints and bird shit. He caught half of a headline, the word 'HORROR' in big bold letters next to a pixelated CCTV image of a woman covered in blood. He hooked a left onto the Strand and kept an eye on the clouds, bulging like overfilled flour sacks.

Gardner quickened his stride and tried to feel at ease in the cheap suit he was wearing. He carried on down Whitehall and the classical buildings imposing themselves between old boys' boozers and souvenir shops. At the back of the Household Cavalry's headquarters Gardner hung a left onto Horse Guards Avenue and tipped his head in quiet respect at the statue of the Gurkha outside the Ministry of Defence. Left again and he found himself on Whitehall Court. Twenty metres down the street he found the place he was looking for.

Compared with the ostentation around it, the building looked subdued. It was three storeys tall with a stucco front and an oak door, above which a dark glass fanlight framed the company name in finely etched gold letters: Talisman Security. The 'International' had been shortened to 'Int'l'. Gardner approached the intercom to the right of the door and pressed the buzzer.

'Yes?' a woman squawked.

'Joe Gardner. I'm here for the interview.'

Static crackled from the speaker. Gardner scratched his freshly clipped beard, straightened his tie.

'Please enter.'

There was the diplomatic click of a lock being released. Gardner gave the brass doorknob a twist and entered the reception. The woman who had spoken to him through the intercom greeted him with a stern face. She was disappointingly old and fat. He was signed in and given a visitor ID badge.

He rode the shuddering box lift up to the first floor. When he stepped out he got a surprise. This floor was nothing like the gentlemen's club décor of the reception. Gone were the dark-framed portraits and the musty smell of old money. Instead he was in a white-tiled corridor with frosted-glass office doors. A fragrance like freshly chopped pinewood hung in the air. He stopped outside the interview room for a moment and wiped his brow.

Gardner had faced down terrorists and been shot at by African warlords, but job interviews scared the shit out of him. Fuck it, he thought. Let's get it over with. He opened the door and entered a long and wide meeting room. A white walnut table faced him. A deck of Cisco phones were lined up on the table, along with a projector, and at one end of the room was a pulled-down white screen.

Three figures were seated at the far end of the table.

On the left was a woman. Slimline body, small breasts, early thirties. Her brunette hair was tied back in a business-like manner and she was dressed in an understated skirt suit. On her wedding-ring finger she wore a discreet band that depressed Gardner.

The guy on the right was almost as thin as the bird. He was sitting stiffly in his chair and scribbling on a notepad. Conservative-blue suit, white shirt, grey tie. His face was smooth and clean-shaven, his fingernails immaculately cut. He didn't look like he had ever lifted a weight, let alone spent a night in the jungle.

Then Gardner set eyes on the figure sitting in the middle, and did a double-take. He blinked. His eyes were not deceiving him. The man was sitting with his hands splayed in front of him and broadcasting a smug, taunting look at Gardner.

'Hello, Joe,' he said.